THE TEMP

KELLY FLORENTIA

S

Copyright © Kelly Florentia 2024

The right of Kelly Florentia to be identified as the author of this work has been asserted by the author in accordance with the Copyright, Designs and Patents Act 1988.

First published in Great Britain by Stylo Books 2024

ISBN: 9798323574407

The story contained within this book is a work of fiction. Names and characters are the product of the author's imagination and any resemblance to actual persons, living or dead, is entirely coincidental.

All rights reserved. No part of this book may be reproduced, stored in a retrieval system, or transmitted in any form or by any means, electronic, electrostatic, magnetic tape, mechanical, photocopying, recording or otherwise, without the written permission of the author.

Prologue

At first, I thought it was a bit of harmless fun, watching him sweating it out in front of the wall-to-wall mirror in his green *Serval* gym vest and black shorts. All that pelvic thrusting and hip swivelling sent temperatures soaring in the packed studio, even though he seemed oblivious to it all. Members couldn't get enough of him, especially the women of a certain age. Bar me, of course. All I was interested in was toning all the saggy bits and getting rid of my spare tyre. My confidence had hit rock bottom. I needed to get back into shape, at any cost.

The waiting list to join his free classes, a deal the trainers agree to at *Serval* in exchange for using the facilities for their paid customers, was as long as my arm. It's not because they're free, although I'm sure that helps. Who doesn't love a freebie? It's because of him. Working-out with him was fun. Exciting. It really didn't feel like exercise at all. I'm not going to lie, I liked him – enough to hire him as my personal trainer. Behind my husband's back.

But that was six weeks ago. Now, just the thought of Frank makes my skin crawl.

Now, he's become a liability.
Now, I want to make him disappear.

Chapter 1

I lock my front door hurriedly, keys jangling, and am instantly flooded with panic. Did I put the alarm on? I can't remember hearing the familiar bleeps. Tom will go loopy if he comes home to an unarmed house. Hesitating, I go to look at my watch and that's when I spot him, standing on the edge of the pavement, outside Mr Stanhope's house next door. He has one hand in his grey joggers, orange carrier bag hanging from his wrist, phone pressed against his black beanie-covered ear. *Shit*, this is all I need. Blood rushing to my cheeks, I make my way along the footpath, heels click-clacking against the paving stones in time with my racing heart. Did I put the alarm on? I must've, I must've.

'Sorry, gotta go,' he says quickly into the mouthpiece. 'I do too. Yup. See you later.' Sliding his phone into his pocket, he rounds on me. 'Bella, I was just about to knock for you when…'

'What are you doing here, Frank?' I interject, adjusting the thick strap of my camera bag that is digging into my shoulder. 'Are you out of your mind?'

'Um, I tried phoning but…'

I click my tongue, not letting him finish. 'What do you want? I'm busy.'

'A quick word, that's all,' he says, in that raspy tone of his.

I screw my face up. 'I'm on my way to see a client,' I admit, self-consciously looking this way and that. 'I don't want to be late. You really do need to go.'

'At this time?' He looks at his fancy watch. I haven't seen it before. He usually wears a Garmin. It's impressive – green dial in a platinum case with a deeper green alligator leather strap. Cost a fortune, no doubt. 'I thought you finished at four on Fridays.'

Did I tell him that? I can't remember. I must've done. We talked a lot during training. He seemed nice, kind. Woke, if you like. Unlike some of the other trainers, he never eyed women up, not even the young, gorgeous ones, even when they openly flirted with him. At one point, I wondered if he might be gay.

'I'm sorry to turn up like this.' He does that thing with his eyes, as if dust has flown in. I always thought it was a tick, that it happened because he was shy, but now I can't help thinking he does it on purpose, to get attention. 'I know you don't like unexpected visitors.' I don't and neither does he. It's a pet hate we share. One of the trivial things we discussed during our twice weekly, sixty-pounds an hour sessions.

'Listen.' I pause, exhale loudly. 'If this is about what happened last Tuesday, I just want to forget it.'

'Bella, please. I don't want any trouble,' he insists, palms up. 'All I want is two minutes of your time, and then I'll be gone.' I huff, look at my watch, tell him to go on. 'The thing is…' A ruckus of voices steals his attention as a throng of youngsters spill out of a house three doors away. 'I was worried about you,' he continues. *Liar.* Although I must admit, he does look a bit rough around the edges – sunken-eyed, uneven skin tone – unusual for him. He spends more on facial products than I do.

'You needn't have been,' I say, trying to mollify him so he can bugger off. 'I'm fine.'

'It's not like you to ignore my texts, to not even read them.' *Shit*. I forgot to turn Read Receipts off. 'And when you didn't show up for our training session …' he falters. 'I was imagining all sorts.' He gives me one of his faux doleful looks, with those chocolate almond-shaped eyes. I stay silent, studying my black stilettoes. 'Bella, if this is because your husband found out about us,' he continues, and my head whips up.

'Us?' I shrill, scratching the side of my mouth as the MPV full of teens roars off. 'What the hell do you mean?'

'Well, he doesn't know you hired me, right?' I purse my lips. I forgot I confided in him about that. It wasn't intentional. He caught me off guard one morning when I was ratty and sleep-deprived, offered a discount to family and friends. When I said I'd put the word out, he immediately asked for Tom's email so that he could send him a direct invite, and the truth flew out of my mouth.

'It's got nothing to do with that,' I say irritably. And everything to do with how much it was costing me. I don't habitually lie to my husband, unless there's money involved. Zelda calls him Ebenezer. Behind his back, of course.

'Can I ask why you've ghosted me then?'

'I haven't. Not intentionally.' My eyes dart up and down our quiet cul-de-sac. The thought of an altercation outside my front door, with my new neighbours peering through their voile nets and smart shutters, fills me with unease. 'Frank, I'm sorry I didn't read your texts.' A loud high-pitched beep startles me. It's Anna, from number nineteen, two doors across, unlocking her car, dark hair held up in a messy bun with a yellow band. I've only spoken to her a handful of times but she seems nice.

Ralf, her fifteen-year-old son, is in my Georgia's English class. I look back at Frank. 'I haven't had a chance to read them yet. Perhaps you shouldn't send so many all at once. It's overwhelming.' Confusion sweeps across his face, or is it incredulity? 'I'm snowed under, lots of admin to sift through.' Frank nods, reminds me that I told him my PA is on maternity leave and I've yet to find a temp. 'Sorry, but I'm going to have to go. I'm cutting it fine as it is and…' I look at my watch – 17.26. 'My husband is due home any moment and if he finds you here…'

Frank laughs, throws a glance at his tattooed left arm, bulging out of his green short-sleeved *Serval* top. 'I haven't come here for a fight.' That's just as well because he'd flatten Tom with one punch. Tom's a slim fifty-two-year-old silver fox, golfing keeps him fit, but he wouldn't last five seconds in a ring with Frank. 'But we do need to sort out Tuesday's misunderstanding.'

'*Excuse me?*' I retort, readjusting the strap of my heavy bag.

Frank rubs the back of his neck. 'Look, some clients get a crush on their personal trainers.'

'I don't doubt it. But I'm not one of them.'

'It's not as if anything actually happened? Our lips brushed but we didn't snog, or anything. No harm done, eh?'

I look at him aghast. 'Firstly, I have *not* got a crush on you,' I insist, flicking a thumb out. 'And secondly.' I flick out my index finger and point it at him like a gun. 'I think you'll find that you're the one with the infatuation.' *Especially as I'm twenty years your senior.* 'I'm a happily married woman.'

He holds his designer stubbled chin. 'Is that so?'

'Yes,' I snap. If he's come here to throw accusations at me, it's not going to wash.

Glancing across the road, I notice Anna seated in her car, phone pressed against her ear, lips moving. She hasn't seen me.

Taking a step to the side, I shield myself behind Frank's V-shaped body, then as I go to speak I hear the sound of raised voices. Ralf has appeared on the driveway looking stylish in a high-collared padded yellow gilet and electric blue flares. With his big afro-blonde hair, he looks as if he's stepped out of a 70s album sleeve.

'It's not fair,' Ralf booms. Frank looks round, biting his thumbnail, as Anna swings her legs around and climbs out of her Volvo.

'Get in the car,' Anna retaliates, pushing the sleeves of her long brown coat up a fraction. 'Hey, Bella,' she calls out. And now she's seen me. With Frank. *Brilliant*. Folding her arms, she looks across at him, features set in uncertainty. 'Everything okay?' Anna wraps her coat around her and I'm sure I catch a flash of red tartan pyjamas.

'All good, thanks, Anna.' I wave a hand. A phone rings. 'Haven't seen you in a while,' I holler. Definitely pyjamas. And bare feet in trainers. Anna presses her phone to her ear again. I don't think she heard me. I turn back to Frank to the commotion of slamming doors and the hum of voices. 'Look, you've had your say. So, if there's nothing else.'

'Well, actually, there is.' There's a pause and then. 'I enjoy working with people who genuinely want to get into shape. It makes it all worthwhile. What happened last Tuesday was just a blip. Nothing we can't sort out.'

'Listen, Frank, whatever you think happened, I am *not* and never have been interested in an affair.' He raises an eyebrow, which is plucked to perfection. 'I would never cheat on my husband.'

'Okay,' he admits, holding his hands up. My stomach unclenches. At last, we're getting somewhere. 'Keeping me a secret from him is kinda cheating, though, isn't it?' Acid flares in my stomach. 'Oh, keep your hair on, Bella. I'm not hanging around here waiting for him to come home so I can grass you up, if that's what you're thinking. I'd *never* betray client confidentiality, no matter what. You have my word.' He places his hand on his toned chest. 'Nor will I mention...' Licking his lips he glances away, sniffs. 'The other little incident you're keeping from your husband.' My muscles seize. *Don't rise to the bait, Bella. Calmly get in the car and drive to Mrs Anderson's – you don't want to keep a client waiting.*

'Good,' I say tightly. 'Thank you.' I go to move, his hand snaps around my wrist.

'But you didn't need to cancel your gym membership over a silly misunderstanding and *sack* me. We had a deal, remember?'

And there it is. The reason he's here. Money.

Chapter 2

I look at Frank, feeling numb. If he's here to blackmail me in exchange for keeping quiet about what he saw, I won't be able to fix this.

'You okay? You look anxious.'

'I'm not anxious,' I say in a panicky tone.

Right, I need to calm down and sort this before it gets out of hand. Frank's lost a client – an income – he's got bills to pay, food to buy, times are hard. I've got to pacify him, appeal to his better nature.

'I thought we were friends,' I say. 'I thought I could trust you.'

Frank's features soften. 'We were. We still can be. If only…'

'It's too late for if onlys.' I rub my temple. 'The dynamics between us have changed.'

'Don't pin this all on me,' he says, annoyance slipping into his voice.

'I'm sorry I had to let you go, but you must understand that I can't train with someone when lines have been crossed.'

'So, you didn't stroke my chest,' he says, challengingly. I shake my head at his expensive Nike trainers. 'You didn't flutter your eyelashes at me?' More head shaking. 'You didn't *want* me?'

His accusing tone makes me jump, catapulting me back to last Tuesday. We're in the studio, hot and sweaty after a tough workout. He's showing me how to do a stretch. I can't remember what it's called now, something to do with three soldiers; the warrior three pose, that was it. I stretch forward on one leg – lose my balance – his hands on my hips – faces inches apart – his hot breath on my face – and then he…

'Oh, come on, you can't deny you like me.' His voice breaks into my thoughts, bringing me back to now, and I shudder. 'Getting all personal, bringing me coffee, breakfast. What was that all about?'

'You're twisting things,' I snap, mouth dry. 'You asked me to bring in a sample of Zelda's bakes.' My sister recently set up her own bakery business from home. I was trying to drum up business for her. Frank's got a big following on Instagram, showcasing his exercise routines and healthy eating plans. I certainly wasn't trying to bribe him into bed with half a dozen protein muffins.

'You told me to hold on to you, then you let go before I was ready.' A little girl skips along the street and we step out of the way, her dark, shiny hair swishing against her narrow shoulders. Her mother follows, phone secured under her hijab, pushing a pram full of grocery bags. 'If I accidentally touched your chest, it was to stabilise myself.' A car door slams. Olivia, Anna's seventeen-year-old daughter, calls out *Mum*. 'But you…' Frank's phone starts ringing.

'Sorry, got to get this.' Taking a few steps back, he turns and faces Anna's house, securing the carrier bag under his armpit. 'I'm free next Wednesday afternoon,' he says to his caller. 'I can book the studio for three. Sounds perfect, yeah.'

A client. What about *my* client? Anger powers through me. I flick my wrist and my phone lights up – 1745. If I don't get a move on, Mrs Anderson will start ringing again. I've already changed our appointment twice today. I don't want her to leave me a bad review on Trustpilot.

Frank, who is now sashaying towards his white VW Golf parked halfway down the road, laughs into his handset, and just then a thought slithers into my mind, risky and perilous like a cobra. If I can slip away while he's on that call, he won't get a chance to blackmail me. It'll give me time to think, discuss it with my lovely friend Linda tonight at her dinner party, come up with a plan. Linda's always had a problem-solving mind – even our school teachers said so. I point my remote at my car before I can talk myself out of it. The boot flies open.

'I'm not spending two hundred quid on a pair of plimsolls.' Anna's raging voice tears through the air. 'If you don't get in the car by the count of three, I'm going to confiscate your phone.'

'What?'

'And your MacBook.'

'Mum!'

'And you'll be grounded for a week.'

'That's child abuse,' Ralf hits back.

And there was I thinking Valley Gardens was drama-free. Peering around the lid of my boot, I spot Frank, leaning against his car, his back to me. I pull out my tripod hurriedly and rest it against the back wing of my car, then squeeze my work bag between the clutter as Ralf threatens Anna with social services. Grabbing my tripod, I hastily shut the boot. But it's too late.

'Kids, hey?' Anna yells, throwing a glance at Frank, who is swaggering back towards me like a runway model. 'Anyway, better drop this lot off. Have a lovely evening, Bella.' She says this in a *have fun with your hunky visitor* way and my face tingles.

'Nice neighbourhood,' Frank remarks as Anna pulls out of her driveway, wearing a huge pair of dark glasses, even though the sun went down hours ago. He takes in the length of me, hands in pockets, triceps bulging. 'Are they always this noisy?'

'They're a lovely family, actually,' I retort, berating myself for faffing about with my bag in the boot instead of making a quick escape. 'Wasn't it you who always said not to judge?'

'Fair point. What are you going to do with that?'

'It's going in the back. No room in the boot.'

'They make them tiny these days, don't they? Here, let me give you a hand.' Frank's arm brushes against mine.

'No,' I snap, pulling away. 'I can manage.'

Lifting his hands up, he says, 'I was only trying to help.' I scowl as I secure the tripod against the backseat.

'Right,' Frank says, as I slam the car door. 'I'm glad we've cleared the air.' He pauses, sticks a finger under his Gucci beanie hat, which rarely leaves his head, even during classes, and scratches. 'So, we're all good now, yeah?'

'No,' I interject, raising a palm. 'You don't get to gaslight me. If you think I was interested in you then you're deluded.' I flash a tight smile at the boy from number 25, who is walking his Siberian Husky. His pooch usually stops outside Mr Stanhope's for a wee. I watch and right on cue, he cocks his leg.

'Are you always this stubborn?' Frank mutters, running a hand over his face.

'For whatever reason you had.' I point my finger at him as the lad and his dog shrink into the distance. 'You wanted more from me.'

'I didn't.'

'What was it, a bet that you'd get the ice queen into bed? Yes, I know what they call me at *Serval*. What did they do to motivate you? Tell you I was out of your league?'

'It wasn't like that.'

'Count yourself lucky I didn't report you to Jane.' Jane, *Serval's* Manager, with her honey blonde ponytail and rock-hard body, is pleasant enough, calls everyone darling, but she's firm – takes no prisoners. You know the kind.

'Where's all this coming from?' he asks. I laugh incredulously. 'I think you need to calm down, Bella.'

'And you need to leave. *Now*.'

'Pfft, I've had enough of this crap,' he says in that clipped whispery tone of his. 'I came here today to have a civilised conversation, bury the hatchet, but look at you, you're hysterical.'

'If you're so sure I flirted with you, that I was gagging for it, then why are you here, hmm?' Now it's my turn to play mind games. 'Why are you worried?'

A muscle in his eyelid twitches. Ocular myokymia. It happens to me sometimes. Tom said it can be caused by being overly tired or stressed. Frank's resolve is weakening.

'I don't want you to start spreading rumours about me, that's all.' Stepping back, he closes his eyes. I watch as his chest rises and falls. I can almost hear him counting to three. 'I've got some high-profile clients.' I inwardly roll my eyes. *Have you, really? Because you've only mentioned it about three hundred times. Shame the only evidence is a photograph on your phone at a charity event with an ex-soap actor.*

'Eighty-per-cent of my clients are female, they trust me, and I'm not having some…'

'Go on, say it. Some Karen?'

'I wasn't going to say that.' He scowls, squeezes his fist around the handles of the carrier bag, knuckles protruding. 'If they get the idea that I'm a flipping pervert they won't hire me, will they? Just don't do anything stupid, Bella.'

'Relax. I'm not going to say anything to anyone.' *Seeing as you know my biggest secret.* 'But only if you promise that this ends now.' I'm about to get into my car when a surge of fear pumps through my veins. 'How did you know where I live?' I never gave him my address. We always trained at the gym or the park track. It could only mean one thing. He's been stalking me.

Chapter 3

'Dee gave me your address.' Dee. *Serval's* PA. Petite, copper-haired, milky-skinned, late twenties, goes red whenever Frank talks to her. My muscles relax. At least Frank isn't stalking me. 'She looked you up on the system.'

'Is that even legal?'

'Actually, yes. The gym was trying to get in touch with you and you weren't picking up.' I frown at the pavement. I did get a couple of missed calls from the gym but I thought it was marketing with an offer to re-join *Serval*.

'Contact me about what?'

Frank sways the carrier bag at me. 'You forgot your boxing gloves when you legged it out of the studio last Tuesday.'

'Dee should've texted me,' I retort, snatching the bag from his hand and peering inside. Yes, definitely my gloves – pink and white. I forgot all about those. 'Or emailed, instead of dishing out my address to staff.'

'Why don't you report her to Jane?' he suggests.

'Maybe I will.' It's hard to believe that Dee gave him my address. She's good at her job, sticks to the rules, and she's terrified of Jane. But then everyone knows Dee has a huge crush on Frank.

Frank shrugs, examines his nails. 'They'll probably sack her. The club is strict on data protection.' I don't want Dee sacked. Frank coerced her into leaking information in that manipulative, charming way of his.

'Anyway, thanks,' I croak, 'for returning my gloves.'

'S'okay.'

'Great. Well, see you around.' Folding myself into the car, I chuck the carrier bag into the footwell of the passenger seat. Is it possible that he only passed by today to return my gloves and clear the air about what happened? Let's hope so.

Fastening my seatbelt, I turn on the ignition. 'Not so fast, Bella.' My eyes close. I knew it was too good to be true. 'Wind the window down please,' he orders, glancing away. I buzz it down halfway. 'I need to ask a favour.' There's a ding of a bell and he steps out of the way as a lad flashes by on a bicycle. *Please don't let him ask me for money.* 'My landlord has just put the rent up and –'

Turning the ignition off, I look at him pointedly. 'So, that's what this is all about, is it?' I rub the back of my goose-skinned neck, and as I glance away, I see Mr Stanhope's slim figure behind the nets next door. 'And there was I thinking you wanted to clear the air, apologise,' I say, scanning my busybody neighbour's window. He's still there, recording us with his eyes so that he can relay everything to Tom when he next sees him. I can't let that happen. I'll stop at the offy on my way home, grab a bottle of gin to bribe him with, tell him Frank was a rogue builder trying to get business out of me, convince him not to mention it to Tom, not now that he's grieving the loss of his favourite aunt, Andriana. 'What are you going to do, hmm?' I say to Frank. 'Blackmail me? Tell my husband I hired you behind his back?'

'I wasn't going to say that.'

'What then? Tell him you saw me with…' I purse my lips. I can't even bear to think about Liam and what we…what *I* have done to Tom.

Squatting to my eye level, Frank fixes me with a hard stare. 'Let's get one thing straight, Bella. I am not here to blackmail you. I'm here to make amends.' Turning away from him, I inhale the fug of his lemony aftershave and stale sweat. 'Losing your business has hit me hard. A hundred and twenty quid a week is a lot of money for me.'

I bite my lips sealing in the words, *then stop buying expensive designer gear and jewellery if you're hard up.* I focus on his Oliver Peoples sunglasses, which are tucked into the collar of his top, as he continues to babble on about what a decent person he is, and just then it occurs to me that this man could potentially end my marriage in a heartbeat.

'Okay, how much do you want?'

Incredulity sweeps across his face. '*What*?' he says, sounding offended. 'I don't want your money.'

'Then what *do* you want, Frank? Because right now I'm a little bit confused.'

A beat and then. 'Let's start again. Wipe the slate clean.'

'I'm sorry, but no.'

'We can put this blip behind us, pretend it never happened.'

'No, Frank, I wouldn't be comfortable training with you now.' Frank is one of the top trainers at *Serval*. I have lost weight and gained muscle, and, thanks to his personalised fitness programme, my confidence has grown. Admittedly, I do miss the buzz of the classes. But there's no way I can be in the same room as him, not now.

'I can get Dee to give you a 25% discount.' I turn on the ignition. 'Fifty then, but I can't get her to go lower than that.'

He shoots to his feet. 'Bella, wait,' he says quickly, tone raspy. 'We need to sort this. Wait…I haven't finished.'

'Stay away from me.' I rev the engine.

Bending forward, he pins me down with a stare, one hand on the roof of the car. 'It's true what they say, you don't know what someone's like until the shit hits the fan.'

'Get your hands off my car.'

Ignoring me, he licks his lips, glances away, and then his head snaps back round at me like a whip and the claws come out. 'Just who the fuck do you think you are, hmm?' he hisses, face contorted in fury. I'm taken aback. I've never seen this sinister side to him before. 'I'm sure Mr Harris would love to know a few home truths about his precious wife.' I go cold all over. How does he know Tom's surname? I registered at the gym under my maiden name – Villin. 'Nice little practice he's got there at Hadley Green.' And I certainly didn't tell him where he works. But he's wrong about the practice. Tom's part of the optical team, but he's salaried. 'I think I've got a bit of blurry vision, actually. Might be due for an eye test.'

I swallow back sour liquid that is charging up my gullet, and just then a thought rockets into my head. Did Dee give him my address, or *has* Frank been following me after all? With a tremulous hand, I put the car into Reverse, leg shaking. The car moves, he staggers back.

I buzz my window up. 'You stuck-up little *bitch*.' Glancing in my side mirror, I flick the indicator on. 'No one dumps me, Bella Villin.' His words fly at me like bullets as I struggle to put the car into Drive. 'There's a six-month waiting list for my fucking services,' he rages, booting the wheel of my car like a thug.

'Move, you bloody thing,' I mutter at the gear lever as he continues to spit vitriol at me. With a trembling hand, I try to force the car into Drive. 'Come on!!!' A clunking sound fills my ears – clunk, clunk, clunk. Shit, he's trying to open the back door. Thank God for central locking.

Next to me, Frank's face is a blur by the window. 'I promise you, you're going to regret this.' Shrinking into my shoulders, I push my foot down on the brakes just as his gob hits the pane. I cringe, even though the window is closed. 'Whetstone Manor. Isn't that where Georgia goes?' *Oh, God, oh no. How could he know that?* I slide the lever into Drive. 'This isn't over, trust me,' he sneers, stumbling away from the car as I put my foot down. 'I'm about to become your worst nightmare, Bella Villin,' he hollers.

Tearing along the street, my eyes dart to the rearview until Frank becomes a tiny figure in the distance, every part of me shaking. If my life wasn't complicated enough, it's about to get ten times worse.

Chapter 4

I press the shiny, round, gold ringer. It shrills loudly. Smoothing down my hair, I straighten my silk pink blouse. I feel like I've arrived for a job interview, which I've buggered up by turning up late and dishevelled, know I won't get, but go through the process anyway on the slim chance that my interviewer might be a reincarnation of Mother Theresa. I'm ridiculously late, thanks to Frank. Mrs Anderson's anxiety levels must be through the roof. I can almost see a mist of her angst seeping through the newly tiled loft conversion. I'll offer her a 10% discount if she gets shirty. Anything to avoid a bad online review. Although she did sound lovely on the phone. 'Where the hell are you?' I mutter to myself. 'I thought you wanted this done and dusted before your husband got home.'

Looking at my watch, I ring the bell again and stand back, feeling small and insignificant after that altercation with Frank. Jesus, have I got myself a stalker? Will I have to go to the police? Tom will find out everything if I do. I shudder at the thought, throw a glance at the shiny green Mini Cooper parked on Mrs Anderson's driveway. It has an air freshener in the shape of a pair of pink trainers hanging from the rear-view. Must be hers. Surely, she must be in. She sounded desperate on the phone this morning. Unless her husband turned up early. But no, she'd have texted to let me know.

Chewing my bottom lip, I pull out my phone, and just then there's a gust of air and the door flies open. Mrs Anderson is tall, trim and attractive, with a messy silver bob, mid-sixties, I'd say. She's wearing metallic brown shadow over her hooded hazel eyes, mascara, and a splash of plum lip-gloss. Sliding a hand into her black chino shorts, she gives me a warm smile and her eyes crinkle – no work done. I like her immediately.

'I hope you haven't been waiting long. I popped into the garden to empty the bin. Didn't hear the doorbell go. Just caught sight of you through the lounge window.'

'I've only just arrived,' I offer, and she nods, casting an eye at her gold wristwatch.

'I was freshening the place up,' Mrs Anderson says, aerosol in hand. 'Ginny just decided to do a poo on the lounge carpet instead of her clean litter tray.' She rolls her eyes. A car door thumps behind me.

'Oh, dear,' I say, waiting patiently for her to invite me in.

'Pets, hey?' Mrs Anderson looks confident and relaxed in her tanned skin. Probably just back from basking somewhere hot and exotic. Maybe Rhodes, given she's wearing a vest with the word emblazoned across the chest. God, isn't she cold? I'm shivering in my wool suit. 'Talk about timing. I'm sure she did it on purpose. Please, come in.' She steps aside and I notice that she's barefoot and has a gold chain around her ankle. Her lofty frame makes me feel like a midget, even though I'm a respectable five-foot-six.

Brushing my hand against the radiator covertly, I discover that the heating isn't on. I'm going to die of hypothermia. The sooner I get this gig done, the sooner I can get to Linda's and tell her all about my episode with Frank.

'Sorry I'm a bit late, traffic was heaving – an accident on the North Circ.' Mrs Anderson gives me a look and my face tingles. She knows I'm lying but doesn't contradict me. I shuffle along the hallway, bag on shoulder, tripod under my arm, all the while going through the usual preambles – Isabella Villin but everyone calls me Bella. 'It's so lovely to meet you in the flesh, Mrs. Anderson.' I give her a smile, eyes drawn to her toenails, which are neatly varnished in lilac, and then I remember my shoes. 'I'll just leave these here, shall I?' My feet almost groan as I slip out of my uncomfortable heels.

'Oh, you don't need to take your shoes off, we're not posh.' *Oh, I think you are, Mrs Anderson. This place stinks of wealth.* My eyes dart to the floor - Chevron parquet – wall to wall. The good stuff – expensive. No scuffs, look new. The place looks like it's just had a makeover. 'And it's Tina.' Mrs Anderson extends a hand and we shake briskly. 'I just like walking around the house barefoot. Drives Ben, my husband, well, soon-to-be ex-husband, up the wall. Accuses me of creeping up on him.' *Ben sounds like a prick.*

'I'd best,' I say, dropping them next to a pair of blue Hunter wellies, 'you never know what germs I'm bringing into your home.'

'Okay,' Mrs Anderson smiles. 'Whatever makes you happy. Just leave them by the door. Can I get you anything to drink? Tea? Coffee?' I shake my head - tell her I've overdosed on caffeine today. 'Okay, shall we start downstairs?' She flicks a glance at her watch again. 'We are running a bit late, aren't we?'

'I'll be as quick as I can,' I assure her.

'I've removed all the clutter, as you suggested,' Mrs Anderson says. I usually tell people to squint and get rid of anything that stands out like a sore thumb. 'And took the photos down, too, just as an extra precaution,' she adds, as I bend forward and fiddle with the switch of the lampshade. 'You never know these days,' she groans, helping me out with the shade. 'This one's a bit tricky – there. You can't be too careful, can you, what with the dark web and all that.'

'It all looks amazing. Makes my job a lot easier. Thank you.' I point to a black and white photograph of a couple on the wall above the chic seventies-style wooden dining table. The young woman looks stylish and gorgeous with dark hair swept off her black flawless face, reminding me of a younger Linda. The man is ordinary, receding ginger hair, pale skin with piggy eyes. Definitely punching, as Zelda would say. 'I'll blur that portrait out, Tina.'

Mrs Anderson follows my eyes, confused, and then her face goes slightly pink. 'Oh God, yes, please. I forgot about that one. That's my son, Rupert, and Gloria, his wife, on their wedding day.'

'They're a gorgeous couple.' Come on, I'm not going to tell her that her son is no oil painting, am I? Mrs Anderson nods proudly as I snap away, tells me they've got three children now, aged eight to thirteen, and a crippling mortgage. She hopes to help them once this place is sold. 'Life does throw you a lifeline sometimes, doesn't it?'

'It sure does, Tina.' If only it would send me one right now and wipe Frank Hardy off the face of the universe.

Chapter 5

'Did you take a photo of the guest bathroom?' Mrs Anderson asks, ten minutes later as I complete the sketch of the floor-plan in the hallway. 'It's just here.'

I shake my head. 'Guest cloakrooms are a bit small. I won't be able to get a good angle.'

'Are you saying I cleaned it for nothing?'

'Afraid so.' I grin, and we both laugh. 'I'm just going to take a few measurements, then I'll get out of your hair.'

'I must say, you've got a fascinating job. Have you been a property photographer for long?'

'Ten years. My best friend, Linda, is an estate agent, gives me lots of leads. Diary's full for the next six weeks.' I point the measuring device across the room and Mrs Anderson ducks out of the way, even though I told her she doesn't have to. I think it's a reflex reaction. 'I was a shop assistant before that, did weddings and christenings at weekends, the odd family portrait.'

'So, you've always been an artist. My son works in publishing. I've got an English degree, must run in the family, eh?'

'Funny you should say that. My mum's an artist.' I jot down a few notes on my iPad. 'Perhaps there is a creative gene in there somewhere. My ambition is to set up my own estate agency. I love bricks and mortar. Maybe one day.' My phone buzzes in my jacket pocket. I pull it out. It's Tom:

Running a bit late. Last minute eye examination. one of the golf lads got red eye. Can meet u at Theo and Linda's instead. I'll jump on a train straight to Southgate. Might be easier.

I harrumph as I quickly type out my reply, offering my apologies to Mrs Anderson.

'Not bad news, I hope,' Mrs Anderson says, sensing my frustration.

'Friends have invited us round for dinner tonight, but my other half is running late.'

'Oh, that's a bummer. Is your hubby in the same line of work?' I snort at that, tell her he's an optometrist. 'How wonderful! Must be useful for your family members.'

'Yeah.' I scratch my eyebrow. 'Tom looks after us all.'

'Well, at least you're earning too and not relying on his salary.' I give her a minuscule frown. 'What I mean is.' She's gone a bit red now. 'If you ever find yourself in my shoes.' She thrusts a tanned bony hand out quickly, sapphire ring gleaming on her finger. 'You won't have to sell your house to survive. Like I am.'

I raise my eyebrows. *Oh, I will if Tom finds out about Frank and Liam.* 'I don't think that'll happen,' I reply a little briskly, and she looks as if I've punched her. I hope I haven't hurt her feelings. 'But then you never know, Tina, do you?' I add politely, 'anything is possible.' Mrs Anderson smiles, face softening. If she knew I signed a prenuptial before we got married, she'd probably put me through that lounge bay window.

The prenup was set up to protect Tom's family inheritance if we divorce. It wasn't Tom's idea. It was Gary's, his father, a consultant ophthalmologist and also penny-wise. The apple doesn't fall far from the tree. I must admit, I get on a lot better with Wendy, Tom's mother. Gary's a nice enough man, but he's worse than Tom when it comes to money, and let's just say that he wasn't best pleased when he found out his only child was going to marry his pregnant shop assistant girlfriend of six months.

Mrs Anderson shakes her head slowly, back against the wall, arms folded. 'Husbands, hey? We give them the best years of our lives and then, puff, it's all over. Ben spends more time at the golf club than with me, and I'm not even joking. I just feel.' She stares at her bare feet. 'Invisible sometimes,' she whispers, then looks up at me, her stoic persona returning. 'So, one night I just said to him, in jest, of course, it's me or the golf clubs, and he chose the clubs.'

'I'm sorry,' I offer, and then. 'He sounds like a moron.' Mrs Anderson's eyes twinkle, likes it that I'm on her side.

'There was a third party involved. Hence the sale of this place.' She gazes around the lounge dreamily, and I can tell that she's in love with her home, and possibly still in love with her husband – because you can't just stop loving someone, can you? 'Cost us a fortune to do it all up. We'll never get our money back. We knew that from the onset but it was supposed to be our forever home.' Her eyes flick to the ground. 'Now I can't wait to get rid of it.'

'I'm sorry to hear that, Mrs…um…Tina.'

'It's fine.' Mrs Anderson wipes her face with both hands as if she's been crying but there are no tears. 'Anyway, you must have quite a lot on your plate, what with a husband and a job, and giving folk like me free counselling sessions. How do you manage? Is Mum around to help out?'

'Nah, she's away most of the time,' I say, gathering my stuff to leave. 'On an artist's retreat in Portugal as we speak, painting the sun setting against the sea.'

'Oh, how lovely. Is she a local artist? I might know her.' I nod, tell her she doesn't live too far from me. 'Really? I'd love to see her work. I'm a bit of a collector. Perhaps, when she's back from Portugal, you could…'

'No can do, I'm afraid. Zelda and I keep telling her to exhibit but she always refuses.' Mum made a lot of money from commissions, enough to buy her lovely home in Oakwood. But she just wants a quiet life now, without the stress. 'She just loves painting.'

'I see. Okay. Is Zelda your daughter?' Tina asks, and I shake my head, tell her she's my sister. 'I wish I had a sister. I've got a brother, Simon, lives in South London. Is it just the two of you?'

'Yes,' I admit. 'We're very close. Love her to bits. Zelda's only just set up her own bakery business, actually. Zee Bakes.' I add, not allowing the shameless namedrop opportunity to go amiss. 'She does free local deliveries if the order is over twenty-five pounds.'

'I'll know where to go if I need a cake. Shame you haven't got family to help out, though. I know how tough it can be.'

'It's not that bad,' I explain. 'I've got an assistant. Maggie. More of a goddess, really.' Mrs Anderson laughs knowingly, tells me she had a Maggie once when she ran her own cleaning business after she gave up nursing, and this time it's my turn to be impressed. 'So, you didn't use your English degree?'

'I wanted to be an actor,' she says wistfully, 'but my parents wouldn't have it, said it wasn't a proper job. So, nursing it was,' she declares. 'Which I loved but had to give up when I had my son. At Ben's insistence. But I couldn't just sit at home with a baby all day, so I set up my own cleaning business from home.

I've always liked a clean house. To my surprise, it took off and I had to hire staff, including an assistant.'

'Maggie goes above and beyond the call of duty. She's a saint. But she's on maternity leave at the moment. So, it's pretty full on for me.'

'Oh, that's a shame. For you, I mean, not her, obviously.' Mrs Anderson pulls out a tissue from the pocket of her shorts and dabs her petite nose. 'Have you considered getting a temp in to cover for her?'

'Yes, but life has been a bit hectic. I'm actually going to post an ad online tomorrow,' I say, and she nods, wishes me luck. 'Right. All done. I'll email you the images once I've done an edit and completed the floorplan. If you need any help uploading them onto the agent's website, give me a shout, and as I said, I know someone who can do the EPC check for you – very reliable and reasonable rates, too.'

'Oh, that'll be brilliant, Bella. I'll be in touch, and I hope Maggie comes back soon, or you find a short-term replacement.'

'Thank you,' I say, crossing my fingers.

'Actually, can you hang on a moment? I've just had an idea.' I throw a glance at my watch as she disappears into the kitchen, returning moments later with a notepad and pen. 'My niece has just moved here from Dublin and is desperate for work, even something temporary. Is your office local?' I tell her I work from my garden office on Valley Gardens, Whetstone.

'Very nice,' Mrs Anderson says. 'I knew someone who lived there. Number 24, moved to Northampton to be near her son. Husband got dementia. Poor love. They were a lovely couple. You might know them – Charles and Dorothy.'

I shake my head, tell her we only recently moved to the area, but number 24 is a few doors away from me. 'Aww, never mind. Anyway, pop all the details on here, hours etcetera. I'll have a word with my niece and, if she's up for it, I'll tell her to get in touch. She's very good at admin, very organised, and will accept minimum wage. Good with children, too. And pets, if you've got any.'

'No pets – yet,' I say, scribbling down the duties, the hourly rate and my number, even though Mrs Anderson already has my mobile and email address. 'Although my daughter is badgering me for a cockapoo,' I smile, handing her the pen and notebook.'

'How old is she?'

'Fifteen.'

Mrs Anderson nods knowingly. 'A difficult age. I'm glad I only had the one. Thanks for coming over and doing this at such short notice, love. You're a lifesaver. Mind how you go.'

And as the front door closes behind me, it occurs to me that Mrs Anderson didn't give me her niece's name. My finger hovers over the doorbell, and just then my mobile buzzes with a message.

Linda: *Can you grab a couple of reds?* (two red wine glasses emojis). *Zelda texted saying Keiko doesn't drink white x*

Keiko's my sister's latest squeeze and her plus one for tonight. Tom won't be happy. He's already bought the wine for tonight. I'm going to be ludicrously late now, thanks to Frank's impromptu visit and Keiko's aversion to white wine. He's already annoying me. I'll grab two bottles of Merlot from the offy when I stop off for Mr Stanhope's bribe gin. Another text pings through from Linda:

And a dessert please. My sponge collapsed! (crying emoji).

I look at my watch 19.03. And now I've got a supermarket stop-off to do. Bloody brilliant. There's no time to waste. I'll put an ad on Elite Jobs tonight. Mrs Anderson was probably just trying to be helpful. I'll never hear from her niece.

Chapter 6

Fatigue hits me by the time I get home, but it's nothing that a quick shower won't fix. I can't let Linda and Zelda down. They've been looking forward to this dinner party all week.

The house is still, dark, apart from the wall light projecting into the hallway like a spotlight. Georgia must've forgotten to turn it off before going to her mate Tilly's.

Dropping my gear by the front door, I slip the Waitrose bag next to the stairway. Then, as I shrug out of my jacket, there's a creak on the floorboards and then I'm illuminated in a flood of bright lights.

'God, you frightened the shit out of me,' I gasp, heartbeat soaring. 'What are you doing here?'

Tom's face is deadpan, blue eyes fixed on me. He's cleanly shaven and smelling gorgeous in black chinos and a white button-down shirt. His greying, mostly white, hair is slicked back with gel. 'I live here, remember? Where the hell have you been?'

I'm speechless for a few moments, not liking his accusing tone one bit. 'I was working,' I hit back. 'Where do you think I've been?'

'At this time?'

'Yes, at *this* time. What's with all the questions, anyway? Are you checking up on me?'

The accusation in my voice irritates him. 'And why would I be doing that, hmm?' He turns up the cuff of his sleeve angrily. Tom's cool by default, but I've lived with him long enough to know when something, or *someone*, has rattled his cage. Was it Frank? Did he wait for him outside and grass me up after all?

'I had a last-minute job,' I say, not meeting his eye. 'Mrs Anderson in Golders Green. She's divorcing and wants a quick sale, and then I had to stop off at a supermarket to get some wine for tonight.'

'I said I was getting that,' he complains, tilting his head towards the kitchen. 'They're in the fridge. Chilean white. They were on offer.' Cheap plonk that'll give us all a headache in the morning, no doubt.

'There was a change of plan. Linda texted. Keiko only drinks red.'

I go to hang up my jacket when he says, 'Georgia said the alarm wasn't on when she got in from school.' Damn, I knew I should've gone back in to check. 'Honestly, Bella, have you any idea how many break-ins there's been on this road?' he points out, tone patriarchal. Anyone would think he was talking to Georgia. But I'm not in the mood for a row. 'You do realise the insurance won't cough up if we don't bother to put the bloody thing on.'

'I'm sorry, okay? I was in a rush. Anyway, I thought you were going straight to Linda and Theo's?'

He looks at me carefully for a few moments, jaw tight, vein on the side of his neck prominent, and then he seems to snap out of it. 'The eye test was cancelled. Lee had an eyelash under his lid. His wife removed it. I came home to freshen up and Georgia roped me into taking her to Tilly's for her sleepover.'

A result for Georgia. She usually takes two buses to get to her best friend's house. 'Bloody stuck in traffic all the way back.' Welcome to my world. 'And then….' His eyes dart to the Waitrose bag. 'What else is in that bag?'

'What?'

'There's more than two bottles of wine in there.'

'I bought four and Linda asked me to pick up dessert - lemon drizzle. Everyone likes that.' My husband gives me one of his looks. 'Two bottles won't be enough for six people, Tom,' I protest. Reaching over, I hook my jacket in between his navy padded gilet and Georgia's oversized leopard print coat, feeling his eyes burning into my back, and then I hear the swish of plastic and the tinkle of bottles. He's looking inside the carrier bag. When I turn to face him, he's holding Mr Stanhope's bribe gin and reading the label, a slow smile on his lips.

'We were running low,' I lie. 'I'll just freshen up and we'll get going. I texted Linda to say I'm running late, so…'

'We've got an unopened bottle of Bombay Sapphire in the cabinet,' Tom interjects. 'You've splashed out a bit, haven't you? I haven't had Hendricks's in ages.' He twists the screwcap. Shit, I'll have to buy Mr Stanhope another bottle now. 'It's your turn to drive, isn't it?' It sounds more like an order than a question.

'Actually, I'm shattered. Do you mind if we get a cab?' I take his silence as a yes. 'I'll get the glasses, then, shall I?' I say dryly. 'Ice and lemon?'

'Just ice, thanks,' he says, peering at the Merlot in the bag. 'By the way, anything else you'd like to share?'

I freeze, stomach tightening. 'No, I don't think so.' I head for the kitchen; he goes to follow me when his phone pings. His footfall stops. 'If that's Theo, tell him we'll be there in half an hour.'

Flicking on the kitchen light, I quickly grab two tumblers, stick a few ice cubes in them and amble back into the hallway, ice tinkling against the glasses.

'Did you hear what I said?' I look up at Tom, but he's busy texting with his thumb, bottle of Hendrick's aloft in his other hand. 'God, what a day...' I begin, holding a glass out to him, and I can't help but wonder who he's texting with such urgency. By the look on his face, it's work related. Maybe it's that golfing chum Lee with the lash. Perhaps his wife poked him in the eye whilst trying to remove it. 'Traffic was heaving and Mrs Anderson was a bit chatty.'

Tom slips his phone into his back pocket, then pours a generous amount of gin into each glass. 'So, when were you planning on telling me?' I go cold all over. *Damn*. Frank did wait for him and now Tom knows everything. The double-crossing bastard. But no, no, not everything. If Tom knew about Liam, my bags would've been packed by the door. 'Any tonic for this?' Tom asks.

'I think there's one or two under here,' I say, grateful for the extra few seconds to think of a justification for hiring a personal trainer behind his back. Rummaging around in the understairs cupboard, I pull out a can of Fever Tree and hand it to him, dread soaring through my body.

'It's not something you can hide, Bella, is it?' Well, technically, it is. I was using my personal account to pay for my PT lessons, so Tom would be none the wiser. 'Can you hold this please?' He hands me his glass and I pray he doesn't notice the tremor in my hand as I take it.

'Do you think we can talk about this later. I told Linda we'd be there by eight-thirty at the latest.'

I go to move, his hand flies up like a shield, and then he cocks his head sharply towards the living room, and it's only then that I see a pair of legs in black floaty trousers and a pair of white trainers in the gap of the door, followed by the rattle of a cup and saucer.

'Your seven-thirty,' he whispers, eyes darkening. 'I mean, you might've warned me.' I open my mouth to tell him that I've no idea what he's talking about but he just talks over me. 'I looked like a right twat. Why did you book her in tonight of all nights, when you knew we had plans? Honestly, Bella, what were you going to do? Leave me sitting at Theo and Linda's with your sister and her new bloke like a gooseberry?'

'No, of course not,' I mumble absently, as he groans that it wouldn't be the first time. 'I honestly don't know…'

'Poor girl expected to find you here,' he cuts across me angrily. 'She was a bag of nerves when she arrived, shaking like a leaf. I had to make her a sweet tea to calm her down.'

I run a hand over my face. Strangely, I felt relieved when I thought Tom knew I'd been spending shedloads of our cash on a personal trainer. Now, I'm back to harbouring two secrets. 'I'm sorry but I don't know who that woman is, or what she's doing here. I certainly didn't invite her over.'

'She asked for you by name,' he seethes. 'Bella Villin. I put her right, said your name is Harris.' I look at him blankly, and he rubs the side of his forehead with two fingers – something he does when he's getting pissed off with me. 'She's here about the temp's job,' he states. 'Apparently, you arranged it with her aunt.'

'Aunt?' It can't be Mrs Anderson's niece already.

'One of your clients.' He scrunches his eyes, frowning. 'Tina.' Crikey. It is. Mrs Anderson didn't waste much time. 'Look, I had to step in in your absence. Explained everything, hours, rate, and she's happy with the arrangement. She seems like a nice enough girl – keen. Look, you need help, Bella. I don't know why you've been dragging your feet. It's not as if we didn't budget for a temp, is it?' No, but I dipped into that budget to pay for a personal trainer instead. 'Anyway, let's just park that for now and concentrate on her.' He jerks his head towards the lounge. 'It would've been nice if you'd told me you were interviewing tonight, that's all.'

'Do you honestly think I knew about this? I only spoke to her auntie.' I look at my watch. 'About an hour ago. Mrs Anderson said she'd have a word with her niece and get her to call me.'

Confusion sweeps across Tom's face. 'Right. I see. Sorry for jumping down your throat.' A pause and then. 'Bit keen, aren't they?'

'Tell me about it.'

'Well, anyway, she's here now, so you might as well talk to her.' Ushering me towards the door, I let Tom take the half-filled glass from my hand like a robot, even though I haven't finished my drink yet. 'Just go in there and have a quick word, then we'll make tracks.' I go to push the door and then he says. 'By the way, I told her she's hired.'

Chapter 7

Mrs Anderson's niece is slipping a bottle of perfume back into her rucksack as I walk into the lounge, and I almost choke on the heady mist. When she sees me, she gasps and shoots to her feet.

'Oh, Mrs Harris, I'm so sorry to turn up like this but Auntie said she'd spoken to you about it earlier and it'd be fine.' I didn't say that. I said I'd be more than happy to consider her niece for the position if she contacted me to arrange an interview, not that she could turn up willy-nilly. On the face of it, she seems nice and has certainly made an impression on my husband. But turning up on my doorstep without an appointment on a Friday evening? It's just not on. 'I'm so grateful for this opportunity, Mrs Harris. Mr Harris has explained all the duties and terms. I've only been here a fortnight. I really need –'

'Woah, woah, slow down,' I say wearily, sinking into my grey, fabric, snuggle chair. I wave a hand. 'Take a seat.'

'Thanks, Mrs Harris.' Sitting back down, she gives me a watery smile, then gazes around the books in our library in awe, hands clasped together in her lap, nails short, unvarnished. She has a soft Irish accent, long red hair tumbling over her shoulders, and aquamarine eyes. There's something familiar about her, as in when you see a celebrity out and about before processing who they are. In this case, it's Mrs Anderson I see – a family resemblance.

'It's Bella,' I smile. 'Boy, your auntie's a fast worker,' I raise my eyebrows, shifting in my seat. Okay, Tom likes her and that's great but I can't hire her on his say so. She'll be working alongside me. It has to be my decision. I'm going to have to ask her to come back for an official interview. 'Look, I'm interviewing –'

'Gosh, auntie Tina called me right away,' she intervenes, cheeks pink, 'said you were ace and that I should get my foot in the door before you hired someone else. I tried phoning but it went to voicemail.' The call from an unknown number while I was in the supermarket. I thought it was a cold call, so rejected it. I'd have saved her a visit if I'd picked up. 'I had to knock on a few doors to find you, mind,' she says, crossing her legs at the ankles. 'Auntie said you lived a few doors from number 24.' Her smile is broad and she has good teeth, straight, natural looking. Her skin is milky white, the kind that easily burns in the sun, and she has a splash of freckles across the bridge of her nose. 'I wanted to be your first applicant. Auntie said you were going to put an ad online.' Her eyes widen and I realise that I'm frowning at her. 'Mr Harris said the job's mine if I want it. I hope that's okay.'

I admire her nerve and determination, and she's certainly enthusiastic, but no, it's not okay. I rub my lips. I hate letting people down, but needs must. 'Um…Miss Anderson?'

'It's Murphy. Daisy Murphy.' Her chest rises and falls against her white shirt and I notice a gold crucifix around her neck with a red ruby in the middle. It looks vintage. The kind of piece you'd find on a stall at Portobello Road market.

'Daisy, I know Tom offered you the job but we do need to go through the process, yes?' She nods furiously. 'Call it a second interview. The thing is, I'm running late and wasn't expecting you, so…'

Blood rushes to her cheeks. 'Oh, *godddd!!*. I'm such a klutz.' She shoots to her feet, flustered, and then launches into a fit of apologies – it was a stupid thing to do, I probably haven't had dinner yet, must want to interview other applicants, ones who are far more experienced and suitable for the job, whatever was she thinking. 'I'm sorry to have troubled you, I'll –'

'Daisy, stop,' I say loudly, putting a hand out and feeling like a bit of a cow for making her feel so awful. I study her for a few moments. She reminds me of a younger me – vulnerable, desperate to please, yet full of passion, hungry for success. 'Please, sit back down.' Maybe I should give her a chance. Tom likes her. I need a temp and can afford one now that I've sacked Frank. Hiring her will save me paying for an online ad, and time interviewing other applicants, many of whom will be completely unsuitable. 'Tom has told you all about the job, right?' Daisy nods and watches me like an excited puppy. I can almost see her tail wagging. She can sense I'm changing my mind, that she's in with a chance. 'Have you done anything like this before?'

'Admin? Pfft, yeah, loads in Dublin. But I'm not gonna lie, I've never worked for a property photographer.' I like her honesty. 'Sounds amazing,' she beams, sitting back down, eyes bright. 'Going into all those people's homes, having a peek at their lives. Houses tell you so much about folk, don't they?' A girl after my own heart.

'Have you got a CV?'

'Sure.' Fumbling around in her rucksack, she pulls out an A4 sheet. 'Sorry, it's a bit squashed.' Ironing it out with her palm, she hands it to me. 'And my passport for ID.'

'Great photo, ' I say, flicking through her passport. She's photogenic. I look like a troll in mine, and Tom looks like one of the Kray twins. The one with the glasses. I scan the CV and read nothing. I look at my watch – 20.08. Linda's going to kill me. 'Right, I'm going to go out on a limb here. My husband likes you and so do I. We need someone we can trust, someone reliable, and as I know your aunt, you're hired.' Daisy's jaw drops open. 'When can you start?'

'Now!' Daisy stands up, sits down, half stands, sits, face on fire. 'I can start *immediately*. I'll work really hard, Mrs Harris. I mean, Bella.' I laugh lightly, tell her I will need a couple of references and she reaches for her bag again, pulls out a manila envelope and hands it to me, and in that moment it occurs to me that each time she hands me something, a blend of stale sweat and perfume dances under my nose. I thought it was me to begin with, but it only happens when she moves. Perhaps she came straight from the gym, hence the manic perfume spraying and trainers.

'I haven't got time to go through them now,' I say, taking the envelope from her hand, 'but I'm sure everything is in order. I'll see you Monday at nine.'

Daisy gets to her feet and shoulders her rucksack. 'Brilliant. Bella, I can't thank you enough for this opportunity. I promise I won't let you down. I'll do anything – your washing, ironing, I'll even scrub the loos.'

'You won't have to do that,' I say, shepherding her into the corridor, all the while hoping that I've done the right thing, acting on impulse. She is a bit chatty, like her auntie.

In the hallway, she tells me a little more about herself – she's thirty-seven, has two brothers, both older, married with grown-up kids, parents have passed, she was engaged to be married but it didn't work out, Mrs Anderson is the only family she has in London, so knocked on her door. 'And I'm so glad I did because now I have this job.' I remind her that it's only for a few weeks – six, tops. 'That's perfect. It'll give me time to find something else. I've always loved London.' Daisy gazes around our large square hallway as if she were standing in Buckingham Palace. 'There's just so much to see and do.'

In my peripheral, I see Tom pouring another drink, phone pressed against his ear. He's going to get pissed tonight. 'Are you staying with the Andersons?' I ask to the ear-piercing sound of Tom's laughter. Daisy stiffens, then yanks the door open.

'I was but it didn't work out. Ben's a bit of an arse.'

A knot forms in my stomach. I hope he didn't try it on with her. 'So where are you staying?' Folding my arms to keep out the evening chill, I follow her eyes to a blue Peugeot estate parked across the road. 'In the car?' I gasp, hand flying to my throat.

'It's okay, Bella. I'm fine. It's surprisingly comfortable in the back. Rupert uses it for camping, said I could borrow it for as long as I liked.' Mrs Anderson's son, the one with the gorgeous wife. 'Auntie lets me freshen up when Ben's not there and feeds me. I'll find somewhere to live soon. I've got this job now; things are on the up.'

'Oh, Daisy, I am sorry. Couldn't your aunt put you up in a B&B?' Daisy shakes her head, tells me Ben has frozen all her cards. I shake my head – tell her he's a cruel bastard, and she laughs, agreeing. 'If you don't mind me asking, Daisy, why come to London if you had nowhere to stay, no job, no money?'

Daisy exhales deeply. 'Had a row with my fella and he chucked me out. My brothers never liked him and made it clear that I'd made my bed. I had nowhere else to go.' What a piece of shit. How could he make her homeless? 'It's okay,' she smiles, almost as if she knows what I'm thinking. 'It was all my fault. I ran up a bit of a debt on my credit card and sold my engagement ring to pay it off – said I'd lost it when he asked, then he only spotted it in the pawnshop. It was his grandmother's and it's a small town. Reckoned we couldn't start a married life based on lies.' I look at her, stunned, but not for the reason she's thinking, I've done far worse. I don't deserve Tom. I don't deserve this life. 'I know, I know, honesty is the best policy. We might've still been together if I'd fessed up.'

My skin prickles. 'I'm not judging you, Daisy. We all make mistakes, wrong choices.' Daisy smiles at me kindly. But she's right. If I'd been honest with Tom things wouldn't be as they are now. Unlike Daisy, I've still got time to fix this. I'll tell him everything – tonight.

'I'll see you on Monday, then, Bella. Bye, Mr Harris,' she calls out over her shoulder. Tom appears next to me on the doorstep, refill in hand. Slipping his arm around my waist, he nestles his head on my shoulder.

'Did I hear right, is she sleeping in the car? he asks as Daisy walks down the path.

'Afraid so.'

'So, she's homeless?'

'Yeah,' I say, then I look at him and our eyes lock. 'Are you thinking what I'm thinking?'

'Just until she gets on her feet. We've plenty of room.'

I race to the end of the driveway. 'Daisy, wait.'

Chapter 8

Linda sprinkles mozzarella cheese on the herby mushrooms while I arrange the lemon drizzle cake on a glass stand, which she told me she bought from Ikea, especially for tonight. The dining table looks stunning, with glistening crystal glasses, gleaming cutlery and gold-coloured tableware adorning a crisp white tablecloth with matching napkins, and there's a huge vase of fresh purple tulips on the sideboard. She's certainly pulled out all the stops for this evening.

'Help yourself to some wine,' Linda says as she prepares the starters at the worktop next to me.

Helping myself to a glass of Merlot, I glance out of the window. Theo is showing off his new summerhouse to Zelda and Keiko, and Tom is making his way along the path to join them, hands in pockets. I suddenly feel a bit jittery about meeting Keiko. I really want this relationship to work out for my sister. There are so many dodgy men out there. I shudder at the thought of Frank. You really never know what someone's like, or could be hiding. Zelda hasn't been lucky in love. Apart from Jake, all those years ago, her only other true love was Chris, her ex-married lover, and I think that's because he looked so much like Jake. The image of Jake sends a shockwave through me. So beautiful, so young.

'These won't take long,' Linda says, wiping her hands on her white chef's apron, which she's wearing over black skinny jeans and a khaki blouse with a gold flower print, matching her blonde, cropped, afro hair. Linda is a natural beauty. Men, and some women, can't keep their eyes off her whenever we go out. 'We'll call them in in ten. How're you anyway, and why are you dressed like Karren Brady?'

I glance down at my blue Hobbs suit and pale pink tie-neck blouse. 'I've had a shit day. Didn't have time to change.'

'You need another one of those.' Linda gestures at my almost empty glass and I nod, drain my glass, while Linda unscrews the cap off the wine bottle. 'Come on, tell Auntie Linda all about it. You look amazing, by the way.' She fills my glass to the brim. 'You need to give me your PT's number.'

'I've quit the gym,' I blurt, shooting a look at Tom in the summerhouse, who has just thrown his head back and taken a gulp from a bottle of beer. I'm going to have to carry him home tonight. 'Cancelled my membership online on Wednesday.'

'What? I thought you loved it there,' Linda says, astonished, 'said it was unpretentious.'

'I did, but I had no choice.'

Linda goes to take a sip of wine but stops midway. 'No choice?'

'He. Frank. My personal trainer. Got a bit fresh with me.'

'No Way!'

'Yes way.'

'What did he do, try to kiss you?'

I nod furiously, then take a large gulp of wine. 'I lost my balance during a stretch after a Muay Thai lesson, he grabbed me to break the fall. When I looked up to thank him, he had that dreamy, lustful look in his eye, then he went for my lips. I was so shocked. I really didn't see it coming.'

'Fucking hell. What did you do?'

'Pulled away, of course,' I exclaim. 'I almost got whiplash.'

Linda blows out air, cheeks puffed 'Well, I hope he's been sacked.'

'I didn't report it,' I reply briskly. I dart a glance at Tom again – he's safely engrossed in a conversation with my sister.

'Why not? I'm sure there are rules about stuff like that.' Linda takes another mouthful of wine.

'I couldn't report him,' I say irritably, suddenly feeling hot. 'I didn't want any comebacks.' Shrugging out of my jacket, I drape it over a bar stool at the breakfast table. 'We'd got quite friendly and I told him stuff that I probably shouldn't have,' I explain, not meeting her eye. 'Anyway, he just tried his luck. Probably thought I fancied him. Most of the women do.'

Linda raises an eyebrow and offers me an olive from a small white bowl. I shake my head, my appetite gone, and she pops one into her mouth.

'Don't you think quitting was a bit harsh, then? Why didn't you just fire him and hire someone else?'

'And have all that awkwardness at the gym? No thanks.' I scoff, tapping my fingers against my chin.

'I see.' Linda flops onto a seat at the kitchen table, nudging out a chair for me with the tip of her Vans-clad foot. 'You said you told Frank stuff you shouldn't have.'

I nod furiously, take a sip. 'Well, he knows I hired him behind Tom's back for a start off.'

'Okay, but you didn't tell him about Liam, did you?'

'That's the other thing,' I gulp, 'and the reason I can't report him to *Serval's* manager.'

Closing my eyes, I'm catapulted to the day my life turned upside down. After seventeen years, I thought Liam was a distant memory. But then one day, two months ago, a DM popped up on Instagram, saying *remember me?* with Liam's face in the little circle next to it. I was gobsmacked. I didn't think I'd ever hear from him again after the way things ended. I was going to ignore his message but curiosity got the better of me and I started typing.

We messaged on and off for a few weeks. There was no flirting between us. Liam's married with three kids. We agreed to not tell our partners we were back in touch in case they got jealous. In hindsight, I think I only went along with it to please him. Liam's wife had a bit of a reputation. I knew her from back in the day – Ona Cummings. She was nice enough but a bit hot-headed and possessive. She once threw a drink over Lisa Marsh, one of the girls from our crowd, because her mechanic husband was chatting to poor Lisa at a party about replacing her brake pads.

Reminiscing about the past and the old gang with Liam was fun, it felt nostalgic, as if I'd gone through a time warp. When Liam asked to move our messaging onto WhatsApp, I agreed. Then one night, while Tom and I were snuggled on the sofa enjoying one of our TV dramas, my phone flashed up with a message from Liam. Unfortunately, I'd just dashed to the loo during a commercial break and left my phone on the coffee table. When I returned, Tom was holding my phone in his hand, face like thunder.

Our row was explosive and I got the silent treatment for days. He only calmed down after I let him read all our messages and agreed to stop all contact with Liam. I knew Liam would be cool with it, after all, he knew what it was like to live with a jealous partner. But I couldn't have been more wrong. Liam wouldn't have it, insisted on meeting up with me. I refused, of course, I'm not stupid. Until he dropped a bombshell that blew my world apart.

Chapter 9

'Have you taken leave of your senses?' Linda exclaims. She's on her feet now, towering over me, hands on hips. 'How could you trust someone you barely know with such an explosive secret? You made me promise not to tell another living soul about Liam, not even your own sister. You even made me swear on Polly's life.' I actually felt bad for making Linda swear on her beloved Persian cat's life. 'What were you thinking?'

'I didn't tell him,' I whimper, as she pulls out gold-coloured side plates from a cabinet. 'I didn't have to. Frank saw us together on the day I met up with him.'

'Oh, I see,' Linda says, her tone depicting *tell me everything now*.

I give Linda a quick rundown of what happened. On the day Liam forced me to meet him at an indie café in Crouch End, Frank turned up. It was only when I got up to go to the loo that I noticed he was sitting right behind me, so close that our chairs were practically touching. I wasn't going to introduce them. But then Liam shot to his feet and stuck his hand out and said, *Liam Cooper, buddy. Bella's old flame. Pleasure to meet 'ya.*

'Wow,' Linda says, 'why didn't you tell me all this before?'

'I didn't think much of it, to be honest. They met, so what? It wasn't until he came round earlier today, threatening to tell Tom everything if I didn't re-join the gym and put the incident behind us, that things got nasty.'

'Fucking hell, that's considered stalking. Did he hear any of your convo with Liam? Because if he did…'

I rub the back of my neck. 'No. I don't think so. He pulled out his earplugs when he saw me and looked genuinely surprised. But I had to make him promise to not say anything to anyone about seeing me with my ex. News travels fast in *Serval* and some of the mums from Georgia's school train there. I couldn't risk it.'

'What was Frank doing in the cafe, anyway? Does he live in Crouch End?'

'No, he lives in Hertfordshire. He'd arranged to meet a private client there.'

'Bit of a coincidence,' Linda says dryly.

'I thought that too, but then a client did turn up. He even introduced us. Claudia, I think he said, and off they went. Anyway, I refused to go back to *Serval*. We ended up having an explosive row outside mine earlier. I'm still quite shaken by it.'

'He must be in love with you.'

I rub my chin. 'I don't know about love. Probably an infatuation. You know, older woman, younger man thing,' I laugh lightly.

'Well, hopefully, he'll disappear now he knows you're not interested.' Linda holds her chin. 'Try not to overthink things.' A beat and then. 'Any news from Liam about...' Pausing, she throws a glance at the summerhouse. 'You know what?'

I shake my head. 'He promised to stay away if I did what he asked.'

'Good. I'm glad he's sticking to your deal. I don't think you'll be hearing from him again.' Linda reaches out and cups my shoulder. 'I'm sorry your life's been a bit of a shitshow lately, babe, but, look, it's done now.' The oven alarm goes off and Linda gets to her feet and grabs a pair of black and white chequered oven gloves. 'You made a mistake. Just put it all behind you and move on.'

'You're right,' I agree, sighing loudly. Chatting with Linda always makes everything seem less daunting. Her energy is electrifying. 'Anyway, let's talk about something else,' I say. I don't want it to spoil our evening. 'On a happier note, I've finally hired a temp.' Grinning stupidly, I get to my feet, and as Linda begins plating the herby mushrooms, I fill her in on Daisy. 'It's only for a few weeks – until she finds another job and somewhere permanent to live.'

'Oh, you two,' Linda croons, wiping a bit of sauce off one of the plates. 'That's such a wonderful thing to do. I was having a discussion about homelessness with the girls at work the other day, it could happen to any of us. Gosh, I wish I could do something like that, make a difference in someone's life,' she muses, chucking a tea towel over her shoulder. 'Can you run this under the tap for me, sweetie?' She hands me a greasy spatula.

'Daisy was so bloody grateful.' She actually cried out loud before bursting into tears, causing Mr Stanhope to yank back his curtain and glare at us. 'It feels so good to do something positive for someone.'

Linda agrees, tells me kindness releases mood boosting chemicals in our brain, which makes us feel good about ourselves. So, in effect, being kind puts us on a natural high. 'Oxytocin, serotonin and dopamine, to be precise,' she explains. 'I read it in a magazine. Has she got any experience?'

'A bit, but I'll need to train her up,' I muse, inhaling an aroma of tomatoes, garlic and herbs as Linda pulls the lasagne out of the oven. 'But that should only take a couple of days.' Ripping two sheets off the kitchen roll, I dry the spatula, all the while gazing at my husband in the summerhouse as he chats with Keiko who is standing by the window, back to us. Probably giving him the third degree, knowing Tom.

I discreetly check Keiko out. Quite tall, not quite as tall as her ex, Chris, but not many people are six foot three. Keiko's hair is short and white. A mature man who looks after himself. Perfect for Zelda. 'Anyway, what's Keiko like?'

Linda takes a deep breath, slamming a drawer. 'That's the thing. I was going to tell you before you dropped your bombshell about that perve trainer. But...' Linda bites her bottom lip. 'Maybe I shouldn't say anything.'

'Go on,' I urge. A knot begins to form in my stomach. Linda is very perceptive. Good at reading people. I hope she's not going to say she doesn't like him.

'I know him, Bells. We had a brief fling before I met Theo. I say fling but it was more of a one-night-thingy.'

The knot unfurls and Keiko regains his jewelled crown. I'm both relieved and gobsmacked. 'Linda,' I exclaim. No wonder she's guzzling the wine like water. 'You didn't tell me, you rascal.' It seems I'm not the only one keeping secrets.

'I was too ashamed. I'd never done anything like that before and regretted it the next day. I even took the morning after pill and went to an STD clinic, just in case. Listen, don't say anything to Zelda,' she urges and I promise I won't. 'She might say something, you know how free-spirited she is. I don't want Theo to find out,' Linda explains, and I shake my head, agreeing. My sister isn't the best person to confide in, which is why I didn't tell her I'd hired a personal trainer, or about meeting Liam. It's not because she's a blabbermouth, nor that I don't trust her. It's just that Zelda sometimes lets things slip unintentionally. Mainly because she doesn't care what people think. Apart from Mum. She definitely cares what she thinks and would never tell her about her affair with Chris.

'You know what Theo's like,' Linda continues. We all do. Theo's jealous streak is notorious. 'I know it's in the past and everything, but still. 'Anyway, I don't think Keiko recognised me, thank God. I just about recognised him myself, to be fair. His hair was different then – dark, curly. It was his voice that did it, he's got a hint of a West Country accent and something about his eyes. I couldn't even remember his name.'

'Did you see him again?'

'God, no. He rang a few times, wanted to meet up. He was down from Gloucestershire, or somewhere, for the weekend. A stag do, I think.' Linda drains her glass. 'It was just a bit of fun for me but I think he wanted more. Shhh, they're coming.'

There's a ruckus of movement, the door swings open, voices, laughter and the clatter of feet fill the humid kitchen, and then everyone is talking at once - my sister pulls me into a hug, and I inhale her mango-scented golden brown hair, tumbling elegantly over her shoulders. Linda is telling everyone off for not wiping their feet – her freshly cleaned tiles are ruined. Theo is holding Polly in his arms and stroking her long grey fur while Tom mutters something about a golf swing, and then I feel a gust of cold breeze as the door flies open again. In my peripheral, I catch sight of Keiko shouldering past Tom and Theo, heading for the sink in a waft of expensive-smelling aftershave.

I don't take my eyes off my sister. 'Introduce me,' I whisper excitedly, digging my fingers into her skin. 'I can't wait.'

We pull apart, grinning stupidly at each other. Zelda curls a hand around Keiko's arm. 'Keiko, this is my sister, Bella,' she says and as he swings round, drying his hands on a tea towel, I look up at him and my heart stops.

Chapter 10

A loud gasp rips through me and the kitchen falls silent, all eyes on me. My skin is tingling. I don't think I can feel my legs. What is happening? Why is Frank here? I scrunch my eyes shut. Am I hallucinating? I must be. Maybe I'm having a post-traumatic episode. Can that cause hallucinations? Frank really did frighten me earlier with his threats and verbal abuse.

'Hey, small world,' Frank says to me and my eyes bolt open. No hallucination. This is really happening. Polly, clearly sensing the tension, meows and leaps out of Theo's arms and legs it out of the room.

'Do you two know each other?' Zelda screeches, eyes racing from me to Frank, and then her expression changes. 'Bella? Are you okay?' Terror rockets through me, rendering me speechless. 'She doesn't look right, Tom.' Zelda's fingers are cold against my skin, giving me goosebumps.

'She was fine in the car on the way here.' Tom lifts his arm and looks at his wristwatch. 'Maybe it's her blood sugar levels,' he says, looking at me anxiously. 'We never eat this late. Darling?' I look at him in a stupor, almost as if I don't know who he is. And then they all weigh in with their diagnosis, as if

I'm no longer present in the room. Their voices pound in my ears.

'She's dehydrated,' Frank insists.

'Overworked, more like,' Linda chips in.

'And not eating properly,' Zelda adds, worryingly.

'It's exhaustion,' Tom confirms. 'I told her to hire a temp ages ago, but would she listen?'

Shut up, I scream silently, shut up, shut up, shut up!

'Shall I get you some water, babe?' I look at Linda's unsmiling face. She's twirling an onyx pendant of an owl between her fingers that's hanging from a silver chain around her neck. 'Bella?'

I can't speak. Invisible hands snake around my neck, squeezing, squeezing, squeezing. I look at my sister, horrified. Frank a blur next to her in a blue polo top, beige chinos, white hair. White, for fuck's sake. WHITE. Tom's hand on the small of my back makes me flinch. 'Honey?'

I hold on to Tom's arm as if it were a cane. Dread winding around me like ivy. Frank can't be Keiko. He can't be. It's impossible. He must be a doppelgänger, with the same voice and intense glare.

'I'm sorry,' I mutter, voice rugged. 'I'm fine. Just felt a bit woozy.' I shake my almost empty wine glass at everyone. 'Probably this on an empty stomach,' I add, and their expressions immediately relax, like deflating balloons. 'I will have that glass of water, please, Linda,' I say, and then the tension in the air loosens. Voices fill the humid kitchen again, pots and crockery rattle, water splashes into the sink; Linda asks Theo where Polly is and hopes he hasn't let her out again.

'Sure you're okay?' Tom asks quietly. 'We could go home if you're not feeling a hundred per cent.' I shake my head, tell him I had a moment but I'm fine now.

'Lightweight,' Zelda mocks, brushing past me to fill her glass with wine from the bottle on the table.

'Hey, we're not all hardened drinkers, you know,' Frank teases, and Tom agrees, tells him to watch her – she'll drink him under the table. I look at Frank in a daze. 'I'm pacing myself,' he says to us, and Zelda snorts, throwing him a backward glance as she fills her glass to the brim and takes a large gulp. 'I can't cope with hangovers these days.'

'There you go, Bells.' I take the tumbler of water from Linda's hand. The ice-cold glass against my skin grounds me.

'So, you know my wife, Keiko,' Tom says, snatching my attention.

'Yeah.' Frank thrusts a hand through his fake white hair, swinging a glance at me. Tom watches him over his bottle of beer.

'Bella meets so many people through work,' Theo points out, gesturing his beer bottle at me. 'I guess that's what makes her such a people person.'

'I'll second that. She's our top photographer,' Linda yells from across the kitchen, sawing into a crusty baguette. 'Five-star feedback all the way.'

'You met through work?' Zelda quizzes. 'That's weird because you're renting, babe.'

'Um…,' I murmur. 'I…' I take a sip of water, hand tremulous. The cool liquid glides down my oesophagus. I can't lie to them. They're my family. My friends. Okay, I've got to play this safe. Tom knows I quit the gym; thank *God* I told him that at least. I spun him a line about it taking up too much of my time. But he still doesn't know I hired Frank. I will definitely have to tell him now, of course, but not here. My priority right now is my sister. I've got to protect her from this… this lunatic. 'We…um...' I clear my throat.

'We know each other from the gym,' Frank explains, getting in there before me.

Acid rockets into my stomach. Linda shoots me a look over her shoulder, confusion washing over her face.

'But not that well,' Frank adds, throwing me a lifeline. He looks at me as if we're in alliance, a ghost of a smile on his lips. But I don't need his help. I need him to get as far away as possible from my sister. How did this happen right under my nose? Zelda told me she met him online. What are the chances of them being a match on that dating app she's on?

'Seriously?' Zelda says, voice high. 'I didn't know you trained at *Serval*, Keiko.' I narrow my eyes at him – he hasn't even told her he works there. He's lying to her about everything - his job, his name, and God knows what else. 'You didn't say.'

Frank scratches his cheek, avoiding my eye. 'I did,' he insists. 'On our first date. I told you I'm at Nuffield, David Lloyd and *Serval*.'

'Nope.' Zelda shakes her head. 'I'd have remembered if you'd told me because our Bella trains there.'

'Not any more,' Tom interrupts, and Zelda swivels her head towards him. 'You cancelled your membership, didn't you? It was too much for her, what with Maggie on maternity leave,' he says, and Zelda agrees, complains that she hardly sees me these days.

'It was taking up too much of my time,' I confirm. I watch Frank carefully. Linda and Theo, a blur behind him, prepping the food on the counter. 'But, hey, what a surprise, Keiko.' I set my tumbler of water down on the table, eyes skimming the kitchen for my wineglass. I'm sure there was another mouthful left in there. I think I'm going to need an entire bottle to get through this evening. Linda catches my eye and I mouth *wine* at her and she nods, grabbing a bottle by the neck.

'Look, sorry to have to ask this, Keiko.' I curl a strand of long fringe behind my ear. 'But I thought you said your name was Frank.' I look at him expectantly, daring him to expose his real identity. At this, Linda freezes midway through pouring and shoots me a look. 'Have I got it wrong?'

Before he can answer, Linda is at my side like a greyhound, handing me a glass of red. Tom looks at it disapprovingly, one hand in trouser pocket, beer bottle in the other. I take a large gulp immediately. 'Gym buddies, eh,' Linda says to me, her look depicting *I've worked out who he is but you're going to have to suck it up for now. He's seen you with Liam and now he's wormed his way into your family. There's too much at stake. He's a psychopath.*

'Sort of,' Frank laughs. 'Working out is my job. I'm a fitness coach.'

Linda's right. I should just suck it up. Go home. Sleep on it. Discuss it with her tomorrow with a clear head. I take a swig of wine, impatience crawling through my bloodstream. I can't let it drop. I need answers.

I open my mouth to repeat my question when Theo yells. 'What do you want me to do with this?' Our heads pivot towards him. He's holding a huge bowl of salad in his big hands in front of his protruding belly. And, with a roll of her eyes, Linda shuffles off, muttering that she has to do everything in this house.

'His name *is* Frank,' Zelda announces, reaching for a baton of pepper from the salad bowl that Linda is now holding in her hands as if it were the Holy Grail, eyes fixed on me, mouth slightly open. 'I'm the only one who calls him Keiko. Apart from his family,' Zelda gives his bicep a gentle squeeze. 'It's a childhood nickname. I think it's cute. Suits him.' With a wink, Zelda feeds him the stick of pepper, and all I want to do is grab

Frank from his fake white hair and bury his face into the salad bowl.

'My name's Francisco,' Frank clarifies, swallowing. A little detail he omitted to tell me during our training sessions. 'Frank to everyone, apart from my family, who still call me Keiko. And now this one.' He pinches Zelda's dimpled cheek playfully and she laps it all up, leaning into him.

'That's Spanish, right?' Tom asks, taking another beer from Theo.

'Portuguese,' Frank corrects then looks at Theo, declining another beer. 'Ta, mate, but I'm going to have a glass of red with dinner.'

'So, what do *we* call you?' Theo asks, pushing his glasses up the bridge of his nose.

Frank flicks a glance at me. 'Frank is fine. It's what I'm used to.'

'You've changed your hair as well as your name,' I press on, glancing at Linda who is flitting from the dining room to the kitchen as if she were on speed.

Frank shakes his head theatrically. 'You noticed.' A cacophony of laughter blasts against my eardrums. I want to scream. This is *not* funny. This man is dangerous. 'I dyed it yesterday. It's for a charity thing.' Everyone *Oooohs* when he says this.

'I can't take all the credit for it,' Frank admits, holding up his hands. 'It wasn't my idea.' I knew it. He's just a hanger-on. Riding on someone else's coattails. Zelda looks up at him adoringly as he rambles on about the process of hair dying. I don't think I've ever seen her so smitten. My stomach squeezes into a tight ball of fury. I can't have him in my family. He's got to go. How could he date my sister behind my back? Unless... His words from this afternoon ring in my ears: *We need to sort this. Wait....* Fuelled with anger, I didn't let him finish. Was he about to tell me he was dating Zelda? Is that why he came to see me today? Why he wanted to smooth things over.

'Me and a few mates from the club are doing it for Children in Need,' Frank continues. 'We started early so we can make as much as we can.' A poster of Pudsey surrounded by several *Serval* staff in green tops flashes in my mind. It's pinned on the noticeboard by the entrance. 'We've raised three grand so far, so if any of you lovely people can donate.'

'Need any help with that, Theo?' Tom says, grabbing a plate of bread rolls out of Theo's hands and heading for the dining room.

Chapter 11

After dinner, Frank rolls up his sleeves and mucks in with the washing up while Tom and Theo carry on getting bladdered at the dining table. He's the perfect guest, the perfect boyfriend. Everyone likes him, which makes me want to stick pins in my flesh.

By the time Linda serves coffee and the lemon drizzle, Frank has everyone hanging on his every word. He lays on the Frank charm thickly as I sit there nursing a glass of wine, rolling my eyes inwardly at everything he says – he was born and raised in Bristol, used to be a social worker, quit because he found it upsetting – always loved sports, plays five-a-side every Sunday and can swim like a fish. His parents urged him to take up swimming professionally but…

At this point, I stop listening and pull my phone out of my bag. There's a message from Daisy – she's finished packing all her stuff – I'm to text her when we're ready to go. After I told her she could move in tonight, she insisted on picking us up. I declined, of course, she barely knows her way around London. But then Tom got involved, didn't he, got her to download

Google Maps. He even punched in Theo and Linda's address for her – anything to save a few quid.

I scroll through my messages to the babble of Frank's annoying voice. No reply to my earlier text to Georgia, which she's clearly read because the words *seen* are set in grey beneath my message. I start typing.

'But then, three years ago, my girlfriend passed away suddenly,' Frank says loudly. I whip my head up, phone in hand. He didn't tell me about a deceased girlfriend. The table falls silent and we all gawp at him helplessly.

'I'm really sorry to hear that, Frank,' I say, setting my phone face down on the table. No one deserves that. Sometimes I wonder what it would be like if I lost Tom and I feel physically sick. 'It must've been a difficult time,' I offer. My husband murmurs my sentiments, and Frank thanks us, eyes sliding to Tom's arm that he's just slung around my shoulder.

'She must've been so young,' Linda comments, resting her elbows on the table, head inclined.

'Nina was forty-eight,' Frank says to his wedge of lemon drizzle cake in front of him, shoulders slumped. 'We had a twenty-two-year age gap, but age means nothing,' he insists, and everyone murmurs in agreement. Clearly, he likes the older woman. For a moment I wonder if he has temper tantrums and lashes out because he's still traumatised by Nina's death.

'That really sucks, man.' Theo shakes his head, as Zelda pats Frank's back as if she's burping a baby.

Frank blushes, throws me a look. 'Thanks, everyone, you're all so kind,' he says in his whispery tone, 'but I'm fine – honestly. She meant a lot to me...' Frank's voice cracks and I tell him to stop, that he doesn't have to talk about it.

'Thanks, Bella,' he sniffs, wiping a tear from his eye with his index finger. 'It's still very hard. Nina was a beautiful soul, you know?' Shaking my head, I lean into Tom, curling a hand around his thigh, and he cuddles me warmly, his warm body melting into mine. 'But I've got Zelda now.' My stomach tightens. *Not for long if I've got anything to do with it.* 'Nina's death made me re-evaluate everything, showed me how short life is. I'm grateful for every day now.' Pausing, he forks a piece of cake. 'This is delicious, Linda. Almost as good as Zelda's.'

Linda gives me a look depicting *if you say anything you're dead*. 'It was nothing, really. Alexa recited the recipe to me and I just followed along,' she says in a singy voice. Tom opens his mouth to protest and I squeeze his knee under the table, shoving a piece of cake into my mouth, and, taking the bait, he praises Linda for her extraordinary baking skills.

'Mmm…yummy,' Theo says, chewing. 'Well done, Hun. I keep telling her she should go on Bake Off.' Theo and I exchange knowing glances. He's a pretty good liar. I'm impressed.

We spend the next few moments devouring our cake in silence. Silver forks scrape against china. Linda's bangles chime on her wrist as she reaches for the bottle of wine. Polly meows by Theo's chair. I stab my last forkful, eyeing the rest of the cake on the stand. Frank's right, it is delicious. Stress always makes me crave sugary foods. Another piece won't do any harm—a thin slice. I'll start my diet tomorrow.

'Anyone else for seconds?' I pick up the silver cake slicer. 'Linda, this is so more…'

'Actually, you look very familiar,' Frank cuts across me. Linda snaps her head up and looks at me like a deer in headlights. My heart stops, cake slicer in mid-air, mouth agape. 'I think we've met before.' *Shit*. He's recognised her.

Chapter 12

'I'm sure I know you from somewhere.' Frank points his small silver fork at Tom, swinging it up and down, elbow on the table, and Linda's body slumps with relief. Widening her eyes at me, head slightly down and inclined, Linda gives me a look, and I raise my eyebrows, just a fraction, in acknowledgement.

'Can't recall, sorry,' Tom says.

Frank narrows his eyes. 'I can't quite place you.' No, because you're a liar. You've only seen him on my phone's screensaver and are trying to wind me up.

'Tom's got one of those faces,' Zelda teases, polishing off her cake while Tom pokes his tongue out at her playfully. 'Urgh. Please, I've just eaten.'

'You might've seen him at the opticians,' Linda offers, slurring slightly, 'no pun.' She laughs into her glass at her own joke. I look at the empty bottle in front of her. It's our sixth. 'Tom works in a practice in Hadley Green.'

Frank shakes his head, eyes on Tom. 'Zelda tells me you're a top optometrist.' So that's how he knew so much about Tom. Knowing Zelda, she bigged him up. Probably told him Tom's a partner. Tom shrugs modestly, even though I know he's loving the attention. 'But, no, my optician is local. Been seeing him for a few years.' He widens his dark eyes. 'Contacts.' I didn't know that. This might explain the blinking. 'Don't worry, it'll come to me. I never forget a face,' he says, shooting a glance at Theo. Was that a dig at Linda?

We all fall silent for a few moments. I help myself to another slice of cake, look at Tom's half-eaten wedge on his plate, and sit back down. 'It was all delicious, Linda, thank you,' I say, and everyone mirrors my sentiments.

'It was an absolute pleasure. Thank you all so much for coming.' Polly meows at Linda, and Zelda looks down at the cat, smiling, as Frank reaches out and strokes Polly's fur.

'So, Muscles,' Tom says, waving his index finger from Frank to Zelda. 'How did you two love birds meet?' The burning question I've been dying to ask all evening. I fork a piece of cake.

Zelda and Frank exchange glances, grinning. 'Do you want to tell them, babe, or shall I?' Frank asks, wiping a bit of crumb from Zelda's top lip with a napkin. A foot touches mine under the table and I shoot Frank a look, but he's gazing at Zelda like a puppy. Is he playing footsy with me while making eyes at my sister, or was it accidental?

Zelda leans forward, forearms on the table, showing a bit of cleavage. I take in her sea-blue eyes, framed in black eyeliner and smoky eyeshadow, and her cerise stained lips. Zelda's always been a stunner. A natural beauty. But it's not like my sister to wear revealing clothes and so much makeup. I can see her black lacy bra beneath her sheer navy low-cut blouse, dotted with white and pink flowers, which she's stylishly teamed up with white jeans and white stilettos. She looks amazing, but it's not her style. Zelda's more Bohemian. Usually barefaced, bar a sweep of mascara and a splash of lip gloss when she's going *out out*, she lives in hoodies, loungers, floaty dresses, long skirts and baggy jumpers. I hope she isn't changing her style to please Frank.

'*Wellllll*,' Zelda begins, 'Keiko is one of my customers.' I almost choke on a mouthful of cake and Zelda gives me a miniscule frown. 'We met online. He emailed about an order. Bella knows all this.' I look at her aghast. *No, I don't. I thought you met him by fluke on Bumble or something.* 'A few days later, he rang and ordered a cake for his Nan's ninetieth as a surprise, no expense spared.' Everyone *Awws* when she says this, apart from Tom who asks if I'm okay and tops up my glass from the water jug on the table.

Clearing my throat, I reach for my glass, and as Zelda continues to relay their love story, my brain starts turning like a Rubik's cube. Frank looked Zelda up on my Followers list on Instagram – wasn't sure if he'd fancy her (her profile picture is a Victoria Sponge), messaged her with a cake enquiry. When he discovered she offers free local deliveries, he placed an order so that he could check her out. Of course, he liked the look of her, who wouldn't? Zelda's the better-looking sister, but we're still quite similar – slanty blue eyes (hers are bigger and bluer) straight nose that tips at the end, wide mouth. I swallow back a ball of fear that is climbing up my throat as I solve the puzzle in my head. This is no fluke. No coincidence. Frank hunted my sister down like a prey. But why? What's his agenda?

'Nothing like word of mouth,' Tom enthuses, breaking me out of my musing. 'You'll be hiring staff soon, Zee. Who recommended her, Frank? Was it you, darling?' *Inadvertently, yes.* I shake my head at the crumbs on my plate in front of me.

Frank takes a sip from his coffee cup, swallowing. 'I came across her on Instagram while I was searching for a local baker.' I give him a sharp look. A search through my followers, more like. 'Nan loved the cake and asked me to thank her. I messaged Zelda a few days later and the rest…' Frank's voice fades.

'Aww…how romantic,' Linda coos, finishing off the last bit of lemon drizzle and licking the spoon at Frank. Linda is now completely pissed. A chair scrapes against the floorboards. A phone buzzes. My eyes skim around the table – Tom is reading a message, Zelda is reaching over for a coffee refill, but Theo's eyes are burning into Frank. I can't let this go on. Frank is toxic. He's only been in our lives five minutes and he's already causing havoc.

I lean across the table. 'Zee,' I whisper, while Frank tells Linda about his nan's birthday party in her residential home. 'Can I have a quick word, please?'

'Sure.' Zelda nods, worry flashing across her face. 'Shall we go in the kitchen?'

Zelda slides her chair back, and just as she's about to stand, Frank turns to her. 'Everything all right, babe?' Leaning forward, he whispers something in her hair, and Zelda tucks her legs back under the table, grinning at her plate, then throws me an apologetic glance.

'I wish this one was more like you, Frank.' Linda says drunkenly into her glass and everyone ignores her, apart from Theo who is looking at her sternly, and blatantly ignoring Tom who is in the middle of telling him about a true crime podcast he's listening to and is now talking to himself.

Frank isn't going to let me speak to my sister in private, is he? I sigh, defeated, as Tom awkwardly relays the rest of his story to Zelda, in a save face fashion, who is trying to look interested but hasn't a clue what he's on about. I decide very quickly that I'll ring my sister first thing, suggest meeting up at the artisan café near her flat then tell her everything. We all need to go home anyway. Linda's had too much to drink and is on the brink of destruction.

'Sorry about that, Bells.' Zelda leans forward, securing her hair behind her ear and whispers, 'Come on, let's have that chat now.'

'No, It's fine. It'll keep,' I say, giving her hand a gentle squeeze. 'Can you do breakfast tomorrow? Zelda nods. 'Great. I'll text you.' I look at the time on my phone – 11.01. 'Right, I suppose we'd best make a move,' I announce, breaking the tension between Theo and Linda. 'Busy day ahead tomorrow. I'll just text Daisy,' I say to Tom, picking up my mobile.

'You two need to come over to ours,' Tom says to Frank and Zelda as I start typing, 'for a proper catch-up. Isn't that right, darling?'

I murmur in agreement, head down, thumbs flying over the tiny keyboard, taking Tom's suggestion tongue in cheek. Zelda will dump Frank once I tell her the truth about him tomorrow.

'How about tomorrow night? We're free, Bella, aren't we?' A hand clenches around my heart. 'Blow the cobwebs off the barbie.'

'Only if you're sure, Bella,' Zelda offers, sensing my reluctance.

'Of course, she's sure,' Tom says. 'Why don't you two come as well?' Theo and Linda exchange glances, shrugging their shoulders and shaking their heads, as if to say, why not?

There's no way Frank is stepping foot inside our house. I try to suppress the heat working its way into my cheeks but it's no good, my face tingles. I need to think of an excuse. 'MetOffice said rain tomorrow, Tommy. And it's too cold for a barbeque, anyway.'

Tom waves a hand. 'A bit of rain won't stop us,' he says drunkenly. 'Will it Theo? It wouldn't be the first time.' I visualise the one we had last February to celebrate Zelda's birthday. Tom poking hot coals on the wet grass. Theo next to him holding a huge red umbrella. Linda, Zelda and I cowering beneath raincoats, aloft over our heads like white-sheeted apparitions, dashing to and fro with platters covered in silver foil, feet water-logged and soggy. It was one of the best barbeques we'd had.

I clear my throat. 'Um…what about Daisy?'

'She can come too,' Tom jokes.

'Look, sorry, guys, don't want to be a party pooper but Zelda and I won't be able to make it, I'm afraid,' Frank announces, and the hand releases its hold around my heart.

Chapter 13

'Why.' Zelda gives Frank a light slap on the arm with the back of her hand. 'Can't' Another slap. 'We go.' Slap. 'To their barbeque?' Slap. 'Spoil-sport.'

Frank fills his lungs and then exhales loudly. 'It was meant to be a surprise,' he says tightly, looking at Tom as if he deliberately ruined everything. 'I've booked us a trip to Monte Carlo.'

Zelda grabs my hand across the table and squeezes my knuckles. 'Are you joking me?'

'We fly tomorrow morning.' Morning? What about our breakfast date where I will expose him for who he really is? 'Calm down.' Frank dodges as Zelda kisses him all over his face. 'It's just for five days.' *Just?* I roll my eyes silently.

'In a hotel?'

'No, in a brothel. Of course, in a hotel. A five-star spa, as it goes. You've spoilt all the surprises now,' he whines, pushing his plate away from him like a petulant child.

'Oh, my dear God.' Zelda holds Frank's face with both hands and gives him a deafening kiss, leaving an imprint of her cerise lipstick on his forehead. I want to scream my lungs out.

Zelda can't go away with him for almost a week without knowing the truth about him.

'How about the following Saturday, then?' Tom suggests, and everyone agrees. 'That's a date then. I'll get those pastourma you like, Theo, and salmon for you, Linda.'

My phone pings. 'It's Daisy,' I yell hastily. 'She's outside. We'd best get off. Don't want to keep the poor girl waiting.'

'I'm sorry, Mrs Harris…I mean, Bella,' Daisy says, once Tom and I are settled in the back of her car, which smells of burgers and unwashed clothes, like a couple of teenagers being picked up by their mother. Daisy cocks her head at the black bin bags on the front passenger seat next to her. 'If I'd known your sister needed a lift, I'd have left this lot in my auntie's garage until tomorrow. Is that her?' Daisy motions at Zelda with her head. 'She's banging.' Daisy shoots a look at me in her rearview. 'You look alike,' she says, and I smile. 'Although you're more Cate Blanchett and she's more Emily Blunt. Good genes.' Tom agrees and I go pink. It's lovely of Daisy to compare us to Hollywood beauties but I'm nowhere near as glamorous as Cate, nor Zelda, for that matter. Mum would always introduce her as the good-looking one when we were little. It hurt at the time but as an adult, I've discovered that beauty is only skin-deep. 'Will they be okay?' Daisy asks, worriedly, nodding at Zelda who is limping along the road, holding onto Frank's arm.

'They'll be fine, Daisy,' I say, tiredly. I do feel sorry for my sister. Half a mile is a long way to walk in uncomfortable shoes. I do hope she doesn't get blisters, but a part of me is relieved that Daisy turned them down when they asked for a lift, because the thought of being squashed on the backseat with them while they smooched like love-struck teenagers turned my stomach.

Daisy fires up the engine, and it growls – diesel. I look out of the window and wave at Linda and Theo, who are standing at the gate. Linda blows a kiss and I pretend to catch it, and then she makes a heart shape with her hands. My lovely friend put on a great spread for us this evening. Shame Frank ruined it. Tom's phone buzzes in his pocket. I give him a look. 'Who's that?' It's been going off all evening. 'Not the eyelash man again?'

'It's Georgia,' he says sleepily, reading it. 'Replying to a message I sent her three hours ago.' I shake my head knowingly. 'She's fine, by the way. They had McDonalds.' Our daughter would live off takeaways if we allowed it.

'Hope you don't mind,' Daisy says, shooting a glance at us in the rearview, 'but could you buckle in? Better to be safe than sorry.'

Tom and I reach for our seatbelts tiredly. A phone chimes. Daisy's. It's a message from her auntie, she tells us, then begins texting hurriedly, auburn hair dangling in her face. 'Sorry, guys. I won't be a mo.'

I gaze out of the window. Ahead, Zelda takes her shoes off and says something to Frank. I watch miserably as Frank picks her up in his arms. A romantic European break, new clothes (she told me he'd bought her the entire designer outfit she was wearing tonight), fancy dinners in top restaurants, versus midday bunk-ups in her flat, the odd clandestine lunch in the countryside where no one knew Chris, and Christmases with us and Mum. No wonder she's besotted with Frank.

Zelda squeals loudly as Frank jogs along the street, holding her on his back. My heart sinks. It'll all end in tears. I can feel it in my gut. I'm about to look away when Frank suddenly puts Zelda down and races back to the house. Zelda must've forgotten something. Probably her phone. Daisy revs the engine. I crane my neck for a better view. Zelda is leaning against someone's wall, texting – not her phone then. Daisy sticks the car into gear with a loud crunch, apologises again for not being able to offer my sister and her boyfriend a lift home, suggests dropping us off and coming back for them, that it's no bother at all.

'There'll be no need for that, Daisy,' Tom says firmly. 'Zelda doesn't live far. I'm sure Muscles can carry her home on his shoulders.' Is that a hint of antipathy in his tone, or might it be the drink? I don't question him. We can discuss Frank in the morning with clear heads, and I *will* tell him he was my personal trainer and how he manipulated his way into my sister's arms. This has gone far enough.

'It's only a ten-minute walk, Daisy. But thank you. That's very kind.'

Daisy smiles at us in the mirror. The indicator clinks and as we pull away from the kerb with a jerk, I catch a glimpse of Linda, arms folded, flicking a glance over her shoulder. Theo has gone inside. Frank is standing in front of her, hands in pockets. My eyes slide to Zelda, she's still leaning against a wall twenty feet away, putting her shoes back on, and then I look back at Linda. Whatever he's saying to Linda, she doesn't look happy. Frank must've recognised her. I bet he knew who she was all along.

Chapter 14

'Is Tom ready for these, Bella?' Daisy is balancing a tray of kebabs in her hand like a waitress – cubes of chicken threaded onto silver skewers between green, yellow and red peppers. Daisy's done a great job. She's cooked for us every night this week, while I've been climbing the walls worrying about Zelda holed up in Monaco with *him*. Daisy's an excellent cook, by the way, taught by her auntie Doris, from a young age.

I glance out of the window. Tom is sweating over a barbeque, warm sun on his shoulders. It's unseasonably warm today, 20c and dry. At least his mood has improved and he's talking to me again.

The morning after the dinner party, I stuck to my self-imposed promise and told Tom that Frank was indeed my personal trainer. In hindsight, it'd been easier if I'd kept quiet, seeing as I'd sacked him, but I had no other choice. After the initial shock of how much it was costing me wore off, he hit the roof – demanded to know why neither of us mentioned it the night before – what were we hiding? – he knew there was something fishy going on – he could inhale the tension between us.

Telling him I kept Frank a secret because I knew he'd blow a gasket over the cost and make me stop using him, only added fuel to the fire – he slammed me for lying, accused me of wasting money on a fitness coach to boost my ego, reminded me how we were up to our necks in debt, accused me of being selfish. In truth, I *was* thinking of myself for once. I remained silent about why I really quit the gym for fear of Tom losing it completely. I couldn't deal with that on top of worrying about my sister's safety. For my wrongdoings, I was sentenced to five days of the cold shoulder and snippy remarks at the dinner table in front of Daisy, who didn't know where to look, and Georgia, who didn't bat an eyelid.

Catching sight of me at the kitchen window now, Tom waves, then wipes his forehead with the back of his hand, searing the burgers over a hot grill, smudges of grease on his white apron. Theo and Frank look on, beers in hand, hairy arms poking out of their rolled-up shirt sleeves. Georgia is perched on the wooden bench behind them in her orange hoodie and black shorts, Zelda next to her looking tanned and glowy after a week in the sun, which is rather surprising, given that she just told me and Linda that they barely left the bedroom – a piece of information I could've done without.

Daisy shifts her weight onto one leg, her body language telling me to make my mind up. 'That is a very good question, Daisy. I think Tom should be about ready to put them on the grill.'

I look at Linda, who is chopping parsley next to me at the kitchen worktop in a calf-length leopard print skirt and white shirt with long pointed collars, whilst giving me a running commentary of a house she sold yesterday. I know she'd rather be outside with the others, enjoying the sunshine, but that'd mean being in close proximity to Frank, whom she's avoiding as much as possible. Linda rang me the day after her dinner party in a state. Frank recognised her, all right. That's why he ran back to the house after we'd all left, leaving Zelda leaning against someone's wall. Linda denied having ever clapped eyes on him – insisted he was mistaken. He wouldn't have it, of course. Frank never backs down. But when Theo appeared at the door, he backtracked and scuttled off after Zelda who, according to Linda, was wobbling along the street in her new stilettoes like a drunken nineteen seventies prostitute.

'I thought the newly-wed couple were going to put an offer in for the period style house I showed them earlier in the week,' Linda blabbers, gold earrings dangling against her cheek. 'But they went for the new build in the end. I don't know what it is with young people today. The older house needed a bit of work but it would've been a better investment. All they're interested in is flashy new kitchens and plastic lawns.' Linda shakes her head at the vibrant parsley, earrings swinging. 'It really gets my goat,' Linda complains, then pauses, and looks from me to Daisy. 'What?'

'Sweetheart, I could listen to your shop anecdotes all day long, but could you take the kebabs out to Tom and then finish setting up the table outside? I need Daisy to give me a hand with the dips and salad.'

Linda holds up a knife, which has bits of wet parsley stuck to it, grabs her Stella Artois and gives me a look that says *do you want to die* while sucking on the beer bottle. 'Daisy, will you take them out to Tom, please?'

Daisy nods and in a heartbeat, she's gone, sauntering along the freshly mowed lawn, in a polka dot red and white dress, high ponytail of red tresses swishing with each stride.

'Daisy, come over,' Georgia calls out, her voice as sharp as the blade of the knife I'm slicing into the red onion.

'Isn't she lovely?' I say to Linda, admiring Daisy from the window, as if she were my daughter, even though I'm only twelve years her senior. 'I don't know how I'm going to cope without her when Maggie comes back,' I muse, dicing the onion like a pro – something Daisy taught me on her second day here. 'Not that I don't want Maggie back,' I add quickly, sniffing. I take a step back and sneeze into the crook of my arm. 'Bloody onions,' I grumble, eyes streaming.

'Yes, she's very sweet,' Linda agrees. 'You okay?' Soaping my hands at the sink, I tell her that apart from obsessing about how I'm going to manage to warn Zelda off Frank today, I'm fine, just allergic to everything. 'Daisy's very easy on the eye too,' Linda continues, a tinge of warning in her tone. 'Tom seems quite taken with her by the look of things.' I follow her eyes as I dry my hands on a tea towel, then dump it over a chair at the kitchen table. Tom is taking the tray from Daisy's outstretched arm, a warm smile on his lips. A kind, fatherly smile.

'We all are,' I say, watching Theo grabbing a skewer off the tray as it slides off and almost stabs Frank in the neck. Frank darts out of the way, without even bothering to look up from his phone. But when Daisy turns on her heel and slowly makes her way back to the house, I don't miss him eyeing her up discreetly. If only we could film with our eyes.

Linda burps. 'Oops, sorry. It's the beer.' She cocks her head at Daisy. 'Does she look at Tom with those *do you want to fuck me* eyes?'

'Linda!'

'Look, I know you're doing your good Samaritan thing, but I'd keep an eye on her if I were you – cooking for you, chauffeuring your daughter everywhere, keeping the house spick and span. She's making herself indispensable. Classic signs of husband snatcher.'

'Oh, stop it,' I protest, 'Tom's like a father to her.' Linda raises her eyebrows, taking another swig of beer. 'Technically, he could be.' Another look. 'A much older brother then,' I say, slipping back next to her at the island worktop. 'Besides, Tom isn't like that.'

'He's a man, isn't he?' Linda says dryly. 'Men's brains work differently. Usually from the comfort of their underpants.'

I give her a side glance. Linda can be so cynical at times.

'Never mind about all that,' I reply, tetchily. Did you see the way Frank was eyeing Daisy up just now?' I wave a cucumber at her. 'That just proves he can't be trusted. Tom agrees.' When I first relayed my theory to Tom about how Frank and Zelda met, he wasn't sure, said it could've been a coincidence. But when I told him I'd shown Frank Zelda's Instagram account and brought in some samples, at his request, he agreed, called him a snake.

'You've been moaning at her to leave Chris for ages and now that she has…'

'Yes, but Frank's not right for her. He's too young for a start off.'

'Fourteen years is nothing these days.'

'I want her to be with someone safe, like Tom.'

'You mean boring?' Linda laughs lightly but my face is deadpan. 'Look, let her have her fun with her bad boy. He is very cute, isn't he? Enough to make any woman commit adultery.'

'Linda.'

'I'm *joking*. Just let them be. Look, she's happy. It'll fizzle out.'

'You know I can't do that,' I say smoothly, 'not after what he's done.' Tom suggested texting Zelda in Monaco and telling her all about her sleazeball lover, the sooner the better, he said. But I could hardly let rip about her boyfriend while she was on holiday with him. What if she'd confronted him and ended up having a steaming row? Zelda's spirited, like our father, and

Frank's got a vicious temper. There are a lot of cliffs in Monaco. It was too risky.

'Zelda's had her fun in the sun, Linda. She needs to know the truth about Frank.'

Linda shakes her head at me incredulously, a faint smile on her lips, then goes back to slicing a tomato. 'She won't thank you for it, trust me. She might even take his side, not believe you. Look how she reacted when you told her he was your trainer.' The moment Zelda arrived back from Monaco she phoned me, excited to tell me all about her holiday and to see if we were still on for today. I'd been waiting all week to spill the beans about Frank, including the incriminating bits I'd kept from Tom, and couldn't wait a moment longer.

'Zelda, I need to talk to you about Frank.' The words spat out of my mouth urgently, like coins from a jackpot fruit machine. 'Can you pop over this evening? Alone?'

'If this is about you hiring Keiko, I already know and it's fine.'

My heart sank. Frank had got in there before me, told Zelda I was one of his clients – claimed he had no idea we were sisters – what a coincidence, then played the hero – said he didn't mention it at the dinner party because I said no one knew I'd hired him – that it was a finance thing – something to do with my husband. Zelda was a bit miffed with me for not confiding in her but completely got why I kept it from Ebenezer.

'Whatever you tell her now, baby, she'll question it, and he'll find a way to worm himself out of it. After all, you didn't even bother telling her you'd hired him, *he* did. One, nil, my friend, one nil.'

I huff in exasperation, dicing half a cucumber as if it were an Olympic event. 'What am I supposed to do, Linda? Turn a blind eye? Pretend Frank didn't hit on me, didn't turn up at my house and hurl abuse at me, didn't kick the wheel of my car? Didn't stalk my sister? The man's a maniac. I've seen his darker side, remember. I couldn't live with myself if anything happened to Zelda.'

'There is another way.'

I stop chopping and look at her. 'I'm listening…'

Chapter 15

'I don't know about you, but I'm stuffed,' Theo says, two hours later, rubbing his bloated belly. We're sitting on the garden patio, enjoying the afternoon sun. Theo is stretched out on the rattan lounger and I'm on a chair next to him. Frank hasn't left Zelda's side all afternoon, not even for a loo break, which has made Linda's plan impossible. Jesus, what kind of bladder has he got? He's guzzled enough beer and wine today to fill a barrel with wee.

'We've still got dessert.' I look up at the cloudless sky. Birds chirp and croak in trees. Their voices a backing track to the hum of conversation and laughter in our garden. It's hard to believe it's mid-March. It feels like a spring day.

'I'm sure I could squeeze some in.' Theo smiles. 'Is it one of Zelda's?'

'No, she didn't have time. I made a crème caramel.' Out of a packet, but he doesn't need to know that.

'My favourite. Nice and light.' Theo points his beer bottle at Frank. 'So, what do you make of pretty boy, then?'

I look across at Frank – he's talking to Tom at the garden table, crowded with plates smeared with food and crumbs, bottles of wine, squashed cans, a jug of orange squash and half-filled glasses. Frank looks relaxed – legs outstretched and crossed at the ankles - hands on the back of his head, revealing patches of sweat under the armpits of his pale blue shirt. Zelda is sitting next to him, looking on, with a faraway expression. I know that look. She's bored senseless. I wonder if she's tiring of him. It'd make life a lot easier if she dumped him of her own accord. At least he hasn't forced her into an uncomfortable ensemble today. My eyes sweep over her starry print emerald green tunic, tanned legs and white trainers. I notice that she keeps looking at her phone – checking the time, or is she waiting for a text?

'I don't really know him that well, Theo,' I offer, wondering how much Linda has told him. 'He was my personal trainer at *Serval* for a few weeks.' Theo nods, she's told him that much, then. I narrow my eyes at a jaybird that's landed on a branch in our magnolia. 'But I think they're unsuited.' I take a sip of G&T. Ahead, Linda tops up Zelda's glass with prosecco, then offers some to Daisy, who declines.

I discovered that Daisy was teetotal on her second day with us. Her glass of merlot, which Tom put in front of her automatically, as if it were a given, went untouched during our Sunday roast. 'If you prefer white or blush, I'll get some in next time,' I told her, when Tom had gone out to chuck the empties into the recycle bin and Georgia had disappeared upstairs. 'It's really no bother at all. I quite enjoy a glass of white, especially during summer.'

'I don't drink,' she confessed, rolling up her sleeves at the sink.

'What, nothing?' I stopped clearing the table and looked at her, several glasses squeezed between my fingers.

'Nope. Mother was an alcoholic and father wasn't far behind her. They weren't good drunks – argued a lot –

sometimes got violent. We had the Garda out occasionally. It put me off booze for life.' I now make sure the fridge is fully stocked with Coca-Cola and sparkling spring water – her favourite tipples.

Linda, clearly tipsy now, insists that Daisy has a drop of fizz in the manner of Mrs Doyle from Father Ted, but Daisy covers her empty glass of cola, which prompts Georgia to stick out her glass instead, arm stiff.

'Oi,' I call out, shooting to my feet, 'you're too young to drink.'

'Oh, let the girl have some fun,' Linda yells, waving the bottle. 'You were a teenager once, remember.'

'No,' I shout, pointing a finger and taking a few steps towards them. 'Linda,' I warn, 'Don't.' At this, Linda shrugs and sways a little as she sits back down on the bench next to Daisy, and Theo raises his eyebrows at me knowingly.

'Motherrrr!' Georgia cries out furiously, as Zelda tiptoes past me, miming *loo*. 'Why do you always have to spoil EVERYTHING? I have had alcohol before, you know.'

'Not under my roof.'

'Oh, whatever!'

'Hey, do as you're told,' Tom says absently, without looking up from his phone, and Georgia folds her arms, muttering under her breath, probably obscenities about me and her dad.

I sit back down to a babble of female laughter. 'What do *you* think of him?' I ask Theo, cocking my head at Frank.

Theo narrows his eyes, 'I dunno.' He twists his wedding ring around his finger. He can't know about Linda's night of passion with Frank. Linda told me he didn't say a word after we left that night. 'Bit flash, isn't he?' I stay silent. 'Full of himself.'

'Personal trainers are like that. Posers. They like to show off all those gorgeous muscles.' I realise what I've said and feel my face tingle.

Theo removes his glasses, unperturbed by my comment, exhales on the lenses and wipes them with the hem of his olive-green casual shirt, wrinkled from bunching up against his skin on the chair. 'Cocky bastard, if you ask me,' he mutters under his breath. He's right, of course, but I don't say anything.

'How's your sister Elaini?' I ask, changing the subject, as Theo slides his glasses on and leans back in his chair. I love it that he hates Frank but I don't want to spur him on. 'Is she coping okay?'

'She had her last chemo on Wednesday. It's really taken it out of her, Bella.' Theo smiles sadly, eyes filling, then he takes a gulp of beer. 'She's seeing the consultant next week.' I've upset him. Theo has a very close-knit family. Why did I have to mention Elaini? The awkward silence is filled with Georgia and Daisy's voices, arguing over a selfie that Georgia has just taken and is threatening to post on Instagram.

'Don't you dare,' Daisy screeches, chasing Georgia around the garden. Georgia screams and Frank turns his head stiffly and watches them, forearms resting against his thighs.

'Gym guy likes the ladies, eh?' Theo remarks loudly, over Georgia and Daisy's squealing. I hope that observation is because he can see him eyeing Daisy up and not because he's suspicious about Frank and Linda, because if he is, then my life won't be worth living.

'He gets a lot of attention from the women at the gym,' I say. 'Mostly middle-aged.' Theo nods, eyes on Frank. Shit, why did I say that? Linda's middle-aged.

The sound of Tom's laughter snatches my attention. Frank is showing him something on his phone. At least one of us is having fun. I can't stop thinking about how I'm going to corner Frank and whether Linda's master plan will work.

Tom, who is now in possession of Frank's phone, throws his head back and laughs some more, which causes Zelda to dart a glance at them as she fills a glass with red wine at the table. I bet Frank's showing him some of his dad joke memes. Tom chuckles as he slides a finger across the screen of Frank's phone, and then suddenly his expression hardens and his head snaps up at me. Acid swishes in my stomach. Why is he looking at me like that?

Tom seemingly doesn't notice when Frank snatches the phone out of his hands until he mutters something to him. Tom looks round at him, nods, says something.

And now Tom is making his way towards us. Frank behind him, head bowed. What has Frank done?

Chapter 16

My heart whacks in my chest as Tom brushes past me, giving me a side glance. I think I'm going to be sick. He knows something. I can almost smell the repulsion on him. But instead of confronting me about whatever Frank showed him on his phone, he tugs Theo's baseball cap, almost knocking his glasses off.

'All right, pal,' Tom says. Pulling out a chair, he straddles it and then turns to me. 'It's been lovely today, hasn't it? All of us together. This is what it's all about.' Sighing, he holds his beer bottle aloft and ducks his head. 'Here's to family and friends – old and new.' I can't read his tone. Does he mean it, or is he being ironic? I take a sip from my glass of G&T. It suddenly tastes sour. I want to spit it out.

'To family and friends,' Theo cheers. I raise my glass, glancing briefly at Frank who is standing on the green a few feet away, legs wide, hips thrust forward. The frayed hem of his blue jeans bright against the vibrant blades of grass kissing his white Nike trainers. Zelda is behind him, a green blur, chatting with the girls.

'Theo and I were just putting the world to rights. Weren't we, Theo?' I force a smile as my phone buzzes in my pocket. Theo nods slowly, pulls off his cap and ruffles his salt and pepper curls, which have flattened and moistened under his hat. Tom looks forlornly into the middle distance. Perhaps I got it wrong. Not everything is about me. Maybe Frank showed him an image he didn't approve of, like a naked young woman. Tom's a bit prudish about stuff like that, says he wouldn't like old gits drooling over his daughter. My phone buzzes again. It must be Mum. I pull it out of my pocket – an Instagram notification.

'What happened to your phone,' Tom asks, peering at my cracked screen. I wave a hand; explain how I dropped it in Tesco car park yesterday. Tom rolls his eyes, says they should make them bounce, they cost an arm and a leg, and I agree, tell him I'll get it repaired at the local shop next week.

'I wish Mum was here,' I say, wistfully, sliding my phone back into my pocket. 'She'd have loved it.' Filling my lungs with a cocktail of campfire and sweet chilli-grilled meats, I lean my head back and close my eyes, picturing Mum in her hay day cooking burgers and sweetcorn on the barbeque in our backyard. Dad close by on a deckchair studying the afternoon races, fag hanging out of the side of his mouth. I loved it – the summer days – the togetherness – our little perfect family, until Dad destroyed it.

'Is it okay if I use the little boy's room?' The sound of Frank's voice makes me snap out of my reverie. He's finally going to the loo.

Tom half stands and gestures with his beer. 'Sure, fella, through the kitchen, straight down the hallway, first on your left.'

'Cheers, Bro.'

I'm about to offer to show him, which is pretty daft really, we're not in Ikea, he won't get lost going to the loo, when he strides off, whistling under his breath and the opportunity is missed. I shuffle in my chair, feeling restless. I need to think of an excuse to go after him.

'Nice barbeque. Meat was really tasty, tender,' Theo says, filling the silence. I wait for Tom to praise Daisy for her culinary prowess, but instead, they launch into a discussion about marinating meats. Tom says he infuses it with secret herbs and spices. *Yes, Daisy's secret concoction.* Theo insists that olive oil and seasoning is all it needs – it's the traditional way. Their voices become a babble of white noise. I can't concentrate. I feel as if I'm sitting on hot coals. I've got to get inside and wait for Frank to come out of the toilet.

'Here's to many more.' Tom clinks his bottle with Theo's. Ahead, Linda is making her way towards us, wobbling slightly in her heels with every other step.

'All right, babe.' Linda plants a sloppy kiss on Theo's lips, then turns to me. 'Just going for a wee.'

Perfect timing. I shoot to my feet. 'Frank's in there,' I announce, almost reprovingly, and Linda's eyes widen. 'Use the bathroom upstairs. Actually, I'll come with. I need to go too.' Getting to my feet, I drain my glass while Tom prattles on about never understanding why women have to go to the loo in pairs. I've been waiting for this opportunity all day and it's finally arrived.

The moment we're inside, I inadvertently dig my nails into Linda's flesh and she cringes. Loosening my grip, I say, 'Go upstairs while I wait for him in the hallway. And give me ten minutes before you come back down.'

'What am I supposed to do up there for ten fucking minutes? I only need a wee.'

'Go on TikTok or something.' Linda gives me a look. 'Linda, please.'

'Okay, okay,' she says, suddenly sober. The hum of Jailhouse Rock floats in through the open patio doors. Someone's put the music on. Probably Theo's Spotify list. He loves Elvis. He's even got a tattoo of him on his arm. 'But be careful and remember what I said – nice and easy.'

I nod, anxiety flaring in my stomach. 'I know what I'm doing.' The sound of a flushing loo drifts along the corridor, followed by the combi boiler thrumming against the wall in the utility room a few feet away. Frank's turned on the hot tap. He's washing his hands. 'Go,' I urge, heat creeping up the back of my neck. 'Hurry, before he comes out.' Linda scuttles off, heels click clacking against the kitchen tiles.

From the hallway, there's the familiar click of the lock and then Frank emerges, wiping his wet hands on the hem of his shirt. Slightly taken aback by my presence, he steps to the side to let me pass, a smile on his lips that reaches his eyes, as if there's been no bad blood between us at all.

'I put the toilet seat down,' he says, and as he goes to walk past, I block him and our eyes lock. This is it, the only chance I'm going to get to wipe him out of our lives.

Chapter 17

'I don't want to use the toilet, Frank.'

'Okay,' he says simply, sliding his hands into his pockets, features set in confusion.

I know I promised Linda I'd keep to our plan, but fuelled with alcohol and that smug look on his face, I blurt out, 'What the fuck do you think you're playing at? Ordering a cake from Zelda, hounding my sister, trying to impress her with expensive gifts and luxury breaks. What is wrong with you?' The words rip out of me like gunshots.

'Whoa.'

'I want answers, Frank, and don't even think about lying to me. Meeting Zelda was no coincidence. You knew *exactly* what you were doing.'

'Ah, mate, come on.' He exhales loudly 'How could I have known she was your sister?'

'Are you serious?' I snap.

'You really have got an overactive imagination.'

I cross my arms, suddenly feeling cold. 'I want you to stop seeing Zelda.'

His eyebrows shoot up. 'Zelda's my girlfriend. Get used to it, because I'm not going anywhere.'

'You really –' I take a breath, and then hold up my hands in surrender, Linda's words belting into my head. She was right. I need to get him onside and then put him off Zelda, which isn't going to be easy now, seeing as I've fucked it up with impulsion. 'I'm sorry. It's been a long day.' I sigh loudly. 'I'm handling this all wrong. Look, while you were away, I did a lot of thinking and you were right. What happened between us was a misunderstanding,' I offer, reciting Linda's speech word for word. 'To be honest, I was flattered that someone like you liked me.' His expression softens, and for a moment I remember the charming, kind, gentle Frank. The Frank I first met, and I wonder if I'm doing the right thing. 'I read the whole thing wrong and I'm sorry,' I finish, looking away. This is no time to back down. Frank will destroy me if I let him.

'Good, that's really good, Bella. I appreciate your honesty. I know that can't have been easy.' I bite the inside of my bottom lip, inwardly screaming. I want to punch him.

'I'd rehire you in a heartbeat, Frank, but right now I really can't afford it. We're not as well off as you think.'

Gazing around the hallway adorned with Mum's paintings, he holds his palms up at the sparkling chandelier above us as if to say *what the hell is all this then?*

'Looks can be deceiving. We borrowed every penny we could to buy this place.' The look on his face tells me he doesn't believe me. 'Frank, you're a really nice guy.' I wring my hands, mouth drying up. 'God, I hate doing this to my sister.' I hesitate for effect. 'Look, just forget it. Go back and enjoy the party.'

'No, go on,' he insists, frowning. 'What were you going to say?'

'Well, the thing is.' I cross my fingers behind my back. *I'm sorry, Zelda.* 'Zelda isn't the woman you think she is.' His frown intensifies. 'She gets these fixations on men.' I fib. 'Then she gets bored and moves on.' This is true, especially since she's been using that online dating app to wean herself off Chris. 'You might think she's really into you but the truth is.' *What is the truth? Think, woman, think!* 'The truth is, she likes nice things and men with a bit of money.' His hand shoots to his chin, eyes flitting around, as if he's lost something. I can't believe I'm saying all these horrible lies about Zelda, but it's for her own good. One day she'll thank me. 'I might be wrong, but you seem like you want to settle down, have kids.'

'That's right. I do.'

'That isn't going to happen with Zelda. I can guarantee it.'

He tuts, irritated. 'Lots of women have babies in their forties, and there's always IVF or adop...'

'It's not because of her age,' I interject. 'She hates kids.' Well, she doesn't hate them but she has opted to be child-free.

I look at the goosebumps that have appeared along Frank's arm. Is he cold or in shock? 'Well, I wasn't expecting that,' he admits, thrusting a hand through his white hair, which now has a few centimetres of dark roots. 'Thanks for the heads up. That's really good of you, Bella. Wow.' He covers his mouth and nose with his hands and I breathe in a waft of spicy aftershave. I'm sure it's one of Tom's. He must've splashed some on in the loo. 'But I think I can handle Zelda.' My face darkens like a cloud before a downpour. There are footsteps on the landing. Linda is on her way back. It hasn't been ten minutes already, has it? He goes to move.

'No, wait,' I exclaim, hand out. 'You don't understand.'

Frank leans forward, face close to mine. The steps creak beneath Linda's weight on the stairwell. 'Oh, I think I do,' he whispers. 'Nice try. But I won't be put off by your lies.' He takes a few steps towards the bi-fold doors, I barrel after him, then he stops and rounds on me. 'Do you know what? I've tried hard to put things right between us, but clearly, you don't want to know.' A phone goes off in the depths of the house. Linda's. Her footfall stops. She's picking up.

'Hiya, Elaini. I was just thinking of you.' Linda cackles, a boozy amplified laughter. It's Theo's sister. 'I must be a witch, yeah.'

'I know all about you wanting to meet up with Zelda alone to talk about me.' I frown, was he eavesdropping on our conversation, or did Zelda tell him? 'I suggest you stop being jealous of your sister and concentrate on your own relationship.'

I laugh when he says this. 'Jealous? Of what? You?' He shrugs, saying nothing. *Arrogant prick.* 'Oh, do me a favour.' I pull a face, as if I've inhaled sour milk from an out-of-date carton. 'I want Zelda to be happy more than anything. I want her to find someone decent, settle down.'

'Sure you do. She told me how you get jealous of any man that comes between you.'

'Ha. I've heard it all now,' I hit back. Zelda would never slag me off to a man she barely knows. 'And, for your information, there's nothing wrong with my marriage.'

His lips twist into a sinister smile. 'If you say so.'

'What's that supposed to mean?' I snort, scathingly.

'It means that if you and John Cummings Saunders are solid.' How does he know who the founder of Moorfield's Hospital is, has he been researching eye specialists? 'Why were you fishing elsewhere and having secret dates with your ex?'

My blood runs cold. I hear wisps of laughter from the garden and the faint hum of music. I should get back outside, but I can't leave this hanging in the air like a poisonous mist sucking all the oxygen out of my lungs. In my peripheral, I catch sight of Linda sitting on the third step of the stairwell, phone glued to her ear. I jerk my head. 'In here,' I say, and he follows me into the kitchen. I've got to put an end to this nightmare before he destroys everything and everyone I love.

Chapter 18

Frank rips a corner of kitchen foil off one of the leftover dishes, then leans the small of his back against the worktop and starts twiddling with the silver tear-off.

'How much do you want to stay out of my sister's life?' Blood hums in my ears. I can't believe I'm doing this.

'Don't you mean the gold-digger's life?'

'Two thousand?'

He snorts. 'Dream on.' Dream on? Does this mean he'll accept a bribe?

'Five, then.' He laughs at this. 'Okay, ten, but that's my final offer.'

'You really mean it, don't you?'

'I can do a bank transfer. The money will be in your account tonight.' God, where am I going to get ten grand from? I'll have to borrow it from Georgia's savings account, then sell one of my mother's precious paintings to replace it. 'Have we got a deal?'

He chews his bottom lip. I can see he's tempted, mulling it over. *Go on, Frank, say yes, take it. Take it now and disappear.* 'Good looking woman, your mate.' He flicks his head towards

Linda in the hallway, twisting the foil between his fingers, and my insides ache. What has Linda got to do with this negotiation?

'I'll go online now and do the transfer for you.'

'You're a fit family.' He rolls the foil between his index finger and thumb. 'Mum's still a bit of all right. Zelda showed me a few photos. A famous artist, isn't she?' A retired artist, made very good money from it, but I'd hardly call her famous. 'I've got a bit of an eye for art, but I'd never spend twenty-seven K on a bloody painting.' My eyes close – he thinks the Villins are loaded.

'Frank, ten thousand is all I can afford.'

He does that blinking thing, as if butter wouldn't melt. 'That temp of yours. Daisy, isn't it? She's a bit of a sort, too. Got a boyfriend, has she? Or does she prefer the older married type?' I want to hurt him. I want to dig my nails into his throat and watch him bleed to death.

'My offer only stands if you agree to it now,' I say.

'Nope, sorry.'

I feel my face flush. 'Right. Fine. You had your chance.'

'Wait, where are you going?' he says with urgency.

'To do something I should've done over a week ago.'

'What are you going to do, hmm? Fill Zelda's head with lies?'

'They're *not* lies. You tried it on with me. God, you even told me I was beautiful, or are you going to deny that too?'

'You are beautiful,' he says, matter-of-factly. 'Like I said, you're a good-looking family.'

'Don't try to be clever,' I snap.

'Look, I'm being lenient here, because I'm a decent guy, but if you push me, I will tell Tom everything I know.'

I glare at him. 'Zelda needs to be made aware of your Jekyll and Hyde personality,' I say calmly. 'You had me fooled too, to begin with. She needs to know she's dating a thug.'

'Thug?' He actually looks shocked. 'I've been nothing but a gentleman towards you.'

'Do you call spitting on my car window chivalrous behaviour?'

'A bit of spittle might've accidentally shot from my lips in anger, but I certainly didn't spit at you.'

'What about kicking my car, then?'

'Do you honestly think I'd cause criminal damage? I tripped over the fucking pavement in my haste to get close to you, to get you to listen.'

I shake my head. An answer for everything, as per. He's really thought this through. Getting Zelda to believe me is going to be tougher than I imagined. 'I'm sorry, Frank, but I don't believe you.'

He studies me for a while, saying nothing, and then, 'Going back to your mate Linda. She's still sexy as hell. Shame it was only a one-night-stand, although I'm not complaining.' And now he's using my best friend as a weapon to stop me from telling Zelda everything. 'That fat lump Theo is a bit of a wet blanket. Jealous type, is he? Linda could do so much better.'

I scowl at him. 'Better? What, like you?' I scoff, and just then a figure appears from the darkness of the alcove and my heart freezes.

'Just grabbing a couple of beers,' Theo says. 'Don't let me interrupt.' My face tingles, Frank shoots me a look. I didn't hear any footsteps. He must've already been in the recess before we stepped in, quietly listening. I feel the blood drain from my face. Frank said he had a one-night stand with Linda and that Theo was a wet blanket. Did he hear all that? But no, no. Theo would have flattened Frank by now if he had, or at least given it his best shot. Theo must've come in through the patio doors of the recess. We flung them open this morning for convenience.

'All right, Bro?' Frank offers, folding his strong arms against his toned chest. 'Bella's just filling me in on a few family tales.'

They size each other up. I give Theo a tight smile and he looks at me kindly. 'We'll be out in a moment. Linda's on the phone with your sister.'

Theo's lip curves downwards, then he nods, takes a swig from one of the bottles and with one final glance at Frank, he's gone, leaving the echo of his footsteps in his wake.

'I hate it when people creep up on me like that.' Frank does a little theatrical shudder. 'What was I saying?'

Irritation rockets through my veins. 'Threatening to tell Theo you slept with Linda isn't going to make me change my mind. I'm going to tell my sister everything. It's my duty to protect her.'

'Duty? Do me a favour,' he sneers, tossing the rolled-up kitchen foil into the air.

'If you're as innocent as you claim, then why are you trying to stop me from talking to Zelda?'

'Because, sadly, your sister thinks the sun shines out of your backside. She'll believe your crap. Anyway, do what you have to do and let her be the judge. But before you go galloping in like a heroine, you might want to know something.'

I cross my arms against my chest. 'About what?'

'Café Crouchy.' I look at him, confused. 'You know, the cafe I saw you and Liam in.' My tummy tightens.

I blow a strand of hair off my face. 'What about it?'

'Remote workers love it, and do you know why?' I shake my head. I'm guessing it isn't for the rich Colombian coffee blend. 'It's soundproofed. So it's nice and quiet, which was handy on the day I saw you because I heard *Every. Single. Word* you said.'

I glare at him. That can't be true. Who soundproofs a coffee shop? A chill tiptoes over my skin, bringing with it a feeling of doom. Apart from the low hum of music, it was tranquil in there. A few people were quietly chatting but most of the customers were working on their laptops.

'You're bluffing,' I retort.

Leaning forward, he whispers what I said to Liam word for word, before he stood up and faced me. My blood runs cold. 'I could end your marriage just like that.' Frank clicks his fingers. I shake my head, mind racing like a car without brakes – I'll deny everything - tell Tom he's lying because I sacked him for making a pass at me. That he's a spiteful narcissist, making it all up.

'Go fuck yourself,' I snap.

But as I go to move he snatches me by the arm. 'Is this some kind of sick revenge for what happened between us at the gym?'

'Let go, you're hurting me.'

'I swear, Bella, if you ruin this for me and Zelda, I will destroy you and everyone you care about.'

Chapter 19

I shrug Frank off me angrily and he stumbles back. 'If you think I'm going to stand by and watch you hurt my sister, allow you to blackmail me, then you can think again,' I hit back, anger soaring through every cell in my body. 'So, go ahead and tell Tom. I'll deny it all. It'll be your word against mine. Who do you think he's going to believe, hmm?'

Frank opens his mouth to speak when a voice says. 'Hey, I was about to send out a search party.' I spin around. Tom is standing behind me, phone in the palm of his hand, as if he was just about to text me. His white cotton shirt is undone to his waist like a seventy's medallion man, gold crucifix glimmering against his chest, face red from alcohol. My mouth fills with saliva – did he hear everything I said?

'We were just catching up,' Frank says, smoothly. 'Bella is thinking of coming back to the gym.'

'Really?' Tom slips his phone into the side pocket of his black combats, then slings his arm around me, stinking of booze. 'I thought you said you were too busy, my love. Mind you, you've got Daisy now.' He plants a wet kiss on my cheek at about the same time as his phone bleeps and vibrates in his pocket. Relief floods through my body. He didn't hear our conversation.

'It was just a thought,' I mutter, still shaken by Frank's revelation.

'Hey, we could get one of those joint memberships, work out together.' Tom lets go of me and starts marching on the spot, head back, grinning like a loon. 'They're cheaper, aren't they?' He stops marching and looks at Frank, bleary-eyed. 'Text me the details, fella. You've got my number.' My guts turn to mush. They've exchanged phone numbers?

There's a ruckus of footsteps and a shuffle of movement. 'I love my sister-in-law, but bloody hell, Elaini could talk for England.' Linda's at my side, straightening her crumpled skirt. 'I need another drink.' She looks at me, our shoulders touching, and I register the flick of concern in her eyes. 'The in-laws are threatening to visit tomorrow.' Her eyes dart around the kitchen. 'Pass me the wine.'

Outside, Linda tops up her glass with merlot, takes a pew next to her husband on the rattan sofa, grabs a handful of crisps from the bowl on the table and starts munching hungrily, giving me intermittent looks that say *I take it the plan wasn't successful.*

Georgia stumbles along the decked patio in her white Converse platforms, a smudge of red lipstick on the side of her mouth, mascara smeared under her eyes. Brushing past me, she announces that she's starving and then, in a voice loud enough for the entire neighbourhood to hear, claims that there's never any decent food in this house. I can tell she's had more than enough to drink. It was inevitable. Probably necked the entire bottle while I was inside trying to convince Frank to leave my sister. Daisy follows her swiftly. 'I'll make her a sandwich,' she whispers reassuringly, gently squeezing my arm. 'You okay?'

'Yes,' I lie, running my hands up and down the sides of my legs. 'Just a bit tired.' Daisy holds my gaze for a moment and then, with a quick look over her shoulder, tells me to relax. She's got everything under control.

A fusion of Georgia and Daisy's chatter and the sound of crockery wafts through the open bifold doors. I should go inside, sort my daughter out with some food, let Daisy get back to the party, but the need to release my sister from the clutches of Frank has intensified tenfold.

I go to stand up, then sit down again, trembling. If Frank blabs to Tom my life will be over. Perhaps I should just keep quiet. Save my marriage. As Linda said, their relationship will fizzle out soon. I shoot to my feet before I can talk myself out of it. I can't bear the thought of Frank being a part of my family.

My eyes race around the garden. Tom is putting the lid down on the barbeque, two magpies are perched on the fence – a good omen – Behind me, Linda is telling Theo about a new series on Netflix - Zelda is sitting on the long bench under the pergola, phone in hand, hair in her face. Frank is nowhere to be seen. Bingo.

Folding my arms, I make my way along the dewy lawn, rehearsing my speech silently – Hey Zee, having a good time? Look, there's something I need to tell you. Frank isn't the man you think he is – he's got an eye for the ladies, was even checking Daisy out right under your nose earlier. No, no, I want to keep Daisy out of this. I'm going to have to be brutal. Frank made a pass at me. I rejected him, quit the gym and fired him. I picture her horrified expression, then plough on. I'm sorry to say this, but he looked you up on my Instagram followers list and I think he's got an ulterior motive for dating you. Maybe it's revenge for turning him down. The thing is, Zelda, he knows stuff about me, things that could destroy my marriage.

But I love you, you're my sister. So, I'm risking everything to keep you safe. Oh, God, will I even get all that out before Frank comes wading in?

Blades of grass tickle my toes that are peeking from my cross sandals. A light, warm wind blows in my face, carrying the musky smell of my sister's perfume. Zelda looks up at me from her phone. 'Hey, Sis, where've you been?'

'Hey, Zee, having a good time?' Nodding, she shoves up, making room for me on the white bench. Throwing a glance at the house, I take a pew. Through the window, I catch sight of Frank wandering around the kitchen and saying something to Daisy. 'I need to talk to you. It's important.' I can feel my heartbeat belting in my abdomen.

'Is everything okay?' Zelda puts her phone down and I take her hands in mine.

'Zelda, I need you to listen to me carefully and trust me on this, okay?' Zelda nods, frowning. 'And promise that you won't…'

A tinkling sound of metal against glass demands our attention. I look around. Tom is sitting on the rattan sofa, Theo and Linda are on the three-seater. Daisy is standing next to Linda, breadstick in hand, a look of intrigue on her face. Georgia is on the lounger, stuffing her face with a sandwich. They're all looking at Frank standing on the decking, bottle and spoon in hand.

'Listen up, guys.' Frank is striding towards us now. He thinks I've trashed him to Zelda and is out for revenge. I close my eyes, breath shallow, waiting for him to expose me to my family and friends for what I really am. A liar. A cheat.

'We meet a lot of arseholes in this lifetime. Fact.' Lukewarm laughter ripples through the air. I can hear the rustle of his footfall approaching. My gut simmers with anxiety. Swallowing sour spit, I squeeze my eyes tighter, clenching my fists until I feel the sting in the flesh of my palms. 'Life is short. So, without further ado.' There's a pause and a shuffle of movement. 'Zelda, we haven't known each other long, but…' My eyes snap open. Frank is on one knee gazing up at my sister. He's holding a ring between his fingers made out of kitchen foil. 'Will you marry me?'

Chapter 20

I twist Georgia's long, golden curls in my hands as she vomits into the toilet bowl for the fourth time. It's just gone midnight. We saw the last of our guests off an hour ago. After Zelda said yes to Frank, Tom opened a bottle of Bollinger that he'd been saving for a special occasion and turned up the music. I'm surprised Mr Stanhope didn't come pounding on our door. The fizz barely touched my lips when Tom made a toast to the happy couple. I was in no mood to celebrate my sister's engagement to a maniac.

Georgia gags again and I stroke her back soothingly. Tom's muffled grunts and snores filter from the bedroom. The sound of water splashing floats from Daisy's en-suite. She's taking a shower before bed. It's been a long day, for all of us.

'Oh, Mum,' Georgia sobs. 'Am I going to die?'

'No, my love,' I soothe, hand on her back, 'but next time listen to your mother. You're too young to drink. Who gave you the alcohol anyway, was it Linda?' Georgia shakes her head, eyes red, features droopy from booze. 'Auntie Zelda, was it?' I say dryly. I could swing for my sister sometimes. She's too lenient with Georgia, forgets she's only fifteen. 'It had better not have been Frank.'

'Mummmah…stop. I got it myself when you went inside.'

'Oh, Georgie.' I push her hair off her flawless face, clammy with sweat, and look into her deep blue eyes - her father stares back at me. She's so like him, it's uncanny sometimes. If it weren't for the shape of her eyes, you wouldn't think she was related to me at all. 'Well, I wouldn't put it past Frank to ply you with booze,' I groan, running her hair through my fingers. 'I saw him chatting to you and Daisy. But grown-ups aren't always right, you know.' Georgia goes to get up, saliva dripping from the side of her mouth. 'All done?' I ask gently, and she nods, wiping her spit with the sleeve of her Barbie pink pyjama top. I hold her in my arms as we walk back to her room.

'Is Auntie Zelda really gonna marry him?' Georgia asks, climbing back into bed awkwardly.

'I don't know, honey. But it seems that way.' I pull the duvet over her slender body.

'She's only known him like three days. Why was everybody clapping like they'd been together for three years or something?' There were boozy cheers and whistles when Zelda said yes, although I'm not entirely certain any of us were actually delighted with Frank's shocking proposal. He obviously did it to silence me, knew I was on the verge of self-destruction, prepared to risk everything to protect my sister from his clutches. But now, with a ring on her finger, albeit one made out of kitchen foil, it'll be harder to convince her to break up with him. I haven't seen her this happy since Jake. In fact, she might not even believe me now – take his side, like Linda said. Frank will convince her that I'm the jealous sister. What a mess.

Kissing Georgia's forehead, I breathe her in, before tucking her into bed as if she were six, then look at her adoringly, heart swelling with love, and in that moment, I wish I'd had more children. 'They've only known each other a few weeks, but I suppose it's their decision, sweetheart,' I offer. 'Lots of whirlwind romances work out.' A knot forms in my stomach because I know that this one is destined for failure.

'Mum, will you stay a while? In case I'm sick again?'

'Of course, I will.' Sitting on the edge of Georgia's bed, my mind drifts back to earlier. Linda found me in the kitchen after Frank's announcement, slamming cabinet doors and wiping down spotless worktops – hot water gushing from the tap, plumes of steam rising from the sink like a mini sauna.

'Bella,' she said, worriedly, turning off the hot tap. 'Are you okay? I didn't see that one coming. What did you say to Frank? You were meant to put him off her not persuade him to walk her down the aisle.'

'Oh, Linda, it's all such a fucking mess and it's all my doing. I…I… when…'

Linda folded me in her arms and held me as I sobbed on her shoulder, shushing me gently. 'I can't believe I've brought this psychopath into my family.'

'It wasn't your fault, baby,' Linda said kindly, even though we both knew it was. 'Talk about a fast mover. I take it my plan backfired. I am sorry, Bells. I wish I'd kept it zipped now.'

I pulled out of her embrace, wiped my cheeks with the back of my thumbs, told her it wasn't her fault, that I stupidly tried to bribe him with ten grand and made matters worse. 'He knew I was going to tell Zelda about his vicious temper and how he tried it on with me, and that he looked her up on my Insta account and tricked her into believing his Granny story. What am I supposed to do now?'

'Tell him to stick his head into a bucket of water three times and only take it out twice.' I laughed when Linda said this. 'Well, you've got a couple of options now,' she went on, 'say nothing and let them get on with it. It might even work out, you never know. They do seem besotted with each other.'

'Oh, Linda.' It's not what I wanted to hear. I sat down heavily at the table, tapping my fingers. 'You don't know the half of it,' I said, tiredly. 'He heard everything Liam and I said at the café in Crouch End and is threatening to tell Tom.'

'I thought he was listening to music on his headphones.'

'So did I.'

'Oh, fucking hell.' Linda squatted and held onto my knees. 'The other option, of course, would be to ring Zelda tomorrow morning and tell her everything you know about Frank, bar my one-night-stand with him, and make sure she knows you'll go along with whatever decision she makes. Clear the air, sooner rather than later. I can't believe he overheard your conversation. The sneaky bastard.'

Blowing my nose into a tissue, I said. 'I'd tell her in a heartbeat if she'd listen. But will she, now that he's proposed? You saw how happy she was. I don't even care if Frank tells Tom he saw me with Liam. It's about time he knew. The guilt has been clawing away at me for weeks.' Inhaling teary phlegm, I shook my head boldly. 'I'll be free then. And if Tom bails on us, I'll just have to suck it up.'

'I'm never getting married,' Georgia says, snapping me back to now. 'Can I live with you forever, Mum?'

'Of course, you can, love,' I soothe. 'What's brought this on?' I wonder if she's upset about a boy. Or a girl. Georgia knows we're supportive of same-sex relationships. A new love interest would explain why she's suddenly wearing so much makeup and got hammered today. Maybe she likes someone at school who's blown her out. She was talking to Anna's son, Ralf, outside his house for quite a while yesterday morning. It did look quite intense. I wonder if it's him.

'Thanks, Mum,' Georgia groans, ignoring my question. 'Love you.'

'I love you too, more than anything.' I go to stroke her hair when she pushes me away and turns on her side.

'I think I'm okay now, you can go.'

Accepting my dismissal like a servant, I get to my feet, sweep up her orange hoodie, black shorts and sole-blackened socks and place them on the chair before switching the lights off. 'Na-night, Georgie.'

I go to turn the doorknob when she says, 'I hope she doesn't marry him. Frank creeps me out.' I stand stock-still. The light goes back on. Spinning round, I open my mouth to ask her why, when she says, 'Night-night, Mum.' And her eyes close.

Chapter 21

Negotiating my way to our bedroom, I mull over what Georgia just said about Frank. What is it about him that gives her the creeps? Did Frank say anything to her? Eye her up? But even he can't be that stupid – not with her father in plain sight. Besides, Georgia would've said. She's no pushover – she's like Tom and her grandfather, Gary - outspoken, says it how she sees it.

'Everything all right, Bella?' Daisy's voice startles me. She's standing in the doorway of her bedroom in a bra and a pair of lacy plum knickers, drying her hair on a purple towel. She looks beautiful. My eyes sweep over her lean, curvy body and sculpted limbs. I'm not sure if it's because Linda planted the seed earlier and Frank's remark about her preferring older men, but seeing her standing there, half-naked, unsettles me. Throwing a glance at our bedroom door, I cross my arms, glad Tom is behind it, snoring his head off. 'I heard voices.'

'Georgia was sick. Too much booze.'

Daisy tuts, concerned. 'Is she okay?' I tell her that she will be, and Daisy shakes her head, warns me that she'll have a stinking hangover in the morning. 'Sorry about this.' Flinging the towel over her shoulder, she points to her underwear. 'I heard Tom snoring, so thought it was safe to venture.' Of course she did. I'm being silly. It's been a long day. We're all exhausted. I push my hands into the pockets of my dressing gown, hating myself for doubting her. It's that Linda's fault, putting ideas into my head. 'I'm going to watch something on Netflix. My head is buzzing. Don't think I can sleep after all that excitement. Night, Bella.'

'Night, Daisy, and thanks for today.' I turn the doorknob. It opens with a creak. Tom's snores amplify. 'Actually, do you fancy a cuppa?'

In the kitchen, I make us two cups of peppermint tea using fresh leaves from the plant in my window box, and we sit barefooted at the oak table in matching white, fluffy dressing gowns. I let her borrow mine and slipped into Tom's.

'Penny for them,' Daisy says, blowing on her hot tea.

'Just thinking about my sister and her new *fiancé*.' Saying the word fiancé turns my stomach. I raise my eyebrows over my cup, take a sip, and burn my tongue.

'He's a lucky guy.' Daisy looks up at the spotlighted ceiling. 'Zelda's gorgeous. Your friends are lovely, too.' I agree, tell her that Linda and I go back a long way. 'Her hubby's a bit quiet, though, isn't he?' I can tell that by this she means moody, but is being polite. 'Very Byronic,' she grins, a twinkle in her eye. That is one way of describing him. 'Don't think he liked Frank much, although he did perk up a bit when they announced their engagement,' she says, and I can tell she suspects something, maybe fishing for information.

'He's a bit overprotective at times.'

Daisy raises an eyebrow. 'Linda is a beauty.'

I agree, and then I say, 'So, what did you make of Frank?' I blow on my steamy tea, breathing in the peppermint.

Daisy shrugs. 'Fit but not my type.' She winks. 'Nice butt.'

'That's down to all that gyming. He's very dedicated.' Not to mention vain.

'Loves himself a bit, eh?' she says, as if I teleported my thoughts directly into her brain. 'I've never seen anyone take so many selfies. He seems nice enough, although there was this one thing.' Daisy looks into space, cradling her mug with both hands. 'That I found a bit weird.'

My eyes widen. 'Oh?'

'You know when I was making the hot drinks in the kitchen? Well, Zelda and Frank were at the table, bent over their phones.' Yes, that's right. We took the party inside. The sun had gone down and it was getting a bit chilly. Plus they wanted to get online and announce their engagement on social media. 'I had my back to them most of the time, but at one point I heard him say he wanted to see the photos she'd taken. I could hear rustling and murmurs, and I got the feeling she was resisting.'

Her comment unnerves me, but then it's not a crime to want to see photos of yourself, especially if they're going to be posted online. Knowing Frank, he'd have wanted to inspect them. Tweak them a bit first. Stick a filter on.

'Their voices grew louder, so I glanced round, asked if either of them fancied a hot drink, and that's when I saw him holding her by the wrist and she let go of her phone.'

The edges of the room darken like a vignette photograph, swallowing me in. 'Are you sure,' I croak, feeling lightheaded, 'that it wasn't playful?'

'It looked aggressive to me. Zelda looked up at me, went a bit red.'

'What happened next?' I urge.

'I asked if everything was okay. They both said they were fine. Frank handed her phone back, then he started rubbing his head with his fingers like this.' Daisy puts her mug down on the table and begins to massage her temples in a circular motion. 'Complaining of a migraine. Zelda said she'd ask you for painkillers.' She didn't. I wonder why. 'And then she wrapped her arms around his neck and they started snogging. I didn't know where to look. It was all so bizarre.' Daisy picks up her mug and shakes her head, baffled.

'Hmm...that is very odd.' I take a sip. I wonder why Zelda didn't ask me for ibuprofen if he was in pain. Unless he stopped her. Unless it was a bogus headache to throw Daisy off because she'd caught him being mean to my sister? I open my mouth to question her some more when my phone starts ringing and vibrating in my pocket. It's Zelda. I glance at the clock – it's a quarter to one in the morning. Did she forget something here? My eyes skirt around the kitchen searching for any of her belongings.

'Hey Zelda. Daisy and – ' I shoot to my feet, Daisy looks at me, concerned. 'I can't understand what you're saying.' Zelda is talking gibberish. I cover the mouthpiece and mime, I think she's drunk, and Daisy nods, goes back to her phone.

'Bella,' Zelda blubs, and I realise that she isn't drunk, she's crying, hysterically. 'Help me...I...please. I don't...'

A shiver races over my skin. Something bad has happened to my sister. Frank has hurt her. I will bloody kill him. 'Zelda, what is it?' Shoving a hand through my hair, I walk into the hallway and start pacing. 'Are you hurt?'

'Yes...I...' I knew it. 'Um... no, I'm fine. It's Frank. He's...he...'

'Has something happened to him?'

'Yes,' she wails, voice like a wounded animal.

So, it wasn't a bogus migraine. The pain was real. I walk back into the kitchen and start motioning to Daisy for my car keys.

'What's the matter with him.' I ask frantically as Daisy swoops around the kitchen, looking for my keys. 'Is he conscious?' Images of Frank gasping for breath flash in my mind. It wouldn't be the first time a fit, healthy, twenty-nine-year-old man had a heart attack or stroke. I want Frank gone, but not like this. Despite what I said in anger, I don't want him dead. I don't *hate* him. I don't hate anyone. I simply hate what he did to me, that's all. 'Shall I call an ambulance?' I suggest. At this, Daisy who is on her knees scrambling around under the table for my keys, looks up at me, wide-eyed.

'*No*,' Zelda screams and I wince. What am I saying? She's probably called the emergency services already. She needs my help. My support. I've got to get round there. Take her to the hospital. They've probably taken him to A&E. I gesture to Daisy, mime that I've got to go out and to keep an eye on Georgia, and she nods, looking worried, and just then she spots my keys in an ashtray, snatches them up and hands them to me.

Dashing to the open window, I pull the handle, inhaling the ashes of our barbeque still hanging in the air. 'I'm on my way,' I say, locking the window. My phone buzzes in my ear. I've got a text. I look at it quickly. Linda:

Bells, r u there? Me and Theo had big fight. knows about my ONS with Frank. Heard him boasting to u. He's gone AWOL. don't know what to do.

Terror pierces through every fibre of my body. This can't be happening. I text back with tremulous fingers, saying I'll call her in a bit, I'm on the phone with Zelda.

'Bella?' Zelda's alarmed tinny voice filters from my handset. 'Bella? Are you still there?'

'I'm here.' I press the phone to my ear. 'Sorry…I'll just change and –'

'No,' she wails, 'there's no time. You need to come over right away.'

'Okay. Calm down, Zelda.' I feel my pocket for my keys, even though I know they're in there, and just then I remember the wine I drank, not to mention the shots I knocked back with Linda before she left, to toast the happy couple, she'd said sardonically. I can't drive. 'Scrub that. I've had too much alcohol. I'm over the limit. I'll jump in a cab.'

'No, please don't come in a taxi,' Zelda yells again, louder this time. How am I supposed to get there in the middle of the night then, Zelda, on a bloody broomstick?

'No cabs. No traces.'

'Why not?' My heart feels as if it's going to rip through my skin. 'You're scaring me now.' Silence, apart from muffled crying. 'Zelda?' I exclaim. Daisy is on her feet, arms by her sides, a blur of white in front of me.

'Oh God, Bella,' Zelda sobs. 'I think I've killed him.'

Chapter 22

'Can't you drive any faster?' I say to a startled-looking Daisy. I hate myself for involving her in this, but who else could I trust to give me a lift to Zelda's? Linda, whom I texted and arranged to meet at Zelda's, downed enough booze to knock out a hippopotamus.

Daisy glances at her rear-view, hands wrapped tightly around the steering wheel, skin tight over her knuckles and sinews. 'I'm doing thirty. I don't want to get pulled over by the cops.' I shake my head, apologise. The last thing we want is the police on our tail.

'Did she say how it happened?' Daisy asks nervously. 'The accident?'

How much should I tell her? Surely, the less she knows the better. 'They had a fight and it got out of hand, and he…he hit her. Slapped her and she fell over, hurt her elbow. She'll be fine. I'll look after her.'

'I knew something wasn't right.' Daisy shakes her head, letting out a long sigh through her nose. 'They both had a lot to drink. My ma got violent when she got drunk.'

I nod as a roaring motorbike overtakes us at top speed, slanting as it takes a bend before being sucked into the night. Only God knows what we're going to do once we get to Zelda's – that's if Frank is still alive.

'Did Zelda say what it was about? Why he hit her?'

I wish Daisy would stop asking me so many leading questions. We're not in a courtroom. Yet. 'An old boyfriend texted Zelda, and Frank read it. He knows her password.'

This is true. After Zelda had calmed down, she gave me a summary of what happened – she'd posted a photograph of her and Frank on Instagram, showing off that stupid kitchen foil ring, with the caption *'He's put a ring on it and I said yes.'* Chris, her married lover, saw it, bombarded her with texts, pleading with her to break off her engagement, promising to get a divorce and marry her. Trouble is, she was taking a shower at the time and her phone was on the bedside table. Frank read them all. They had a big fight. He grabbed her throat, she couldn't breathe, thought he was going to kill her – she fished around on the worktop for protection, picked up a silver letter knife, a souvenir from their trip to Monte Carlo, and dug it into his flesh – he staggered into the garden and collapsed on the lawn.

'Oh, that was a bummer,' Daisy says. 'My ex knew my passcode, too. I kept changing it, but he kept finding it out.' My tension mounts with every kilometre. *Please let him be alive.* 'Don't worry, Bella, it'll be okay,' Daisy says, clearly sensing my tension. 'We're almost there.' Reaching over, she gives my hand a good old shake, and I nod, eyes on the oncoming traffic, their headlights like fireballs. If only she knew that my sister may have just murdered her fiancé. Zelda will go to prison if he's dead and it'll all be down to me.

Chapter 23

We turn into Zelda's narrow, tree-lined road. The street is quiet, eerie. Apart from a yellow glow from one or two bedrooms, the rest of the nineteen-thirties semis are in darkness. Everyone's asleep.

'Which house?' Daisy asks, slowing down.

I don't want her to park too close to Zelda's flat. Those Ring doorbells can pick up motion from passers-by and record everything. Zelda gave me strict instructions to avoid attracting any attention, specifically the rumble of Daisy's diesel car. 'Just pull up here,' I say, gesturing at the kerb where two wheelie bins have been haphazardly abandoned.

The car stops, Daisy pulls on the handbrake and kills the engine, then goes to undo her seatbelt. 'What are you doing?' I ask, hand on the metal lever of the door.

'I'm coming with you.'

'No, Daisy, it's fine. Go home and get some rest. I'll be spending the night with Zelda.'

Daisy shakes her head defiantly. 'I'm not leaving you here.' She gestures with a nod. 'Not with that maniac on the loose. I'll wait in the car until you're done.'

'Daisy, it's twenty past one.' I look around the motionless street. Trees shiver in the light wind. Streetlights cast shadows on the pavement. A vixen screams in the darkness. 'I can't leave you here on your own. Please, just go home. I'll call you if I need you.'

'I tell you what, I'll lock myself in the car and phone you if a serial killer tries to kidnap me.'

'Don't even joke about that.' I'll never forgive myself if I put her in danger.

'I'll wait fifteen minutes, do a bit of Tiktok, if you're not back by then then I'll go home, how's that?'

'Ten.'

'Deal.'

I half walk, half run to Zelda's, glancing behind me. Daisy's car lights are on. Damn, she'll get a flat battery. I pull out my phone and text her. Within seconds her lights go out. Zelda's front door is ajar. I can hear the wisps of voices as I push it open.

'Oh, thank God.' Zelda runs into my arms, face wet, smeared with teary makeup. Linda raises her eyebrows as if to say, what a bloody mess. Then Zelda backs away and wraps her hands tightly around my wrists, eyes feral. 'You will help me, won't you? I can't go to prison. It was self-defence. He was going to kill me. Tell her, Linda.' Zelda snatches Linda's lime green-sleeved arm and she stumbles forward.

'It was an accident,' Linda confirms, as if she was a witness. 'He's having a snooze on the grass. He'll be fine,' she says unconvincingly.

'Shhh,' I soothe, stroking Zelda's hair as she sobs uncontrollably onto my shoulder, 'you won't go to prison.' And then mime at Linda - *is he dead?* Linda shrugs, eyes full of terror.

I hold Zelda at arm's length. 'Right, let's go into the garden and see how he's getting on, shall we?' I say, as if we're going out to check on the progress of her violet hydrangeas that Mum planted for her before she left for Portugal.

We follow Zelda through the kitchen diner to the back of the flat and out into the cold, crisp darkness. 'There,' she says, pointing with a tremulous finger. I put my phone torch on. Frank is sprawled out on the lawn. I make my way along the path, adrenalin soaring through my blood vessels. Swallowing hard, I shine the torch on his motionless, limp body. His face looks grey, lifeless. There's blood on his neck, angling over his left shoulder and onto his blue shirt like a running stream, heading towards the little polo player motif on his chest. But it's impossible to see where the wound is without cleaning him up. I kneel beside him and try to find a pulse – nothing.

'Is he dead?' Zelda asks hysterically, gathering her pink cardie around her.

'Um...' I rub a hand over the grass. It's dewy. Then look at my hand. No blood.

'Bella?' Zelda exclaims.

I look at the white bunnies on her pink cardigan. 'Yes.' I reply with downcast eyes, doom washing over me like a storm. 'I think so.'

Linda's hand flies to her mouth. 'Shit, fuck. FUCK. I'm going to be sick.' And with this, she heaves and vomits into Zelda's hydrangeas.

My eyes skim around the houses, to the milieu of Linda gagging and Zelda's muffled whimpering. Ian and Janette's garden resembles a building site. Zelda said they moved into temporary accommodation while their house is being renovated and, thank goodness, they're in the middle of rewiring the house, so all their security gadgets have been disabled.

Killing my phone torch. I tiptoe along the green, feeling the dew of the grass between my toes. In my haste to get here, I put on the first thing I could find at the front door, a pair of Georgia's leopard print flip-flops. Good job we're both a size six. I peek over the hedge – two fences are broken on the other side and there are ladders strewn on the gravel, one propped up against the house, there's an orange digger and abandoned tools. My eyes slide to a huge excavation at the back of the house, floodlit by the moonlight, revealing exposed pipes. Zelda said something about a basement. I presume that'll be it.

I survey the scene like a detective. Lillian's house, on the other side, is lit up, but Zelda said she's away for the weekend. It must be a security timer. The flat upstairs is in darkness. Silvanna and Giovanni have gone back to Italy, which is a blessing because they'd have seen and heard everything. I look for CCTV cameras but see nothing. Zelda's garden isn't overlooked. Tall conifers line the back fence and the lawn backs onto a lake and gardens. No one could have seen or heard a thing. We're safe.

'Oh, my *God*. I'm a murderer.'

I spin around, breath ragged. Zelda is standing over Frank's body, quivering. 'Keep your voice down,' I hiss, rushing up to her and snatching her by the hand. 'Let's go back in and discuss it.'

'Shouldn't we call for an ambulance?' Linda suggests frantically, trying to keep up with us as I march Zelda along the patio.

'It's too late for that.' I step back and flick a finger out. 'Get inside.'

Chapter 24

The deafening silence at the kitchen table is punctuated by Zelda's hiccupy sobs, the hoot of an owl and the gekkering of foxes.

'We need to call the police,' Linda insists. 'God, my mouth is so dry.' Getting to her feet, she snatches a glass off the drying rail and fills it with tap water.

'They'll lock me up,' Zelda murmurs tearfully. 'I'll be an old woman before I'm released.'

'Not if you explain that you acted in self-defence,' Linda claims, sitting back down, glass in hand. 'We'll get you a good barrister. Theo's cousin Andrea is…'

But Zelda shakes her head to and fro, to and fro. 'Bella, please don't call the police. I'll die in prison.'

'It'll be manslaughter,' Linda explains. 'You might not even go to prison.'

Zelda uses her hands as earmuffs, rocking back and forth in her chair. 'They won't believe me. Please, Bella, don't call them. How will it look when they dig up my file?' I bite the flesh inside my bottom lip, that thought did occur to me, too.

'We can't just leave him there,' Linda says to me firmly. 'Look, if we don't call the emergency services it'll be conspiracy to murder, you do realise that, don't you?' Silence. 'Right, I'm ringing them now.' Linda's hand disappears into her handbag.

Leaping to her feet, Zelda grabs Linda's arm with both hands. 'No, don't,' she cries, wrestling her for the handset. 'If you do, I'll kill myself. I mean it.'

I comb my hands through my hair as they continue to squabble, their voices growing louder and louder and louder, and then, 'Oh, just shut the fuck up and let me think.'

The room falls silent. All I can hear is the thump, thump, thump of my racing heart. This morning I didn't think my life could get any worse, but what happened with Liam pales into insignificance compared to this. Zelda has killed a man, albeit in self-defence. *Her* fiancé of a few hours. *My* ex-fitness instructor. *Linda's* one-night stand. We're all connected to him in some way. Linda's right, we can't just leave him there. We will have to call the police, but I can't relay this to Zelda, not while she's like this.

'Can't we get rid of the body?' Zelda asks. 'I saw a thriller on TV where...'

'Are you out of your mind?' Linda yells. 'We'll all go to prison once they dig him up from your garden. Our DNA is all over him.'

'We *were* all at a party with him,' I offer. 'He's bound to have our DNA on him. The police won't question that.'

Linda's eyes have become like discs. 'You can't be serious?'

A beat and then. 'No, no, of course not. We're not going to bury him.' I drum my fingers against the table, filling the silence. 'Did Theo turn up?' I ask, hoping a change of subject might calm Linda down.

Linda shakes her head. 'I've no idea where he's gone. He just stormed off. He'll probably sleep it off at his sister's and come home tomorrow.'

'Zelda,' I say gently. Zelda's head shoots up, eyes round. 'How did this happen?'

'I told you on the phone,' she says, annoyed.

'Tell me again, from the beginning, and don't leave anything out. We need to get our stories straight.' Zelda looks from me to Linda, and Linda nods reassuringly, drops her phone back into her handbag and tells her that we'll look after her, no matter what.

Zelda takes a deep breath. 'We came home, and he went upstairs and locked himself in the bathroom. I think he was doing a bit of coke.'

'Drugs?' I say, horrified.

'No, Bella, he necked a can of cola,' Zelda snaps. 'Of course drugs.'

'You let him do drugs in your home,' I exclaim. 'Where Georgia has sleepovers?' Only occasionally, but still.

'He did it once, and I told him off. He promised it was a one-off, but then started spending ages in the bathroom. I saw a bit of powder on his nose a couple of times, but I didn't want to argue with him. I'm not his keeper.'

'Zelda, you should've given him his marching orders the first time he did it.'

'Oh, will you get off my case?' Zelda yells, head in hand. 'I don't need this shit right now.'

Linda gives me a look, then turns to Zelda. 'Go on, Zee.'

Zelda takes a few breaths. 'He was acting a bit weird after we left yours. Almost fell asleep in the cab, could barely walk in a straight line when we got out. I knew it was the booze. I told him I'd put the kettle on and make us both a nice cuppa. He agreed; he had a headache earlier.' I nod but don't say anything.

I don't want to snitch on Daisy. 'He even asked me for a slice of my lemon cake.'

'People get the munchies on coke,' Linda says, 'Or is that weed?'

'Weed,' I say, as if I'm an expert.

'Anyway, I left him to his tea and cake and said I was going for a shower. Chris had been texting me all afternoon but I didn't reply in case Frank got suspicious.' That's why she was reluctant to hand over her phone earlier. 'Once I was safely in my bedroom, I replied to Chris. We exchanged a few emotional messages and agreed to meet up to discuss things. Don't give me that look, Bella, you can't help who you fall in love with.'

Liam flashes in my mind – his pleading face, his soft voice saying things he shouldn't be saying, things that were buried long ago. 'I wasn't going to say that. I'm not judging you. None of us are saints. Carry on.'

'I was going to let Frank down gently. I mean, I don't even know why I agreed to marry him. He just took me by surprise, that's all. I got caught up in the moment.' Linda gives me a look. 'When I came back into the kitchen, he was acting bizarre.' Zelda pauses, takes a sip from Linda's glass, which has an imprint of her crimson lipstick on it.

'Go on,' I urge, covering her tremulous hand with mine.

'He was sitting at the table with my laptop staring at my bank's log-in page, and then he asked me to lend him some money.' Linda and I frown. 'I was like, what the fuck? I wasn't going to give him any.'

'Of course not,' I tut, 'you're not stupid.'

Zelda looks at me for a moment, and then. 'He asked me to do a bank transfer for fifteen hundred quid – the landlord was breathing down his neck – threatened him with eviction – he promised to pay me back next week when he got paid. I told him I didn't have that kind of cash.'

Linda shakes her head. 'He must've thought you were a pushover.'

'More fool him,' I add, 'he really doesn't know the Villin sisters at all.' I laugh lightly.

'You're not going to like this next bit.'

'Go on,' Linda says gently. 'You can tell us anything, we won't be judgy.'

Zelda takes a deep breath. 'I already lent him two grand.'

Chapter 25

'Are you winding us up?' I exclaim. Zelda shakes her head. 'You actually handed over two thousand pounds to a man you'd been dating for five minutes?' I cringe at my hypocrisy – wasn't I willing to give him ten thousand to leave her just hours ago?

'It was to make a payment on his car – he was in arrears. *What*? They were threatening to repossess it,' she exclaims, 'He showed me the emails.'

'How could you be so bloody naïve?' I cry.

'Bella,' Linda says wearily, 'calm down.'

'Calm down? She got fleeced by a moron. Have you any idea how many cakes she has to bake to earn that much cash?'

'I felt sorry for him. He was always so generous, paid for everything – bought me expensive stuff. Took me on that luxury break. He was even talking about booking an overnight stay at The Savoy for my birthday, with a west-end show and dinner at the Ivy Grill. That watch he wears is a Patek Phillipe. It's worth over a hundred and fifty thousand pounds.' The one I saw on his wrist the Friday before last. It looked expensive, but

I didn't think it was worth that much. 'I thought he was good for it.'

Folding my arms, I shake my head at my sister. 'If it was so valuable why didn't he flog it?'

'It was his grandfather's. An heirloom.'

'Oh, Zelda. What were you thinking?'

'Shut up, Bella. She got a decent holiday out of it and expensive clothes,' Linda says. 'Just write it off, Zelda. Money comes and goes.'

'Trouble is, I need it now to pay my own rent.' Zelda rubs her eyes with the heels of her hands.

'Come on, let's not divert.' Linda sighs heavily. 'We've got a dead man in the garden, remember.'

Linda's right. 'Come on, tell us what happened next?' I say, 'after you refused to hand over any more of your hard-earned cash?'

'He didn't believe me. He was like, how can you not have fifteen-hundred-quid when you run your own business, when your mum's paintings sell for thousands?' Mum's artwork again. 'Honestly, by this time I just wanted him to go. I told him it wasn't working out and we should call it a day. He could transfer the 2k I lent him into my bank account whenever he could. And that's when he went mental.' That's exactly how he reacted when I refused to re-join the gym. 'He started pacing up and down the kitchen, scratching his arms and neck, called me a mean bitch, said I was still in love with my ex, accused me of using him, called me horrible names.' Zelda pauses, looks at me.

'Go on, sweetheart,' I say.

'I tried to calm him down, explained that my decision had nothing to do with Chris – we were moving too fast, too soon. He wouldn't believe me, called me a slag, refused to give me my money back, suggested I flog all the designer gear he bought me instead. Then he sat down and started scratching his legs, saying he didn't feel right, that I'd poisoned him with my lemon cake.' Zelda's eyes dart from me to Linda, face incredulous. 'I was like, hello, you did just snort a bag of shit you bought from some corner street dealer. Maybe that's why you're feeling ill. Then he seemed to snap out of it, started pleading with me for another chance, said he'd fallen in love with me, that he'd sooner kill me and go to prison than lose me. I went to pick up my phone to call you, Bella, when he grabbed me by my ponytail and pinned me against the wall, holding me by the jaw. I couldn't speak and then he goes, "No one dumps me. I'll leave when I'm good and ready." And then…'

'It's okay, honey,' I say, 'take a few breaths.'

'Take your time, sweetie,' Linda adds, curling a hand around Zelda's forearm.

Zelda inhales deeply, then lets out a trembly breath through her mouth. 'He squeezed my jawbone. I thought it was going to crack. I couldn't move my head, and then he began to unbuckle his belt with his free hand.'

I close my eyes. He was going to rape her.

Chapter 26

'Jesus,' Linda mutters, looking away.

'What on earth was he going to do to you?' I gulp. My poor little sister must've been terrified.

'Maybe strangle her and make it look like a sex game gone wrong,' Linda says softly. 'I read a novel once where that was the twist.' Linda looks at me. 'Really good, if you want to borrow it.'

Zelda clears her throat. Linda apologises deeply, says she sometimes gets mental absence when she's under pressure. 'He wasn't going to *rape* me,' Zelda clarifies. 'He was complaining about cramps in his stomach, said he had acid reflux from the rich food and undid the button of his trousers. But then his phone started ringing in his pocket, thank goodness, and he let go of my throat. I wanted to scream, but my throat was so sore. Who would hear me anyway? All the neighbours are away. He kept me clamped against the wall with his body while he rejected the call. I tried to calm him down. I mean, obviously, he wasn't right in the head. I promised to stay with him if he changed, marry him. I even offered to give him the fifteen hundred quid he wanted; said I'd ask you for it.' Zelda nods at me. 'But he just laughed. Then he said something odd.'

'Oh?' Linda says, inching closer.

'He called me a lying bitch and said he won't be bribed by the stinking Villins again. I think he meant you, Bella, because he can't have meant Georgie.' I look at her, then at Linda, but say nothing.

'He put more pressure on my throat with his fingers. The room began to sway and dim. I could hear him panting. I opened my eyes as wide as I could and focused on a rash that had appeared on his neck while trying to prise his hands off. But it was no use. Even in his intoxicated state, he was too strong. I knew I was going to die.' Zelda gives the bowl of ripe fruit on the table the thousand-mile stare. 'My life literally flashed before me,' she whispers. 'I had to do something. I rooted around on the worktop – felt a steel implement, and then my hand came down and I stabbed him.'

Linda gasps, as if she's watching a thriller on Prime. 'Did you stab him in the jugular?'

'I don't know,' Zelda whimpers, 'It all happened so fast. I just wanted to get him off me. I thought I only scratched the inside of his shoulder. There was blood. On my hands. On the letter opener. On him.' Zelda sobs quietly for a few moments and then she turns to me, inhaling teary phlegm. 'What do you think he meant by he won't be bribed?'

Linda gives me a long, hard stare and then nods. 'Go on,' she says, wearily. 'Tell her.'

I open my mouth. It's dry. I take a sip from Linda's glass and then begin; the words toppling from my lips, tripping over each other. 'I met Frank at the gym on my first day. He coaxed me into hiring him; he was nice, friendly. We used to chat – a lot. I trusted him. I'm not even sure why…' Linda and Zelda listen in silence, like jurors, as I relay my story from start to finish, including his threat to ruin me if I tried to split him and Zelda up. 'I warned him off you, Zee, but he wouldn't listen. So, I bribed him. Offered him ten grand to get out of our lives.'

'He knew I was your sister?' Zelda gulps, ignoring everything else I just said. 'Tried it on with you?'

'Yes, in the studio gym.'

'Came after me because you rejected him?'

'Zelda, I'm so very sorry.'

'Are you saying he targeted me to spite you?' I shake my head, apologise repeatedly. 'And then he fleeced me. Do you think it was because I told him Mum was a famous artist?'

'I think so, love. It would explain his motive.'

'But Mum doesn't sell her paintings anymore? She lives off her pension.'

'He doesn't know that, does he?' Linda offers.

'Oh, my God, he used me,' Zelda gasps.

'I'm sorry,' I say again, like a broken record. 'You don't know how many times I tried to tell you but…'

'You knew what he was like, what he was capable of, and you kept quiet.'

'*No*. I was about to…'

'You let me go out with a psychopath?' Zelda scratches her arms as if she's riddled with germs. 'Have sex with him?'

'It wasn't like that. I was going to tell you right away but...' I throw a glance at Linda and she shakes her head encouragingly. 'It's complicated.'

'Really? Well, I've just killed my fiancé, so I've got all fucking night.'

'Zelda, please let me speak,' I manage.

'He could've killed me tonight,' Zelda cries, pointing towards the garden. 'That could've been me out there. And now I've got a dead man on my lawn and blood on my hands because of *YOU*.' She jabs her finger at me bitterly.

'It wasn't like that,' I cry. 'I wanted to tell you from the first day but it wasn't something I could just blurt out in front of everyone, was it? And then you went on that romantic break.' Zelda is looking at me through narrowed eyes. 'I swear on Georgia's life, I was about to tell you earlier today, but then Frank made that outrageous announcement and proposed.' I pause. Linda complains of feeling cold, and without saying a word, Zelda gets up, jabs at the thermostat next to the stainless-steel sink and sits back down.

'Oh look, you're right,' I admit, head in hands. 'I should've told you the very first day at Linda's. I knew he had a big ego and a temper but I didn't think he was capable of anything like this.' I pause and then. 'Look, it might've been a combination of the drugs and drink that made him go crazy,' I offer, as Zelda sits back down. 'I honestly, hand on heart, had never seen him behave as you're describing.' Zelda's head snaps up at me, and then everything freezes. It feels as if the atmosphere in the room has dropped to minus five.

'As I'm *describing*?' Zelda's voice is faint. 'You don't believe me, do you? You think I murdered him.' I shake my head no. 'Poisoned him with the lemon cake.' More head shaking. 'And now I want you two to help me dispose of his body.' Jesus, where is this coming from? She gets to her feet. Linda tugs at Zelda's sleeve, tells her to sit back down – that wasn't what I meant – we all need to calm down. Zelda ignores her, immobilising me with her scowl. 'You think I killed him in cold blood.' Pressing her palms on the table, she leans forward, face close to mine. 'Just like you thought I did to Jake all those years ago.' Her fist hits the table. 'Don't you!!?'

Chapter 27

Zelda had been dating Jake for a year when it happened. Mum warned her on the first day she brought him home for tea, said she'd get hurt by the likes of him. They were from different worlds. Jake's parents were rich, successful professionals, with two beautiful homes, one in Hampstead and the other on the south coast. Mr and Mrs Arquette would drive down to their getaway home most weekends to escape the madness of London, leaving their only son to party to his heart's content. Their north London house was notorious for pool parties and magnums of champagne.

One summer night, Jake and Zelda decided to surprise his parents in Whitstable. It was unbelievably hot. We couldn't sleep and temperatures were soaring. We all longed for the sea and clean air. Jake couldn't drive. But Zelda had just passed her test. Mrs Arquette's Ferrari was parked on the carriage driveway, gleaming in all its redness. The keys were a stone's throw away, hanging on a hook in the hallway. Jake persuaded Zelda to get behind the wheel – promised her she was insured - the policy was for any driver. Dizzy on love, adventure and innocence, Zelda agreed.

They jumped into the sports car and hit the road with the wind in their hair. Zelda said Jake was high as a kite, swigging neat vodka straight from the bottle. When they got off the motorway, he opened the passenger window and sat on the ledge, woohooing, screaming that he was the king of the world. Zelda said she felt nervous, pleaded with him to get back inside but he wouldn't listen. She didn't see the bend, nor the oncoming lorry. She slammed on the brakes, the car fishtailed and she lost control of the wheel.

Jake died instantly. There was an inquest. Neighbours said before the accident, they heard loud voices and screaming from the house in Hampstead. The police interviewed Zelda. 'We were just mucking around in the pool,' she said in her statement. 'Our voices accelerated.' The gossip and rumours didn't help. Paul, one of Jake's friends, said Jake was seeing another girl behind Zelda's back, and that he was going to end it with Zelda that weekend. None of it was substantiated, or true. Jake was in love with Zelda. Everyone knew that. He even gave her a ring.

But the seed was planted, so I questioned Zelda, as any big sister would – had they argued in the car – did he chuck her – was she upset – driving too fast – did she lose control of the wheel? I told her to tell me the truth, that I'd have her back. Zelda looked at me silently and then she got up and left the room. She didn't speak to me for two weeks.

It was the worst time of our lives. We got eggs thrown at Mum's car. *Murderers* graffitied on our front door. Mum couldn't take any more abuse. Her paintings were selling like hotcakes and her accountant suggested she invest it in property, so we moved. Zelda got done for driving without insurance and permission from the driver. But after discovering that the brake pads and rotors on Mrs Arquette's car were worn out, the coroner ruled that the fatality was an accident. And as there was no evidence of foul play, the police let Zelda go. Jake's parents never forgave Zelda for the death of their son.

'Of course, I believe you,' I say now. 'It just came out wrong. I'm sorry. Zelda, come on. What are you doing?'

'You knew Frank was a nutjob.' Zelda buzzes around the kitchen, opening and closing worse-for-wear cabinet doors, one of which has been hanging off its hinges for ages. 'But why bother warning your sister, who was sharing a bed with him, when you had more pressing things to do.' She pours two inches of gin into a glass and downs it like water. 'Like getting that new skivvy of yours to cook you all a three-course meal on your top-of-the-range Aga, for your perfect family, in your flashy new home?'

Shock courses through me. Where is this coming from? 'My life isn't a bed of roses,' I say, wearily. 'We're up to our necks in debt.'

'Oh, come off it,' Zelda snaps, 'you want for nothing.'

'Girls, come on,' Linda pleads, eyes darting from me to Zelda worriedly.

'We work bloody hard,' I contend, shooting to my feet. Linda holds her head in her hands. Zelda takes a swig of gin straight from the bottle, eyes not leaving me. I can't believe we're arguing. That Frank is still managing to do this to us. I sit back down. Rubbing my temple, I stare at my sister – she looks broken. Zelda hasn't had it easy. I know that Jake's death, all those years ago, still haunts her, and she's always struggled financially. 'Look, I know things have been difficult for you but now you're self-employed…'

'Business is going down the pan,' she interjects.

'But I thought you had a waiting list?'

'I let a few clients down at the last minute.' Zelda squeezes her top lip between her fingers. 'It was when I went on that stupid holiday to Monaco with Frank. Most of my clients were mums from the local school. Word gets around. They're all using Lena now,' she groans, as if we know who Lena is. 'A girl from Kosovo. Her daughter goes to Mortimer. She's just started up – undercutting me on prices too. I heard she's very good.'

'The quality won't be good if she's using cheap supplies,' Linda suggests, and Zelda shrugs. 'They'll soon come knocking on your door again, hon.'

'Linda's right.' I curl a hand around Zelda's forearm and give it a gentle squeeze. 'Things will pick up again, I'm sure. I've had slumps in the past.'

Zelda gives me a dark look. 'You're forgetting one thing – you've got a husband to support you.'

'Okay, I have.' I sigh, drawing my hand back. 'But I've got problems too, you know.' A big fat one called Liam. 'Come on, love, where's the strong Zelda I know? The woman who refuses to be defined by a man?'

Zelda throws her hands up in the air. 'You should've told me about Frank from day one. Stopped me,' she says, her anger returning. 'Why did you meet up with Liam, anyway? You've got a good guy. You've got it all. Why fuck it up for a bunk up with your ex?' I go to speak, explain that it wasn't like that, but she talks over me, face twisted in fury. 'God, I'm surprised Tom has stuck around. I'd have left you years ago.' Her words slice through my heart like shards.

'Oh, so Tom's a fucking archangel now, is he? A good catch? You've certainly changed your tune,' I snap, reminding her that *she* was his first choice all those years ago, and she turned him down, said he was too nerdy.

'You know what I mean. The way you've...'

'Enough, Zelda,' Linda intervenes. 'I know you're upset, but there's no need to be so harsh. Bella wanted to tell you about Frank the moment you arrived yesterday, but I put her off.'

Zelda looks incredulous, eyes wild. 'So, it's your fault.'

'Zelda,' I exclaim. 'This isn't anyone's fault. It…'

'What were you doing?' Zelda says to Linda, talking over me. 'Protecting your ex-lover?'

The room goes silent and I'm suddenly aware of the fridge freezer whirring. Frank told her about his one-night stand with Linda.

Chapter 28

Linda's eyes rocket towards me. 'Don't look at me,' I say.

And then they start to squabble about Frank, their voices growing louder and louder in my ears – Linda denies it profusely but Zelda won't have it, says Linda ogling him at her dinner party didn't go unnoticed. Linda leaps to her feet and starts yelling, pointing her finger at Zelda, words flying from her full lips like bullets - she's not that desperate - has a real man on tap at home - she's risking her life and her marriage to help her tonight – what an ungrateful cow.

'Enough.' I shoot to my feet and spread my arms out like an eagle. 'Taking lumps out of each other isn't going to help. What's done is done. Let's all just calm down and figure out what we're going to do about...' I flick my head towards the garden, '*Him*. The room falls silent again. A fox screams. Someone's foot taps under the table. 'Zelda, where did you put the weapon?'

'I washed it and put it back on the microwave.'

'What a stupid thing to do,' cries Linda, still reeling from Zelda's accusations.

'I had to get his blood off my hands.'

A loud thump startles me. 'What was that?' I ask.

'It sounded like pounding,' Linda replies.

Zelda shrugs. 'Probably the central heating. It's ancient. Startles me sometimes.'

'So, anyway…' I continue. And then there's another thud, like a box being kicked. 'There it is again?'

'Must be a fox,' Zelda says, irritably, combing her hands through her hair. 'Knocking something into that gaping hole next door. They're always doing it. Their builders chuck their empty pizza boxes on the floor. It's a haven for vermin.'

'I saw that,' Linda pipes up, 'what on earth are they doing?'

'A basement,' Zelda whines, running a hand over her face, 'and kitchen extension. It's been going on for eighteen months. They've made our lives a misery. Lillian, next door, spoke to them several times but they won't listen. She works from home, too.'

'Eighteen months? That's taking the pee,' Linda protests. 'We had that down our road during the first lockdown. Theo called the council and they issued them with a noise abatement order. They get fined up to five grand if they break it. That soon made them considerate neighbours. Why isn't it boarded up anyway? What if a child ran down there, or a dog? It looks dangerous.'

'There was a panel with a door and lock, but it collapsed in the wind and they didn't bother replacing it.'

'Surely, that's a health and safety issue,' I intervene.

'Who fucking cares?' Zelda cries. 'I've got more pressing things on my mind right now. Like a corpse in my garden.'

'Sorry, you're right,' I say, and then there's another loud crash, like a building collapsing. 'That's definitely no fox.'

We leap to our feet and race to the back door, knocking into each other in our haste. I rattle the handle but it won't open.

'I locked it behind us,' Linda says, 'and put the key on the side. I think. Where's it gone?'

'Oh, fucking hell, Linda,' I yell.

'The French doors in the lounge,' Zelda enthuses.

Zelda bolts out of the kitchen and we barrel after her. Once she finally finds the keys, she unlocks the patio doors, hands visibly trembling. We fly into the garden, panting, chests heaving, and then we all stop still and stare at each other, horrified. Frank has gone.

Chapter 29

'For fuck's sake,' Linda cries. 'Where is he?'

Zelda falls to her knees, palms pressed together. 'I didn't kill him. Oh, thank God.'

'Shit,' Linda continues, elbowing past me and peering over the back gate, 'do you think he wandered off into next door's building site?'

'God knows,' I reply, heart whacking against my ribcage like a squash ball. I'm glad he's alive, although he doesn't deserve to be. But at least my sister hasn't got blood on her hands. That said, I haven't got a clue what to do now. Frank isn't going to just let this go.

'Why would he wander into the building site?' Zelda asks, scrambling to her feet. 'There's nothing in there and he knows the owners are away.'

I pull my dressing gown around me tightly, blocking out the chill. 'I'd imagine he's gone to A&E to get that stab wound looked at. That's what I'd have done.' Via the police station to report Zelda for assault, but I don't tell her that. The last thing I want is to freak her out again. 'But we'd best check all the same,' I suggest. I look at the back gate, which is swung open.

He must've left it open in his haste to get away. 'Let's go out the front and have a look. He can't have gone far, not with an injury like that.'

We hound the streets, each of us in different directions, eyes like scanners, but Frank is nowhere to be seen. He seems to have disappeared into thin air. 'Let's have a look down the driveway, see if he left a trail, spots of blood, something we can follow,' Linda suggests, and Zelda yelps, like a frightened dog, clutching the sleeve of my dressing gown. 'Come on, there's no time to waste.'

We walk along the downward slope of the shared driveway, negotiating our way around three concrete gully surrounds, bags of sand and several stacks of chipping stones. The moment we reach the excavation, I hear the sound of running water. I gather my dressing gown around me. It's darker and creepier than I remember back here. Maybe it's because there's no friendly light on next door and the upstairs is vacated, pitch black.

'God, Zelda, how can you live here on your own?' Linda says. 'I'd shit myself.'

'It's all I can afford.'

'What's that noise?' Linda whispers. 'It sounds like a stream.'

'Next door's drains. They've got a leak,' Zelda explains. We inch closer. The cavity is deep and dark. I pull out my phone and shine the torch in the excavation.

'Can you see anything?' We all peer into the pit. Linda and Zelda shake their heads. Zelda was right, it's full of rubbish, rubble and stacks of builders' shipping pallets. My eyes race over the litter. A white carrier bag, flapping in the wind, desperately trying to free itself from the neck of a large bottle of cola catches my attention, next to it lie several empty pizza boxes and yellow polystyrene food containers, with smears of red sauce and bits of food stuck to them. I can see now why Zelda says it's a haven for vermin. No sign of Frank. 'Let's go further in,' I suggest, 'along the side slope and look inside the pit properly. Does that lead into the garden?'

'There's no way I'm fucking going down there,' Linda shrieks, taking a step back.

'Zee?' My sister is transfixed on the excavation as if she's under some kind of spell.

'Sorry, yes, it does,' Zelda says, tuning back in. 'But he wouldn't have gone down there, Bella. There's no exit at the bottom of the slope. It's closed off and dangerous. You can't go down there without a hard hat. Ian popped in and explained it all to me last week and Frank was here, so he knows it's a no-go zone.'

'We've got to do something, girls, and fast,' Linda insists, pulling out a box of Marlborough Lights from her crossbody bag and lighting up. 'We should've called the police right away. Are they Frank's?' She blows smoke from the side of her mouth, closing one eye.

We follow Linda's gaze. There's a pair of army green wellingtons at the side of the garage. 'No, they're my gardening boots. I was meant to put them in the garage this morning, but forgot.'

'Right.' Linda blows the smoke high and I look at it longingly. 'Here,' she says begrudgingly, handing me the fag, 'it'll take the edge off.'

'Look, we know Frank's injured,' I point out, flicking ash off her cigarette. 'So, he can't have gone far.' I take a deep inhalation, relishing every second.

'But I didn't kill him,' Zelda says.

'Did you drive here or get a cab?' Linda asks me, ignoring Zelda.

I shake my head, blowing out smoke. 'Daisy dropped me off, but I told her to go home if I wasn't out in ten.' I give Linda her ciggie back and check the time on my phone. 'That was over an hour ago.'

'Why don't we just leave it,' Zelda pleads, shuffling from foot to foot. 'He's gone now, so must be okay.'

Linda takes a final lug and then stamps the cigarette out with the sole of her shoe. How she walked half a mile to Zelda's in the middle of the night in those heels is a skill in its own right.

'Listen, I know it was self-defence, lovely, but you stabbed him, remember,' Linda warns gently. 'It's still a criminal offence. And the fact that you didn't call the emergency services is going to make you look guilty if he decides to press charges. Depending on his story, you might get done for attempted murder.' Zelda's face pales and I can see that the idea of Frank lying to the police, blaming her, didn't cross her mind.

'We've got to find him and make sure he doesn't report it,' I say, 'Bribe him again, offer him more. I can get a hold of ten grand, more if I have to. Sell a couple of Mum's paintings, that should fetch another ten, twenty grand.'

'You can't sell our heirlooms,' Zelda groans. 'They're Georgie's. Might be worth a fortune one day. Besides, why should we pay him off? He was the one who tried to kill me.'

'You're absolutely right, Zee,' Linda says. 'Look, we can still call the police and tell them everything. It's not too late.'

'Of course, it's too late, Linda, it's been over two hours since the assault. They're going to want to know why Zelda didn't report it immediately. It's going to make her look like the guilty party now.'

'Hmm…he is the one with the stab wound and Zelda has got previous with the police.'

'They're going to arrest me, aren't they?' Zelda quivers, her panic returning. 'I'm going to prison. This is the end of my life. Frank has ruined me.'

Chapter 30

'It's going to be all right, sweetheart,' I insist as Zelda continues to sob quietly. 'We'll think of something.' We will think of nothing and all end up behind bars and need therapy to get over the trauma for the rest of our lives. 'Try not to worry.'

Linda shakes her head, pulls out another cigarette, then, clearly thinking better of it, pushes it back in. 'If Frank goes to the police, they'll do forensics on this place, find specks of his blood in here, in the garden, not to mention cocaine. We're all accessories to a crime now.'

I rake a hand through my hair, damp with sweat. 'We need a solid plan.'

'He'll have us all behind bars,' Zelda sobs. 'I'm so sorry for dragging you both into this. I was so frightened. I didn't know what to do.'

Linda's face softens. 'Look, I can't stand the son-of-a-gun. Anyone would've done the same to protect themselves in your shoes. It was self-defence. It's not as if it was premeditated. Any judge and jury will take that onboard once you're in the witness box. They're not stupid.' A pause and then, 'Shit, what if he collapses in the middle of the street and bleeds to death?

The sooner we find him, the sooner we can get him some medical help. Otherwise, we'll all be up on a murder charge.'

My stomach twists. I didn't think of that. Linda's right. 'Zelda, can you drive? We can cover more space if we try looking for him in a car.' Zelda shakes her head, tells us she'd been drinking too, and isn't in a fit state to drive anyway. 'Okay, I'll ring Daisy, see if she can come back and help us find him.'

Zelda squats by her garage door and covers her ears, rocking back and forth and chanting *What've I done?*

Daisy's phone rings out. She must be asleep. I hate to do this to her but I've got to wake her up and get her back here. I hang up the moment I hear her chirpy voicemail greeting and press redial. It rings and rings and rings and then, 'Hi Bella, everything okay?' she says, voice raspy.

'Sorry to wake you, Daisy,' I apologise. 'But is there any chance you could come back to Zelda's? We've got a bit of an issue and need your help.'

'It's fine.' Daisy yawns loudly into the mouthpiece. 'I'm still outside.' Another yawn. This woman is an angel sent from heaven. I close my eyes briefly, then give Linda the thumbs up. 'What's up? Is Zelda okay?'

'Did you see Frank wandering around outside at all?' I demand. Daisy tells me she didn't, had her head over her phone most of the time, then had forty winks. 'Okay, I'm going to come out in a moment and I need you to drive me around a few blocks. Will that be okay?' Silence. 'Daisy?'

'Um…can I ask why?' I can't tell her the truth. I don't want her involved beyond necessary.

'Well, you know Zelda and Frank had a fight.' I pause, waiting for a reaction, but am met with silence. 'Linda and I tried talking some sense into him but he wouldn't listen,' I lie. 'There was an..um…' My eyes dart from Linda to Zelda who are both looking at me in wide-eyed anticipation. Linda is biting on a red-varnished thumbnail. 'There was a bit of an accident. He did some cocaine and fell over on the concrete patio in the garden.' Daisy gasps. She's very anti-substance abuse. 'I think he's hurt himself. There was a bit of blood.' I squeeze my eyes shut, press the phone against my shoulder and take a breath. 'He stormed out a few minutes ago, but we need to find him …in case…' In case what? In case he goes to the police and tells them that my sister tried to kill him? 'In case he's hurt.'

'Oh. Right,' Daisy says. 'Is he on foot? Only if he's driving, he might've taken himself to A&E.'

I didn't see his white VW Golf parked outside when we arrived, but that's not to say he didn't park it further along the road. Is he in a fit state to drive? I doubt it, given the state of him. But if he managed to get behind the wheel, he could be at the police station at this very moment reporting the incident. And just then, right on cue, a siren wails and we all look at each other like deer in headlights.

'It's the police,' Zelda whimpers, eyes full of terror. 'They're going to arrest me. Lock me up. It'll be his word against mine. They won't believe my version of events. Frank is too sharp, too clever. Oh, Bella, I didn't mean all those horrible things I said to you. You're a brilliant person. The best sister anyone could ask for.' She draws her sleeve along her nose, wiping away teary mucus. 'Tom's lucky to have you.'

I go over to her and pull her to me with one arm. 'I promise you, on my last breath, you won't go down for this.' And then, remembering Daisy's on the line, I let go of Zelda and quickly mute the call, praying she didn't hear any of that. 'I will fight tooth and nail to prove your innocence and get you acquitted. 'The sirens scream in my ears. They're getting closer.

'Oh, fucking hell,' Linda says, frantically. 'Tell them it was self-defence, Zee, he was going to bloody kill you. You were fighting for your life, grabbed the letter knife to defend yourself, get him off you.' Linda pauses, takes a breath, eyes shining with adrenalin. 'And then he went outside and collapsed on the lawn ... Zelda, are you listening? Stop it, stop.' Linda wrenches Zelda's hands away from her ears. 'You tried to wake him, couldn't. Felt a pulse. Didn't know what to do. Panicked. Phoned Bella. We came as fast as we could. We were about to call for an ambulance, heard a noise, realised he'd got up and scarpered. Okay?' Zelda doesn't answer. 'Okay?' Linda yells.

'Okay.' Zelda is sobbing uncontrollably now, and I just watch her, uselessly, aching with grief. The wailing sirens are longer now and harder. They're moments away.

'Listen to Linda,' I insist, my confidence waning by the second, 'she's got an A-level in Law.'

'They'll go easy on you once they hear all the facts,' Linda promises. 'It'll be your first offence. Well, proper offence.' A roar in the sky snatches our attention. Overhead, a helicopter hovers like a huge insect, pinning us down with its red and indigo flashing lights. 'Jesus Christ,' Linda yells as the helicopter's blades belt out above us like machine guns. 'You're not a serial killer. What on earth has he told them?'

Blue and yellow lights illuminate the road ahead. They're here. They are after my sister's blood. Linda takes a few tentative steps forward and peers at the police car parked diagonally outside Zelda's flat. Zelda screams, sirens yelp on a loop. I cover my hands over my head. I can't let them lock her up. I've got to do something.

'Shit, they're getting out of the car,' Linda hisses. '*Shit.*'

Chapter 31

The siren continues to scream in my ears, and then it suddenly stops. This is it. They're coming in to arrest Zelda. I can almost hear the rustle of their uniforms, the cackle of their walkie talkies as they make their way along the uneven garden path.

'I am *so* sorry, Linda,' Zelda cries, eyes wild. 'I'll tell them you had absolutely no knowledge of this. I promise. I'll say…'

Linda takes a hold of Zelda by the shoulders firmly and starts giving her another pep talk while I look on, legs like lead. 'Look, there's every chance that you'll…' Linda's voice fades into white noise. In my peripheral, I see the police car moving.

'Shhh…' I hold a hand up to silence them. 'Listen.' There's a low rumble of a helicopter and then the sudden flare of a siren again, distant this time. 'Look,' I cry, pointing at the road ahead. 'No flashing lights. They must've been passing through,' I enthuse. 'Used this road as a shortcut.'

We all exhale sharply, as if we've been holding our breath under water in some kind of sardonic fitness contest. Linda presses a hand against the garage door and holds her chest. Zelda squats on the step of the back gate, face in hands, shoulders shaking. I look up at the ink sky, silently thanking the universe.

'I thought I was going to have a heart attack,' Linda gasps.

Daisy's muffled voice filters from my handset, which I'm holding against my shoulder. I forgot she was there. I unmute her.

'Sorry, Daisy, couldn't hear you,' I lie, heart belting. 'Can you repeat that, please?'

'Christ above. I'm not surprised,' Daisy says. 'Those sirens were deafening. Three cop cars just rocked up. They couldn't get past the narrow street. Someone had double parked. A taxi, I think, on an airport run. Two people came out of a house a few doors away with suitcases.' So that's why they stopped outside Zelda's. I was wondering why they needed a helicopter and several police cars to arrest an unarmed woman on suspicion of assault. 'Look, I'm just getting out of the car. Can you hear me now?'

'Yes, you're much clearer now, Daisy.'

'Great. So, did Frank drive here, then?'

'Um…not sure. Hold on. Zelda, was Frank's car outside?'

Zelda shakes her head, wiping her teary face with her hands. 'I picked him up,' she says, voice nasal from crying. 'He was going to stay the weekend and didn't want to lose the space outside his flat.'

'He's on foot, Daisy.' I cover the mouthpiece and tell the girls to get inside. 'I'll be out in a…'

'Have you tried calling him?' Daisy interjects as I follow Linda into the flat, Zelda close behind me, and I get the feeling Daisy's not up for this. And who could blame her? She didn't sign up to be my dodgy midnight chauffeur. She's only my temp. A surge of guilt skims through me. I should tell her to forget it, to go home and get some rest. But I can't. The need to help my sister is bullying its way through every ounce of reasoning I have.

'That's a good idea, Daisy. We'll try that first. I'll ring you back, save you waiting.' Daisy agrees, and I end the call, tell Zelda to ring Frank, something we should've done straightaway. Frank's phone goes straight to voicemail and I tell her to hang up.

'Okay, this is what we're going to do.' I pause, lick my dry lips. 'If Frank reports it, we'll tell them what really happened. Well, a diluted version. Frank attacked you in a jealous rage. He was going to kill you and you had to find a way to fight back.' I slide my thumb over the corner of Zelda's red silicone phone case in my hand, gazing at my haggard face in the mirror while an insane plan starts taking shape in my mind. 'You grabbed your mobile phone.' I hold it up as an exhibit. 'And lamped him on the face with it.' Zelda swallows, shakes her head. Linda looks shellshocked. 'The impact of the blow shook him up, he let go, and then he fled.' I turn to Linda. 'Why don't you go home love, we can say that I came here alone. I don't want you involved in this.'

'Yes,' Zelda agrees. 'You've done enough for me already.'

'No way.' Linda shakes her head. 'I'm staying put.'

'No, Linda, *please*,' I insist. 'I know you want to help but this is too risky, too dangerous.'

'It's not up for discussion, Bella.'

My eyes fill with gratitude. Zelda mouths *thank you* at her. I turn back to Zelda, sniffing back a tear. 'Right, the moment he left, you called me, distraught, frightened he'd come back.' I look at Linda. 'I called you, asked you to meet me at Zelda's. I wanted as much backup as possible. Frank's a strong man, remember.' Linda nods. 'He was never on the lawn unconscious. Okay? Never.'

'What about his wound?' Zelda cries.

'You've no idea how that happened.'

Zelda shifts from foot to foot, as if she's marching on the spot. 'But I'm not very good at lying. What if I mess up and they catch me out?'

'She's right,' Linda pipes up. 'It'll be false evidence. Will Zelda withstand a police grilling?'

'You won't mess up.' I curl a stand of hair behind my sister's ear tenderly. 'We'll back you all the way.

'Okay,' Zelda nods furiously, sniffs. 'Thank you. You two are the best.'

Linda sighs, tone hesitant. 'Frank's injury is going to be a problem. Will they really believe she had no knowledge of it? The police aren't stupid.'

'Frank was off of his head on cocaine and alcohol, got into a fight once he left. He's obviously a user, mixes with the wrong crowd of people. It'll be his word against Zelda's.'

'They'll still do forensics on this place,' Linda warns. 'A sniffer dog will pick up Frank's scent on the lawn, even a droplet of blood on a blade of grass is enough.'

'So what? He was her boyfriend. Accidents happen all the time – he cut his hand gardening or barbequing.'

'What about the letter opener? The dagger might still have traces of his blood on it. It gets into all the nooks and crannies. I remember a case study I read about once where they found dried blood on the knife that was used to murder someone, even after it'd been washed. That's how they caught the assailant.' Linda rubs her lips. 'It's too risky. She's tampered with evidence. No doubt, Frank will deny attacking her. He'll probably try to frame her; say she lost her mind and stabbed him in a jealous rage after finding out he'd tried it on with *you*.'

'Oh, God, Bella.' Zelda starts breathing heavily. I think she's hyperventilating. 'Linda's right.'

'We'll get rid of the letter knife,' I blurt, without thinking. 'They can't do her for attempted murder if there's no weapon. Where is it, Zelda?'

'I put it back on the microwave.' I tell her to go and fetch it and she dashes off to the kitchen, while Linda goes off on one – what do I think I'm doing, we're in too deep, what if Frank dies and the police want to search our houses too, do I want them all to rot in prison?

'Here.' Zelda holds the weapon out to me with both hands, while Linda continues to whine in the background.

'Linda's got a point, Bella. Helping me is one thing but lying to the police...'

'We can't just dump it,' Linda points out. 'What if someone finds it?'

'They won't. I'll make sure it disappears.'

'So, you're a magician now, are you?' I don't answer.

'What about the lawn?' Zelda cries. 'What if there was a lot of blood? What if they check it? Maybe I should just take my chances – tell them the truth.'

'Google how to get rid of blood on grass, Linda.'

Muttering to herself, Linda starts jabbing at the screen of her phone. 'Dilute bleach with water and pour over the area, or burn it.'

'We'll mop the floor tonight, clean the entire kitchen, including all appliances. We'll dig up the lawn and burn it, then returf it in the morning. I've got turf in my garage. We were going to replace a dry patch that went brown and crispy.'

'Burn and returf the lawn in front of the entire neighbourhood in broad daylight?' Linda says, astonished. 'Have you completely lost the plot?' Actually, right now, I think I might've.

'Just bleach it then,' I reply briskly. 'I'll get rid of this.' I pat my pocket, feeling the long blade of the letter knife. 'Okay?'

'But, Bella,' Linda cries. 'It's illegal.'

'Okay?' I yell, ignoring Linda.

'What's going on?' We all turn towards the voice, like deer in headlights. 'Get rid of what?'

Chapter 32

Daisy is standing in the doorway in my dressing gown, looking drained. On her feet are my black and white animal print faux fur cross slippers. In my haste to get here earlier, I didn't notice her wearing them. I don't remember lending them to her. I usually keep them in the bathroom. But now is not the time to question Daisy about a pair of slippers, not when I've got more pressing things on my mind, like how long was she standing there and how much did she hear?

'Get rid of what?' Daisy repeats. A strand of red hair escapes from her messy bun and hangs loosely on the side of her face. I watch as she steps into the hallway, almost as if a slow-motion dial has been pushed. Stripped of make-up, Daisy's skin is pale but she's still stunning. I tear my eyes away from her seductive beauty as Linda's voice bellows in my ears – *Does she look at Tom with those do you want to fuck me eyes?*

'Yes, um…' I begin, pushing Linda's voice out of my head, 'we need to get rid of…'

'We need to get rid of an old bicycle of mine that Zelda has been storing in the garage for me,' Linda interrupts, saving the day. 'Zelda's landlord wants it gone.'

Daisy doesn't look convinced. 'But I heard you say it's illegal.' She touches the ruby that's set in her gold crucifix, pasted against her smooth, glowing skin. 'Is it stolen?'

Linda chews the inside of her lip, throwing me a worried glance. 'Stolen? Don't be silly.' Linda snorts, eyes sliding back to Daisy. 'Bella suggested dumping it, but we can't. Fly-tipping carries a hefty fine and…'

'Oh, my God.' Our heads swivel towards Zelda, who is rifling through her handbag. 'My debit card is missing. Frank must've taken it.' Is this true, or is she playing Daisy? I study my sister's face, but it's unreadable. 'Come on, we've got to find him,' she urges, shouldering her bag as we gape at her. 'He knows my PIN. We can worry about your bicycle later, Linda.'

'Jesus, what a shit,' Daisy says, annoyed. 'Come on. My car's outside.' Daisy gathers herself to leave with motions of urgency, and then she freezes, 'Oh, wait.' She touches Zelda's arm. 'You'll need to report the card missing. Ask your bank to suspend it, just in case.'

'That's a point.' Zelda's hand shoots to her forehead, eyes on me. Her card isn't missing. She's lying. But Daisy is sharp as a whip. We're going to have to be very careful around her. 'I should, shouldn't I?'

'Good thinking, Daisy,' I interject. 'Ring your bank now, Zelda.'

'But aren't we –'

'You two stay here,' I say to Linda and Zelda, 'in case Frank comes back. Lock yourselves in and call me if anything happens. I'll go and look for him with Daisy.'

'Maybe I should go with Daisy,' Linda offers, 'someone will have to confront him and you two look like you're on the game in those negligees. The last thing you want to do is get arrested for soliciting kerb crawlers.' Daisy and I exchange glances, a small smirk on her full, pink lips. Is she wearing lip-gloss? Surely not.

'Just stay here, please, Linda,' I say firmly, tying the belt of Tom's dressing gown around me tightly. 'I've got this.' I sniff the air. 'Is that bleach?' I ask, hoping they'll take the hint and clean the place up, get rid of any traces of blood. 'Or gas?'

Daisy takes a lungful of air, curling a loose strand of hair behind her ear as if it'll intensify her smelling senses. 'I can't smell anything.'

Linda, taking the bait, says, 'I can smell it too. A slight whiff.'

'Relax,' Zelda breathes. 'I bleached the kitchen floor earlier.' My sister's getting good at this. 'Phone me if there's any news, Bella.'

I tell her that I will as I usher a very whiny Daisy through the front door – she can smell something now – a hint of gas – they must call out an emergency plumber, google one now – the house might blow up. Over my shoulder, I tell the girls to make sure it's not a gas leak, just to keep Daisy happy.

Closing the door behind me, I make my way along the path, Daisy in my wake, and just then I swear I see a flash of Mrs Anderson in her green Mini Cooper, crawling outside Zelda's flat before accelerating into the darkness.

Chapter 33

I buckle in as Daisy turns on the ignition, Mrs Anderson buzzing in my mind. What on earth was she doing here at this time of the morning? Unless… 'Daisy,' I say, as she pulls away with a hurried jerk. 'Did you call your auntie at all tonight?'

'Aunt Tina?' Daisy yawns as she flips on the indicator at the end of the road, head swivelling from left to right. 'No. Why?'

Perhaps I was mistaken. It is late, I am traumatised, not to mention absolutely shattered. Mrs Anderson isn't the only sixty-something woman driving a green Mini Cooper. It's almost four in the morning. Still dark. People will be heading off to work, or the gym, or coming home from a late shift. It could've been anyone. 'It's nothing,' I reply in a yawny voice as we turn onto the High Road.' It's true what they say, yawning is contagious. 'Listen, Daisy, I'd appreciate your discretion on this. It's just that Tom can get a bit…'

'My lips are sealed,' Daisy says before I can finish.

'Thank you.'

Daisy nods, eyes on the road, clasping the steering wheel with locked arms, and then suddenly her eyes widen. 'There,' she exclaims. My head almost does a ninety-degree turn. 'By the cash machine. Behind us.' She darts a look at her rear view. 'It's him. Quick.' She's right. I'd recognise that beanie hat and V-shaped body anywhere.

We pull up hurriedly outside a pound saver shop as I fidget in my seat with urgency, as if I'm sitting on nettles, eager to leap out of the car and race after him before he gets away. I unbuckle my seatbelt just as Daisy pulls on the handbrake. 'Wait here,' I instruct. 'I won't be a moment.'

'Shall I ring the police?' Daisy asks, panting. 'He's obviously trying to steal money from Zelda's account.'

'No,' I yell. 'I mean, not yet. Just stay put. I'll be as quick as I can.'

I rip along the pavement, flip-flops flapping against my feet, pulling Tom's dressing gown around me. The knot I tied has loosened and I'm only wearing a flimsy nightdress underneath. Frank is standing in front of the hole in the wall, beanie hat pulled over his white hair. 'Frank,' I cry, 'Please, I just want to –'

And as Frank turns to face me, the words die on my lips. He takes in the length of my body, blue eyes wide and wild. My face burns as I self-consciously fold the dressing gown around me. It isn't him.

'I'm…I'm…sorry.' I begin. The man shifts forward, throwing me a lustful look. His ginger hair, which is sprouting from his black grubby beanie, is pasted to his leathered forehead. I inhale a fug of liquor, tobacco, and stale sweat. 'Wrong person,' I wheeze. I need my blue inhaler. Ginger man scratches his bristly cheek, eyes flitting to my breasts. No, no, it's not my breasts. He's eyeing my pockets; he can see the bulge of the letter-opener. He must think it's a purse. I've got to get away from him. Fast. Backing away, I turn on my heel and start running, the T-bar of my flip-flops digging between my toes, slowing me down. Behind me, I hear the sound of footsteps. I flick a glance over my shoulder. He's getting nearer.

'Oi, you,' he calls out, voice gruff.

I up my speed, eyes skimming around the dimly lit empty road lined with shops, desperately searching for Daisy's blue Peugeot. A car horn blasts in the distance and I jump. I can hear ginger-man's urgent footfall. How many women are murdered on their way home after a night out? Am I about to become another statistic? Panic steers my limbs around a parked car. *Damn it, Daisy, where the hell are you?* And just then a car horn hoots again, followed by a blinding beam of headlights flashing. It's Daisy. She's parked further along than I thought. Daisy is now out of the car, arms flaying in the air, beckoning me to hurry up.

'Daisy,' I scream. My dressing gown has now completely opened and is ballooning around my scantily clad body. I flick a glance over my shoulder and see a blur of the ginger-haired man, bent over, catching his breath.

'Hurry,' Daisy shouts, 'Get in.'

But as I reach the car, my knees give, legs wobbly. Daisy is now looking past me, horrified. Her hands fly to her mouth as a big hand clamps around my shoulder. Ginger-man pants. Daisy screams. I lose my footing. There's a crunch as my face hits the pavement. And then there's darkness.

Chapter 34

I can't open my mouth. I try to swallow but my throat feels like miniature razorblades are working their socks off in it. Every muscle in my body aches – limbs like lead. Am I paralysed? I wriggle my fingers and toes. They tingle. Not paralysed. My hand stings. Someone has nailed me down, impaled me to the floorboards, gagged me. Forcing my eyelids open again, I drink in a mist of white light. I'm not sure where I am but I'm not at home, of that I'm certain. The room is bright and stuffy. How did I get here? What happened to me?

Closing my eyes, I try to retrace my steps but my brain is exhausted. I'm about to drift off when Zelda and Linda's faces snap into my mind. I was with them but something happened to me, something bad. I was attacked. By a man. Was I mugged?

'Where...where am I?' I manage, forcing my eyelids open. There's a blurry face hovering over me now in a pink top. A man. I inhale his scent. I know him.

'Nurse.' The voice is full of alarm. 'Nurse!'

I open my eyes and the pixilation slowly dissolves. 'Tom?' I croak, 'How?'

'Don't get up,' Tom urges. 'You're in A&E, you had a fall.'

A fall? I wasn't attacked. Relief floods through my veins. 'In hospital? Why? I…'

I flop back onto the hard pillow and as I shut my eyes, the last few hours slam into my head – Frank's body on the lawn, Zelda crying, hysterical. She's killed him. Linda wants to call the police – then the lawn again, Frank no longer on it - flashes of light, blue and white and yellow – sirens shrieking – Daisy and I driving around Southgate looking for Frank – Daisy's voice – *there at the cash point* – was it Frank? No, I don't think it was. It was a ginger-haired man. He was chasing me – he was going to hurt me. Did he push me? Where's Daisy? Why is Tom here instead of her? Did Ginger-Haired-Man hurt her? What have I done to that innocent girl?

'Where's Daisy?' I mumble, throat dry. 'Is she okay?'

'Shh…Don't worry. Daisy's at home with Georgia,' Tom says. 'She called me right after they contacted the emergency services. I met her outside the hospital and put her in a cab home. There was no point in both of us staying. The poor girl looked shattered.'

I sigh with relief. She's safe. 'Why am I here? I'm fine. I want to go home.'

I go to whip back the covers, but Tom stops me. 'You had a fall and might be concussed.'

'Concussed?' I groan. 'No. There's nothing wrong with me. I shouldn't be here, wasting NHS's valuable resources.'

'Try not to upset yourself, Bella. Daisy told me everything.'

Bile rises in my chest. 'What did she say?' Before I left the house, I slipped a note on Tom's bedside table, telling him Daisy and I had gone to Zelda's because she'd had a fight with Frank and wanted my support. Has Daisy grassed us up? Did she tell Tom that we went on a manhunt looking for Frank in the middle of the night in our nightwear?

'I know about the cashpoint. So, don't even think about denying it,' he says firmly, and the room darkens. She did tell him everything. I can't be angry with her. Tom must've put the pressure on, had her against the ropes. He can be quite intimidating when he's upset. She was vulnerable, frightened.

'Tom, I can explain.'

'No need.'

'But…'

'Look, I know you were trying to help her. I get that, but…' Tom rubs a hand over his unshaven face. I can see that he's furious with me, but desperately trying to hold it together. 'You just don't know when to stop, Bella, do you?'

My eyes slide to the window ledge where there is a vase of artificial flowers. 'I didn't know what else to do,' I whisper. 'She needed me.'

'You can't save everyone.' Zelda isn't everyone. She's my sister. 'Look, giving Daisy a temporary home and job is one thing, but risking your life to help her was…'

'Daisy?' I interject.

'Well, yes. You were on your way home and she asked you for a cash sub to pay back a loan to her auntie.' I look at Tom aghast. Daisy didn't grass us up. She cleverly devised a believable scenario and fed it to Tom, who lapped it up. 'You stopped at a cash point in Southgate, remember,' he says, trying to jog my memory, 'but then this guy, who was behind you at the machine, started chasing you and you thought he was going to mug you.'

'Yes, that's right.' I nod, confirming Daisy's lies and hating myself for putting her in such a difficult position. 'It's all coming back to me now. Daisy's bastard uncle said he wants the money first thing tomorrow morning, or else.' Tom smiles and shakes his head, glad that I'm remembering. 'Was the man trying to rob me?'

'No. He was returning something you dropped. Poor sod was mortified. Just recovered from an op. Gallbladder, the paramedic said – apparently, he could barely keep up with you.' Tom smiles. 'He's the one who rang the emergency services.'

'Dropped what?' I ask in a loud voice, causing a blue uniformed nurse to look round from the bed across from me.

'Your debit card. It fell out of your robe pocket. Well, my dressing gown. Here.' Tom pours half a tumbler with water from the jug next to my bed and feeds me a few sips. The tepid liquid soothes the razorblade sensation in my throat. 'They gave you a bag of saline.' My eyes dart to my right hand. It has plastic tube poking out of a white plaster. The needle is still in my skin, stinging. 'You were very dehydrated.'

'Debit card?' I repeat. That can't be right. I ran out of our house like a greyhound when Zelda called, grabbing my phone in my haste. In fact, I had nothing else on me apart from…. Dread rockets through my body as I feel the pockets of my dressing gown. The letter knife. It's gone.

'Yes. Daisy recovered it for you. Don't look so worried. It's in her handbag, safe and sound.'

'Did you take anything from my pocket?' I demand.

'What?' Tom screws his face up. 'No, I…'

There's a kerfuffle of voices, footsteps, the swish of fabric, and then a woman's voice says, 'Ah, Mrs Harris. Nice to have you back with us. I'm Mrs Michaels, one of the consultants, and this is Dr Loizia – Valentina. You had quite a nasty fall, I hear. How're you feeling now?'

Chapter 35

'Mum,' Georgia cries. She drops her half-eaten toast onto her plate and launches herself at me. Closing my eyes, I wrap my arms around her and she melts into me.

'I'm fine,' I say, turning my forehead away, to make sure she doesn't brush away the ointment Dr Loizia gently applied to a graze on my head before discharging me half an hour ago. 'It's just a scratch.' I breathe my daughter in as the seriousness of what happened finally bulldozes into my brain. Zelda may have killed Frank, and I have managed to lose the weapon she used to slay him with. I wonder if perverting the course of justice carries a prison sentence. What if I go to jail for twenty years? I will miss out on so much of Georgia's life – her graduation, passing her driving test, relationships, maybe even grandchildren.

'Gosh, Mum, you're shaking. Are you sure you're okay?'

'Can I get you anything, Bella?' Daisy half stands, chewing a mouthful of cereal.

'No, I'm fine. Sit down and finish your breakfast.'

'Dad woke me up before he left, said you fell over and fainted and were carted off to A&E in an *ambulance*! I couldn't sleep after that. Why did auntie Zelda call you out in the middle of the night, anyway, just cos they had a fight?' I tell her she was upset. They'd split up and she needed my support, which is partly true.

Daisy gets to her feet, coffee in hand, and saunters towards me. Pulling me into a hug, coffee arm outstretched, she says, 'Glad you're okay.' Then presses her lips against my hair. 'I've got the letter knife in my drawer upstairs.' Every hair on my body stands on end. My temp has criminal evidence nestled inside her knicker drawer. She's an accessory to the crime now. I swallow what feels like a pebble stone.

Daisy backs away from me slowly, giving me a knowing look, then quickly spins on her heel and rushes back to her seat. I look at Tom in a daze as he necks a carton of semi-skimmed. 'What? I was parched.' I stay silent, trying to process what Daisy has just revealed, even though I hate him drinking anything straight from the carton and spreading germs, especially now that Daisy is living with us. 'I'm going up for a shower and a kip. You coming?'

I shake my head, tell him I'm starving. 'Aren't you due at the practice?' I ask, throwing a glance at the clock on the wall as I pull half a loaf of bread out of the fridge. The sooner Tom is out of the house, the sooner I can question Daisy about the letter knife and get her to hand it over. 'It's almost nine-thirty.'

'Bella, it's Sunday,' Tom says, scratching his head.

'Oh, yes, sorry.' I faff about with the loaf. I can't concentrate. I pop two slices into the toaster with tremulous hands.

'Dad,' Georgia calls out as he reaches the door. 'You can't go to *bed*.'

Tom pauses, one hand on the doorframe. Why not?' he says tiredly.

'You're meant to be giving me a lift to Parliament Hill? Football practice? I've got to be there in, like, an hour.' Tom's face is deadpan. 'Please don't tell me you're not taking me now cos of Mum's fainting drama.' The sympathy didn't last long. She's lucky I love the bones of her.

'Can't you jump on a bus, sweetheart? I've been up half the night. I'm shattered.'

Georgia eyes flit from me to her dad, face like thunder. 'I'm not getting three buses dressed in my football kit. I mean it, Mum. Oh, *Dadddddah*.'

'I'm sorry, Georgie,' he mutters. 'Can't one of the mum's give you a lift?'

'You always ruin everything for me. Why can't you be like normal parents? They're always taking their kids, like, everywhere, even to Central. You're always working or sleeping. Or having shitting seizures in the middle of the street. Jeez!!!' Then she turns to me. 'Mum, can you take me?'

'Georgia I….'

'Oh, I hate you both! *Grrr*.'

'Calm down, Georgia. I'll drive you,' Daisy offers. 'Your folks had a difficult night. Go up and get ready.'

Georgia races to Daisy. 'You.' Georgia cups Daisy's face with both hands. 'Are.' She gives her a hard kiss on the cheek. 'An absolute.' She kisses her other cheek. Harder. 'Lifesaver.' I couldn't agree with her more.

Daisy laughs as she recovers from Georgia's endearing assault. Daisy and I watch, shoulder to shoulder, as Georgia ambles out of the kitchen, knocking into her father in the doorway, complaining all the while – she can't believe he let her down at the last moment, typical, it's a good job we hired Daisy, at least we got one thing right. I raise my eyebrows at my husband to the backdrop of Georgia thundering up the stairs.

Tom rolls his eyes at me before chasing after her. 'Sweetheart, wait!'

Once Georgia and Tom are safely out of earshot, I round on Daisy, grab her hand and pull her down onto a chair at the kitchen table, throwing glances at the door in case Tom comes back. 'Daisy,' I pant. 'I'm so sorry. The letter knife. I put it in the pocket of Tom's dressing gown when I wore it on Friday morning. I've been looking everywhere for it.' I pause, do a hysterical little laugh for effect. 'Honestly, I'd forget my head if…'

'I know,' Daisy cuts across me.

'Pardon?'

'I heard you talking at the door about dumping it. You weren't talking about Linda's bicycle.' She jerks her head towards the ceiling where her bedroom is. 'It was that.'

'No.' I close my eyes briefly. *Fuck*. 'Daisy, it's not…'

'It's okay, Bella.' Reaching forward, she curls her hands around my shoulders firmly. 'I know you guys are in some sort of trouble and I'm guessing Frank's involved.' I shake my head to and fro, to and fro. 'I want to help. You took me in when I was desperate. Saved my life. Now it's payback time.'

'No.' Tears sting my eyes. 'You don't owe me. I didn't help you out in exchange for anything.' I look at the clock. It's twenty to ten. Linda and Zelda will be awake. It's not an unreasonable time to call on a Sunday. I need to return their calls, let them know I'm okay. But first I need to find out exactly what happened when I fainted and how much Daisy knows. 'What happened after I fell over?'

Daisy sits back in her chair. 'The man at the cash machine gave me the letter opener, said it flew out of your pocket as you ran away. He was mortified when your flip-flop overturned and you fell over and fainted, blamed himself for alarming you. We had to call an ambulance, Bella, you were spark out.' I nod, tell her she did the right thing. 'I rang Tom while we waited for the paramedics to arrive. A few moments later you regained consciousness but were completely out of it, saying crazy stuff about Frank, something about him trying to kill Zelda. I told the gentleman you were a bit confused, thanked him and said I'd take it from here, that I was your sister.' She laughs lightly, and I smile. 'Hope that was okay,' she adds, going red. 'It was the only way to get rid of him.'

'Of course it was. Good call.'

'He was gone before I drew my next breath. He'd had an op and was still recovering. Stank of booze, though.'

'Yes,' I agree. 'I smelt it on his breath when he spoke to me.' I bite my bottom lip. At least I didn't mention Frank's body and Zelda stabbing him. 'I'm sorry, Daisy, and thank you for looking after me. Now, about the letter opener, you've got it all wrong. It's an office device,' I say, and she frowns. 'It was my dad's, a bit of an heirloom, hence my panic.'

'It has a Monte Carlo stamp on it,' Daisy says. 'Zelda and Frank just got back from there.'

'Yes, they did. What a coincidence.' I laugh lightly. 'Dad was stationed in the south of France, loved Monaco, used to tell us stories about his time there.' Her features soften. She's buying it. I plough on. 'I don't know what you overheard outside Zelda's, but I can categorically tell you that we were not talking about getting rid of my letter opener. Linda's bicycle really is in Zelda's garage and we need to get rid of it. Theo refuses point blank to have it back in the house.'

'Oh, right. I see. I just... Gosh, I'm so sorry for thinking the worst. It's lack of sleep,' she laughs and my muscles unclench. 'Theo is a bit of a moody chops, isn't he? And slightly scary.'

'Exactly. So, if I could have it back please.'

'Oh, absolutely.' She gets to her feet. 'Good job Ginger-Haired-Man found it, eh? Might be worth a few bob if it's antique.' I close my eyes as I follow her out of the kitchen and up the stairs – feeling sick with nerves and deceit.

Later that night, I stare into the darkness, with the weight of Frank's disappearance pinning me down like lead, willing sleep to come, but it doesn't.

Chapter 36

The moment daylight breaks, I whip back the duvet and throw on the first thing I find. I then scribble a note for Tom, and one for Daisy, saying an urgent job came up via text. I place Tom's on the bedside table, and slide Daisy's under her bedroom door, before slipping quietly out of the house, stomach twisted like a wrung-out rag.

I arrive at Waterlow Park in Highgate in just under twenty minutes. On the bridge, I retrieve the weapon from my handbag, which I wrapped and secured in a terry tea towel and a brick to give it extra weight, and drop it into the lake. Job done.

'How'd it go, Bette Davis?' Linda yells over the thunder of several kanga drills, the moment I step into Zelda's lounge for our Monday morning meeting.

'What?' I say tetchily, inhaling a fug of musky smoke, cheap air freshener and the slight mist of doom. 'What's an old Hollywood movie star got to do with anything?'

'Great disguise,' Zelda smiles, pointing at my face, and it is only then I realise that in my haste to get away from an old chatty couple, with two barking dogs, at the exit gate of Waterlow Park half an hour ago, I forgot to remove my head scarf and dark glasses when I climbed into my car and I now look like a Hollywood diva.

'Everything okay?' Linda is sitting in an armchair, glasses perched on the bridge of her nose, iPad in hand. 'No one saw you, right?' I hesitate, for a nanosecond. I can't tell them about the frantic dogs and the elderly couple. It might make them anxious. 'How's the injury? Is that why you're wearing the sunnies? Sorry, I didn't think.'

'It's just a scratch,' I say, dismissively, 'concealer is a godsend.' I look at two flowery mugs on the coffee table, trembling from the vibration of a blaring dumper going up the shared driveway. 'Everything went to plan,' I confirm, pulling off my sunglasses and untying my headscarf. 'No one saw me.'

'Well, you should try telling your face that,' Linda snuffles.

'Sorry, Linda. I barely slept.'

'How're you feeling after the fall?' Zelda asks. I tell her that I'm fine now. It was a fuss over nothing. 'And you're definitely sure no one saw you in the park.' Zelda looks at me anxiously.

'*Yesss*,' I hiss, annoyed. The dog owners saw me in the park, but they didn't witness me chucking the weapon into the lake. So, technically, I'm not lying. 'The letter opener has vanished.'

'Thank fuck for that. You had me worried for a moment.' Linda yawns, while Zelda flaps around with a can of air freshener, and I notice that Linda's eyes are a little bloodshot. Poor Linda. I'm going to have to make it up to her. Once this is over, I'll treat her to a weekend health spa in the New Forest. Linda coughs raucously. 'Can you please stop doing that?' she cries, fanning a hand in front of her face. 'I can't fucking breathe.'

'I'm sorry. I just want to get rid of the smell of bleach,' Zelda yells, aerosol in hand, over the sudden blare of a drill that sounds like a machine gun.

'You've got cement on your shoes,' Linda points out. 'Mine were soiled too.'

I look down at my black kitten heels, spotted with grey dots. 'Shit,' I groan. 'They're new.'

'I'll give you a wet cloth to wipe them down before it sets,' Zelda offers, ushering us into the kitchen. 'A lorry load of cement arrived for next door this morning. Their hose had a tiny leak. Splashed it all over my front lawn. Landlord will be livid.'

The next twenty minutes are filled with a mixture of yells and tears as we scream at each other across the kitchen table to be heard. They big me up for getting rid of the evidence and I tell them I'd do it again in a heartbeat, for either of them. Although, if I'm honest, I'm not sure this is true. Criminality is not my forte. There's a heaviness in the pit of my stomach that won't shift.

'Have you guys checked Frank's socials?' Linda asks, as we gather ourselves to leave.

'He's not on Facebook or Twitter,' I say. 'Or TikTok, as far as I know.'

Zelda nods. 'I checked his Insta and there's been nothing since last Saturday. But he doesn't update with any regularity, so that doesn't mean anything.'

'He might be lying low. Maybe he just wants to forget all about it,' Linda says, shrugging on her jacket. 'He obviously hasn't reported it to the police.'

On the doorstep, there's a stumbling of hugs and kisses, and as Linda gets wolf whistled by one of the builders next door, who looks about Georgia's age, an email alert pings on my phone.

'Sorry,' I say, 'got to read this. It might be work.' I pull out my phone. One new message. I tap on Inbox. It's from a sender called *killingsteve1984@gmail.com* with the caption HELLO ISABELLA. 'It looks like a spam message,' I announce. One I should probably delete without reading, but I'm a big fan of *Killing Eve* and it has made me smile.

Curiosity bubbles in my stomach as the message loads to the hullabaloo of Zelda and Linda discussing the building work next door. But as I read the email, my breath snags in my throat and my ears start buzzing.

Those with blood on their hands must pay.
F.

Chapter 37

'I think I'll have the calamari to start.' Tom muses, eyes on the menu.

We're at *The Stage*, our local gastro pub, having a date night. It's just had a refurb and the great reviews have been pouring in. Georgia is having dinner with Tilly and her family at *Lemonia* in Primrose Hill. And Daisy is eating out with a friend who's visiting from Dublin. They've been out shopping all day. I gave her the day off. A thank you for holding the fort for me while I've been convalescing after my fall and that email I received from KillingSteve1984 four days ago. After I recovered from an asthma attack, Linda and Zelda insisted it was spam, or a random troll, but I wasn't convinced. It was signed F. Surely, that's too much of a coincidence. In the end, I agreed to take a few days off to get over the trauma of recent events.

'Samantha said the sea bass is exceptional, so I'll follow with that.' Samantha is Tom's sixty-year-old foodie colleague. Everything she recommends is usually delicious. 'What about you, sweetheart?'

'Um… I'm not too sure,' I murmur, scratching my wrist. 'Something light. I had a big lunch.' I had an apple, and that was a struggle.

'This is the selection for the offer.' Reaching over, he points at the Early Bird card attached to the menu. 'We could share a starter and dessert if you're not that hungry?' This is something we often do. 'Look.' He points. 'They've got salmon en-croute. You like that.' I don't think I could stomach anything with pastry. I was thinking of having something like a seafood or goat's cheese salad.

'Sharing sounds like a great idea.' I stare at the menu, the words a blur. I can't concentrate. I wish I'd kept myself busy with work now. The time off has only intensified my anxiety. Is it possible for us to just carry on as normal? Baking cakes, selling houses, having date nights, after what we've done?

Frank's bleeding body on the lawn flares in my mind and I suddenly feel hot. 'Gosh, it's boiling in here.' I shrug off my black cardigan and chuck it over my handbag on the seat next to me, then pinch the collar of my dress and give it a few tugs, letting in some air.

'I'm actually fine,' Tom says. Jutting his bottom lip out, he runs a finger along the wine list as I try to convince myself that KillingSteve1984 isn't Frank. He is alive and well, wants nothing more to do with the Villin sisters, hence his silence. I stare at the Early Bird menu and read nothing.

'You're going to gnaw that thumb off.'

'What?'

Tom gestures at my mouth, and it's only then that I realise I've bitten my nail down to the skin. 'Look, is everything okay? You've been quiet all evening. Fidgety.' I look up at my husband. He looks tired. His skin is dry and he has purply bags beneath his eyes. 'Because if you're still not feeling a hundred-per-cent.' Pausing, he sighs. 'Listen, maybe this wasn't such a good idea.'

'I'm fine,' I say hastily, frowning at the menu and pretending to read it. 'A night out is just what I needed. It's a great idea. Thank you.'

Tom smiles at me, eyes creasing at the sides. 'Only if you're sure.'

'Absolutely.' My eyes flick over the menu, words swimming in my vision. 'I'll have the same dish as you, I think.'

I look up at an unsmiling waiter, who's just arrived at our table, pen hovering over notepad. 'Are you ready to order, guys?' he says, throwing a glance at the entrance as it swings open.

The evening flies by and the conversation flows. We talk about Daisy and how brilliant she's been, especially with Georgia. Then we swiftly move on to our heavy workload, agree that life is short, we've got to slow down, spend more time together. But when Tom quizzes me about Frank and Zelda, my heart freezes. I tell him, hastily, that they've decided to call it a day, and he nods, says he wasn't right for her and then he says something odd. 'I hope the bastard rots in hell.' I shoot a glance at him as he smiles up at a waitress, who is clearing our table. 'Can we please have a doggy-bag for this,' he asks, pointing at my barely touched plate.

'Bit harsh,' I hear myself say, as the waitress disappears into the depths of the pub, long braids snaking down her elegant back. If I didn't know him better I'd think Tom might have something to do with Frank's disappearance. I imagine Tom waking up in the middle of the night and reading the note I left him – *Gone to Zelda's. They've had a fight. Won't be long* – furiously throwing on his clothes, grabbing his car keys, turning into Zelda's road right on cue as Frank stumbles onto the street. Frank hailing him down, bleeding, asking for help – clambering into his car, complaining how we left him for dead, relaying what happened at the gym, saying I was gagging for it – Tom's hands tightening around the steering wheel, like they sometimes do when we're having a full-blown row, calling him a liar before hitting the brakes and tossing him out onto the pavement, leaving him to bleed to death.

'I mean, he was so bloody full of himself, wasn't he?' Tom clarifies, snapping me out of my terrifying reverie. *Wasn't he?* Past tense.

'I imagine he still is.' I laugh lightly into my glass so that he can't see the alarm on my face. 'But yes, he was,' I take another sip. '*Is*,' I say, tongue slightly slurred. I've had enough. It's time to go home before I say something I shouldn't.

'Man's a complete knob. Good riddance to bad rubbish. I just hope he doesn't manage to get back into Zelda's good books. She did seem besotted with him.' I take another sip of wine, hating myself for thinking my husband was capable of such a despicable act. 'Zelda will meet someone else,' Tom affirms, and I'm sure I see a glint of darkness in his eyes.

Chapter 38

The Stage's loos are modern and plush, with streaked black marble flooring, green and gold leaf wallpaper, gleaming white ceramic bowls and shiny stainless-steel taps. Very instagramable, as Georgia would say.

I turn on the tap and pump soap into my hands from the silver dispenser. Apart from the wobble I had just now about Tom having a hand in Frank's disappearance and his hatred of him, I really have enjoyed tonight, and I know I'm ready to go back to work. The door swings open and two women totter in, their strong perfume flooding the toilets. They stagger behind me towards the cubicles, calling each other Babe and discussing the evening in a slurry tone – it's so sick in here – doesn't Craig scrub up well – Miranda's a total bitch, isn't she? – those fillers and Botox make her look like Frankenstein.

Their voices fade as they lock themselves inside the cubicles, their heady perfume still hanging in the air. They'll have the hangover from hell in the morning and regret everything they said about poor Miranda.

'Any news about the house?' one of them yells as I rinse my hands. 'I was gonnou ask you before but forgot.'

'Josh wants to knock it down.'

'The price?'

'Nah, the shed.'

Giggling to myself, I shake the excess water off my hands, then immerse them into the gap of the dryer to the backdrop of a flushing loo and the clatter of doors swinging open, followed by a flash of the women teetering towards the basins. On close inspection, they look older than I thought – probably mid-forties.

'Liam still wiv that girl?' the woman with spidery eyelashes asks her pink-lipsticked friend, and my heart spasms. Liam. Did I really need reminding? I was having such a lovely evening.

'He was gonna dump her on Valentine's Day,' the friend replies, sliding up next to me and smearing more pink lipstick all over her mouth. 'But didn't want her to think he was doing it to avoid buying her a present.' I stifle a laugh that is charging up my throat as I fish out my lip-gloss from my handbag. 'They're still together, though. He brought her round the other day.'

'What's she like?'

'Quite shy. Liam told me off after she left – said I was rude to her.'

'Oh, you couldn't be rude to anyone. What did you do?'

'I know,' she exclaims, and then, 'Sorry, babe,' she says to me after she unsteadily nudges me on the elbow, causing my lip-gloss wand to slide along my cheek. 'I went upstairs and left her on her own while Liam popped out to get us a takeaway. I said hello first, though.'

'Some people are so bleeding touchy, aren't they,' Spidery-Eyelashes says as I wipe the gloss from my cheek with a tissue, taking off a line of foundation with it and leaving a red blemish in its place. 'Liam needs reminding who picks up his manky socks and washes his dirty boxers. I'm glad I haven't got kids.'

Traffic starts building up in my mind as the door closes, shutting out their voices and drunken laughter. I think about my time with Liam. Like Pink-Lipstick-Woman's namesake son, he was a total slob around the flat – socks and underwear discarded on the bedroom carpet, cupboard doors left open, wet towels all over the bathroom floor. Cleaning up after him became a way of life. Pressing my lips together, I drop the lip gloss back into my handbag as a blur of faceless women swim in and out of my vision. God, what did I ever see in Liam? I wish I'd never responded to his message on Instagram. I wish I'd blocked him.

I do a little shiver, catching sight of a middle-aged, fair-haired woman checking herself out in the mirror before moving to the hand dryer, her back to me. Lost in thought, I didn't register her sliding up in her long, red cardigan. Combing a hand through my hair, I dash behind the red-cardiganed-woman, hoping she'll hold the door open for me. 'Thanks,' I cry in anticipation. The door slams in my face. Why are people so bloody rude?

Back at our table, I find the unsmiling waiter clearing up. 'Sorry,' I say, 'did you see where my husband went?' Perhaps, he's gone to the loo, too.

The waiter gestures towards the door with his head. 'Just left, madam.'

I inwardly scream. Why did Tom leave without waiting for me to return? I specifically told him not to pay until I got back. I wasn't gone that long and, for a change, there was no queue in the ladies. I go to leave and then, 'Did he leave you a tip?'

The waiter runs a cloth over the table. 'It's okay, madam,' he says over his shoulder.

I knew it. I can't believe how mean Tom is sometimes. Admittedly, the waiter was a bit miserable but who knows what battles he's fighting. I fish around in my handbag for my purse and hand him a five-pound note.

'Thank you so much, Madam,' he says, smiling for the first time this evening. I race across the restaurant. 'Don't forget your doggy-bag,' he calls out, but I'm gone.

There are a few patrons hogging the pavement as I slip out into the cool, evening air. My eyes flit around the street wildly, searching for Tom, and then I spot him, about thirty feet away near a taxi bay. He's standing in front of a group of revellers, talking to a couple who look like they're killing time, waiting for their cab to arrive.

I start walking. Stop. Crane my neck for a better view as the group of revellers bundle into a waiting cab. The man is about Tom's age, maybe a bit older, late-fifties, wiry long hair but balding at the top. He looks like he's come straight from work in his dark suit and white shirt, tie loosened, round belly hanging over his trousers. My eyes dart to the woman, who has her back to me. I know her. I'd recognise that long red cardigan anywhere. It's the woman from the toilets who slammed the door in my face just now.

Tom is laughing at something the man is saying now and the woman is looking at her watch, shuffling impatiently on the pavement in her red stilettos, that match the colour of her cardigan. The lady in red. Wasn't that a song? I frown, her profile looks familiar. We know them, obviously. I think they're Linda and Theo's friends. We met them at one of their many parties. I should go over and say hello. I go to move when a taxi pulls up. The round-bellied man opens the door, then turns and yells out, 'Cheerio, Tom.'

I watch as the woman folds herself into the backseat of the cab. When she looks up, I see her face properly for the first time and everything stops. The rowdy group behind me cheer. A bus pulls up next to me, wheels screaming. Maybe it isn't her. Maybe my vision is playing tricks on me. I have had two big glasses of red. That's equivalent to about five drinks, isn't it? I start walking fast, wishing I'd worn my flats instead of these three-inch heels. Tom has his back to me now, one hand in pocket, the other pressing his phone against his ear. I'm a metre away when the cab pulls away and just then the woman glances out of the window, giving Tom a polite nod and tight smile, and I know without a shadow of a doubt that it's her. Mrs Anderson. Daisy's auntie.

Chapter 39

I hear a babble of voices coming from upstairs the moment Tom pushes the front door open. There's a faint smell of popcorn in the air, too. I glance at my watch. It's almost eleven. I'll have to go up and tell Georgia to switch the TV off shortly, or politely ask Daisy to turn down the volume. We don't want Mr Stanhope banging on our door, complaining about the noise.

'Bit loud, isn't it?' Tom comments, picking up on my tension. We kick off our shoes in synchronisation.

'It is a bit.' I slip my black heels next to Georgia's red trainers, the same shade as Mrs Anderson's stilettos. Her tight expression in the back of the taxi loops in my mind. Our cab pulled up just as I approached Tom at the taxi bay. With the phone pressed against his ear, he ushered me into the back of the cab urgently, miming *Sorry. Nick from the practice.* Naturally, I didn't want to disturb his important conversation about Mr Horsham's glaucoma, so didn't get a chance to quiz him about Mrs Anderson. Thinking back, Tom was chatting heartily with her companion as if she were invisible, and she did seem a bit edgy, bored, impatient to leave. Did Tom meet

Mrs Anderson for the first time tonight? They do say we've got six degrees of separation. It could all be a huge coincidence.

'We don't want old Stanhope on the warpath, do we?' Tom groans, and I agree, remind him that he's called noise pollution at eight in the evening in the past. Wrenching up my dress, I slip out of my tights, and just as I open my mouth to ask him about Tina Anderson, his eyes slide to my thighs. Unbuttoning his shirt slowly, from the bottom up, he takes in the length of me. I shoot a glance at the upstairs landing. A sound of howling, followed by screaming travels down the stairwell. They must be watching a horror film. Tom is still undressing me with his eyes. Surely, he's not going to seduce me in the hallway. One of the girls could pound down the staircase at any moment. Catching us at it could traumatise them for life.

'Come here,' he says, voice low.

What's got into him? He's not usually this frisky, not of late anyway. It's that 14% volume wine he guzzled at *The Stage*. My eyes drop to his torso – not gym-toned by a long shot, but sexy all the same. Tom suddenly stops undressing and pulls me to him. I inhale his scent. Warm, familiar, spicy. 'We can't,' I breathe, 'not here. Let's go upstairs.'

'Where's the fun in that?' he whispers, backing me up against the banister. 'God, it's been ages…'

'We can't do it here,' I murmur, as he gently guides me towards the staircase. 'The girls.' We gaze at each other, drunk on lust, and then I feel the softness of the stair carpet on the back of my thighs. Parting my lips with his warm tongue, we kiss hungrily. My eyes close, Frank's face darts into my mind, his breath on my lips, hands on my arms, and then the TV amplifies, followed by the thump of footsteps on the landing.

'Stop,' I pant, pushing him off me. 'We've got a houseguest, a teenage daughter upstairs.'

Tom looks at me for a few moments, breath hot against my face. 'Yes, yes. You're right,' he says, suddenly snapping out of his lustful zone. We pull apart, dishevelled, heart racing. 'Sorry, I got carried away,' he says, to the backdrop of a loo flushing, and, with a hand through his messed-up hair, he grins and backs away slowly, fastening his shirt with one button, before disappearing into the kitchen.

Bending down, I tidy our shoes in a neat line against the wall. Above me, footsteps stomp on the landing, followed by the clamour of a door closing, drowning out the sound of the TV. It was Georgia needing a wee. Daisy's got an en-suite.

I ruffle my hair as I study my reflection in the silver framed hallway mirror. I barely recognise the woman that is staring back at me. How can I feel thirty-five yet look like this? My skin is dry and dull. My cheeks have puffed out and my jowls seem more prominent in this harsh lighting. Turning to the side, I pinch the fat around my middle. I've put on half a stone since I quit the gym. My spare tyre is back with a vengeance. I joined *Serval* because I had low self-esteem and wanted to get into shape. I now look even worse. I'm surprised Tom still finds me desirable. Blood rushes to my face and I have to look away from my reflection.

I've got to sign up with another gym, find myself a decent personal trainer this time. Maybe a woman who will knock me into shape. Tom won't mind now that he knows how important it is to me. We agreed after Frank, no more secrets. I bite my bottom lip. I still haven't told him about Liam, though. If he finds out what happened from someone else it'll end us. I will lose everything – my home, my family, my life. I can't let that happen.

Fuelled with Dutch-courage, I yell out Tom's name. There's a shuffle of footsteps and then he appears, staring at his phone, half his shirt hanging out of his trousers. 'Tommy,' I say, and he looks up at me. 'We need to talk.'

Chapter 40

'Sounds ominous,' Tom says, flicking the lights on in the lounge. 'What's this about?' I follow him swiftly, rubbing the back of my neck.

'The thing is,' I begin, inhaling a faint fug of polish.

The TV flickers on. 'Hang on,' he says, not looking at me. Tom hits a few buttons on the remote control, settling on a football match. 'You don't mind if I watch the highlights while we're talking, do you?'

Fessing up about Liam isn't something I can do while he's watching football. 'Don't worry, watch your match. It can wait.'

He smiles up at me, settling back on the sofa. 'Only if you're sure.'

'I am,' and then, 'Feet,' I say and he removes his size elevens from the freshly polished coffee table. Daisy must've given the room a once over. I'll have a word with her about it in the morning. She's not our housekeeper. 'Do you want anything else to eat? We forgot the doggy-bag at *The Stage*,' I lie. Tom shakes his head- tells me it'll give him heartburn. I leave him to his football and head for the kitchen.

'How the hell did you miss that?' Tom's voice booms from the lounge as I flick the kettle on. Mr Stanhope will definitely be calling noise pollution tonight. 'It was an open goal, for fuck's sake.'

Smiling reflectively, I lean against the worktop as the kettle rumbles and thrashes, my eyes darting around our huge, gleaming, state-of-the-art kitchen. With its sleek teal cabinets, stylish island, chic wooden breakfast bar, and forty-seven-inch screen mounted against the bare brick wall, it is breath-taking. The kind of kitchen you see celebrities posing in with their perfect families and French Bulldogs in *Hello*. Am I about to lose everything for one stupid mistake?

I gaze up at the full moon through the skyline windows, wishing it would purge my guilt. The kettle judders on the worktop. How did a girl like me end up with a life like this? I loved our old mid-terrace, but you couldn't swing a cat in our kitchen. Zelda was gobsmacked when she first saw this one, said she'd kill for a kitchen like mine. The idiom sends a chill along my spine and I do a little shudder. *She didn't kill Frank. She can't have. He got up and walked away, for goodness' sake.*

Exhaling loudly, I go to move, and just then I hear something rattling outside. I stop stock still and listen. Silence. I take a step forward. There's a thump followed by a knock on the door – tap, tap, tap. My stomach surges. Someone's outside. I'm about to call Tom when a thought rams into my brain. Could it be Frank? I silently recite the ominous email from KillingSteve1984, word for word – *Those with blood on their hands must pay.* Linda and Zelda were wrong. It wasn't spam. F *is* Frank.

I cock my head and listen, mouth drying. Nothing, apart from the click of the kettle and white noise coming from the TV in the lounge. I inch closer, straining my ears but am met with silence. Surely, there's no one out there. No, of course not. I'm overreacting, that's all. It was probably an animal looking for food. I rub my forehead, what is wrong with me? Frank isn't hiding in our garden. I'm about to walk away when I catch sight of a fleeting shadow outside. That was definitely no animal. Adrenalin soars through my blood as I lurch forward and fumble with the lock. The door flies open. A gust of wind sweeps into the house.

I step into the night, cold seeping through my skin, chilling my bones. The wind has picked up and it's whistling in my ears. 'Hello?' I cry, rubbing my arms and wishing I'd kept my tights on. Trees shiver in the gust, casting shadows on the rattan furniture besides the fluttering parasol. I take a few tentative steps forward. 'Is anyone there?' I gulp, voice trembling. But my words are swallowed into the darkness.

'Frank?' My cold breath plumes. 'Frank, is that you?' What am I doing? Frank won't answer, even if he's here. He wants revenge. He's going to hunt us all down one by one and make us pay. I mean, I know it sounds farfetched but he did try to strangle my sister. What's to stop him from murdering me in cold blood right now? My daughter will be motherless. Tom will be a widower.

A fox screams nearby and my stomach spasms. I need protection. My eyes race around the patio, pausing on a brick that is weighted on the feet of a metal solar chicken light. Tom put it there to stop the wind from blowing it away. The sound of squeaking and juddering catches my attention, forcing me to spin round.

Without thinking, I tiptoe along the patio, grit and cold pinching my bare feet, and peer over the wall. A wooden door swings in the whistling wind. My body sags with relief. It isn't Frank. It's Maureen and Stewart's back gate. It's been left open. It wouldn't be the first time. Maureen has banned Alex, their twenty-four-year-old son, from bringing his muddy boots into the house after rugby practice. He now has to leave them in the garden until they've been cleaned. Sometimes, after a few drinks with the lads, Alex forgets to put the latch back on before going inside.

Securing their gate on the latch, I berate myself for being so paranoid. Frank isn't a serial killer. He's probably sunning himself somewhere on the Mediterranean coast this very moment, cocktail in hand. *Get a bloody grip, woman, and sort your mess out before you lose everything.*

Chapter 41

The moment I walk into the lounge, Tom flicks a finger over his phone and places it next to him on the sofa, folds his arms across his chest and frowns intently at the 55-inch screen. It was his photos app. I saw a blur of faces, probably an old photo of us.

'Good match?' I ask, sitting down heavily next to him, fingers warm from the hot mug in my hand. I peer at him as he stares at the TV screen. The lust and urgency to get me into bed has clearly gone.

'Bit boring, to be honest.' Tom yawns, stretching his arms above his head. I follow his gaze to his phone as the light dims and goes out. 'Left a review online.' Leaning forward, he picks up a coaster and places it in front of me, and I place my mug down. 'For *The Stage*,' he clarifies, throwing me a smile.

Right, I decide very quickly to ask him about Mrs Anderson before I broach the subject of Liam. I scratch my neck as a player misses a goal and the crowd groans. 'I was meaning to ask you,' I say. 'You know that couple you were talking to outside the restaurant.' Reaching over, I pick up my mug of tea. Tom frowns, grabs the remote. 'Well, the woman actually.' I take a slurp, and Tom throws me an annoying glance as he turns up the volume. He hates the sound of slurping and chewing. He passed on one of his patients to Samantha once because the poor man was breathing too loudly during his eye test.

'What the one with Lawrence?' he says, as if Lawrence is an old friend of mine.

'Yes,' I trill, then lower my voice. 'Do you know her?'

Tom shakes his head, goes a bit red. Is it the heat? It is quite hot in here. I touch the radiator behind the sofa. It's still warm. 'Not really.' How can you not really know someone? You either do, or you don't. 'I've seen her a couple of times recently, picking Lawrence up from the golf club.'

Chewing my thumbnail, I give my husband a sideward glance. His eyes don't leave the TV. Lawrence loops in my mind. I remember Tom mentioning him now – good handicap. Could've been a pro. Bit smug, if my memory serves me correctly. Has a son who's a golf coach. Mrs Anderson must've just started dating Lawrence on the rebound. I hope Lawrence doesn't take advantage of her.

'You'll never guess who she is,' I say, excitedly. Ignoring me, Tom leaps to the edge of his seat, eyes wide, fist clenched on his knee, and then he covers his hands over his face as another goal is missed. I nudge him with my knee. 'Did you hear what I said?'

'Sorry, love. Who who is?'

'That woman with Lawrence.' Tom waits, poker-faced, then does a jittery shrug as if to say, *well, are you going to tell me or not?* 'She's Daisy's auntie,' I exclaim.

Tom's face pales as a roar from the television explodes into the room. A goal has been scored and he missed it. 'No way,' he says, lowering the volume.

Finally, a reaction. I do a little nod, sucking my cheeks in smugly. 'She's the client who recommended her on that Friday, remember? I photographed her house. Small world, eh?'

'Seriously?' He shoves a hand through his hair and leaves it there. 'I can't believe it. What were the odds of that?'

'I know,' I say, staring absently at the TV as footballers pile on top of each other.

'Gah, we lost.' Tom starts flicking through the channels. 'Daisy's auntie, eh? Why didn't you come over and say hello?'

'I was about to when they got into the cab. I don't think she recognised me.' I squint at the family photograph of the three of us above the fireplace. Mum took it two years ago on the balcony of her lovely home, which overlooks the golf course. It was such a beautiful picture that we got it printed on canvas. 'Probably too loved up with Lawrence. She was standing right next to me in the pub loos, applying lippy in the mirror. Maybe she's long-sighted,' I muse.

'Wow, what a coincidence.' Tom leans back on the sofa and stretches his legs out in front of him, crossing them at the ankles. 'To be fair, I don't know Lawrence that well. He's not part of our group.'

'Oh, I thought he was,' I say, stroking his cheek. It's stubbly but soft.

'Nah. It's always small talk with him. I see him at the club sometimes and the Christmas dos.' Picking up the remote, Tom lowers the volume, turns to me and fixes me with a stare. 'I really enjoyed our date night. Just me and you. Like old times.' *I wouldn't go as far as that, Tom, I got pregnant almost immediately. We hardly had any fun nights out at all.* 'You and Georgia are everything to me,' he breathes, 'I know I don't say it often enough. But if you ever…' he falters. 'I want you to know that I'm your best friend as well as your partner.' I think Linda would object to that. 'What I'm trying to say is.' He exhales through his nostrils. 'I'm here if you need me. If you ever want to talk. About anything. Anything at all.' He looks at me carefully. 'If you're in any kind of trouble.' A knot forms in my stomach. Does he know about Frank? But no, how could he? 'In sickness and…'

I press my fingers against his lips to silence him. 'Tom, there is something.' He frowns, narrowing his eyes. This is it. The moment I've been dreading. My heart thumps hard, cascading to my stomach. I take a breath and then I blurt, 'I haven't been completely honest with you, and I know I should've told you this a long time ago, but I…' I glance at the ceiling, fiddling with my wedding ring. 'There's no excuses. I've been an idiot. So much could've been avoided. If only I'd…'

'Just tell me, Bella.' Picking up the remote control, he switches the TV off. The screen blackens in synchronisation with my heart.

'It's about Liam,' I utter. Tom's face darkens immediately. This is going to be painful. It will crush him. I will hurt him. But sometimes we've got to do what's right and not what's best for us. 'I met up with him. Once. Well, actually it was twice.' Tom looks at me, wordless, then gets to his feet and shoves a hand into his trouser pocket. 'It's not what you think, Tommy.' He starts pacing, rubbing the back of his neck. I slide to the edge of the seat. 'I shouldn't have answered his message that time. I should've deleted it. I shouldn't have let my curiosity get the better of me. I know that now.' I look up at him pleadingly. 'But it wasn't a date.' My eyes close. 'I had to meet him because…'

'I know why you met him.'

My eyes snap open. 'What?'

He snatches his phone off the sofa and starts scrolling, then hands it to me. I stare down at the lit-up screen and I know that if I was standing up my legs would buckle and I'd collapse. I glance up at Tom but he has his back to me, leaning against the fireplace as if he's doing a push-up.

Covering my mouth with my cold hand, I look at the couple in the photo. It's slightly out of focus, taken from outside through the window, but the faces are as clear as day. Liam is cupping my cheek and we're gazing at each other across the table like lovers. My intestines collapse. I think I need the loo.

'Frank,' I manage, squeezing the phone in my hand. The prick took a selfie of us at the café in Crouch End. He must've gone round the block and come back for this shot because I watched him walk away.

'He was showing me a few goofy photos from their trip to Monaco at the barbeque last Saturday,' Tom explains. 'He told Zelda he'd deleted them and made me promise not to tell, and then suddenly I caught sight of this one. It was too late for him to backpedal.' I stare at Tom in a stupor, and for a split second I wish Frank was dead. 'I think he did it on purpose, to be honest, wanted me to see it. That's why he gave me his phone.' Heat spreads through me like wildfire. 'I asked him to send it to me. I've been waiting for you to tell me. I wanted to hear it from you.' He pauses, looks at the sparkling chandelier.

'Tom,' I begin urgently, 'the photo was taken out of context. I was crying, Liam tried to comfort me but I slapped his hand away.'

'I don't care about the photo. It's what he said he overheard that's been bothering me.'

'Did he …'

'Yes,' Tom confirms, and I feel as if I've been plunged into an ice-bath. I can't feel my limbs. 'He played the part to begin with, didn't want to cause any trouble and all that. But he didn't need much persuading to share your secret. Blokes solidarity and all that. Fucking tosser.' I chuck the phone onto the sofa and cover my hands over my ears as Tom rambles on and on about Liam – he's a loser – a jack-the-lad homewrecker – how could I do this to him – to us? *No, no, no. Please make him stop.* 'I don't know what Frank's beef is with you, or what he was trying to achieve.' His words smother my airways. I feel as if the oxygen is being sucked out of the room. I glance up. The furniture is swaying. What's happening? Am I going to faint again? 'But now that I know, I can't unknow, can I?'

'Tom, please.'

'I can't ignore that…' Tom's lips tremble. 'That Liam is Georgia's dad.'

Chapter 42

'Tommy, please listen to me.' I rest a hand on my trembling thigh. 'Where are you going? Tom. Wait.' A buzz of laughter from the TV filters through the ceiling as he stomps out of the room in a rage. For a few moments, I just sit there frozen, feeling light-headed, disorientated. Frank has destroyed me. The vindictive bastard. God forgive me, but I wish my sister *had* ended him. What am I going to do now?

Shooting to my feet, I barrel after Tom. 'You can't walk away from this. We need to discuss it.' Tom ignores my pleas, opening and closing cabinet doors manically. I gawp at him as he crosses the kitchen and opens the freezer. A gust of arctic air snaps at my legs. 'Tom, please.' With his bare hand, he scoops up a handful of ice cubes from a plastic bag. They rattle as they hit the glass. 'You said I could talk to you about anything, remember?'

I watch, rooted to the spot, as he grabs a bottle of cognac off the worktop by the neck. It's the one Daisy uses for cooking. Cheap and, undoubtedly, not the smoothest of blends, but I don't suppose Tom really cares right now. It isn't every day you're told that the child you've been raising for the last fifteen years isn't biologically yours. Wrapping his lips around the mouth of the bottle, he takes a swig, as if his life depended on it, squeezing his eyes shut as he swallows, face ablaze.

'Just calm down, will you?'

Tom's eyes snap open, round and wild and challenging. 'You,' he seethes, jabbing a finger at me. 'Don't get to tell me how to *fucking* feel.' Spittle flies from his mouth, foaming at the corners.

'Please just listen to me,' I say, breath shallow. He pours a generous amount of tawny liquid into a tumbler and knocks it back in one hit. 'What Frank told you was…'

A crashing sound from upstairs snatches our attention. He stops pouring mid-flow and looks at the ceiling.

'Shit,' I say, following his gaze. 'I hope that's not Georgia, listening.' I hesitate. 'I'll be back in a minute.'

I take the steps two at a time, heart pounding, gently ease Georgia's door open and sigh with relief. She's asleep, mouth slightly ajar, TV flickering on the wall in front of her bed, volume high. The sound of the cistern filling from Daisy's room filters through the open door as I watch my precious daughter sleeping soundly.

'It's okay, darling,' I whisper, standing over her, 'I won't let Frank destroy our family. I promise.' Dropping a light kiss on her silky blonde hair, I close the door gently behind me, race down the stairs and storm into the kitchen. Tom is sitting at the table looking ashen.

'You okay?' I ask.

'Do I look okay?'

'Sorry. Stupid question. She's asleep, by the way,' I mutter, pulling out a chair opposite him. 'Daisy must've dropped something in her bedroom.' Tom acknowledges this piece of information with a grunt. 'About what Frank said…'

'Don't even think about spinning any more lies.'

'I wasn't going to.' I exhale loudly. 'I wanted to tell you about Liam. I just needed to sort out a few things first and then…'

'When?' he snaps.

I look at him, puzzled. 'What?'

'When were you going to tell me?'

The deafening silence is punctuated by the hum of the fridge and then the creaking of footsteps above us. I hope it's Daisy, unable to get back to sleep after a wee, and not Georgia eavesdropping at the top of the stairs.

'I was waiting for the right moment.' I press my hands flat on the table, fingers splayed, and focus on the gold band around my finger, and just then I picture our shotgun wedding, as Gary called it, where not a drop of alcohol passed my lips – the stuffy registry office of the Wood Green civic centre – Linda and Zelda, bridesmaids next to me. Tom's mate, Toby, by his side in a too tight navy suit – my protruding belly – I was definitely showing by then. And then a table for twenty at the Apollo restaurant in Bayswater where everyone got pissed apart from me. 'But you were bereaved and…'

'Don't you dare use my aunt as an excuse for your lies,' he roars. I look at the ceiling, imagining Daisy sitting up in bed, listening, kindle in hand, wondering what a psycho family she's got herself mixed up with.

'I'm sorry,' I whisper. 'It's just that you warned me off Liam and I didn't know how to…' And then suddenly a thought rockets into my head and the reins pull on my vocal cords. 'Hang on a minute.' Cocking my head, I press my torso against the edge of the wooden table and narrow my eyes. 'You said Frank told you everything last Saturday, sent you the photo. You've known about Liam for almost a week, yet carried on as normal. You even wanted to fuck me just now on the staircase.' I glower at him. 'So why the sudden incredulity?'

Tom's face tightens. 'I thought he was lying. I thought you were going to deny it,' he says through gritted teeth. 'I've been going crazy since I found out. I couldn't even discuss it with anyone. In the end, I convinced myself you'd bumped into your ex and that clown took a photo of you and *him* to cause trouble between us because, let's face it, it's obvious you didn't want him dating Zelda.'

I nod fanatically. 'You're absolutely spot on.' Holding my hands up, I swallow hard. 'Frank's a vindictive liar. I've known him for weeks, remember? Long before any of you guys met him.'

'Only this time he wasn't lying, was he?' Tom says dryly. 'This time he was telling the naked truth.'

Chapter 43

'No, Tom, you've got it wrong,' I insist. 'Frank's a liar, he was...'

'Jesus, does a word of truth ever come out of your mouth?' Tom cuts across me. 'Dad was right about you all along.' Right about what? What did Gary say about me, the fucking arsehole. I told you he's never liked me. 'Do you know what I think, Bella?' I do a little shaky head thing, almost like a tremor. 'I think you're only saying all this now because you got caught.' I shake my head to and fro, to and fro. 'I don't think you were ever going to tell me about Liam.' *No, no, no. I was!* 'I think you were going to just carry on letting me think I'm Georgia's dad.' His words come at me like sharp knives. 'Because God forbid anyone tries to ruin your perfect life.'

'You've got it all wrong,' I retort, fresh tears blurring my vision. 'If only you'd let me explain, I....'

He raises his palm to shut me up, takes a gulp of cognac and swishes it around in his mouth like a rinse. I bite the flesh inside my bottom lip to stop myself from bawling. 'Okay, I admit I've been a bit economical with the truth.' I pause, tap my fingers against the table nervously. My entire body is trembling. 'But I was only trying to protect you.'

Tom raises an eyebrow. '*Oh, Please.*'

'Just give me a chance to tell you what happened. The truth. And why Frank is trying to destroy our marriage.'

'Bit late for that.'

'Please hear me out.' Tom shrugs as if to say, go on then, then takes another big gulp of cognac.

I take a deep, shaky breath and begin – I hired Frank as my personal trainer, didn't tell him because I knew he'd blow a gasket about his fees. But I needed to get into shape. It was important to me. I was beginning to feel invisible. I was putting on weight, getting saggy, feeling low. 'We were getting on brilliantly and then one day he tried it on with me.' Tom looks incredulous. 'Tried to kiss me. I pushed him away; told him I was happily married. But he wouldn't take no for an answer. That's why I quit the gym.'

'Another lie,' Tom groans, 'why am I not surprised?'

'On the day we went to Linda and Theo's, I found him outside our house.' Tom gives me a sharp look. 'And before you say anything, I didn't give him our address. He got *Serval's* assistant to look it up on the system. He told me he was returning my boxing gloves but then tried to persuade me rejoin the gym, called his come-on a misunderstanding. Gave me some sob story about his landlord putting up the rent. God, that man spends money like water. I don't know where he gets it from. Maybe he's an escort.' I laugh lightly but Tom is looking at me as if he wants to kill me.

'Anyway,' I continue, 'when I refused, he completely lost it.' Tom frowns. 'He was scary, intimidating. Later that night, low and behold, he turns up with Zelda on his arm.' I exhale a trembly breath. 'Frank is clever, Tom.' I wipe a tear that is curving over my cheek. 'Everything he does is calculated. Planned.'

'Have you quite finished?'

'Yes,' I say, wiping my nose with the back of my arm. 'Well, say something then.'

Tom snorts and looks at me in a way he never has before. The chair grazes against the tiles as he shoots to his feet and marches out of the kitchen. 'Nice try,' he yells over his shoulder. 'Frank's version is almost identical, only the roles were reversed.'

Shit, he doesn't believe me. Getting to my feet, I take a few breaths, holding onto the backrest of the chair for support because I'm not sure I can trust my legs to hold me up. I can hear Tom clattering around in the front room, the thud of the sideboard drawers – *slam, slam, slam* – his heavy footfall, and then a drone of voices – he's turned the TV back on.

Creeping back into the living room, I slide onto the seat next to him as he stares at the screen, face ablaze, lips a downward curved line.

'Tom.' I go to touch his arm but he tuts and shakes me off. 'I'm not leaving until we've discussed this,' I say smoothly, sounding braver than I feel. 'Everything that Frank told you is a lie.' He gives me a sharp look. 'An exaggeration of the truth,' I correct. 'Yes, he earwigged on my conversation with Liam at the café, but he doesn't know the facts – took everything at face value and added lots of spice, and as for me fancying him. Pfft, fat chance.'

Tom looks at the remote on the coffee table. He's going to turn up the volume to drown out my voice, something he does to his mother when he wants her to shut up, something he knows I detest as much as Wendy does.

'Please, don't,' I say quietly, grabbing his hand mid-flow as he reaches for the remote. 'Okay, I'll tell you everything. The whole truth.' I follow his eyes to my hand, yellow wedding band gleaming on his finger, and that's when I spot it – an A4 white envelope on the shelf of the coffee table. It wasn't there before. I'm a hundred per cent certain of it because the latest copy of Good Housekeeping was in its place. That's what all that opening and closing of drawers in the kitchen was about – he was looking for something. This.

I peer at it discretely. It looks official. Is he going to serve me with divorce papers? Is that why he didn't confront me about this for almost a week? Was he biding his time? Sorting out the paperwork? I don't know what to do. I can't breathe. I can't focus.

'Ouch,' Tom groans, and I notice that my nails are digging into his flesh. I let go. 'I was going to mute it,' Tom clarifies, rubbing the imprint of my half-moon fingernails on his skin. 'Go on then,' Tom says coldly, throwing a glance at the 1950s style sunburst clock on the wall. 'Say what you've got to say. It's getting late. I'm tired. I want to be in a fit state to do my eye examination in the morning.'

I fill my lungs with his cognacy breath and look at the glass in his hand. 'I could do with some of that.'

Tom hands me the drink. 'Knock yourself out.'

I take a gulp, ignoring the cough syrup taste as the liquid burns my mouth and slithers down my throat. 'Thanks.'

Tom rubs his eyes with his fists tiredly, then rests his forearms on his thighs, legs wide apart and looks up at me. 'Well?' He glances at the clock again. 'I haven't got all night.'

I clear my throat. 'I *was* unfaithful to you. I slept with Liam.'

Chapter 44

'It was just the once, not long after we met,' I say as Tom continues to glare at me. 'In hindsight, it was a stupid thing to do, but I was missing him – everyone kept telling me to stop pining for him, to concentrate on my future. I wish I'd listened.' I pause, waiting for a reaction. Tom tugs at the loose skin of his thumbnail with his index finger. He can't even bear to look at me. I plough on. 'Liam begged me to go back to him, promised marriage, children. I felt wanted, special, my life would be complete. I went back to his – stayed the night. It was the weekend you were at that Stag do in Manchester.'

Tom nods, 'Toby's. That didn't last long.' No, it didn't. They divorced six months later.

'I regretted it immediately, and that's when I realised I was no longer in love with him. I told Liam I'd met someone else. Someone kinder, stronger, stable.' Tom gives me a watery smile. I inch closer. I can feel his body heat. 'Liam seemed to take it in his stride.' I don't mention that he got out of bed, hopped into his jeans and slammed the door behind him so hard that I thought the entire building was going to collapse. 'I doubt very much he meant all those things he said to me before we got into bed.' Tom grimaces, takes a glug from his glass. 'I'm sorry, Tom, I shouldn't have done that to you, but it was early days. We hardly knew each other. I thought we were a fling. How was I to know we'd end up getting married?' I comb a hand through my hair.

'Anyway, I never heard from Liam again, until he looked me up online. I don't even know why I responded to his stupid message. I think I was just being nosey. Wanted to find out how his life had panned out. Show off about mine.' I laugh sourly. 'He hasn't aged well. But then he was into all sorts.' I stare at the A4 envelope, wishing I had x-ray eyes. 'I thought he might've mellowed over the years. People do, don't they?' I muse. 'He certainly seemed like he had, from the messages, I mean.'

Tom follows my eyes to the A4 envelope but says nothing. 'I honestly believed Liam wanted a friendly catch up. But, of course, he had an ulterior motive, which didn't come to light until I told him we couldn't continue messaging because you weren't okay with it.' I look at the glass in Tom's hand. If he grips it any tighter I'm sure it'll smash.

'Then the truth came out. Liam had been stalking me online for quite some time and found out I had a fifteen-year-old daughter.' I inhale deeply, shake my head. I feel so ashamed. 'He did a bit of maths and asked me if she was his. He never was good at arithmetic.' I smile sadly. 'I told him Georgia was your child, that he got his dates wrong.' I roll my eyes but Tom doesn't flinch. 'Anyway, he wouldn't have it – threatened to get his solicitor onto me if I didn't agree to a paternity test.'

'And did you?'

'That's when we met up at the cafe – he showed me the kit with the instructions. I promised I'd do it and send it off, then text him the results – he refused, didn't trust me, wanted to meet Georgia, get a sample of her hair, or something.' Tom stiffens. 'It never happened,' I say firmly. 'I'd never do that to our daughter.' My eyes widen. 'Or to you,' I add hastily. Tom knocks back the last dregs from his glass, places it on the coffee table, and lets out a painful breath through his nostrils. 'In the end, he agreed to let me do it.' I close my eyes. 'Provided he watched.'

'Watched?' Tom leaps to the edge of his seat, hand balled on his knee.

I should stop now but I can't. I've got to tell him everything. 'I dropped Georgia off at school, as usual. Just before she got out, I told her I needed a cheek swab for a new Covid variant.' Tom looks at me, eyes full of curiosity, or is it shock? I can't be certain.

'Liam parked up behind us and watched me do it.' I pause, swallow, 'I put it in the phial and once she was out of sight, I shot out, rounded the car, and handed it to him, with strict instructions to never, ever contact me again.'

'And he was all right with that, was he?'

I shrug. 'The agreement was, if the results were negative, he'd leave me alone.'

'Pathetic wanker,' Tom mutters.

'I toyed with the idea of binning the test, but I couldn't take the risk of him taking action – putting Georgia through it – dragging her through the courts. It wasn't worth it. This is an important school year for her. I couldn't…I didn't…'

'Okay, okay, I get it.' Tom picks up his glass, realises it's empty and puts it down again. 'Did he get the result he wanted?'

'Obviously not. I haven't heard from him.' I snort, give him a sideward glance. 'Georgia is a Harris, Tom, through and through. You've got to believe me. Liam is *not* her father.'

'And you're a hundred-per-cent sure of that, are you? I don't answer. Is anyone one hundred percent certain of anything? 'Thought not.'

'No, wait, I...'

'And it was just a one-night-stand sixteen years ago?' Tom interjects.

'*Yes*. As soon as I...'

'No affair?'

'I swear on Georgia's life.'

Tom scratches his chin. 'Then or since.'

'*No*!'

'Okay.' Tom exhales at the muted screen. 'I believe you.' *Thank you, God.* Leaning my head back on the headrest, relief washes over me, and then I feel something on my lap. It's the A4 envelope. It is sealed and addressed to Mr T. Harris. 'Open it,' he dares, a coldness seeping from his skin and penetrating mine.

'What is it?' I gulp, glancing down at it with trepidation. It's the divorce papers. We will sell the house. Go our separate ways. Georgia will have to flit between two parents. My eyes skim over the envelope. Normal post – second class — nothing suspicious about it at all.

'Go on,' he urges, 'open it.' I go to pick it up and then, 'But before you do, I want you to know one thing. The contents in that envelope change nothing. You, me and Georgia, we'll always be a family, okay?' I nod, eyes stinging with tears. At least he wants an amicable separation. We will be like my friend Rosie and her ex-husband Peter. They still go away together as a family. They even stay at each other's houses during the Christmas and Easter holidays and bring their respective new partners along. One big happy family. I don't think I could do that. I don't think I could bear to see Tom with another woman.

I tear the envelope open with tremulous fingers and pull out two sheets of paper. The heading is in big, bold black writing – Alpha Omega Diagnostics. My eyes flit over the contact details, a London address. I start reading.

DNA Test Report

Name of Child: Georgia Hannah Harris.

Alleged Father: Thomas Joseph Harris.

Every hair on my skin stands on end. *What the hell?* My eyes scan the report — rows and rows and rows of numbers and letters and graphs swim in my vision.

'I used Georgia's toothbrush.' No wonder she couldn't find it on Tuesday morning. He didn't utter a word when she accused me of using it and chucking it in the bin. 'Ordered the kit online. A courier dropped it off at the practice, picked it up the next day. It only took forty-eight hours. I couldn't open it. I was going to burn it tonight, without reading it. Georgia is *my* daughter, whether she shares my DNA or not. She means the world to me. Sperm doesn't make you a dad. There's no way I'm going to let that lowlife take her from me.' I nod, eyes filling with fresh hot tears. 'But for us to move forward, I had to be sure that there was no affair because you must admit, you have been acting weird lately – disappearing in the middle of the night, hushed phone calls in the bathroom.' If only he knew they were with Linda and Zelda discussing Frank.

'I promise you, Tom.' I place a hand on my heart. My celestial being jumps up and down with joy – he doesn't want a divorce. 'There's been no affair, no relationship.'

'Okay. And there's nothing else I should know?'

I stare at him in a daze. Yes, there is, actually. I may be an accomplice to attempted murder. My sister stabbed her boyfriend and I got rid of the weapon she used to kill him with. I might rot in prison and you will have to bring up Georgia on your own.

'Well?' he says.

I fiddle with my wedding ring. He's giving you another chance, Bella. Don't fuck it up. Tell him. Tell him everything. Rid yourself of this burden. He'll understand. Look at how well he's taken the news about Liam. 'No,' I hear myself say, voice hoarse. I can't betray my sister.

Tom's eyebrows shoot up. 'You don't sound too sure.'

I swallow. 'No,' I say firmly, sitting up straight. 'There's nothing else.'

He nods at the papers in my hand. 'Go on then, put me out of my misery.'

I shake my head. A big tear splashes from my eye and lands on the report as I read it. 'Oh, Tom,' I cry, clamping a hand over my mouth.

Tom's eyes fill. 'Shhh…it's okay.' He pulls me to him and I sob onto his chest. 'It's okay. We're a team. We'll get through this.' Taking the papers from my limp grasp, he scrunches them into a ball. 'I love Georgia with every part of me. Nothing will break our bond.' A beat and then, 'We will have to tell her, though. It's only fair. She might want to meet him.'

Pulling away from him, I take the papers from his hand, unfurl them, and read the result again before handing it to him:

Probability of Paternity – 99.9998%

Chapter 45

We're snuggled together on the sofa, watching a rerun of *Would I Lie to You* on Dave. The barely audible cackle of laughter and the buzz of the panel's voices fill the soothing silence. With the exception of Tom getting up briefly to make us both a Vodka Martini to celebrate the news, we haven't moved an inch. I moved through that period of tiredness. Makeup sex might've had something to do with that, and I'm now awake and alert. Tom is high as a kite. It's almost as if he's become a father again for the first time.

'Shall we go up?' Tom's voice breaks into my thoughts. 'It's almost one in the morning.'

'In a minute.' I snuggle closer to him, not wanting this moment to end.

Tom sighs. 'I meant what I said,' he says, playing with my hair. 'It wouldn't have made a difference if Georgia wasn't mine. But God, it's a relief to know she is, do you know what I mean?' I murmur in agreement. 'Your hair's grown. I like it. Why don't you leave it long again?'

'I like this length.' I look up at him indignantly. 'Don't you like it?'

'Of course I do. You always look lovely.' Even with all the fat I've accumulated? I don't think so. But I take the compliment and snuggle against him, hearing the soft rhythm of his heartbeat, feeling the rise and fall of his chest. 'I knew you'd tell me, you know. That's why I held on to the DNA report.' He wraps his arms around me, chin resting on my head. 'You're rubbish at keeping secrets from me.'

'Hmmm...' I murmur. Apart from one big, fat one that could give me a custodial sentence. 'I certainly...' I begin, and then there's a thunder of footsteps on the stairwell, followed by Georgia belting into the room, face flushed with anger.

'What the actual fuck?'

'Language,' I say, pulling away from Tom.

'What is it, Georgie?' Tom asks, tucking his shirt back into his trousers quickly. 'Why aren't you asleep?'

'Flies,' I mime, dropping my gaze and Tom quickly does up his zip, while Georgia's eyes dart around the room wildly, muttering obscenities – she can't fucking believe it – we're so fucking lame. I just about manage to grab my bra off the seat next to me and shove it behind the cushion before she averts her gaze back to us. She nods at our cocktails on the coffee table. 'How many of those have you two had?' She looks at her phone. 'It's gone one. I thought you were still out.'

'We've been home ages,' I say. 'Didn't you hear us come in?'

Georgia readjusts her silky blonde hair, which she's loosely tied into a bun on top of her head, face set in annoyance. 'I fell asleep watching TV.' She eyes me up and down suspiciously. 'It's ridiculously late. Shit, man.'

Tom gets to his feet, hands on hips. 'Calm down, Georgie. We're the parents, not you. And less of all that swearing. That's not how we brought you up.' He side-glances me. 'This is all that lad's influence from number nineteen.' He throws a finger in the direction of the front door. 'Rebellious little shit. Did you hear the lip he was giving his mother the other day?'

'Ralf's not that bad,' I protest, 'Anna's a good disciplinarian. He's at that age.'

'Why aren't you picking up your bloody phones?' Georgia demands. Her eyes flit from me and rest on Tom, narrowing in irritation.

Tom sits back down and peers at his handset on the coffee table. 'Nothing on mine. Oh, wait. Two missed calls earlier. I had it on silent.'

'Mine was switched off,' I admit. Tom's suggestion so that we could enjoy the evening without interruption. 'Were you trying to get a hold of us, Georgie?' I stand up and go over to her. 'Is everything all right? You're not ill, are you?' I go to touch her forehead but she ducks like a professional boxer.

'Mother, can you please put your phone back on?' she snaps, looking straight ahead at a bronze sculpture of a naked woman on the sideboard. A housewarming gift from Mum, which none of us really like. 'Auntie Zelda and Linda have been driving me nuts all night.' My heart stops. Why have they been phoning Georgia? It must have something to do with Frank. My pulse quickens. 'Jesus, you two. I'm not your fuuuc...' Tom gives her a look and the F word dies on her lips. 'I'm not your personal assistant. Grrr...I hate my life.'

Georgia stomps across the room, then collapses onto the sofa as far away as possible from her dad and starts texting, hands flying over the lit-up screen frantically. Acid whooshes in my stomach. Something is very wrong. Snatching my bag off the floor, I unzip it hurriedly, pull out my phone and switch it back on. The white apple flashes and then my phone buzzes and buzzes and buzzes – 10 missed calls from Zelda. 6 missed calls from Linda. 12 new messages.

Linda:

Message 1 – *Bells, please pick up.*
2 – *Where are you?*
3 – *Ring me now. Urgent.*
4 – *Pls call asap. William sniffing.*

William is our code for Old Bill. A wave of fear washes over me and merges with the nausea that is swishing in my stomach. The police have been round to Linda's. Frank must've reported us, or worse still, been found *dead*. I quickly retrieve Zelda's messages with cold, tremulous fingers.

Message 1 – *Bella. Please. Where are you?*
2 – *Pick up!!!!*
3. *I'm ringing Tom.*
4 – *Bloody answerphone.*
5 – *Georgia says you're not back.*
6 - *Call me NOW!!!*
7 - *It's URGENT.*
8 - *At police station. They've brought me in for questioning.*

A chill runs charges through my body. Zelda's been arrested. It's over. I need to contact Sean, our solicitor. I open my Contacts app and start scrolling.

'Bella, what is it?' Tom's voice.

'I've got to ring Sean…I…' The handset shakes in my trembling hands.

'It's the middle of the night. You can't ring him now. What's happened?'

'Zelda, she's at the station and…I…'

'Oh, the police came round,' Georgia says, matter-of-factly.

Our heads snap up in synchronisation. 'The *police*?' Tom says, incredulously.

'When? What did they say?' I ask in a panicky voice. '*Georgia*, what did they say?' I demand, and Tom gives me a look.

'All right. Keep your hair on, Mother. About nineish.' Georgia's eyes don't leave her phone. 'Daisy spoke to them. I think they were looking for you, Mum.'

Getting to his feet, Tom shoves his hands into his pockets, shooting a worried glance at me. 'Why is Zelda at the police station, Bella, and why do the police want to question you? What did she say in her texts? Has Frank been back? Did he hurt her?'

'No. I don't know,' I whimper, waving the phone at him as if Zelda will materialise from it like a genie and back me up. 'I've got to go to her.' I start rifling through my bag. 'Where are my car keys?'

'Bella, you've just knocked back a large vodka martini. You're in no fit state to drive. Is she still there?'

'I'm not sure,' I mumble absently. 'She must be. Oh, here they are…' I shoot to my feet.

'Everything okay?' Daisy is standing in the doorway in a new dressing gown. It's a pink fleece and has her initial on the breast pocket.

'Oh, Daisy, I hope we didn't wake you,' I say, even though I know we did. Daisy shakes her head. 'Georgia said the police were here earlier.'

Daisy nods. 'They asked if you were home and if I knew where Zelda lived. I said no, of course. I'm no grass.' She says this in a tone suggesting that Zelda and I are criminals and that she is on our side because she's cut from the same cloth. Tom stiffens next to me. I want to die. 'I told them I'm the new home help, don't know a thing.' Daisy shrugs, glances at her nails, which are freshly manicured. Tom nods, tells her she did right by not getting involved in our family affairs, and she blinks, throws him a tight smile. 'They gave me this.' She fishes in her pocket and pulls out a business card and hands it to me. 'Said if you could give them a call in the morning.' I look at the card – DC Pernice. 'Are you okay, Bella? You've gone very pale.'

Georgia looks up from her phone, tells me to get some sleep, that I'm not getting any younger. Daisy gently reprimands her, reminds her that fifty is the new thirty. I'm not quite fifty yet, I want to say, but gnaw my thumbnail instead. Frowning, Tom gives me a worried look, then turns up the volume on the TV. It's a newsflash. 'Look, it's that man they found in Limes Park last Monday.' Man? What man? 'I heard it on the radio this morning. Only up the road from Zelda's. They must've identified him. Poor sod. I knew he'd…'

Tom is talking but I'm no longer listening, something about Georgia, football and parks and never letting her go out alone again. I turn my head towards the TV in a daze, as if everything has stopped - time, my pulse, movement. The headlines, in bold white font against a thick red strip at the bottom of the screen, sway in my vision – *Limes Park Murder Investigation.* It must be Frank's body. I look at Daisy, who is now sitting on the armrest of Georgia's chair, then at Tom. His lips are moving, but I can no longer decipher what he's saying. A message buzzes through on my phone. I look down at it in horror.

Zelda – *It's all over. I'm done 4.x*

Chapter 46

I race into the kitchen, leaving Tom glued to the news, and Daisy and Georgia discussing a dance on TikTok that's gone viral. I've got to find out what's happened to my sister. With tremulous hands, I ring Zelda. It goes to voicemail. I press redial again and again and again, then ring her landline. I wait and wait and wait, and then, 'Heya…'

'Oh, Zelda, thank God they've let you go.' I give the kitchen door a light kick with my bare foot, drowning out the girls' voices. 'I've...'

'Sorry, I'm out. Leave a message.'

Bloody answering machine. Where the hell is she? Still in custody? Surely, they can't detain her without any evidence. I'm about to phone Linda when there's a loud thud on the front door, followed by the shrill of the bell. Acid rams into my stomach. It's the police. They've come to arrest me too.

Opening the door a crack, I peek around it and watch as Tom pads into the hallway. The back of his shirt is sticking out and he shoves it back in as he reaches for the latch. Any moment now, armed police officers will barge into my house and handcuff me. I squeeze my eyes shut to the clunk of the front door being wrenched open.

'Gregory. Everything okay, mate?' It's Mr Stanhope – not the police. Relief slithers through my veins and I let out a little sigh. We're too loud, of course we are. The poor man can't sleep. I glance at the time on my phone – 01.16. We're lucky he hasn't contacted noise pollution. With my back against the door, I cock my head, lips apart, focusing on the shiny Ninja air-fryer I recently bought online, another of Daisy's recommendations, they're quicker and healthier and, to Tom's delight, cheaper than an electric oven. Their voices are low. Tom must be apologising, telling him that he didn't realise how late it was.

'It was my duty,' Mr Stanhope says loudly. Duty? He must've rung the council, after all. 'I couldn't lie to the police.' Police? My eyes widen as a second bout of fear grips my lungs. Dropping my phone onto the kitchen table, I race to the front door.

'Ah, there she is,' Mr Stanhope says, as if I'm his long, lost cousin. His light brown hair, threaded with white, is neat and side-parted, he's cleanly shaven and wearing a caramel shirt beneath a brown V-neck sweater. Mr Stanhope always dresses smartly, even at home.

'Mr. Stanhope, I…' He gives me a look, sucking in his cheeks, one hand in his beige slacks. He constantly reprimands me for calling him by his surname, but it's a hard habit to break. 'Greg, I..' Another look. And then I remember that only his ex-wife, who cheated on him repeatedly during their thirty-year marriage, calls him Greg. 'Gregory, I'm sorry if we were a bit too loud but we …'

Closing his eyes, Mr Stanhope raises his palm and inclines his head. 'I'm not here about the noise, Bella. Although, I must say, the television is unacceptably loud.'

'Yes, of course. I'm sorry,' I mutter. 'It won't happen again. We were out tonight and Georgia fell asleep with…'

'He's here about Frank,' Tom interrupts, and my insides turn to mush. I hold onto the doorframe to stop myself from wobbling as laughter filters through from the living room.

'Oh. I see,' I manage, trying hard to look normal. A siren wails in the distance, travels through the midnight air like an umbilical cord and drills into my stomach. They're coming for me. They've detained Zelda, that's why she's not picking up. I wonder if they've arrested Linda too. Poor Linda. I will give a statement. I will say she had no involvement in this whatsoever. It's a Villin crime. 'What's happened?' I croak, clearing my throat. 'Is Frank all right?'

'I don't think so,' Mr Stanhope says, scratching his nose.

'What do you mean?' I ask, mouth drying. I throw Tom a look, his face is serious. *He knows, Bella. He knows. He knows. He's worked it out.* What have I done to my family? Two weeks ago, I was a normal, forty-nine-year-old mother, wife, businesswoman, and now I'm a lying, cheating, criminal.

'As I explained to Tom just now, he's been missing for several days,' Mr Stanhope says in his nasally, eloquent tone. 'Didn't show up at work, even though he had clients booked. *Serval's* manager said it's not like him at all.' They've spoken to Jane. My mouth fills with saliva. I swallow it back. Where is he? *Please God don't let him be in the mortuary.* 'And now the police have said…' He weaves his fingers and presses his hands against his chest as if he's delivering a church sermon. 'I'm sorry to call round so late but I thought you'd want to know the news as soon as.' *Sweet Jesus*, Frank *is* the Limes Park victim. Zelda has murdered him. 'I did try earlier but…' Mr Stanhope pauses, coughs into his hand. 'There was no one in.' He looks at me in a way that suggests someone was in but they wouldn't answer the door. 'I heard voices not long ago. I thought it best to deliver the news myself rather than you hear it from someone else.'

'Yes, of course,' Tom says, face grave. 'Thank you, Gregory.'

My eyes fill and I blink, inhale congested phlegm that is building up behind my nose. 'Gosh,' I manage. Tom fishes a tissue out of his pocket and hands it to me. 'How dreadful.' I blow my nose, then look at Mr Stanhope carefully as he and Tom discuss police procedures. Neither of them sounding very convincing.

Oh, Zelda, what've we done? We've behaved abominably. Callously. What if it was the drugs that made Frank lash out? We might've saved his life if we'd called for an ambulance. We're monsters. I can just hear the judge's sentencing now. *Bella Harris, you assisted in the demise of Frank Hardy in a cruel and ruthless act. I sentence you to...* Tom touches my arm, breaking me out of my reverie, asks if I'm okay.

'Yes, I'm fine, love. Just a bit shocked, to be honest.' I force a smile, folding my arms. In my peripheral, I see Mr Stanhope scrutinizing me with his small, round, grey eyes. I don't think he's ever really liked me. He looks up to Tom because he's a professional, but I get the feeling he thinks I bring down the tone of the neighbourhood, with my north London accent and working-class background.

'So, um...did they say why they wanted to speak to you in particular, Gregory?'

Mr Stanhope's expression hardens. I've offended him. He regards himself as a pillar of the community. The unofficial neighbourhood watch.

'What my wife means, Gregory, is why disturb our neighbours before speaking to us first. It is, after all, a family matter. Frank is Bella's sister's boyfriend.'

'Oh, no, they didn't call on me. They were just leaving your house, Bella, and I happened to be taking the bins out.' Yeah, right, at gone nine? Snooping more like. Malc and Suzy, from next door but one, had a pest control van parked outside their house last month. Mr Stanhope was out there like a shot, disposing of a carton of milk into the recycle bin.

'I asked one of the officers if everything was okay,' he goes on. 'If I could help at all, explained how I knew the family well.' The urge to slam the door in Stanhope's face, run to the bathroom and vomit in the toilet bowl grips me hard. 'They didn't tell me much, mind. I don't suppose they would disclose confidential information. But did ask if I'd seen your sister, knew of her whereabouts.' My legs are starting to shake. I'm not sure how long I can keep up this calm pretence. 'DC Pernice said whatever information I could provide would be most appreciated and off the record.' Corrupt police – why am I not surprised? 'I told them I know where Zel…'

'Right, I see,' I interrupt. I want him to leave now. Mr Stanhope barely knows Zelda. I think he's seen her a handful of times, exchanged nods, said hello, nothing more. Zelda isn't one for chitchat. 'Well, anyway…' My phone rings in the distance. I left it on the kitchen table. 'I'm sorry, Gregory. I've got to get that.'

I go to walk away when he says, 'I had to tell them about the altercation you had with Frank Hardy, Bella.' His words drive into the back of my head like darts. My phone continues to ring. 'It was on the eighth of March. I made a note of it in my diary, just in case.' I stand stock-still, face burning. *Just in case of fucking what?* I turn on my heel, wanting to drain every ounce of blood in my body for burning my face, for making me look guilty. 'What do you mean?' I look at Tom. He says nothing, lips a thin, dry line, creases on his face somehow deeper.

'I was saying to Tom, before you appeared.' Mr Stanhope pinches the bridge of his nose, then throws a hand out. 'I saw Mr Hardy here, Friday before last. The two of you were having words outside,' he clarifies, and everything dims, like the lights in a theatre. 'It seemed quite heated.' *Shut up, shut up, shut up.* 'And, if I'm honest, aggressive.' I'm glad I managed to tell Tom about Frank turning up, but I don't want Stanhope to think we were fighting because the police might see that as a motive. I want Stanhope to retract his story, tell the police he got it wrong. 'I'm sorry, Bella, but I had to tell them. I'm duty bound.'

I swallow what feels like a beach pebble in my throat. 'Gregory, that wasn't....' I look at Tom for support but his eyes have hardened. 'We weren't.'

'Wait, what exactly are you suggesting, Greg?' Tom thrusts his chest out and lunges forward, and Mr Stanhope backtracks, clearly intimidated by Tom. I squeeze my eyes tightly shut as they blast into a heated argument about witnesses and facts and the reliability of what you actually saw and what happened. Their voices drill into my ears, louder and louder and louder. I want them to stop. Please make them stop. I clamp my hands over my ears and then out of nowhere I blurt, '*Shut up.* A man has been *killed*.'

And then there's silence. They swivel their heads round and look at me, frozen. And I know, without a shadow of a doubt, that this is the beginning of the end. It has finally hit the fan.

Chapter 47

'Killed?' Mr Stanhope says, face pallid.

'Bella?' Tom's voice has a hint of a warning tone to it.

'Hang on just a moment. Are you saying Frank Hardy is dead?' Mr Stanhope asks. His manner is dark, suspicious. I don't like it. My mind is buzzing, spinning. Is this a trick question? Why is he saying this? Frank has been confirmed dead. He just said so. Didn't he? He's the Limes Park victim that was on TV just now. My sister is being held in custody for his murder. My eyes dart from Tom to Mr Stanhope, and for a moment they look like giants looming over me as I shrink into myself, wanting to fade, vanish.

'I…um…' Stanhope and Tom continue to look at me – waiting. 'I thought…' And then I hear an amplified roar of laughter from the TV in the living room. Someone has opened the door, and then the warmth of another body next to me and the aroma of perfume, strong and exotic.

'Everything okay?' Daisy asks, taking a bite of an apple. 'Gosh, what's with the long faces, who's died?' she says through a mouthful of fruit. I look round at her pleadingly, eyes stinging. She stops chewing, swallows, wipes the side of her mouth with her knuckle. 'Shit, has someone actually *died*?'

'Look, I think there's been some kind of...' Tom begins.

'It appears, Daisy,' Mr Stanhope says firmly, cutting across Tom like an opposition MP in the House of Commons. 'That Bella thinks Mr Hardy has been murdered.' I didn't say that. Why is he twisting things? Stanhope rubs his thin, dry lips with his finger, regarding me beneath knitted brows.

'Mr Hardy?' Daisy asks, bewildered. 'The actor!!!? Oh my God. I love him. He's only young. Shit, what happened? Was it cancer?' Her hand flies to her chest. 'Don't tell me it was suicide. So many artists can't take the pressure of trolling. I blame social...'

'Not the actor, Daisy,' Tom interjects, running a hand over his face, 'Frank.' Daisy frowns and her forehead creases. 'Zelda's Frank.'

Daisy makes an O shape with her lips, looks at me and blinks. 'No way? When?' She gasps, apple in hand.

'The police came round earlier,' Mr Stanhope clarifies, and Daisy shakes her head, said she'd spoken to them too. 'They were looking for Zelda, said her boyfriend was reported missing.' *Missing?* Not dead? A cocktail of relief, fear and panic rips through me.

'They didn't say anything about Frank to me. They just asked if Zelda was in and if I knew where she was,' Daisy says to Mr Stanhope, then looks at me and mouths *Sorry*. She thinks she's said too much. I tell her it's okay, that Mr Stanhope clearly knows more about the case than we do. 'They said they had this address for Zelda on their records?' Daisy shrugs.

'She lived with us for a while. When we first moved in.' Tom sighs loudly through his nostrils. 'She was in-between flats. Don't tell me she still hasn't updated her records?' Tom says to me, tiredly.

'It hasn't been that long.' I rub the back of my neck. 'You know what she's like.'

'I think we're missing the point here,' Mr Stanhope says, miffed. 'Bella, why would you think Mr Hardy is deceased?'

I swallow. All eyes are on me. 'I didn't mean him,' I stammer. I look at Tom for support but his face is blank. 'I was talking about that poor guy on the news just now.' I wave a hand in the direction of the blaring TV. 'The one found in Limes Park.' They continue to stare at me. Stanhope flicks a glance at Tom. He doesn't believe me. 'It really freaked me out. Sorry about the confusion.'

The silence is long and agonising, and then Tom says, 'Poor sod.' And the mood immediately softens, almost as if a switch has been flicked on. 'Limes is great during the day but at night…'

'I gave them her address, by the way,' Mr Stanhope announces, and our eyes rocket towards him. How could he possibly know where Zelda lives? 'I helped her move, remember?' he says, clearly noting my confusion. Of course, he did. Zelda had a lot of stuff, was low on cash, and Tom was too stingy to hire a man with a van, so asked Stanhope if he'd help transport some of her belongings in his VW estate. Zelda didn't even see him that day. I'm sure of it. She was inside rearranging furniture and unpacking boxes.

'I reckon Mr Hardy might be on the run,' Mr Stanhope says, 'they wanted to know if I'd seen him recently, how well I knew your sister, what she was like. I told them I knew her very well indeed.' *Liar.* 'That I was close friends with the family.' This man is unbelievable. 'Oh, they were all ears when I told them I'd been to Zelda's flat,' he chuckles smugly, rubbing his thumb and index finger together. 'She makes a lovely cup of tea, your sister, and her clementine hot-cross buns are exceptional.' So, not only did Zelda see Stanhope, she invited him in for tea and bloody cake. 'I explained that she was a baker by trade, ran her own business and that she struck me as an open-minded person.' He cocks his head and bends slightly forward. 'A free spirit, if you like, but feisty with it.' Very perceptive of him. I couldn't have described her better myself. 'A bit standoffish, if I'm honest, but pleasant once you get to know her.' I bet she barely spoke to him.

'Did they mention anyone else?' Such as Linda or me? *Please say no.*

'Only if Zelda had mentioned any of Frank's friends. If Diane or Nina rang a bell. I said, no, of course. I wouldn't dream of prying.' I try hard to stop my eyebrow from arching. 'When I asked them if he was in some sort of trouble, they shut down.'

'Nina,' I repeat, then turn to Tom. 'Isn't that the girlfriend that died?'

Mr Stanhope takes a sharp intake of breath. Tom nods. 'He told us about her over dinner at Theo and Linda's, remember? Said she was ill.'

'Actually, no, he didn't say that,' I contradict, 'he told us she'd died suddenly, not the cause of death.'

'Bloody hell,' Daisy says, 'a dead-ex?'

Mr Stanhope is looking at us aghast. 'They did ask me to call them if I had any new information,' he says to no one in particular, a note of glee in his voice. 'And, of course, now I'll have to if you say his ex-girlfriend mysteriously died.'

For fuck's sake, why does he have to twist everything I say? 'No, I…Nina…'

'He told us Nina had died but that doesn't mean it's true,' Tom suggests, coming to my rescue. 'Maybe she dumped him and he wanted a bit of sympathy from us.' He waves a hand out. 'Maybe she's dead to him – metaphorically.'

'Or she might be actually dead,' Daisy pipes up. 'He might've killed her.'

Chapter 48

'Now, let's not get ahead of ourselves, Daisy. This isn't Crime Watch,' Tom laughs lightly, giving her a reproving look. 'I'd leave it to us now, Gregory,' he adds smoothly. 'We'll speak to Zelda and update the police with any new information in the morning.' Mr Stanhope goes to protest but Tom cuts across him. 'She might've heard from Hardy by now, know where he is. Let's gather all the facts first, yeah? You don't want to be wasting police time, pal.'

'Yes, yes, that's true,' Mr Stanhope says to my bare feet, which I can scarcely feel. The wind has eased but it's still bitter. I go to move when Stanhope looks up at me sharply. 'You will let me know what your sister says?'

'Of course,' I concede.

'Absolutely,' Tom says, at the same time.

I'm relieved that the police are only looking for Frank because a missing person's report has been lodged. But if they were only questioning Zelda about Frank's disappearance, why did she send me that sinister text just now?

'Yes, thank you, Gregory,' Tom says, 'for letting us know.' Tom takes Stanhope's hand and curls the other around his forearm, and they shake heartily.

'Bella, if you find out any information from you sister, do contact the police.' I nod, tell him I will. 'Perhaps this Diane the police mentioned might know something. Did you say you know her?' *Of course I don't know her. Why would I?* I open my mouth to tell him when a face matching the name begins to form in my mind. Frank has a client called Diane – late fifties, recently separated, tall, with very long blonde hair that was always up in a bun, and muscles to die for. Could it be her?

'No,' I say firmly, rubbing my arms as a shiver powers through me. It probably isn't her. 'I don't know her. I still can't get over the Limes Park victim. His poor family,' I add, and everyone murmurs in agreement.

'I've been following that story online,' Mr Stanhope says, 'what with it being a local crime.' How the three of us missed this important piece of information I will never know. We wouldn't make very good detectives. 'Actually…' Mr Stanhope holds his chin. 'Maybe I shouldn't say this.' But you will anyway. I cross my arms. I'm freezing. 'I only saw Mr Hardy twice, once outside, as I mentioned, and then again at your barbeque, over the fence. But there are similarities with the Limes' victim.' My guts spasm, sending a searing pain into my ribs. *No, please don't say it. Don't say it could be Frank. He's missing, that's all. Done a runner with Zelda's two grand.* 'The description the papers have given are quite fitting – age, build, colouring.'

Daisy gasps. 'Do you think it could be *him?* They were calling for witnesses on the news just now, asking anyone who thinks they might know him to come forward.'

'Nah,' Tom says, dislodging something between his teeth with his fingernail, 'The Limes' guy is smaller. Hardy is built like a pit-bull.' I close my eyes, *thank God.*

Tom sniffs the air repeatedly like a hound. 'Can you smell that?' he asks, swiftly changing the subject.

We all start sniffing, noses twitching. 'I can't smell anything,' I say, and Daisy agrees, then sniffs the edge of her dressing gown, asks if it's ylang-ylang because she just smashed a bottle of it in the sink. The shelf collapsed. So, that's what the loud crash was earlier. 'I'll pay for a new one,' Daisy offers sheepishly. 'I overloaded it with Aldi finds. Sorry.'

'It's okay, Daisy,' I say, and Tom gives me a look. 'That shelf has been loose for weeks.' I've been nagging Tom to fix it, to no avail. 'I'll get a handyman in to repair it.'

'I'll fix it next week,' Tom insists. But we both know that won't happen.

'There's a whiff of bonfire,' Mr Stanhope offers. 'It's that couple at number thirty-eight. They're always burning stuff.'

Tom sniffs repeatedly. 'No, it isn't smoke. It's something else. Oh, there is it again.'

We all shake our heads. 'Might be your aftershave,' I suggest, wishing they'd all disappear so that I can go into my garden office and ring Linda for an update.

'No. It smells like my auntie Andriana.'

I smile. 'She always wore musk, didn't she?' Our house reeked of it for hours after she'd visit.

'Musk, yes,' Tom says excitedly.

I sniff the air again. 'But I can't smell it.'

'It's definitely musk,' Tom murmurs. 'Look, sorry. I'm going to have to go. I need to google something.' Tom's crafty excuse to leave.

'That's a very attractive crucifix you have there,' Stanhope says to Daisy as Tom disappears into the kitchen, 'that ruby is quite unusual. I dabble in antiques. Is it a real piece?'

'I should think so,' Daisy scoffs, stroking it with a slender finger. 'My mother bought it for me when I was an infant.' Poor Daisy. She always wells up when she mentions her mum.

'Daisy.' Georgia's voice echoes from the living room. 'Come and see this. Quick.' And Daisy is saved by Georgia.

'Nice to finally meet you, Gregory,' Daisy says chirpily. 'Better get back to Georgia,' she whispers to me, hand on my shoulder.

'Likewise,' Mr Stanhope calls out to Daisy's back. And then we're alone. 'Anyway, best get back to Arthur.' Mr Stanhope's cat. 'He'll be wondering where I've got to. Have a good night, Bella.' Hands in pockets, he goes to turn and then stops mid-circle. 'And don't forget to let me know what your sister says about Mr Hardy.' He smiles, but I don't miss the flash of accusation in his eyes. 'Night night, Bella.'

I amble back into the kitchen and snatch up my phone from the table. Two missed calls and a voicemail from Linda. I press my phone against my ear and listen to her message – *she's sorry for not picking up earlier – Theo was hovering and watching her like a hawk. 'I can't say much now,'* A pause, an inhalation, must've been smoking, *'I'm in the garden having a quick fag.'* I knew it. *'But look, don't worry, it's all sorted. Zelda has... Oh, shit, he's coming out. I'll speak to you tomorrow. Sleep tight, Bells. Love you. Mwah.'*

Holding the phone to my chest, the reels in my head start spinning – why was Theo watching her so closely? Is he suspicious, or has he got a guilty conscious? He did go AWOL when he found out Linda had a one-night stand with Frank on the night Zelda stabbed him. That gives Theo a motive, doesn't it? Did he go out looking for Frank in the early hours of that morning? Did he find him injured and finish him off? A shudder runs through me and just then my phone buzzes in my hand with a text – Zelda:

1. *Total nightmare of a day. I'm okay. Haven't been arrested. Sorry about text before, it was meant to say, I'm done, as in I've left the police station. But cab went over a bump as I was typing and my finger slid upwards and accidentally hit the number 4 before typing a full stop. I didn't notice until now when I reread it.*

Thank God for that. I smile as I read her next message, thoughts of Theo murdering Frank and dumping him in a ditch dissolving.

2. *Frank reported missing. All is well-ish. Will explain tom.*

I'm about to reply when *typing* appears at the top of the screen. I wait it out and then another message buzzes through:

Can I use your office in morning? Neighbours have warned me of very loud building work – noise levels will be off the scale. They've made my flat intolerable to live in (an orange angry face emoji) *Need to catch up on invoices. Promise not to leave a mess.* The last time I left Zelda alone in my office I had to fish crisps out of my keyboard with tweezers for a week. *Know ur picking Mum up from Heathrow. Leave key in usual place if you're out early. No need to reply. Going to sleep now. Shattered. Speak tomoz.* Signed with an emoji kiss, a red heart, and two women with their arms wrapped around each other.

Chapter 49

'I'd change before leaving, if I were you,' Tom says, the next morning, as we're preparing breakfast. We move around the kitchen in synchronisation. Just as we have hundreds of times before. Only this time it's different. This time this thing, this invisible shield, hangs between us. I know what it is. It's the aftermath of my revelation about Liam. I learned early on in our marriage that Tom is one of those people who gets shocked into submission when they're insulted or mistreated, and then, when they've slept on it, rebel. But I don't rise to the bait.

'Do I stink?' I raise my left arm and sniff. 'All my shirts are in the wash.'

After our midnight drama with Stanhope, I left Tom in the kitchen googling phantom smells and went straight to bed. With a fitful sleep, I was the first one up this morning, slipped into my wide-legged trousers and blouse, which I was wearing all day yesterday, emptied the dishwasher, texted Mum about her flight home, fluffed up the cushions in the lounge and made a cooked breakfast for Georgia and Daisy. I then sat at the table and watched them ravish it, nursing a cup of tepid black coffee, barely registering what they were talking about – head full of Frank and Zelda and Liam.

'I'll spritz myself with that perfume Daisy bought me yesterday.' A thank you gift for everything we've done for her, from a boutique shop called *Icecube*. 'I haven't got time to wash and iron a blouse. I'll be late for my appointment.'

'I'd use something stronger if I were you,' Tom says, pulling out a carton of milk from the fridge. 'Those cheap scents don't last long.' I grimace but say nothing. 'You, okay?'

'Yes, why wouldn't I be?' I ask. Tom pulls a face, as if I'm being defensive. 'Are you doing a full day today?' I quiz, clearing up Georgia's empty plate off the table and chucking the bacon rind in the bin.

'Yep, back-to-back appointments.' He places two Weetabix biscuits into a white bowl. 'Roll on Sunday.'

'We need to slow down,' I muse. 'Maybe think of moving again. Somewhere quieter, greener.'

I flick the kettle on again, even though it's just boiled and Tom gives me a sideward glance, eyebrow raised as he splashes milk over his cereal.

'Move? After we've spent so much money on this place? That's just boiled, by the way,' he points out, screwing the cap back on the milk.

I busy myself with cups and tea bags. 'Hertfordshire is nice. Cheaper, too. We could pay off all our debts and still have money left over and…'

The milk carton hits the worktop so hard it makes me jump. Tom is looking at me through angry eyes, fists clenched against the worktop, skin taut against his knuckles. 'We agreed that we're not moving until I retire. For fuck's sake, Bella, you can't run away from your responsibilities. My work is here. Our families are here. Not to mention Georgia's private school.'

'Keep your hair on,' I say defensively, throwing a glance at the door. 'It was just a suggestion. And will you please keep your voice down. The girls are upstairs getting ready.'

'I'll do as I please, thank you very much. It's my house, even though it seems to have turned into a bloody hotel.'

'What's that supposed to mean?' I retort, 'You're the one who hired Daisy and agreed to let her stay. Why are you being weird? I thought you liked her.'

'*Excuse me?*' he says indignantly. 'I'm not the one who…'

'Sorry,' a voice says, and we both swivel our heads towards the door. 'Hope I'm not interrupting anything,' Daisy says, face pink. She's standing there awkwardly in her new pink bathrobe looking beautiful and angelic.

'No, of course you're not, love,' I say, praying she didn't hear Tom calling our house a hotel. 'Is everything okay?'

Daisy wrings her hands, takes a step forward, shooting a quick look at Tom. She heard everything. Tom pulls out his phone and scrolls through it, glancing up at Daisy with mild irritation.

'Um… I wanted to let you know that I've found a job. It's at a car dealership in Brentford. Money is good, great perks. Cars are top of the range. Prestigious clientele.'

'Right,' I manage, hoping it's true and that she's not just saying this because of Tom's hostile remark. 'Well, that's wonderful, Daisy. Congratulations.'

'I don't want to leave you in the lurch,' she says hurriedly. 'But they want me to start on Monday.'

'This Monday?' I exclaim, and she nods. 'It's a bit short notice, love. Maggie isn't due back for a few weeks.' I look at Tom for backup, but he just rolls his eyes.

'Oh look, don't worry. Forget I said anything. I'll turn it down. I…'

'No, it's okay, sweetheart,' I say, coming to my senses. I can't stand in her way because of my own selfish needs. This is a brilliant opportunity for her. 'You must accept it. It was just a bit of a shock, that's all.'

'Will you be moving out too?' Tom asks.

'Tom,' I snap, giving him a sharp look. 'You can stay as long as you like, Daisy.'

Daisy laughs lightly. 'It's okay. I know I've overstayed my welcome.' *No, you haven't. I love having you around. We all do.* 'You guys have been saints, but...' she pauses, looks at Tom again. Is that unease I see in her eyes? 'I can't thank you enough.' I go to protest but she talks over me, 'I'm looking at two flats today. They sound really good. Fully furnished, close to amenities.'

'Oh, Daisy.' I go over to her. 'Only if you're sure, love.' She tells me that she's a hundred-per-cent sure, and after a brief chat about her new job and the properties she's viewing today, she's gone.

Chapter 50

'You could've been a bit more subtle,' I say to Tom, tone clipped, once Daisy's safely out of earshot.

'She can't stay here forever.' Tom adjusts himself in his seat. 'Look, we put the girl up, gave her a home, a job. We didn't know her from Adam.'

'That's beside the point. You were rude.'

'Rude? I'm not the one who's got the TV on all night.'

'Stop being a child,' I hit back.

'She charges up a billion appliances. And who has two showers a day?' I shake my head at him. I might've known it was about money. 'Do you know how many litres of water a shower pumps out per minute?' *No, but I think I'm about to find out.* 'Twenty,' he exclaims. 'Twenty,' he repeats for emphasis, *'per minute!'* I didn't realise it was as much as that. No wonder he's in and out in two ticks. 'She's in there for twenty minutes. That's four-hundred litres.' A pause, and then. 'Did you know she left her hair straightener thingy on and went out?' Georgia told me about that and I made her promise not to tell her dad, but she obviously did. I wonder why.

'Shhh,' I hiss, fishing a teabag out of a cup. 'Being pissed off with me about Liam doesn't give you the right to take it out on our poor temp. She's not your punch bag. I explained why I had to do what Liam wanted. What was I supposed to do, let him drag Georgie through the courts?'

'What you were supposed to do was tell me the truth.' Returning the milk to the fridge, he gives the door a hard slam. 'It's obvious you don't trust me,' he scoffs, sitting down at the table with a bowl of cereal that has turned to mush, hair sticking up.

'That's not fair.' Pulling out a chair, I sit down next to him, placing his T initial mug near the edge of the table. 'I really don't understand you sometimes. If you weren't okay about it, why didn't you say so last night?' I lower my voice and look at the door, 'Instead of wanting to have sex with me?' He doesn't answer. 'I'm not sure what else you want me to do.' More silence. 'Look, I thought we sorted all this out.' I lower my voice to a whisper. 'The test proves that you're…'

'It's not about that,' he snaps, blowing on his tea. 'I want to know what's going on with *Frank*.' His words ram into me like a bulldozer and I have to hold on to the edge of the table, even though I'm sitting down. 'Why did you tell Stanhope he was dead?'

'What?' I do a little laugh. 'I explained last night. I was talking about the Limes Park victim. Maybe I overreacted a bit. It's the menopause, making me all teary and emotional.' I look at his face for a reaction but he carries on eating his cereal, tapping at the screen of his iPad with his other hand. 'I cry at everything these days.' He slides a finger along the screen. 'So, it's the silent treatment, is it? I honestly don't know what's got into you this morning.' I take a sip of black tea. 'You're always ratty when you haven't had enough sleep.'

Tom looks up at me from his iPad. 'What's got into me? You're the one who's acting like the bloody gestapo.'

'You're being ridiculous,' I cry, my limbs buzzing with nerves.

'I'm being ridiculous now, am I?' he hisses, pinching the screen of his iPad and peering at a huge eyeball with a blister in it, which makes me recoil. 'On top of being rude, weird and a child?' And just then his phone lights up on the table and I looked at it instinctively. He jerks his head towards his phone. 'Pick it up,' he says through a mouthful of cereal. 'Go on. Read it,' he dares. I roll my eyes and he snatches the phone off the table and chucks it across to me. 'In fact, read all my texts, why don't you? Unlike you, I've got nothing to hide.'

'Stop acting like an idiot.' I'm on my feet, looming over him, arms folded. Another message flares and this time I manage to see who it's from. Dad – *I'll call you later.*

Picking his phone up, Tom points it at me. 'So, I'm an idiot now, am I? Any more insults you want to throw at me today?' he seethes, slipping his phone into the pocket of his pink shirt without reading the text. 'I don't think you're in a position to get all sanctimonious after the web of deceit you've weaved recently. And now Frank has vanished off the face of the earth. The police are coming round to our home. I mean, really, Bella?' His eyes are bulging. 'I'm not sure how much more I can take.'

My cheeks burn. 'I told you; I don't know where Fra…'

'Actually, stop.' Closing his eyes, he raises his hands, then pushes his chair back and stands up. 'The less I know about it the better.'

'You can't leave like this,' I cry, standing in front of him.

'Move.' His tone chills me to the bone. I step to the side and he shoots into the hallway, thrusting a hand through his sticky up hair, all the while droning on about a busy day ahead – a staff meeting, followed by Mrs Shahid's conjunctival cyst, won't even have time for a bloody lunch break.

'Then stay and finish your breakfast. *Tom.*' I barrel after him.

Outside, he unlocks his car and throws his stuff on the back seat as I launch into a pathetic, pleading monologue – I hate it when we fight - I do trust him – why is he being so arsy with me. 'Look, I don't know anything about Frank's disappearance,' I insist, which is true. 'And neither does Zelda.'

'Isn't she due round?' Tom throws a look up at the house. I tell him that's the plan. She'll be working from the garden office. 'Right, well, make sure she's gone by the time I get home.' My hand shoots to my chest and I take a step back as he folds himself into the car. Why doesn't he want Zelda in our house? 'Don't insult my intelligence, Bella, I know you're involved in something illegal.' A shiver rips along my spine, rendering me speechless.

'But Zelda…' I gulp.

'I'll talk to you tonight. I'm running late.' Revving the engine, he looks at me, chewing the inside of his bottom lip, as if he's about to say something but isn't sure. I take a step closer and curl my hands around the open window, bending slightly, but then he seems to snap out of it, flicks a glance at the house again with tired, red-rimmed eyes and puts the car into drive.

'What time will you be…'

'I dunno,' he cuts across me. 'I'll message you later.' I watch from the edge of the driveway, stunned, as he speeds off, wheels screeching, brake lights flashing at the end of the road.

Suddenly aware of a cold, gritty bite beneath my bare feet, I hurry along the driveway, Tom's accusation looping in my mind. I don't know why I'm shocked. It was only a matter of time before he caught up with us. A ruckus above me snatches my attention. I look up at the house as the window closes. Daisy is standing there, staring down at me. *Shit*. How long has she been there? Did she hear my brawl with Tom? I give her a little wave as I hurry inside, head down, feeling her eyes burning into me.

Chapter 51

Zelda straightens her navy cable-knit sweater and then looks at me with those big, sad eyes of hers. 'I thought they came to arrest me for killing Frank,' she whimpers, 'that he was the guy they found in the park. I heard it on the local news that evening, tried calling you but it kept going to voicemail.' I hate myself. I'm a rubbish sister. I should've kept my phone on for emergencies instead of switching it off for a bloody date night with Tom.

I gaze at the red polo player emblem on her jumper. 'Fourteen quid off Vinted,' she says gently, almost as if I'm judging her for wearing designer clothes. I'm not. I wasn't. I just needed something to focus on because I couldn't look her in the eye.

'I've let you down,' I whisper, brushing away a tear from my cheekbone with the heel of my hand. I imagine her at the police station all alone, sitting on a plastic chair beneath sharp fluorescent lights, an untouched tea in a polystyrene cup in front of her, two officers on the other side of the cheap formica desk, like vultures.

'Don't be daft. You're not my keeper.' But I am, your keeper. I am. You're my little sister. It's my job. It's always been my job.

Blinking, I take in the length of her. She looks different somehow. Frail, thinner, slight. Is it possible to lose so much weight in a week? 'Oh, come here.' I pull her to me and wrap my arms around her body, feeling her vertebrae against my fingers. She has lost weight.

'They asked me to go in for a voluntary interview.' She rests her chin on my shoulder. 'Pounding on my door as if it was some sort of drug's raid.' Pulling away, I hold her at arm's length, then curl a long strand of hair behind her ear as she goes on to say how she ended up ringing Linda because she couldn't get a hold of me, told her everything. Linda great – comforting, supportive. 'It was a fucking nightmare, Bella.'

'I can imagine.' I glance at my watch – 08.15 flashes up in bold white font. It'll take me forty-five minutes to get to my client in Hertfordshire. I've got an hour to spare. 'Come on, I'll put the kettle on,' I say, and she nods, padding behind me into the kitchen. 'Did you have a duty solicitor?' I ask over my shoulder.

'Some bloody useless kid.' Zelda pulls out a chair at the table and flops into it, arms folded, legs apart.

'I would've rung Sean, love,' I offer, 'I wish you'd tried my landline.'

'You unplugged it, remember?' Oh, yes. It's been unplugged for months. There's a fault on it. It keeps ringing randomly, waking us all up in the middle of the night. Four engineers later and we've still got the same problem. We gave up in the end and pulled it out of the socket. As Georgia pointed out, who uses their landline these days? Only last night it would've been crucial. I could've helped my sister.

'I'll let them brew.' I flick a hand towards the two mugs on the worktop as I pull out a chair next to her and throw another glance at my watch – 08.17.

'Gotta be somewhere?'

'A gig in Hertfordshire.'

'Oh, I don't want to keep you from your work.' Zelda goes to stand, but I pull her back down by the arm.

'I've got plenty of time,' I say, even though I know I'll be cutting it fine. 'So, what happened last night? Tell me everything.'

I listen in silence as Zelda tells me how the police turned up at her flat looking for Frank, said he'd been reported missing. 'I told them I didn't have a clue where he was. I hadn't seen him since last Saturday. When I confessed that we'd had a bit of fight and I broke off our engagement, they looked at each other. I hated myself for saying it, for being such a stupid klutz. And then I blushed, didn't I, and they looked at each other again.' Zelda takes a deep breath. It's actually more like air hunger. 'I thought they were going to tell me he was dead,' she exclaims. Another long breath, which she blows out through trembling lips. 'Arrest me on suspicion of murder. The cops told me he was reported missing by Diane.'

'Diane from *Serval*?' Zelda nods. 'Why would she report him missing?'

'They said she's his *fiancée*.' My eyebrows shoot up. 'I know. The two-timing shit. They wanted to know if he'd asked me for money. Apparently, he owes Diane a substantial sum. I said the only girlfriend he talked about was his dead-ex, Nina Ivanov.' Zelda's cheeks go red. 'God, it's hot in here. Is the heating on?'

Getting to my feet, I cross the room. 'Mr Stanhope mentioned Diane and Nina last night. Ouch, it's hot. Georgia must've turned it up when she showered this morning and forgot to turn it off.' More like didn't bother, but I spare Zelda the details. Tom and Georgia have a turn-on-turn-off-the-heating contest daily.

'Stanhope?'

'He spoke to the police while we were out. They came looking for you here,' I murmur, turning the thermostat off. 'They didn't have your new address. You really need to update your contact details, Zee.' Zelda nods, says it's on her 'to do' list. 'Gosh, I can't believe he was engaged to Diane. I wonder how much she lent him,' I muse, going back to the teas, and I wonder why he refused my ten grand.

'They were meant to be going away on Wednesday.' Zelda explains as I place a cup in front of her. 'Frank told me he'd be at a fitness conference in Newcastle for a few days. Diane started to worry when he wasn't returning her texts or answering his phone. She went round to his flat and the landlord told her she hadn't seen him all week. Diane rang the hospitals, then went to the police. She was worried, I suppose.'

'Shit,' I mutter.

'Anyway, Louis, a gym colleague, I met him once briefly at a pub.' I tell her I know him, nice-looking, mid-thirties, dark hair. 'Yes, him. Well, he's the one who told the police Frank was dating a Zelda Villin. Given that Frank was reported missing by his fiancée and I was the last to see him, they asked if I'd go in for a chat. I panicked. I didn't know my rights. Linda told me I didn't have to comply but if I didn't go, depending on what information they had, they could arrest me and make me give a standard interview in custody at some point. Maybe they thought we were swindling people together, that I was in on it, or I had something to do with his disappearance. I couldn't risk it.'

I rake a hand through my hair. 'Good job you rang Linda.'

'She was brilliant.' We take a sip from our cups in synchronisation. 'Anyway, I thought it was in my best interest to go to the station with them, show them I was willing to help with their inquiries, had nothing to hide. I did insist on legal representation, though. Linda told me to say that.'

I hold my chin as Zelda goes on to tell me how the police asked her question after question about her relationship with Frank – if she knew Diane Perry, or Nina Ivanov, who's very much alive, by the way. 'On and on and on,' Zelda groans, pressing the heels of her hands against her temples. 'In the end, they thanked me and said they'd be in touch if they needed anything else.'

'Gosh,' I muse. 'But why did Frank tell us Nina was dead?'

'I wondered that too. So, when I got home last night, I googled her.'

'And?'

'I messaged her on Instagram. She's only his bloody *wife*,' Zelda admits, and my jaw almost hits the floor.

Chapter 52

'He left Nina three years ago,' Zelda explains. 'Cleared out their joint account, went to work and never came back. She's moved on now, living with someone, has a toddler and one on the way, doesn't want to get involved.'

'I can't believe it,' I say, astonished. 'It's obvious he's done another runner after fleecing you and Diane. Did the police say they'll prosecute him for theft when he shows up?'

'Nope, there's nothing they can do about the money, as we gave it to him willingly.' So, if they're not after him for his fraudulent activities, they must be concerned about his welfare. Why is Zelda so calm? Maybe it's a delayed reaction. An image of him bleeding to death in a ditch flickers in my mind. I bat it away. 'Besides, he's potless, spends money like water.'

'His Patek Philippe watch must be worth a few quid,' I offer, trying to stay positive. 'Do you think it's real?'

'I doubt it,' Zelda admits.

'You can get good fakes for fifty quid from Malaysia,' I confess, and Zelda agrees. 'I noticed his watch the very first time I saw him wearing it. I think it was that lovely emerald green face and leather strap.' I tap my finger against my cup. 'I wonder if the police will contact you again.'

'PC Pernice rang me this morning,' Zelda says, and my eyes widen.

'And?'

'They've had an update. Frank finally replied to Louis's text messages. They traced his location from his mobile number.' Relief sluices through me. He's alive. That explains Zelda's calm demeanour. 'They also checked his bank account. Two cash withdrawals were made. CCTV outside the cash machine matches the description they have of him.'

'Where is he?'

'St Ives.' Zelda takes a slurp of tea.

'He's in Cornwall?' I exclaim.

'Cambridgeshire,' she clarifies, draining her cup. 'Louis told the police he's gone to see his parents in Huntingdon. Mum's very poorly, apparently.'

'Did he tell them he'll be coming back?' *Please say no.*

'Not for the foreseeable. Linda thinks he won't show his face around here again after what he's done.'

'That's true.' A pause and then. 'Anyway, at least we know he's not dead.'

We sit in silence for a few moments and then Zelda says, 'Bella?'

'Yes, love?'

'Can I ask you a question?'

'Of course.' I grab both her hands and look her in the eye.

'I don't know how to say this, really.'

I squeeze her slender fingers. I know what she's going to say. She wants to ask me for a loan to pay her rent because that wanker stole her money, but doesn't know how to style it. 'You know you can ask me anything, right?' I say, already preparing the bank transfer in my head.

Zelda nods. 'Why do you smell like a charity shop?'

'What?' I think I'd have preferred her asking me for money. Tom told me I stank earlier but I thought he was being spiteful. 'Do I smell?'

'To put it mildly,' she giggles. I look at my watch, wondering if there's enough time to put on a quick wash. 'I'm sure Mum won't mind. Drench yourself in some perfume.'

'I'm not picking Mum up.' I get to my feet and start unbuttoning my shirt while Zelda starts to hum David Rose's Stripper. 'Oh, be quiet.'

'Mum's getting a train back?' Zelda asks as I chuck my blouse into the washing machine and set it to a fifteen-minute quick wash. 'She won't be happy about that.'

'Daisy's picking her up.' Daisy pounded down the stairs the moment I stepped inside after my brawl with Tom earlier, and threw her arms around me – she'd seen and heard everything from her bedroom window. When she asked if there was anything she could do to help, I suggested, in jest, picking my mother up from Heathrow and, to my astonishment, she agreed.

'Daisy?' Zelda says incredulously as I slide a hand through Daisy's black hoodie, which she abandoned on one of the chairs. 'What's she gonna do, stand there with a cardboard name display?'

'Georgia's going with her. Daisy's found another job near the airport and is viewing two flats in Ruislip this morning, so will be nearby. I've got a lot on and it made sense.'

'I didn't know she was leaving the garden shed.'

'Garden office,' I point out, reminding her that it cost forty-five grand, and just then my phone starts ringing on the worktop where it is charging – Linda calling.

'Going for a wee,' Zelda mimes, as I put Linda on loudspeaker.

'Morning gorgeous, I…'

'Do you want the good news or the bad?' Linda interrupts, without any preambles.

'Oh, the good, please. I can't take much more bad news today.'

'Well, they're both bad, actually, but one is worse.'

'Please don't tell me Theo is still reeling about Frank because…'

'No, it's not that. Everything is fine between us.'

'What is it then?' The washing machine spins. 'Linda?'

'Today's gig's been cancelled. Owner's brother has passed away.'

'Oh, that's sad.' I open my calendar app and delete the appointment. 'I'd be a wreck if one of my loved ones died. But what can be worse than news of a death?'

'The Limes Park guy.'

'What about him?' I ask. It can't be Frank – he's on the run, texting Louis from Cambridgeshire and withdrawing money from cashpoints.

'He's been identified.'

'Is it someone we know?' I gulp. The washing machine chugs.

'Yes.' A pause. 'Are you sitting down?'

I flop onto the chair. 'I am now. Go on, who is it?'

'Liam.'

The hairs on my arm stand on end. 'Liam who? It can't be…'

'Liam Cooper. Your ex.' The machine spins at about the same time as my stomach. 'He's the Limes Park victim.'

Chapter 53

I heave over the toilet bowl, saliva dripping onto my chin. Liam is dead. Murdered. How is that even possible? Who could've done this to him?

'Are you okay, Bella?' I shake my head at Zelda as I get to my feet. 'How did it happen? Did Linda say?'

'No,' I manage, staggering back into the kitchen.

'But who could've killed him? It doesn't make sense.' Zelda turns the tap on.

I roll up my sleeves and notice that there's a bit of drool on the right-hand cuff. 'I've no idea,' I say, rubbing it with my finger.

'Here, drink this.' Zelda hands me a glass of water. I don't usually drink tap. Daisy said it's polluted. Tom insists it's perfectly fine to drink, meets the water quality standards. The liquid shakes as I draw it to my lips.

'Is Linda certain? He's not the only Liam Cooper in north London. I bet there are dozens of them around.' Grabbing her phone, she starts jabbing at the screen.

'It's him,' I say, voice barely audible. 'Linda's sure. There was a photo online. She said they'll be updating the story throughout the day. God, I hate to think what his wife and kids are going through.'

Zelda stares at her lit-up screen, lips parted, and then chucks her phone onto the table and steps away from it, her expression confirming Linda's story. She's taking this a lot worse than I expected. It's terrible news, but she was never a Liam fan.

'It's a lot to take in, isn't it?' I say. 'Look, I need to go up and change. I got a bit of sick on Daisy's hoodie.'

I go to move but Zelda grabs my arm, digging her nails into my flesh. 'Oh, God, Bella. I've done something stupid.'

'Zee, what is it? You're shaking.'

She looks at me, eyes full of unease. 'I haven't been completely honest with you.'

My stomach clenches. 'Why do I get the feeling I'm not going to like this?'

'Because I don't think you will. Sit down.'

'Whatever it is you've got to say can't be worse than finding out my ex has been murdered.'

'Sit,' she demands, chest heaving.

I do as I'm told, feeling numb. Zelda pulls out a chair and sits down next to me. Legs wide apart, elbows on knees, hands pressed together against her mouth. 'Daisy told me something at the barbeque last Saturday.'

'Daisy?' Pulling a face, I scratch the side of my neck.

'Yeah,' Zelda confirms.

'Go on.'

Zelda shakes her head. 'You're not going to like it, Bells.'

My phone buzzes on the table with a WhatsApp message. I quickly read it before it disappears. It's from Maggie.

Guess what? Mum has agreed to babysit.

The screen goes black. I go to look away but then another message pings through.

Can come back to work as soon as. x

'It doesn't matter whether I'm going to like it or not' I flip the phone over to avoid any further distractions. 'I need to know what's going on.'

'Who just messaged you?' Zelda nods at my phone. 'Was it Tom?' I shake my head. 'Daisy?'

'No,' I snap, 'it was Maggie if you must know. She wants to come back to work. Look, I'll ring her later. Come on, tell me what Daisy said.'

'Promise me you won't freak out.' There's a warning edge to her tone, which I don't like. 'No, I can't tell you, you're already freaking out. You're doing that thing with your lips.'

'What thing?' I say, annoyance bubbling in my chest.

'Sucking them in and then covering the top half with the bottom and then switching over and biting the bottom one.' God, she makes me sound like Les Dawson.

I purse my lips. 'I promise I won't freak out,' I say calmly, even though I know I probably will. 'Or do the lip thing. Come on, Zelda, this is serious.'

Zelda shoots to her feet and starts pacing, rubbing her lips with her fingers. 'Daisy told me something about Tom, something very serious.'

Chapter 54

I watch Zelda pacing up and down the kitchen, arms folded. 'I need you to tell me what's going on between Tom and Daisy,' I say firmly.

'Okay, okay. Just chill, will you?' A beat and then. 'After she made us the hot drinks, Frank went off to the loo,' Zelda clarifies, 'leaving us alone in the kitchen.'

'And?'

'And Daisy confided in me. I didn't think much of it at the time, but now.'

I frown at her, pulse picking up speed. 'Go on.'

'On the day she turned up for the interview, you were out.'

'Yes, I was on my way back from her auntie's via the supermarket.'

'Tom asked her to wait in the living room. When he went off to make her a cup of tea, the doorbell went. Daisy thought it was you, got up and went and stood by the door to check you out. She was nervous as hell. But it wasn't you. It was a man, introduced himself as Liam.' My skin freezes. I don't like where this is going. 'Tom said you weren't home, but Daisy reckons Liam didn't believe him cos he kept looking over

Tom's shoulder. At one point, Liam caught a glimpse of her and she had to duck out of the way. Tom got wind of it and pulled the door behind him, so Daisy could only catch wisps of their conversation.' Her words penetrate through my skin and seep into my bones. 'Then Liam started shouting, said you were a lying, evil bitch, asked if Georgia was in.'

'Georgia?' I manage, dread coursing through my veins. 'Why?'

'I dunno. Daisy reckons Liam sounded like he was three sheets to the wind – her exact words.' A little smile threatens my lips. I can imagine Daisy saying this. 'There was a kerfuffle, and the door flew open. Tom had Liam against the wall in an armlock, threatened to kill him if he ever tried to contact you again, or found out he'd been sniffing around his daughter.'

'Oh, no.' I swallow back saliva that has filled my mouth. Liam must've got the paternity test results and was in denial — got hammered and came round to confront me. He was probably going to accuse me of tampering with the kit, knowing Liam. 'Why didn't you tell me all this before, Zelda?'

'Tom made Daisy promise not to tell you in exchange for securing her a job. Daisy only mentioned it to me because she wanted to find out who Liam was, if he was a threat to you. She is very…um…' Zelda hesitates. 'Fond of you, isn't she?' I nod, tell her she's very grateful for everything I've done for her, and Zelda rocks her head from side to side as if my statement could be feasible. 'Anyway, I told her he was just an ex who looked you up on online and to forget about it. Liam was harmless, wasn't he? I didn't want to cause any trouble for Daisy, and, if I'm honest, I didn't think it was such a big deal. Liam was off his head. I thought he was just pissed off with you because you cut all ties with him. But now…'

'But now, what?'

'Tom did threaten to kill him, Bella, and now Liam *is* dead.'

'No,' I say, rubbing my thigh. This would mean that Tom's known about Liam and the DNA test for weeks. 'Tom wouldn't…he couldn't…why would he…unless.' I close my eyes. I'm back on the sofa with Tom, A4 envelope in hand, running my thumb along the bubbled seal, wet from the rain, or was it?

'Unless what? Zelda asks, but I ignore her. Mind buzzing. A second-class stamp for something as important as a DNA result? That doesn't sound right. Tom is forever complaining about the cost of postage stamps, emails everything, and, at a push, will only use second class. The report snaps into my mind. It did look a bit basic – as if someone had just rustled it up in MS Word. Could it be…?

'Bella. Bella?' Zelda shakes me out of my daydream. I didn't even feel her hand curl around my wrist. I give her the thousand-mile-stare. Is it possible that Tom read the results, binned the original and put a fake report in the envelope to keep our family intact, safe? 'Answer me, Bella. What is wrong with you?' Tom did bang on about being Georgia's father no matter what – called Liam a lowlife, said he'd never let him take his daughter from him. 'Bella, please, you're doing the lip thing again.' But no, no, I'm overthinking. Tom isn't a killer. Besides, he is Georgia's dad. I'm certain of it. I worked out the dates and everything.

'I've got to go,' I snap, shooting to my feet.

'What? Where?' Zelda's voice follows me into the corridor, her footfall hurried.

'I won't be long.' I slide a hand into the sleeve of my trench coat.

'Bella, please, if you think Tom…'

'If I'm not back before you leave.' I yank the door open. 'Lock up and put the spare key through the letterbox.'

'Hang on,' Zelda cries, but I'm already climbing into my car. 'Let me help you, Bella, I'm your sister.'

'Let me know if you hear from Mum, too,' I say, ignoring her pleas. 'And tell Georgia to stay with her. I'll pick her up later. I want to talk to Daisy alone when she gets back.'

'Bella,' Zelda cries as I fire up the engine. 'You shouldn't be driving. You're too wound up. Bella!'

I press my foot down hard on the accelerator. Anna, from across the road, swings out of her driveway. I swerve around her, wheels screeching, and tear down the road, flicking a glance in my rear view. Anna is out of the car, talking to Zelda, arms flailing. But I don't stop. I need answers from my husband, and I need them now.

Chapter 55

'Bella,' Amy trills as I breeze into the surgery. 'How lovely to see you.' Amy looks stunning and relaxed behind her computer screen, albeit slightly misplaced; with her Nordic looks and impeccable fashion sense, you'd expect to see her working the floor of a luxury fashion brand in an exclusive store than sitting behind an optician's desk.

I lean my forearms against the reception desk and look down at her, heart hammering against my arm. 'How're things? Good holiday?'

'Oh, it was absolutely fab,' she enthuses in her Essex accent. 'Ricky and I can't wait to go back next year. Have you ever been to Regnum Carya?' I open my mouth to speak but she just talks over me. 'It's am-a-zing. All inclusive. We had such an incredible time.' In my peripheral, I notice Tom's room is slightly ajar. He's in-between patients – perfect timing. 'Our friends, Bex and Adam came with, they've got two little ones. Benjamin, four, and two-year-old, Ellie, and...'

'Sounds wonderful, Amy,' I interject. 'I'd love to hear all about it but I am a bit strapped for time.' I give my wrist a quick swivel. 'Is Tom about? Just want a quick word.' I make to walk towards his room.

'Sorry, Bella, he's gone for an early lunch.'

I freeze. 'Lunch?' I spin round. 'At nine-thirty?' I pivot my wrist again for impact.

'Well, brunch. He had a window between nine-thirty and eleven.' *Lying bastard.*

'Oh,' I say, taken aback. 'I thought he was booked solid today. Any idea what time he'll be back.'

Amy shakes her head. 'Afraid not. You know what he's like with his work lunches.'

'Work?'

'A meeting with a supplier. A millennial. They do snazzy, unique designer frames. These Gen Ys are popping up all over the place, so prices are competitive.' My eyes narrow. Amy's face drops. She thinks she's landed him in it. 'I'm pretty sure that's what he said but I could've misheard,' she says, adjusting her black Alice band which has gold stars all over it. 'I was literally in the middle of doing our social media stuff.'

'Actually, yes, I remember him mentioning it now,' I lie. 'Brain like a colander.' Amy smiles, tells me she's the same, then launches into an anecdote about how she left one of the gas rings on and went to Tesco, and another time put the coffee jar in the fridge. A phone rings – saving the day.

'Okay, I'll leave you to it,' I say, securing my bag on my shoulder.

'Eyes on The Hill, how can I help?' I wave at Amy, and then she says, 'Can you hold a moment, please?' She covers the mouthpiece. 'Bella,' she whispers, waving me back, 'he's at the bistro on Margaret Street. I booked the reservation for him this morning, if that helps. If you hurry, you might catch him before he goes in. You lit just missed him.'

Power walking along Margaret Street, I knock into a commuter who stares at me, then sway to avoid a group of students, their laughter and banter ramming into my ears. I scan the street ahead for Tom's familiar white mane, and then I spot him, waiting at the kerb for the lights to change. 'Tom,' I scream, '*Tom*.' He turns around, eyes skimming the street, then turns back towards the traffic. I'm sprinting towards him, breath ragged. 'Tom, wait up,' I wheeze, and then we're standing on the pavement, face to face, like strangers. Could the man I've been sharing my life with for sixteen years be a killer? Pedestrians skirt around us at the crossing, impatient to get across before the lights turn green, one man tuts loudly in my ear.

'What're you doing here?' Tom asks, baffled. 'Is everything okay? Is it Georgia?'

'Georgia's fine,' I pant, catching my breath. 'I need a word.' He goes to object, says he's seeing a contact. Can't it wait until tonight? 'No, it can't. It's important.' I beckon towards a bustling pavement café. 'Let's grab a coffee.'

A few minutes later, we're sitting at a table waiting for our drinks to arrive. 'Well? Are you going to tell me what's going on? I've an important meeting to get to.' I give him a look suggesting what happened to his busy schedule. 'It was unexpected. I had a cancellation. Look, what's this about?'

'Liam's dead,' I say, and his face pales.

'Your ex-Liam?' I shake my head. 'Wow. When? Was he ill?'

'Nothing like that. He was found dead in the woods. He's the Limes Park victim.'

'Jesus.' Tom's hands fly to the back of his head. 'Poor sod. What a way to go.' A dog barks. Children squeal. There must be a school nearby.

'I know Liam came round looking for me that Friday evening,' I say as a car horn screams in my ear. 'I know you threatened him.'

Tom shakes his head, goes a bit red. 'Bloody Daisy. I knew I couldn't trust her. That woman has been nothing but trouble since we took her in. Bloody sponger. It's obvious she's got a *thing* for you,' he scoffs, sounding as if Daisy is in love with me.

'Don't be so bloody stupid,' I snap. 'Daisy's been a godsend.'

'Oh, get real. I've seen the way she looks at you. Lifting his hands up, he wriggles his fingers. 'Bella, can I get you a coffee?' he says in a baby voice. 'I'll clean the shower, Bella, you put your feet up. I'll get the tea on tonight; you've had a long day.'

'Daisy's trying to help me out, that's all. In case it slipped your mind, I've got a full-time job, a demanding teenage daughter, an ungrateful husband and a bloody huge house to clean because you're too *stingy* to hire a cleaner.'

Tom rolls his eyes, lips dancing to the tune of sarcasm. 'Why is she always borrowing your clothes, then? I caught her sniffing your dressing gown the other day. Don't you think that's a bit weird? Bloody two-faced bitch.'

'It wasn't Daisy who told me,' I confess. Nearby, a group scrape their chairs against the pavement, preparing to leave. A blonde, thirty-something woman downs a cup of something quickly as a sharp-suited bloke in square rimmed glasses tugs at her arm, hurrying her along. 'Well, not directly. Daisy confided in Zelda and …'

'Oh, I might've known she'd have something to do with it,' he laughs sardonically.

I immediately resent him for belittling my sister. 'You've never gotten over what happened that night at the Temple Bar, have you?'

Tom screws up his face. 'What're you on about?'

'For blowing you out,' I hiss. On the night I first met Tom, I was out with Linda and Zelda. We ordered some cocktails at the bar – it was two for one happy hour. When Zelda handed the bartender her credit card, he nodded at Tom, who was at the other end of the bar with Toby, said it'd been taken care of. It wasn't long before the guys made a beeline for us. I fancied Tom immediately, but he was more interested in Zelda. When she rejected him, he moved on to me. And the rest, as they say, is history.

'A narrow escape, more like,' he scoffs. 'Woman's a nutter.'

'Rejection hurts, but you've held onto a grudge for far too long.' Not to mention made me feel like shit for making it so obvious. Tom shakes his head; tells me I need therapy. 'Anyway, I'm not here to discuss Daisy or Zelda. I want to know if...' A waitress has appeared at my side with a tray of coffees. We sit in unbearable silence as she places two flat whites in front of us. Once she's safely out of earshot, I round on him. 'Did you have anything to do with Liam's murder?' I accuse, and his features twist in incredulous horror.

'You truly have lost the plot.' I stay silent, waiting. 'Are you crazy?'

'Well, you did threaten to kill him,' I point out.

'That was only a...' A rosy-cheeked waiter interrupts with a bowl of sugar, which he places in front of me. 'Did he tell you he was Georgia's dad? Was that it? Did you tamper with that paternity test?'

'Are you being serious?' He tears a sachet of sugar and pours it into his drink.

'Anyone can rustle up a basic DNA report using a template online.'

'I don't believe this.' Tom picks up his phone, jabs at the screen, then holds it out to me. I pinch the screen and start reading.

From: @alphaomegadna.com
To: Tom Harris. Ref: TM789126 Report.

Dear Mr Harris, further to your request, please find enclosed a copy of your recent DNA test report. I scan the report — the exact copy he showed me. He's not lying.

'Satisfied?' I don't answer. A plate smashes from the depths of the cafe. A few people cheer. A tall, slim waitress with chocolate skin rushes past our table. 'Look, if there's nothing else. I've got work to do.' Tom gulps half of his drink in one, complains that it's tepid and costs a fortune.

'Can't you stay a while longer? We need to talk. Things between us are...'

'Sorry, no,' he says, 'not when you're like this.' A pause and then. 'I wonder what Georgia would make of it all.'

'What do you mean?' Surely, he's not threatening to tell her I tricked her into taking a swab for DNA testing.

'We'll talk later, Bella.' And with another final gulp, he's gone.

I watch in a daze as Tom's swallowed into the crowd. The DNA report might be genuine, but that doesn't mean he didn't kill Liam. I take a sip of coffee, wondering if I've been sharing a roof with a killer, when my phone starts ringing.

'Linda,' I sigh, pushing a hand through my hair. 'You won't believe what a morning...'

'I've got news,' she cuts across me, breathlessly. 'Liam's story has been updated.'

'And?' I'm on the edge of my seat.

'He wasn't murdered, after all. The coroner's report says it was drug-induced.'

Chapter 56

Zelda launches herself at me the moment I walk through the door. I had her on loudspeaker on the journey home, told her how I'd falsely accused Tom of murdering Liam and if my marriage wasn't in trouble before, it is now. 'I received another email from killingsteve1984,' I say now.

'What did it say?'

Pulling out my phone, I locate the message and start reading out loud. 'Are you satisfied now, you heartless cow? This isn't over by a long shot. I'd sleep with one eye open if I were you. F.'

'Bloody bastard,' Zelda seethes. 'That's a threat. We should inform the police, not that they'll do anything about it. Hang on a minute, you need to see this.' Zelda scrolls through her phone and then holds up a photograph. 'It came though just as you left.' I peer at the screen. It's of a man's hairy arm.

'What's this?' I say, shrugging out of my coat. 'A new fetish?'

'Look at the bigger picture.'

'Oh, blue skies. Lovely.' I hang my coat on the hook as Zelda goes on about looking at what's in plain sight. Taking the phone from her hand, I pinch the screen and then every hair on my body stands on end. On his wrist is an expensive looking watch with a green face and emerald green leather strap. In his hand, a Starbucks cup with the initial F written in a black felt-tip pen. I read the message beneath it – *Hasta la vista*. 'So, he has done a runner,' I mutter.

'I phoned the police, forwarded the photo. DC Pernice said the case was now closed but to contact them if he made a threat. Well, he's just threatened you.'

Over a late breakfast of freshly made croissants and coffee, we agree to park the Frank story. I've no proof that KillingSteve1984 is Frank, so going to the police would be futile.

'How did you leave it with Tom, then?'

I rub the back of my neck. 'I tried phoning after Linda gave me the update on Liam, but he wouldn't pick up. I'm such a shit wife.'

'To be fair, he did lie to you about Daisy. I mean, bribing her with a job to keep quiet.' Zelda shakes her head. 'That would really freak me out.'

'I suppose,' I say, 'but he had good reason.'

Zelda chews, shrugs her left shoulder, and then her phone lights up next to her. She picks it up and frowns at the screen, then rolls her eyes. 'Chris.'

'Oh, Zelda, please don't tell me…'

Zelda holds up a hand. 'I dumped him but he won't take no for an answer. You're right, Bella, he's never going to leave his wife and family, and I was stupid to believe he would.'

'Well, I'm glad to hear it.' I tear off a piece of pastry.

'Anyway, moving on, I read the article about Liam online.'

I sit in silence as Zelda tells me how the police thought Liam's death looked suspicious but had nothing to go on, until a bat watcher came forward with new evidence – video footage of Liam running through the woods half naked, slipping and hitting his head, then getting up and staggering into the woods, where he must've collapsed and died.

'Bat-Watcher left his camera on a tripod and went off to have a sandwich and a cuppa in his car. He didn't see the recording until a few days later when he uploaded the SD card onto his computer. Police discovered Liam's clothes scattered along a path and a skid mark, matching the tread of his shoes. There was some of his blood on a tree matching his DNA. There's a chance he took his own life. A lot of people use drugs – even prescription ones. Liam's poor wife, though. She must be in bits. They've got kids, haven't they?' I nod, swallowing, hold up three fingers. 'What would drive a father of three to do something like that?'

'Depression is a demon.' A beat and then, 'They weren't his biological kids, by the way.' I press a finger into the flakes of pastry on my plate, avoiding her gaze. Should I tell her about Georgia, how Liam harassed me, badgered me for a paternity test? Zelda will want all the details. I'm not sure I'm up for an interrogation. It's water under the bridge, anyway. 'His wife had them with her ex-husband. Liam adopted them. Loved them to bits. Sent me several photos of his family.'

'Oh.' Zelda frowns, takes a gulp of coffee. 'Right. Well, you don't have to share the same DNA to be a dad,' she points out, quite rightly. 'I wonder what pushed him over the edge. Sounds like he had it all.'

'Who knows?' I say, feeling sick. Surely, he didn't kill himself because he discovered Georgia wasn't his. No, I'm being silly. Why would he? 'Maybe it *was* accidental.'

'Yeah,' Zelda agrees. 'Liam was always a bit of a renegade. I often wondered what you saw in him. Apart from the obvious.' She grins wickedly. 'He was gorgeous.'

'Looks aren't everything.' I glance at my watch and it occurs to me that I haven't heard from Daisy. She said she'd message once she picked Mum up. Not like her. She's usually very efficient. I hope nothing's wrong. 'Have you heard from Mum yet?'

Zelda shakes her head. 'I rang just before you got here but there was no reply. They must be stuck in traffic.'

'Right, shall we make our way round there? We can let ourselves in. Surprise her.'

'I'll drive. My car is parked across the road.'

We're sitting in Zelda's Fiat 500, a few minutes away from Mum's when my phone starts ringing and vibrating in the breast pocket of my denim jacket. 'It's Georgia,' I say, as we go over a bump in the road. 'They must be home. Hello, darling, how…'

'Oh, Mum, where are you? I'm at Gran's. Please come now.'

'We're almost there, love. Has something happened?'

'Mum,' Georgia cries. 'Please, hurry. Nan and Daisy are fighting.'

'Fighting?' I turn to Zelda, who is singing along to Lady Gaga's Bad Romance on the radio. 'Turn that bloody thing down,' I holler. 'I can't hear what she's saying.' The music dies. 'Say that again, darling. I didn't hear you. I thought you said Nan and Daisy were arguing.'

'I did,' she cries. 'They're shouting.'

'What's wrong?' Zelda says, eyes flitting from me to the road.

'Georgia said Mum and Daisy are having a fight.'

'A fight? What the fuck? Ask her what…'

'Shhh…' I wave a hand as we drive over a bump. 'Georgia, do you know what they're arguing about? Did something happen? Did Mum upset her?' Mum isn't the most tactful person I know, takes pride in shooting from the hip.

'I don't know,' Georgia whimpers. 'There was a bit of tension in the car. Nan started praising you for helping Daisy out, saying you've always had a kind heart. Daisy looked upset, put out. The flats she saw today were minging. The foyer in one of them stank of piss and the other had a filthy mattress against the wall of next door's flat, with a syringe next to it.' Daisy was upset because the flats weren't suitable. So what? There'll be other flats. 'Oh, Mum, will you be long? I don't know what to do.'

'We're almost there, Georgie.' We turn into Mum's tree-lined avenue.

'I…. Oh, God, *Mum*.' I hear a crash and a scream in the background, and in that moment my motherly instincts kick in and my pulse goes mental.

'I'm here, baby.' We pull up outside Mum's semi, blocking in Daisy's blue Peugeot in the driveway. 'Can you open the door?'

'Oh fucking hell, Mum, she's gone berserk. Daisy, stop.' There's a kerfuffle. Another loud crash. A scream. 'Put the knife down!' And then the line goes dead.

Chapter 57

I step into Mum's bright corridor, Zelda in my wake. The house is still, silent. All I can hear is the sound of my ragged breath and my raging pulse thundering in my ears. Georgia left the latch on but she's nowhere to be seen. Zelda goes to close the door behind us. 'Leave it,' I whisper, 'I told Mrs Anderson I'd leave the door open for her. She'll be here any minute.'

While Zelda was rummaging around in the boot for Mum's door keys, which she's lost yet again, I'd quickly rung Tina and told her Daisy was acting strangely, and although she seemed put out when I gave her Mum's address and begged her to come over, she agreed when I told her she was armed and potentially dangerous, said she'll be as quick as she can.

'Bloody Tina Anderson,' Zelda mutters, 'this is all her fault, recommending her unstable niece for your temp job.'

'Be quiet, Zelda.' I take in the pile of mail on the sideboard, the blue light of the modem next to it, Mum's Reiss red puffer jacket, draped over the banister.

'God, it stinks in here,' Zelda whispers, pulling her sweater over her nose. It does. The pungent odour makes me retch. 'It smells like a decomposing body,' she coughs. 'Not that I know what that smells like.'

My eyes race around the hallway, resting on a vase on the floor by the kitchen door containing a bunch of wilted yellow roses, rotting in murky water, a film of slime at the halfway mark of the glass urn. 'There,' I whisper, pointing at the culprit. 'Looks like someone was about to throw them out.'

'Mum,' Zelda screams, and I silence her with a daggered scowl.

'Keep your bloody voice down. We don't want to make anyone panic.' Inclining my head, I crane my neck and listen. Nothing, apart from Zelda taking a deep inhalation beneath her sweater.

'Do you think she's...' Zelda pauses, eyes round with terror. 'Hurt anyone?'

'*No*,' I snap. 'Daisy wouldn't harm a fly. There'll be a reasonable explanation for all this, I'm sure.' I'm not but wishful thinking never hurt anyone. I go to move when I hear the groan of floorboards. I raise my eyebrows towards the ceiling. 'Come on.'

The stairs strain beneath our footfall. On the landing, Mum's bedroom door is slightly ajar. The others are all closed.

'Someone's in there,' I say, 'don't make any noise.'

We creep into Mum's room as quietly as we can. It's empty. My eyes dart around the room taking in the familiar furniture. The balcony doors are flung open and the drapes are billowing in the light wind. I can see the white metal bistro table and chairs, where Mum often sits painting, a row of neglected pot plants lining the side of the balcony's patio, and then I spot a figure in the gap – Daisy's, and then the sound of weeping - Mum's. *Please, God, please don't let there be any casualties. Please let my family be safe.*

'Daisy, please come down,' Georgia whimpers. Her voice is distant, hollow. She's not on the balcony. 'I'm sorry I called Mum. I wasn't telling on you. I was just…scared.'

'Come on, love.' Mum's voice, hoarse, panicky. 'I'll make us all a nice cup of tea.'

'Right, that's it. I'm ringing the police,' Zelda hisses, pulling her phone out from the back pocket of her jeans.

'Don't,' I hiss. 'It might make her panic. She might hurt herself.'

'If we don't act now then someone is going to get killed.' I shush her angrily. 'Don't say I didn't warn you.'

'Please be quiet, Zelda, and stop being so melodramatic. Daisy isn't capable of murder.' Zelda doesn't look convinced. 'Just let me handle this, okay? She's my temp. I know her.'

I go to move, but Zelda's quick. Elbowing me out of the way, she charges towards the balcony and yanks the curtains back. I chase after her, grabbing a fistful of her sweater in my hand and then we both stop stock-still and watch in startled silence. Daisy is leaning against the Juliette balcony, back to us, blood dripping from her hand and spitting onto the concrete patio, speckled with Mum's colourful acrylics.

Zelda speaks first. 'What the actual fuck, Daisy? Have you lost your mind?' Daisy doesn't move. It's as if she's wearing headphones, blocking out all noise.

'That's really going to help, isn't it?' I complain. I move forward. Zelda grabs my arm with both hands. 'Get off me,' I whisper angrily. 'Let me do this my way. *Please*.' Zelda holds her hands up in surrender, head inclined. 'Daisy?' I call out, stepping forward. 'Daisy, love, it's Bella.' At this, Daisy suddenly awakens, spins round.

'Bella,' she says, as if everything is normal, as if she hasn't got a twelve-inch knife in her hand, as if there is no blood pumping from it and spattering onto the floor like a murder scene. Daisy follows my eyes to her injury and tuts. 'Had a bit of an accident.' She waves the bloodied knife around. 'Your mum tried to wrestle it out of my hand while I was chopping carrots for tonight's tea. We were just about to call you, actually. Bloody sharp these things, aren't they?'

I edge nearer. 'Why did she try to snatch it off you?' I say as calmly as I can.

Daisy shrugs. 'Probably likes being in control. Most mums are like that. Think they know best. Oh, shit.' She wipes her bleeding hand on the edge of her blue top, then lets it flop by her side. I watch as it bleeds out again. 'It's just a scratch,' she says, dismissively.

'She's batshit crazy,' Zelda mutters. 'Why are you being so calm? Call the police.' I don't answer, eyes focused on Daisy. 'Mum, are you okay?' Zelda yells.

'Zelda, is that you? Listen, we're fine. Is Daisy okay? Is she hurt? It was an accident. Daisy, I'm sorry, love. I didn't mean to snatch the knife off you.' So, it's true. But something in Daisy's eyes tells me all is not well. 'I was just trying to help speed things up a bit. I've got a knack, you see.' Mum laughs lightly. 'I've been chopping veg for centuries.'

Daisy rolls her eyes. 'See what I mean?'

'She's fine, Mum.' I yell. Daisy's hand twitches, and my eyes dart to the knife in her fist. 'Georgia?' Taking a step nearer, I crane my neck and peer into the garden until Georgia and Mum come into view. Mum is squeezing Georgia in her arms – no blood, no injuries, just two frightened faces.

'Mum, is Daisy okay? I was going to go after her but Nan wouldn't let me.' Daisy snorts when she hears this. Zelda groans behind me, something about not blaming her.

'I couldn't chase after her,' Mum quivers, 'not with my arthritic hip, and I didn't want Georgia to…,' she falters. 'I wanted Georgia to stay down here with me in case I sat down and couldn't get up again.' Mum laughs nervously.

'Daisy, why don't you put the knife down, love?' I suggest, moving slowly towards her. 'We don't want any more accidents.'

Daisy looks at me in confusion, then at the knife in her right hand. 'Ha, I forgot all about that.' She sets it down on the table, straightens her pale blue blood-stained blouse, and then follows my eyes to her wound. 'It's okay,' she says. 'It's the fleshy bit of my palm. Looks worse than it is.' She presses the wound with her left palm. 'I came up to run it under the bathroom tap and find some antiseptic, but ended up in here' She gazes at the golf course that backs onto Mum's garden. 'What a view, eh?'

Sighing wistfully, Daisy takes in her surroundings. It's clear she's having some sort of mini breakdown. But what set her off? I bite my bottom lip. She has been under a lot of pressure lately – chucked by her fiancé in Dublin – abandoned by her brothers – Tina's husband giving her grief – homeless – adjusting to a temp job and a new home – and now having to uproot again. It's enough to send anyone over the edge. Getting her involved in the Frank saga didn't help. She looked so frightened that night. God, what have I done to the poor girl?

'I'd better get this cleaned up.' Daisy turns to me.

'Mum,' I shout, 'is the First Aid box still under the sink?'

'I'll get it,' Mum replies.

'Zelda, grab a towel out of the linen cupboard.' Zelda glares at me. 'Now,' I yell and she shuffles off in a fury.

I walk over to where Daisy is standing to the backdrop of Zelda's footfall on the landing, followed by the clank of a cupboard door opening, a shuffle and then she's back, handing me a blue, frayed towel, which is falling apart. 'What?' she says, 'you're cleaning up a wound not giving her a luxury facial.'

'Come on, love,' I say, taking Daisy's wrist and wrapping the towel around her hand. 'Let's go down and get you cleaned up.'

I flick my head towards the knife and mouth, *pick it up*, as I shepherd Daisy out of the room, and for once, my sister doesn't object.

Chapter 58

'There you go,' I say, looking proudly at the bandage on Daisy's hand as Mum shuffles in with a tray of tea and biscuits, looking tanned and radiant in her yellow blouse and white slacks.

'Thank you,' Daisy manages, back to her old self again. 'I'm sorry about before. I didn't mean to scare anyone.'

Rocking back on my heels, I get to my feet and brush myself down. 'I did a first aid course at school. Thanks, Mum,' I say, taking a mug off the tray. I'm glad we've got Daisy in a stable state, but I still want to know what caused her to uncharacteristically lash out like that. My eyes slide to the blood stains on her blouse. Was it an accident, or did she deliberately cut herself? Does she self-harm? I didn't see any signs of it, but then I had other things on my mind.

'So, is someone going to address the elephant in the room, or are we just going to sit down to tea and biscuits?' Zelda says, putting an entire Jaffa cake into her mouth.

'They're not biscuits, they're cakes,' Georgia comments, taking one from the plate in Mum's outstretched hand.

'Yes, I always found that strange,' Mum muses. She offers one to me. I shake my head, I've never been a fan of Jaffas, and she sets the plate down on the oblong wooden table. 'I mean, biscuits are crumbly, aren't they? Whereas this…'

'Will you just *stop*.' Zelda shoots to her feet and jabs a finger at Daisy. 'What were you thinking holding my mum and niece at knifepoint.'

Daisy looks up at her, then at me pleadingly. 'I wasn't. I didn't…'

'Oh, Zelda, that's not what happened,' Mum interjects, coming to Daisy's rescue.

'Nan's right. It was an accident. I'm sorry if I scared you, Mum. I panicked.' I tell Georgia that it's fine. Phoning me was the right call.

'Zelda, will you please calm down,' I say firmly.

'*Me?* I'm not the one who was waving a twelve-inch knife in my hand,' she spits, and I give her a look depicting maybe not now but you did stick a letter knife into a man's neck that almost killed him. 'That was different,' Zelda protests, reading my mind. I raise my eyebrows, even though I know she's right and that Frank deserved every bit of pain and fear he felt. '*Jesus*,' she mutters, and, in a huff, sits down and snatches another Jaffa cake off the plate.

'Zelda's right. I was out of order.' Daisy leans back in the armchair, cradling her injured hand, eyes on the ceiling. 'I don't know what to say. It all happened so fast. I…' she tails off.

'It's okay, Daisy, I'll explain.' Mum settles down on a high-back chair, tea in hand. 'Georgia was in the front room playing with her phone on Ticktack.'

'Tiktok,' Georgia corrects, taking a sip of tea and pulling a face. 'Urgh. This needs more sugar.'

'Anyway,' Mum says, as Georgia scuttles off to the kitchen. 'Daisy and I were in the kitchen sorting out dinner. Georgia was hungry and so was I. I hate inflight food. I had a few things in the freezer and picked up some essentials from M&S at Heathrow. Daisy offered to help me, bless her. I called out to Georgia to get rid of those rotting flowers.' I was right about the abandoned vase. 'We were having a bit of a chinwag about…' Mum pauses, glances at Daisy, but Daisy is giving her untouched mug of tea the thousand-mile-stare. 'Well, I was telling her about my girls, you know.' *Oh, Mum, I do know.* Mum has a habit of boasting about our achievements to anyone who'll listen. Daisy's lucky she didn't get the photo album out. 'Then she asked why I didn't have any more children, try for a boy.' Mum sets her mug down on the table. 'It's a reasonable enough question. You were just making conversation, weren't you, love?'

'Bit personal,' Zelda groans.

Actually, Zelda's right. It was a personal question. I hate it when people ask me why I didn't try for another. Mum might've had secondary infertility for all Daisy knew. She didn't. Mum's never been motherly. Dad was more hands-on with us – taking us to the park swings, the cinema, fairground, while Mum got on with everything else.

'I laughed,' Mum goes on. 'I mean, I love the bones of you girls, but I'm not mum-of-the-year material, am I? I mean, you two were quite enough for me, thank you very much. You went quiet on me then, didn't you, love?' Daisy looks destroyed. Did she lose a baby? Is she infertile? It's not something we ever discussed. 'But being the stupid woman that I am, instead of steering off the subject of children, I berated her for cutting the carrots too thickly, said my Bella could do a better job when she was twelve.' I rub my forehead. It's not the most tactful thing to say to someone you barely know. 'I was joking,' she clarifies, sensing my disapproval. 'Oh, I don't know why I said it, I'm sorry, Daisy. I didn't mean to offend you.'

'You didn't,' Daisy says to the TV, flickering in the corner of the room. 'It's just that I was the house cook growing up. I know how to prepare food.' I'll second that. I will miss her cooking. 'But I should have just let you take the knife and carry on. I mean, it is your house.' Georgia bustles back into the room and Daisy draws her legs in to let her by. 'I shouldn't have put up a fight. I'm sorry I shouted at you, Sandra. I've got a bit of a short fuse.' Has she? I hadn't noticed, but then I don't know her that well. 'I had a bad day.' With her two middle fingers, she rubs her forehead and sighs. 'When I saw the blood, it made me panic and I just …' she falters. My entire body sags with relief. That explains it all – she suffers from hemophobia.

'Daisy didn't have a great upbringing,' Georgia interjects, and we all swivel our heads towards her, and then her phone starts ringing in her hand. 'Parents were both alkies.' Getting to her feet, Georgia presses the phone to her ear. 'Hi, Dad.'

My heart freezes. Tom only rings Georgia during working hours if it's an emergency. What could be so urgent? I imagine Tom going back to his practice, still reeling from my accusations. Is he going to go grass me up to Georgia about the DNA test now that I accused him of murder?

Chapter 59

'Can you just hang on a sec, please, Dad?' Georgia covers the mouthpiece. 'Daisy's dad used to give her Chinese burns for misbehaving and pull her ears until they bled if she burnt the Sunday roast. You'd run upstairs and lock yourself in your bedroom, blood pouring. Init, Daisy? The sight of the red stuff makes her panic now.'

Daisy's eyes harden, her look depicting *traitor*. 'Sorry, Daisy, but they've got to know why you freaked out. Otherwise, they might think you're doolally and lock you up in a funny farm.' Georgia giggles. 'Oh, and her mum used to lock her in the cupboard under the stairs for being naughty. Yeah, Dad, what's up?'

'Daisy, is this true?' Mum gulps, to the backdrop of Georgia's footsteps clattering in the hallway, her voice fading with each step.

'Why didn't you say something, love?' I ask, the fear of Tom grassing me to Georgia taking a backseat to Daisy's wellbeing.

Zelda runs a hand over her face, looking contrite. 'Shit, no wonder you're traumatised.'

'Daddy couldn't hold his drink – didn't know what he was doing, and Mammy was only trying to teach me a lesson.' Daisy picks at a loose thread of her bandage. 'That's how parents disciplined their kids back in the day, wasn't it?' Zelda and I look at each other.

'Well, no, I never did that to *my* kids.' Mum shakes her head. 'I mean, they got the odd clip around the ear, but nothing more.'

'That's abuse,' Zelda croaks, clearly shaken by Daisy's revelation. 'You must be suffering from PTSD.'

'PT what?' Mum quizzes, curling her sleek white hair behind her ear.

'Post-Traumatic Stress Disorder,' Zelda clarifies. 'It's a condition caused by a traumatic experience.'

'Right. I see. Well, you should get some professional help for that, love.'

'I haven't got PTSD. I'm fine.'

I disagree. I think Zelda's spot on. That, together with the hemophobia, will explain her outburst today. 'The system should've taken care of you,' I say. 'Honestly, some people shouldn't have kids.' Mum murmurs in agreement when I say this. 'But hey, you've got us now, right?'

Daisy's head snaps up. 'Why are you chucking me out, then?'

Heat gushes my face. 'I'm not,' I protest, suddenly feeling defensive. 'You can stay as long as you like. I'm sorry Tom was a bit short with you this morning. He's got a lot on his plate.' I laugh lightly, eyes flicking from Mum to Zelda who are looking at me as if I'm a monster who's throwing a homeless, abused girl onto the streets. 'Georgia said the flats you saw today weren't very good, but there'll be others – no rush,' I say, feeling as if I'm sitting in a witness box being scrutinised by a harsh jury. 'Maggie said she's ready to come back to work. I mean, if I could keep you both on, I would.' A drill goes off and I look at the wall. Mum rolls her eyes, flicks a hand out and says she's got new neighbours, moved in while she was away. 'Look, I'll talk to Tom, see if we can arrange something for you. How's that?'

'That control freak?'

'What do you mean?' I'm taken aback by her feralness. Tom is a stingy arsehole, but he's been good to her for most of her stay.

'I mean, he calls all the shots, holds the purse strings. Manipulates you.'

'Of course he doesn't.' I give a little mirthless laugh, looking from Zelda to Mum for backup, but they're wearing their harsh jury expressions again. 'I do what I like with my money.' This isn't strictly true. Tom has taken to opening my credit card and bank statements since I omitted to tell him I'd hired Frank, and then pretends he opened them by accident.

'Actually, she's right, Bells,' Zelda looks at Mum. 'We've thought it for years.'

'Oh, come off it,' I protest. 'He's not that bad.'

'He's old-fashioned.' Mum waves a hand. 'That's all.' At least Tom has one supporter. 'Your father was the same.'

'It's coercive behaviour, Sandra,' Daisy points out. 'It's criminal. Anyway, I don't want your charity, Bella. I know when I'm not wanted. Funny how you weren't so eager to get shot of me when you needed my help to hide the weapon.'

Needles pierce into my guts. '*Excuse me?*' I utter. Zelda looks at me, face reddening.

'Weapon?' Mum asks, with fake laughter.

'It's not funny, Sandra,' Daisy rages, blood rushing to her cheeks. She has got a short fuse, after all. 'Your precious baking-genius daughter stabbed her boyfriend and your expert veg-cutting eldest was going to help her cover it up.' I feel the room swirl, the sensation making me bilious. There's only one way she could know all this – she was standing outside Zelda's door that night for a lot longer than she let on. 'It's been all over the news,' Daisy adds for good measure. Right, she thinks Frank is the Limes Park victim. But why this sudden anger? Tom rudely asked her to leave this morning and I suppose I went along with it. But is she really that vindictive?

'No, that's complete bollocks,' Zelda gulps. 'Look, Mum, I'm gonna level with you.' Mum folds her arms in readiness, lips pursed. 'While you were in Portugal, I dated a guy, Bella's ex-personal trainer, who turned out to be a bastard. We had a fight and he disappeared, that's all. Did me for two thousand quid.'

'Two thousand pounds? Oh, you idiot,' Mum barks and Zelda reddens, humiliated, hurt.

'Disappeared?' Daisy scoffs. 'Dead more like.'

'No, Daisy, he's very much alive. In fact, I got a text from him this morning.'

'Where from, the morgue? We all know he's the Limes Park victim. That's why the police came round to Bella's fishing for information.'

Mum looks as if she's about to have a heart attack. 'Is this *true*?'

Closing my eyes, I run a hand through my hair. 'No,' I say, 'Frank isn't the Limes Park guy.' Daisy opens her mouth to protest when I blurt, 'They've identified the body. It's Liam Cooper. Look it up on your phone, Daisy.' Daisy's face pales. She didn't know.

Chapter 60

'Liam Cooper?' Mum's on the edge of her seat. 'That young layabout you went out with and wanted to marry?'

'Yes, Mum,' I say wearily.

'He's dead? How?' Mum's eyes are round and wild.

I run a hand over my face. 'I can't go into it now, Mum.'

'Frank may still be alive,' Daisy pipes up, and Mum's eyes rocket towards her. 'But I'm telling you the truth, Sandra. They left him for dead in the garden.' Zelda and I steal an anxious glance at each other. This is more than PTSD and hemophobia.

'Okay, we had a fight,' Zelda swears. 'All couples do. Yes, it got a bit heated but I didn't attack him.' I look at Zelda who has her hands behind her back and I know that she has her fingers crossed. 'Daisy's confused, maybe because of the blood loss.'

'There's nothing wrong with my brain, thank you very much. I know what I heard.' Daisy looks at me with such loathing, that I can almost feel the pain physically, like a vapour of hatred seeping through my skin and squeezing my heart. 'You thought he was dead and just left him there, didn't you?'

Yes, yes, yes!! We did. It's all true.

'Now you're being ridiculous,' Zelda snorts.

'Bella,' Mum says, clearly upset. 'Please tell me none of this is true.'

I put on my best poker face. 'Of course, it's not true. Zelda's right. It was a lovers' tiff. I went round there. Frank was alive and well,' I lie, 'Honestly, Daisy, I don't know where you...' But my voice is lost in the sudden cacophony of their brawl. Daisy is contradicting Zelda – Zelda is telling her she's hallucinating, imagining things.

Mum is on her feet now, towering over Daisy, demanding answers.

'Fine,' Daisy yells. 'Your perfect daughters almost killed a man, Sandra.' My heart crushes. I don't think I can move. 'They're *murderers*.'

We all fall silent. Mum looks at us, a slight tremor in her hand. 'She's talking nonsense. Bella?' Holding my chin, I nod, mouth, *she's not well.* 'I'll excuse you this time because I know you're suffering from PPI.' I bite my lip, sealing in a nervous laugh. 'But I'd like you to take that back, please.'

'Dream on, Grandma,' Daisy scoffs. A thump against the wall snatches my attention, followed by drilling. They must be putting up shelving or pictures.

'Right, that's it. I want you to leave,' Mum says, pointing at the door. I think it was the grandma reference that did it. 'I won't have malicious lies spread about my daughters,' she yells above the noise. 'Come on, get out.' But Daisy just sits there, a wry grin playing on her lips. 'Come on. *Out*.' Bang, bang, BANG. 'I said out.' Mum goes to manhandle Daisy but she won't budge. '*Get out, get out, get out,*' Mum shrieks at the wall, veins in her neck protruding.

The noise next door suddenly stops dead. Daisy shuffles to the edge of her seat, injured hand aloft, and unzips her handbag. She's fishing around for her keys, thank goodness. 'I'll need to move my car,' I say wearily. 'I've blocked you in.' But instead of leaving, she pulls out a tube of sweets, pops one into her mouth and settles back into her seat, arms folded. 'Oh, Countdown,' she announces, parking the sweet on the side of her mouth. 'Put the volume up, Sandra. Me and Mammy used to love this, even though she was useless at it.'

'What kind of person are you?' Mum whispers. 'My daughter takes you in, puts a roof over your head, food in your belly, and *this* is how you repay her?'

'I'm not a charity case, Sandra.' Daisy sucks on the sweet loudly. 'Bella was at a loose end. I helped her out.' She looks at me, eyebrow raised. 'In more ways than one.' *Sweet mother of God. My lovely temp has been possessed by Satan.* I fold my arms, glance at my watch. Where the hell is Tina? What's keeping her?

'This has gone far enough,' Zelda interjects.

Mum throws her hands up in the air. 'Call the police, Zelda.' Zelda and I exchange glances. The police? After what Daisy has accused us of? I don't think so. We didn't kill Frank, but Zelda did stab him and we failed to call 999. Linda said that's conspiracy to murder. We'll get locked up if Frank decides to give a statement, especially with Daisy's testimony. 'Well, don't just stand there like two bloody statues.' Mum's voice makes me jolt. 'Oh, for God's sake, if you want a job doing.'

Mum goes to walk past me. I block her with a sidestep. 'Mum, she's clearly not well,' I whisper.

'Well, I can see that.'

'They might section her if you call the emergency services, especially after the knife incident earlier.'

'Well, maybe that's the best thing for her.'

'Oh, Mum, don't. Her auntie is on her way to collect her. She'll be gone soon.'

'I'm not deaf, you know,' Daisy interjects, getting to her feet. 'Go ahead, call the police. I've got a thing or two to tell them about your family anyway, and while I'm at it, I'll tell them how you tried to stab me as well.' Daisy thrusts her bandaged hand out at Mum, taking in the length of her in disgust. 'The apple doesn't fall far from the tree, does it?' Mum shakes her head, muttering to herself. 'Oh, stop fretting, grandma. I'm going.'

Daisy knocks into my shoulder as she thunders towards the door. Zelda looks at me pleadingly, arms and legs crossed, bottom lip clenched between her teeth. I hesitate, mind racing. Should I go after her? She's already threatened to tell the police everything. And what did she mean by me needing her help to hide the weapon? Did she follow me to Waterlow Park that day? *God*, she'll direct the police straight to the evidence.

'Daisy, wait,' Zelda says, as if she's reading my mind. 'Please don't go, not while you're so upset.' In the mirror above the fireplace, I watch as Daisy pauses, one hand on the doorframe. 'We overreacted,' she says to her back. 'And we're sorry. Aren't we, Bella?'

Daisy turns around, holding my gaze in the mirror. 'Yes, we are.' I shake my head so violently it hurts. 'We're *very* sorry.'

Daisy seems to like my endorsement. Shuffling back in, she sits on the armrest of the sofa, legs wide, speckles of blood on the hem of the right leg of her flared jeans. 'You two must think I was born yesterday.' I look at the grandfather clock in the corner of the room. Bloody Tina Anderson. What's taking her so long? I rue the day I ever set eyes on her.

'What's the matter, Sandie?' Mum hates being called that. 'Cat got your tongue?' Daisy glares at Mum. Mum looks horrified. I bet she wasn't expecting this homecoming while she was sipping her G&T on the flight back to Heathrow.

'Daisy, what do you want from us?' Zelda asks.

'If you need money until you sort yourself out,' I offer.

'I don't want your money,' Daisy says coldly.

'Then what *do* you want?' Mum pleads.

'What's going on?' Our heads swivel towards the loud voice. Tina is standing in the doorway in black chinos, a red blouse with huge pointed collars and a beige trench coat. An A4 manila envelope is clutched to her chest. A pair of expensive looking glasses are hanging from her elegant neck on a chain.

'Oh, thank God you're here, Tina,' I manage. 'Daisy's very upset. She's not herself…'

'Darling, what's wrong?' Tina asks Daisy, ignoring me. 'What happened to your hand? What's all that blood on your clothes?' Her head snaps up at me. 'Did you do this to her?'

'What? *No*. Daisy had an accident.'

'Bella's right,' Mum concedes. 'We were in the middle of cooking and…'

'Let me see that.' Tina puts her glasses on and frowns at Daisy's bandaged hand. 'Come on, I'll take you to A&E.'

'There's no need, Tina. I cleaned it up for her.'

'I'm okay.' Daisy says. 'Well, I will be once I get away from this toxic lot.'

'Toxic?' Zelda snorts with fake mirth. 'Is that why you can't bear to leave my sister's house?'

I take a lungful of breath. 'Daisy, I've done my best for you. I'm sorry if you feel let down. The job was only temporary. That was clear from the start.' I turn to Tina. 'We've treated her like family.'

'I should hope so.' Tina's mac swishes as she sits down, showing a bit of the lining - Burberry.

'Tina, I know you're protecting your niece and family comes first but…'

'Uh-ah, she's not related to me.'

'What?' I say, flicking a worried glance at Zelda. 'But you…'

'Daisy's your sibling, actually. Well, half-sister,' she says. And then everything stops, freezes, as if someone has hit a pause button.

'Right,' Georgia says, charging back into the room. 'What have I missed?'

Chapter 61

It takes several seconds for me to process what Tina has just said. *What the actual fuck?* The temp can't be our sister. I look from Daisy to Tina. Their faces are stolid. A feeling of unreality sweeps over me.

'God,' I say, tugging at the neck of my black cashmere jumper. 'It's so hot in here.' Inhaling a fug of perfume in my hair and fried food on someone's clothing (Tina's, I'm guessing), I glance at the bay window longingly, wishing someone would open it and let some oxygen in before I die of suffocation. But no one is moving. Everything is still.

'Are you okay, lovey?' Tina asks Daisy, breaking the silence. 'I'm sorry I put my foot in it, but they needed telling. It's what we agreed.' *Jesus Christ*, who are these people that've tricked their way into our homes, our lives?

'Is this some kind of sick joke?' Zelda explodes. Mum stays silent, face incredulous.

'It's okay, Mum,' I say tiredly. 'Don't worry. This is all my fault. I'll get it sorted.' I look at Tina. A drill goes off next door. Georgia demands to know what's going on. 'There's obviously been some sort of mix-up.'

'No mix-up, Bella. We've got evidence.' Tina says, and I feel the floor beneath me move like a wave in the sea. What kind of evidence? Proof that Dad had another affair? God, I'm surprised Mum stayed in the marriage for as long as she did. I collapse onto the two-seater brown leather sofa next to a confused looking Georgia, the croissant we had earlier swimming in my stomach.

Zelda, who is now occupying the three-seater opposite me like an empress, narrows her eyes at Daisy, face ablaze. 'How old are you again?'

'I'm thirty-seven.'

'Right. I see.' Zelda looks at Mum, but Mum is staring at Daisy agape, which doesn't sit well with me at all. 'Listen, you two, Dad fucked off to Australia years ago. We're practically estranged. So, if you were banking on having a stake in this house, of our mother having dementia and falling for your scam, you're out of luck.' Mum shoots Zelda a look and adjusts the collar of her yellow blouse in protest. Mum prides herself on being a young seventy-eight-year-old – walks daily, swims every Saturday morning, plays Wordle, paints, travels, and is always splashing out on the latest lotions and potions from QVC. 'Sorry to disappoint, ladies, but you've had a wasted trip.'

'Will someone please tell me what happened?' Georgia yells. The room falls silent. The drilling has now been replaced by constant tapping. 'Why has everyone suddenly turned against Daisy? She didn't hurt Nan on purpose, Mum. I told you it was an accident.'

'It's not that, Georgie.' I clear my throat. 'The thing is, sweetheart. Daisy is claiming to be our sister.'

Georgia's eyes glimmer. 'You're shitting me.' I shake my head. 'Seriously? Oh, my fucking God.'

'Stop blaspheming,' Mum cries, making a small sign of the cross against her chest.

'Sorry, Nan, but this is mega.'

'*Claiming*, to be our sister,' Zelda reminds Georgia. 'Not *is*.'

'I always knew there was something special between us – a link – a vibe.' Georgia leaps to her feet. 'OMG. I've got a new cool aunt.' Jumping up and down on the spot, Georgia starts scrolling through her phone. 'Let's take a selfie to celebrate.'

'Georgia,' I warn, but she ignores me, takes a pew next to Daisy on the armrest, forcing Tina to get up and sit next to Zelda. A phone pings, not mine. A loud sneeze filters through the walls, one of those noisy achoo ones. Georgia is now holding her phone aloft, pouting at the screen, head pressed against Daisy, and that's when I see it - the chin, the nose, the way their right eyebrow arches slightly. I feel sick. Is it possible that Daisy is telling the truth?

'This'll go viral on Insta,' Georgia beams. I watch as they both grin at the phone camera, Daisy's smile not quite reaching her eyes, while Tina looks on like a proud mother. The scene plays out like a horror movie. I look at Zelda who is busy texting then at Mum, who is gazing at them dubiously.

'Say cheese.' *Oh, God. Oh, no.* Georgia's got over seven thousand followers on Instagram. All her school friends will see it. Their parents will have a field day at our expense. Ralf from across the road will show his mother, Anna, and she will tell her neighbours Amber from number seventeen, the legal secretary who loves a good old gossip, and her miserable husband, Dave, who can't sparkle without a drink, she might even drop it into conversation to Julie and Charlie who've just moved in at number twenty-one – I often see them chatting outside. We'll be the talk of the neighbourhood, especially once Mr Stanhope gets wind of it. My face burns. I can't let that happen. I've got to stop her. I hear the click of a camera.

'Give me that!' Powered with adrenalin, I shoot to my feet and slap the phone out of Georgia's hand. It almost topples out of her grasp but she manages to snatch it before it hits the carpet – reflexes like a feline, inherited from me. 'Put that thing away,' I yell, hot and ruffled. She doesn't move. '*Now*,' I holler, throat raw from the strain.

For a moment, Georgia looks at me challengingly, but then slips her phone into the pocket of her bright green hoodie. 'All right, Mother, don't get your knickers in a twist,' she says, skulking back to her seat. 'But you've got to admit, it is cool, isn't it, Daisy?' Daisy smiles. 'I knew there was a bond between us. I just KNEW IT! Wait until I tell Ira and Mazi. Man, I'm so gassed right now.'

'Gassed?' Mum croaks from the corner of the room, as Zelda slips her phone into her pocket. I hope she wasn't texting bloody Chris. She always turns to him in a crisis.

'It means excited, Nan.'

Mum rolls her eyes. 'Give me strength.'

Daisy goes to move. 'I shouldn't have come.'

'Sit down,' Mum orders, wearily.

Zelda and I give each other a look that says *what is she doing?* Daisy hesitates, glances at Tina, and when Tina gives her a small nod, she sits down on the edge of her seat, almost as if it'll collapse beneath her weight. 'Right.' Mum takes a breath, straightens her lapel and holds it like a barrister. 'Let's get some answers to this bullshit.'

Chapter 62

'I'm sorry, Sandra, but none of this is bullshit. It's all true,' Tina says gently.

'Con-artists, the pair of you,' Zelda seethes. 'Next, you'll be telling us that dad had an affair with *you* and this one here is your love-child.' I hate to admit it, but the thought did flicker through my mind.

'Tina.' I swallow hard. 'Did you trick me from the onset?' Her silence tells me that is exactly what she did. 'Is your house even for sale?' Tina shakes her head, eyes downcast. *Fucking hell.* I was meaning to look up her house on Rightmove but was far too busy obsessing about Frank and Liam. 'It *was* you crawling outside my sister's flat last week, wasn't it?' Tina and Daisy exchange glances. 'And you saw me last night at the pub and ignored me. Why?' I demand furiously.

'If you stop shouting and whinging, Bella, I'll explain.'

'I'll tell you what I think, shall…' I begin.

'Mummmm,' Georgia groans. 'Let Tina speak.' The room falls silent.

'I couldn't speak to you last night because my husband was with me and I'd get rumbled.' I don't believe it. She's not even separated. 'Please don't look at me as if I'm something nasty you trod in. I couldn't betray Daisy.' Tina looks at Daisy. 'My precious foundling.'

'Oh, God,' Mum utters through her fingers, and in that moment, I feel as if the temperature has dropped to zero.

'Foundling?' I manage, holding the base of my throat.

'Daisy was left on the hospital steps in a cardboard box, wrapped in a blanket, in the middle of January.' We all gawp at Tina, wordless.

'I was dumped,' Daisy says quietly, eyes scooting from me to Zelda, whose mouth is hanging open. Mum says nothing, but her whole being has deflated. She looks tiny in that chair, almost as if she'll disappear.

'One of the nurses found her and brought her up to maternity. Nurse Daisy Manning. That's who she's named after. Only two days old, she was, poor little lamb,' Tina continues. Georgia gasps loudly, clamping a hand over her mouth and looks at me, eyes filling. 'She was in care for several months, finally got adopted by a wealthy couple who were desperate for a daughter.'

'A slave more like,' Daisy mutters, picking at a loose thread on her bandage.

'They were a middle-class family,' Tina continues, 'had two boys, wealthy but pure evil.'

'Come on, Mum. Don't fall for their lies,' Zelda cuts in, not sounding at all convincing. 'They're obviously a couple of fraudsters after money.' Mum says nothing – face frozen.

'We took it in turns to feed and change her in maternity. Put the word out, hoping her biological parents would come forward, but no one came for her. Technology wasn't as advanced back then. We couldn't trace the patients. We checked the register, of course, but just hit a brick wall. Daisy's been looking for her birth relatives for some time now, haven't you, love? And as for fleecing the elderly, Zelda, Daisy's got enough money of her own.'

My guts spasm. Daisy told us she was homeless. I felt sorry for her. Was it all lies - the boyfriend who threw her out because she pawned his grandmother's ring – the brothers who refused to help her – sleeping rough in the car? It must've been. But why? To punish Dad for abandoning her through us?

'God, they're a noisy lot next door,' Tina says, and the sound of a power tool snaps into my ears. 'It would do my head in.' She squints at her gold watch. 'I think it's considered noise pollution at this time on a Saturday.' But Mum says nothing. 'Right. Well, anyway, at least Daisy's useless parents did one good deed.

Daisy nods. 'They left me and my brothers a fair amount.' Zelda raises her eyebrows. Georgia gasps, clearly impressed by Daisy's wealthy status. 'Owned half of Dublin.'

'You deceived me,' I mutter through my fingers. 'You deceived us all. Tom, Georgia, Zelda, even Linda was taken in.'

'For what it's worth, I am sorry,' Daisy mumbles, as a power tool whines. I look at her, my expression depicting *sorry isn't going to cut it*. 'I had no choice.'

'Bullshit.' Zelda gets to her feet and starts banging on the wall, shouting at them to pipe down. 'Everyone has choices, and you chose to lie to my sister for personal gain.'

'No,' Daisy insists, getting to her feet, bandaged hand close to her chest. 'It wasn't like that.' She wipes a tear from her left eye. 'I swear. I was just looking for a way in. I wanted to tell you, Bella. I almost did a few times but…'

I rub my temple. 'Why should I believe a word that comes out of your mouth?' What is real about Daisy Murphy? Everything she's told us so far is a lie. 'Zelda's right, you are out to fleece us.' The words slip out of my mouth effortlessly, even though I'm not sure I believe them. Her eyes close and for a horrible moment she morphs into my dad, not so much now, but when he was younger, and I know, without a shadow of a doubt, that Daisy Murphy isn't out to fleece anyone. Everything Tina Anderson has said is true.

Mum's on her feet now, arms stretched out like a mediator, chest rising and falling rapidly. 'Let's all just calm down, shall we, and discuss this like adults.' I square up to Daisy, heart belting. The tension in the air seeps through my pores, sinking into my bones.

'Bella, I won't tell you again,' Mum says, and Daisy and I slip back into our seats like begrudged teenagers, giving each other looks. 'How did you find us, Daisy?'

Poised on the edge of her seat, Daisy sniffs, wipes her tear-stained cheeks with the heel of her hand, and then, 'After Dad died, I found an old biscuit tin in the basement. Inside was a newspaper cutting of my story and other bits of keepsakes. I didn't do anything with it for ages. I was shocked, in denial. Once I'd processed it all, I got in touch with the hospital where I was abandoned. The nurses and staff had all retired, moved. But Tina's details were still on the system.'

'Good job I left a forwarding address when I moved to London, eh? We spoke regularly on the phone after that, became friends.' Tina throws Daisy an adoring glance. 'She's like family now.'

'Like a niece,' I say dryly.

Tina looks at me gravely. 'Anyway, I invited her to London and said I'd help her find her family.'

'Tina suggested trying a DNA database. I figured I had nothing to lose by giving it a go. I went through the process, thinking it'll lead to nothing, and then bingo. A match. A father.' *Sweet Jesus.* Mum yelps like a wounded animal, eyes full of hurt, betrayal. I will never forgive Dad for this.

'Mum, have you still got my spare inhaler.' I can't breathe. 'Mum!' Mum waves a crumpled tissue at the sideboard irritably, and I remember it's in the top drawer.

'Grandpa,' Georgia exclaims, as if Dad is sitting in front of her. Clearly impressed with Dad's philandering instead of being mortified by his unforgiveable betrayal. 'You old rascal.'

'I think you should sit down, Sandra,' Daisy says, but Mum just stands there, defiant.

'Come on, Mum,' Zelda groans as I shake my inhaler ferociously. 'Daddy would never have done anything like that to you. Don't fall for her sob story,' she says, her conviction waning by the second.

'She's right,' I agree hastily, wanting it to be true more than believing it.

'I'm sure your father was a decent man and a good parent,' Daisy replies as I wrap my lips around the mouthpiece of my asthma pump. 'Pity your mother couldn't keep her knickers on.'

Chapter 63

'Mr Gray ring any bells, Sandie?' Daisy says, as we all gawp at her.

'Dear Lord.' Mum flops into her chair as if she's been pushed.

'Nan!'

'*Mum*,' I cry, 'tell her she's lying.'

'Oh, I've heard it all now.' Zelda's face twists in repulsion. 'Just…just get out, will you, and take your aging fake aunt with you.' The words sprout from Zelda's lips like venom.

'Barry Gray,' Mum mutters at the carpet, then jerks her head up. *Who the fuck is Barry Gray?* 'You spoke to him?' With a deep inhalation, Daisy nods. Tina confirms this, says she was there when they Facetimed. 'What did he tell you?' she demands.

'He said you'd had a fling, got pregnant and insisted on an abortion. In the end, he reluctantly agreed. Shortly after, he relocated to Birmingham. Ran a pub until he retired – still there with his family.'

'Relocated, my arse,' Mum retorts, and I feel the blood drain from my face. She's not denying it. It must be true. But when?

How? We'd have noticed Mum's bump if she were pregnant for a start off. 'What else did he say?' Mum probes.

We listen in stunned silence as Daisy tells how Barry's eldest son, Mark, bought his dad an ancestry DNA kit for his birthday. 'You can imagine how Barry reacted when he found out about me, and I was just as stunned when he emailed.' Leaning forward, Daisy picks up her mug and takes a sip of tea, no doubt stone cold by now. 'Barry wasn't surprised when I told him my story, said you were a nasty piece of work, Sandra, with no time for children.' The hairs on my neck flare. Zelda looks at me, shakes her head.

'Oh, Daisy, that's mean,' Georgia says, offended.

'Hey, that's not true,' I snap, mirroring my daughter's reaction. Admittedly, she's never been mumsy, but she's not cruel. Mum always put us before her own happiness after Dad left, often going without meals to feed us.

'Barry told me you had two other daughters, even remembered their names.' Daisy laughs lightly. 'He warned me not to contact you, said I'd regret it. But I was adamant. I wanted to know who my mother was. I wanted to look you in the eye, Sandra, and ask you why you abandoned me.'

Mum presses her fist against her lips. 'Vindictive lying bastard.'

'Lying bastard?' I repeat, confused. Is she denying it?

'You guys weren't difficult to track down with a name like Villin,' Daisy says. 'So…' Daisy stretches her arms out wide as if we've won her in a raffle. 'Here I am,' she trills in a singy voice. The irony in her tone is palpable, rendering us speechless.

Closing my eyes, I rub my forehead. A migraine is starting. And then I hear the sound of clapping – slow, measured, theatrical. 'Great performance.' Zelda's on her feet. 'But you heard what Mum said. Barry Gray is a liar. Now, will you please crawl back to whatever rock you surfaced from and leave us alone.'

Mum blinks and a single tear slides along her cheek. 'It wasn't like that. I didn't…he…Stanley…my ex-husband.' A pause, a sniff. 'Stanley told me you were going to be placed with a loving family who couldn't have children,' Mum confesses, and in that moment my whole existence turns on its axis.

Zelda looks as if all the blood has been drained from her body. 'Fucking hell.'

'Mum? How is this possible?' Did our parents drug us for nine months?

'I am SO stoked. This is brilliant, Nan.'

Georgia's excitement sends a crash of anger and disappointment shooting through me like a missile. 'Oh, Georgia, will you please shut up,' I snap, feeling a searing pain shoot from my temple to my eye. 'This is serious.'

'After Stanley took you, I changed my mind,' Mum says through thin, quivering lips speckled with stale pink lipstick. 'I wanted you back, but it was too late. You'd already been placed with a family. I begged him to tell me where you were but he refused point blank – said it was part of the agreement. Accused me of being an unfit mother – said he'd call social services if I didn't shut up about it. Get me sectioned. Take my girls away. I was on antidepressants, couldn't cope with the loss.' Mum looks at me, eyes watery, and my anger melts away like a snowflake.

'Oh, Mum,' I say. 'Why didn't you tell us?'

'We started arguing a lot more,' Mum continues, ignoring me. 'Eventually, I persuaded him to get in contact with the family, said I'd kill myself if he refused. I watched him pick up the phone, dial the number and speak to someone. I could tell something was wrong by the tone of his voice. When he put the phone down, he turned to me and said the young couple had moved and that their adopted baby had…' Mum chokes on her words, rubs her arm. God, no, please don't let her have a stroke. 'They said it was a cot death,' she gulps. Pins pierce my stomach repeatedly. Dad didn't make that call, did he – he fobbed Mum off to shut her up. I bet he had his finger pressed on the plunger during the entire fake conversation. 'I'm so sorry, girls.'

Bitter saliva fills my mouth. I swallow it down and look at Daisy, who is twisting the crucifix around in her fingers, features set in confusion. 'You thought I was dead?'

Mum nods, squeezing the damp tissue in her hand. 'I believed him – why would he lie to me? But none of it was true, was it? He just made it all up. Dumped you outside a hospital, came home, had his tea, laughed his head off watching an episode of Morecambe and Wise and went to bed. The evil bastard. Divorcing him,' Mum says to me and Zelda, voice breaking, 'was the best thing I ever did.'

Zelda sighs, throws me a fleeting glance. 'To be fair, Mum, you did cheat on him and have another man's child.' Mum turns away sharply, as if she's been slapped. 'Is that when you disappeared for almost a year,' Zelda continues. 'When you went to look after Grandpa?' My heart crushes. Of course it was. Why didn't I make that connection? I bet Grandpa wasn't even ill.

Mum nods. 'I stayed with him a couple of nights, then moved into a B&B until I had the baby. Meanwhile, Stanley was going to put the house on the market, sell up and join me with you girls once I'd given birth. Barry could never know. We'd start afresh in the Isle of Man, where no one knew us. Those were Stanley's terms.'

'Wow, Nan,' Georgia gasps.

'The cross.' Mum sniffs. 'They let you keep it.'

'It was in the biscuit tin I found.' Daisy's voice is barely audible. Mum dips her head, shoulders shaking.

'Oh, Nan,' Georgia rushes over to her, and I watch as my mother weeps in my daughter's arms. I feel numb. I can't believe I've got a half-sister I knew nothing about. A sibling who's been sharing my home for weeks. A mother who's been harbouring a secret for almost a lifetime. But most of all, I'm sickened that the man I'd looked up to is nothing but a selfish, ruthless, monster.

'Mum, why didn't you tell us?' I ask again.

'Oh, love,' she sobs. I couldn't.'

'Well, this is all very endearing,' Zelda sniffs. I know that look. I know she's feigning indifference, 'But you could be anyone. Mum's daughter is dead. A cot death. Our father isn't a liar. He placed Mum's baby with a loving, childless couple who were desperate – made their dream come true.'

Tina sighs loudly. 'I suppose you'll want to see some proof.' Tina's hand disappears into the manila envelope that she's been guarding close to her chest since she got here. 'Here,' she says, and as she hands me several A4 sheets, I catch Daisy shaking her head at Tina nervously, eyes flared, frightened. My heartbeat belts. What is she hiding now? What is it she doesn't want me to see?

Chapter 64

I thumb through the pages eagerly, blocking out the babble of voices. A copy of the newspaper cuttings – *Baby found on Trinity Hospital stairs.* A photo of baby Daisy, wearing a gold crucifix around her little body with a glimmering ruby in the middle. Oh, and now the prize – Ancestry Report for Daisy Murphy. I scan it hungrily:

Sort by Relationships

Match categories:

Parent/Child – Barry Gray.

And then, highlighted in yellow, there it is. The proof we all need. *Jesus wept.*

Georgia Harris – Possible relationship: First cousin once removed – Half uncle, aunt – Half nephew, NIECE! *Oh, Liam, what've you done? You said it was only going to be a paternity test, you little shit.* My pulse slams against the wall of my chest.

'Bella, Bella, did you hear me?' Tina's voice becomes audible again, 'Let Zelda see the documents, please.'

'What? I utter, hair in my hot face. I feel as if I'm floating. I can't show this to Zelda, she'll blurt it all out, everyone will question me. Georgia will want to know how her details ended up on a DNA database without her permission, and, more importantly, who put them there. But before I can say anything else, Tina snatches the papers from my limp grasp.

'No,' Daisy barks, hand out, and Tina recoils.

'But don't you want them to…'

Daisy gives Tina a look, eyes hardening, and all I can do is sit there, panting, wishing I could dissolve into the fibres of the sofa. 'That report contains confidential information,' Daisy says through gritted teeth, then looks at me, face softening. She knows about Liam and the paternity test. Of course she does, she must've emailed him thinking it was Georgia, and he told her everything, including where to find us. And now, Daisy is trying to protect me. I want to hug her. 'Look, Tina, you shouldn't have even shown it to Bella, not without my consent.'

'Yes, of course.' Tina gives me a fleeting, nervous look. 'You're right. I'm sorry. I didn't think.'

'Typical,' Zelda groans, impatiently. 'Bella, did you see anything, anything at all that confirms Daisy's related to us?'

'I um…' Swallowing, I glance at Daisy. 'I didn't get a chance to read it all properly before…'

'Bella?' Mum says crisply, clearly sensing my tension. She's no fool. 'If there's anything you think you should share, please do. This is important.'

'Yeah, Mum, come on,' Georgia agrees.

Zelda looks at me carefully. She knows something's up. 'I don't think anything can shock us more today, Bella.' *Oh, there is, Zee, there is.* The room falls silent. I can feel everyone's eyes burning into every cell of my body.

'Well, Barry Gray *is* the father, as Mum confirmed,' I curl my hair behind my ears. 'Which means it's true.'

'Bollocks. It means nothing.' Zelda's eyes slide to the papers in Tina's lap. Shit, she's going to snatch them. She goes to move but Daisy is like lightening. 'I'll have those, Tina, thank you very much.' Daisy folds the sheets with one hand and for a moment I think she's going to tear them up, but then stuffs them into her open bag on the floor next to her.

'There is no proof, is there?' Zelda spits. *There's concrete proof, Zelda. Concrete.* 'You're just pissing in the wind.'

'Zelda stop,' I say gently. Going over to her, I squat and curl my hands around her forearms and make her look at me. 'It's true, love. It happened. We've got to accept what our father did.' Her face reddens. 'Look, maybe he wasn't thinking straight. Maybe…'

'I'm not accepting anything,' Zelda fumes, pulling away from me. 'If you three have been taken in, I haven't. Those documents only prove that Barry Gray's her dad. End of.'

'Zelda, love,' Mum says.

'I should go, leave you to digest it.' Daisy goes to stand up. Tina fastens the belt of her coat in readiness, glancing at her watch. I bet she can't wait to get out of here.

There's a kerfuffle of movement, zips hissing, fabrics swishing, and then. 'Daisy, wait,' Georgia pleads, then turns to me and Zelda, 'I know you're upset about Grandpa, auntie Zelda. I would be too if I found out my dad had done something as horrible as this. But it's not Daisy's fault, is it? Yes, your parents divorced when you were little, but at least you grew up in a strong family unit. At least you knew where you came from – who you are.' My eyes fill. How can my fifteen-year-old child mature in such a short space of time? 'Wouldn't you want to find your biological parents if you were in Daisy's shoes? I deffo would.' Zelda and I exchange looks. Tina nods, mumbling in agreement. Daisy leans against the doorframe, cradling her injured limb, while Mum continues to destroy the tissue in her hands, muttering to herself. I think she's cursing Dad. 'Daisy didn't ask for any of this. Okay, she might've gone about it the wrong way, but we all love her. Why should this change anything?' She turns to Daisy. 'Why don't you and Nan just do a DNA? Keep everyone happy.'

'How did all this happen, Mum?' I ask. 'I thought you and Daddy were happy.'

'It's complicated,' Mum says irritably. 'Look, your father was away working for months on end. I was young, head in the clouds. Barry was a looker. We had a brief fling, that was all. When I told Barry I was pregnant, he said he couldn't leave his wife and kids – not that I asked him to - said he'd see me and the nipper right, on the quiet. It's not what I wanted to hear.'

'So why did you keep it?' Zelda demands, and Daisy gives her a deathly glare. Zelda presses on. 'You had options even then, surely.'

'An abortion was out of the question. I was too far gone.'

'Hello?' Zelda says, 'Didn't you miss any periods?'

'I thought I was going through the change. My mother had an early menopause. But I wouldn't have done it, anyway.' Mum shakes her head defiantly. 'I fobbed Barry off, told him I'd gotten rid of it, he was off the hook. About eight weeks later, Barry was gone. A stroke of luck, Stanley called it. We could stay in our home after all. I'd stay at the B&B until I had the baby, with regular visits from Stanley, and he'd tell folk I was looking after my poorly dad. I had terrible morning sickness, couldn't travel.'

'Hyperemesis gravidarum,' Tina says. 'Some women suffer with it throughout their pregnancies.'

'Is that what it's called? Anyway, I'd come back with the baby. No one would know it wasn't Stanley's. But after the birth, Stanley took one look at Cindy and ran for the hills. It was your shock of red hair.' Mum smiles at Daisy. 'He was a very proud man.'

'You were going to keep me?' Daisy's eyes fill.

'Of course I was. *Of course*. Well, at least that was the plan until Stanley changed his mind. He gave me an ultimatum. You, or him and the girls. What kind of choice was that?'

A bloody impossible one.

Chapter 65

'Cindy,' Daisy sniffs, ten minutes later, once Mum lets go of her. I thought Mum was going to squeeze her to death. I don't blame her. It isn't every day your long lost, presumed dead, child walks into your life. 'Was that my birth name?'

Mum nods as Georgia walks in with another tray of hot drinks, sets it down on the coffee table and tells everyone to help themselves. 'Lucinda, after my mother.' Nana Lucy. A no-nonsense woman who despised Dad, the feeling was mutual, but worshipped the ground Mum walked on. She'd have lynched Dad for abandoning her namesake granddaughter. 'I always liked strong names – Isabella, Zelda, Lucinda.'

'Lucinda. I like it.' Daisy gives mum a watery smile.

'I've never stopped thinking about you, every single day. I can't believe Stanley lied to me. It's unforgiveable,' Mum seethes. 'Letting me mourn all these years for a child that's alive.' Mum sets her mug down on the table 'You've got my nose,' she coos, touching her own face. 'And Bella's smile, and your profile is just like my mother's. Zelda looks a lot like her.' Zelda shuffles in her seat, takes a slurp from her mug and winces, complaining that it tastes like dishwater – whatever that tastes like.

'Daisy, why weren't you upfront with us?' I ask, intrigued. 'Why the cloak-and-dagger approach?'

'Daisy didn't want to deceive you, Bella,' Tina replies, like her spokesperson. 'We were just looking for a lead. The was no record of a maternal family member on the DNA reports.' Tina coughs into her hand and looks at me as if to say *apart from Georgia Harris with Liam Cooper's email.* 'Daisy got your surname from Barry,' Tina continues. 'We found Bella online quite easily.' *Especially as you had all my details at hand.* Tina turns to Daisy, 'It was Facebook, wasn't it?' Daisy shakes her head, tells her it was Instagram, Georgia makes a vomit sound, says Facebook is for old ladies. 'Anyway, we couldn't come in all guns blazing. The shock might've sent you running for the hills.' Oh, I don't know. Maybe initially, yes, but I'd have been intrigued enough to agree to a meet-up.

'We needed a strategy.' Tina pauses, takes a sip of coffee. 'A way in. An invite. Daisy was nervous as hell about telling you who she was, especially after Barry's warning.' That is feasible. But lying to us for weeks? What's the worst that could've happened if she'd fessed up?

'I stayed undercover because I couldn't bear to be rejected twice,' Daisy admits.

'So, we came up with a plan,' Tina says to me. 'I'd pretend I was putting my house on the market and hire you to take the photographs. The idea was to meet you, try and find out about your mother.' That's why she was asking so many questions about Mum, and there was I thinking she was just being lovely.

'What did you expect my sister to do, give our mum's address out to a complete stranger?' Zelda snaps.

'No,' Tina says tersely. 'I'd simply gauge the situation. Find out if Sandra was still alive, if she lived in London, if she was still married. That sort of thing. And I'm not sure what would've happened after that.'

'We didn't think that far ahead,' Daisy adds. 'I just wanted to meet you on neutral grounds. See if I fitted in. If you liked me.'

'I suppose we thought the dots would join up spontaneously.' Tina takes another sip. 'The good news was that you are still alive, Sandra. The bad news was that you were in Portugal.' Tina looks at me. 'I couldn't ask you when she'd be back, not without sounding like a stalker. I was asking too many questions as it was. You were getting suspicious.' I wasn't, actually, but perhaps my body language suggested otherwise. 'I managed to find out you were an artist, Sandra, and lived quite close to Bella. I thought I was on a roll then. I mean, imagine, if you were well known. We could buy tickets to one of your exhibitions, and Daisy would meet her mother.' Tina clicks her fingers. 'Just like that. But, alas, Bella wouldn't divulge anything more. And that was the end of that. Our plan had failed.'

'Not quite, Miss Marple.' Daisy throws Tina a smile.

'When you said you were looking for a temp, Bella, a thought shot into my head. It was the perfect solution. Daisy could meet you, find out when her mother was coming home, where she lived, and, in the meantime, get to know her sisters, and her adorable niece, too.' Tina flicks an affectionate glance at Georgia and she laps it up, shimmying smugly. 'We decided that if Barry was right and you were a rotten lot, Daisy would simply go back to her life in Dublin, no one would ever know.'

'A right pair of detectives, aren't you?' Zelda groans, picking at a fingernail.

'I think it's genius,' Georgia trills, hands in namaste against her chin.

There's a moment of silence and then Mum says, 'Wait, a moment. Earlier you said Bella and Zelda had tried killing someone.' Panic pierces my chest. I forgot all about that. 'Why did you say such a horrid thing?'

Daisy shakes her head. 'It was all lies,' she says to the navy patterned carpet, and my heart breaks into a million pieces. Loyal to the core. 'I wanted to hurt you, Sandra, that's all.'

'By accusing them of being *murderers*,' Mum says crisply. Daisy nods and Mum's eyebrows shoot up.

'You can't blame her,' Tina offers. 'After the homecoming she just received.'

I look at Mum. She's deep in thought, fist pressed against her lips. God, I hope she doesn't press Daisy on this. Daisy's fragile at the moment, she might break under Mum's detective-style questioning.

Suddenly, Zelda shoots to her feet. 'I can't deal with this shitshow. I'll text you later, Bells.' Rushing over to Mum, she gives her a quick peck on the forehead. 'Great to have you back, Mum,' she whispers, then shoots across me.

'Zelda,' I barrel after her. 'Zelda, wait.' The front door slams so hard that my teeth vibrate. I sigh loudly as I pad back into the living room, making a mental note to call Zelda this evening. This news is going to take some digesting.

'I should go,' Daisy announces as I flop back down on the sofa. 'I shouldn't have done this to you. Not like this. It was a crazy idea. I'm sorry, Bella, you've been nothing but kind to me and all I've done is lie to you. Taking in a homeless stranger, that takes some heart. You really are an earth angel.'

'Hear hear.' Georgia applauds.

'It was my fault,' Tina objects, rubbing the back of her neck tiredly. 'I was the one who came up with the ridiculous plan.' She sighs loudly at the ceiling. 'It just felt like the right thing to do at the time.' Daisy objects, tells her she can't thank her enough for everything she's done for her.

'You did what you thought was right, Tina, and you brought my daughter home. I'll always be grateful to you for that.'

And just like that, I lose a temp and gain another sister.

Chapter 66

'Muuuuum,' Georgia yells. 'Auntie Linda's here.'

'I'll be down in a minute, sweetheart.' I lean over the banister, catching sight of a blur of yellow swishing by as Linda clambers after Georgia in the hallway. She's wearing her new Karen Millen trench coat. Theo bought it for her. A peace-offering for giving her a hard time over that one-night-stand she had with Frank a million years ago. 'Linda,' I yell, clipping on my right earring. 'Help yourself to coffee or tea.'

Heading back into my bedroom, I tuck my olive-green blouse into my black skirt, throwing a glance at the time on Alexa Echo Show on my bedside table. It's eight-thirty. Daisy said she'll be meeting us at the house at half-nine. We've plenty of time, but I feel anxious as hell. It's not newbie nerves, it's more to do with the potential tenant who will be viewing the property. *You'll be fine, Bella. She won't bite.*

Tom had laughed when I told him Linda and I were starting our own agency. 'I'll give you three months, tops,' he said, sardonically. 'Sorry, Bella, but you haven't got a business brain between you.'

But I've already proved him wrong. Linda and I set up Belinda Estate and Lettings two months ago and we've already sold seven properties and let out sixteen.

Daisy was our first client. Tina Anderson was right about Daisy having plenty of her own money. It was sitting in the bank earning a pittance. Linda suggested investing it in property. So, when Zelda's neighbours, Janette and Ian, ran out of money and into debt, forcing them to put their house on the market via our agency, Daisy got in there first with the asking price. The process was swift, and they exchanged three weeks ago.

Zelda got first dibs and has moved into the first-floor flat with loft conversion. The kitchen isn't massive, but it's big enough to accommodate her cake business and a far cry from the dismal flat she rented next door, with its prehistoric kitchen, mould infested bedroom and ancient bathroom. Daisy isn't charging Zelda a penny, not even mates' rates. All she'll have to do is chip in for the bills. I swear that girl has invisible wings.

Daisy, much to Mum's annoyance because she wanted her youngest daughter to live with her forever and not just a few weeks, has moved into the basement flat. 'I love gardening,' Daisy said when I warned her that she won't get much light down there and basements are notorious for flooding. 'I'll be fine. Plus, I'll earn a bit more from the two-bedroom ground-floor flat.' I couldn't argue with that. The ground-floor apartment with balcony overlooking the incredible views of Green Bay gardens and lake is a bit spectacular.

A text pings through. I look at the screen. It's from Tom:
Picking Georgia up from football practice and going to Wagamama. Fancy joining us? Xx
I quickly type:
No.

I chew my bottom lip, finger hovering over send, delete it and type again:

Thanks. But you guys should spend some quality time together.☺

I read it back, then press Send. Tom and I are officially separated. We agreed that our marriage wasn't working out – the trust had gone – and I couldn't live with his stinginess a moment longer. The truth is, all I've ever wanted was to be loved. To be put first. To be someone's number one priority. If I'm honest, I don't think I had any of that with Tom. I'd go as far as saying that he only married me because I was pregnant with his child. Zelda was his first choice when we met all those years ago. Tom just settled for me. Second best Bella, that's what I am. Maybe I should have it printed on a t-shirt, or tattooed inside my wrist.

A week had passed before I told my family that Tom and I were estranged. It was during a family dinner to celebrate Daisy's homecoming. I wasn't surprised by Mum's reaction. She loved Tom. She even cried. Blamed me, said I was being hasty, 'So what if he's parsimonious?' she'd said. 'I can think of worse traits.' Zelda agreed with the latter part of Mum's assumption and I began to doubt everything again. Until Daisy spoke.

'I wasn't going to say anything but now I will.' Daisy set her cutlery down. 'On the night of all that hoo-ha with Frank and Stanhope and the police visit, I walked in on Tom having, what looked like, a steamy conversation with a woman on Zoom.' Zelda gasped, looked at me, grim-faced, while Mum made a noise that sounded as if she was suffocating.

'I thought you'd gone to bed,' I said. We all had, bar Tom who was googling smells and the afterlife.

'My head was buzzing. I couldn't sleep. I went down to make myself a cup of camomile. The moment he saw me, he slammed the lid of his laptop down, and just sat there, deep in thought, hand still on his laptop, face all flushed and sweaty. I guess he didn't know how much I'd heard. I wasn't going to mention it, but his reaction made me suspicious. After a few moments, I asked him, casual as you like, who that blonde bird was. He laughed it off, said it was a colleague, called their conversation a bit of banter. I was like, what, at this time of the morning? Then he made me promise not to tell you, Bella, reckoned you had a bit of a jealous streak.'

A cold silence snapped around the table. Mum, Zelda and I exchanged glances. 'I gave him the benefit of the doubt,' Daisy continued. 'I didn't want to cause any trouble between the two of you. But he did get a bit frosty with me after that.' That was why he suddenly wanted her out. She knew too much, couldn't trust her.

Tom didn't deny it when I confronted him – called the affair stress-sex. 'Natalie was a client,' he explained, which broke all the rules in itself. Health professionals aren't supposed to date patients, are they? He went on to say that when Liam came to our house that night looking for me, Tom had lost it, thought we were lovers. 'I am sorry, you know,' he said, in Wendy and Gary's hallway when I went round to take him a few of his things.

'For what? Bribing Daisy, or sleeping with someone else?'

'All of it. I was lost, weak, and Natalie just...'

'Took the edge off?' I finished. 'Most people have a few large G&Ts.'

He inhaled deeply through his nose. 'I still love you and I want us to fix this.'

'It's too late, Tom. I'm sorry. I'll send the rest of your things on.'

Then as I reached for the doorlatch he blurted. 'I know you were in love with him.' I paused, frowned at the door. 'I heard you talking to Liam on the phone.' My frown deepened. 'Oh, don't play the innocent. On the night of Linda and Theo's dinner party, after I'd warned him off you. You couldn't wait to lock yourself away in the bathroom and phone him, could you? Well, I wasn't tucked up in bed, as you thought. I was standing outside, listening.' I spun on my heel then, and looked at him incredulously. 'I heard you pleading with him to give you another chance. Begging for his forgiveness. *Pathetic*.'

'You're insane,' I retorted.

'That's what all those gym visits were about, weren't they?' he hissed. 'Losing all that weight. You wanted to look good for *him*.'

I shook my head. 'You really are deluded. Hang on, I know what you're trying to do, accuse me of infidelity to make yourself look better to save face. But you're the one who got caught with his pants down.' I went to open the front door when his hand slammed against the panel. I could feel his hot breath against my ear, smell the alcohol on his breath. He was pissed.

'But it's what you said to him next that sent me into the arms of another woman. Do you remember what it was?'

I turned around and squared up to him. 'You were drunk then and you're drunk *now*.'

'Thought not,' he whispered. 'I'll refresh your memory, shall I?' He cleared his throat, then said, '*Please, don't push me away. Just say the word and I'll leave him.*' My face twisted in confusion and I gave a little mirthless laugh, told him he was pathetic. 'But he didn't want to know, did he? Refused to leave his wife and kids for you. And you...' He poked my shoulder. 'Got so mad that you chucked your phone across the bathroom.' I shook my head in disbelief, told him he was mad. 'That's how you shattered your phone screen. You didn't drop it in the Tesco carpark at all, did you?'

My phone rings on the bedside table, breaking me out of my reverie. I peer at it and my heart stops. It's Fiona, Liam's widow.

Chapter 67

I've never been a Fiona fan. I mean, she's not the most level-headed person on the planet. Linda almost fainted when I told her that Fiona was *killingsteve1984@gmail.com* and not Frank, as we all suspected. I should've worked it out, really. We all called Fiona, Ona, back in the day, apart from her ex-husband Steve, who insisted on calling her Fi, which she loathed.

Liam once told me that Steve took out a restraining order on Fiona because she refused to accept that their marriage was over. I gasped when he said she'd keyed Steve's brand-new Range Rover. What a vindictive, thuggish thing to do. But that was just the tip of the iceberg. Liam also confided that she'd stalked his new girlfriend and almost ran the pair of them over as they were leaving their local pub. 'She was in a bad place, Bells,' Liam confessed. 'On antidepressants. Drinking far too much, not eating properly. She's a different person now. Therapy helped. Apart from the jealousy thing, that is. I think that's just how she's wired. But, hey, none of us is perfect. I've got a good life with her and the kids.'

Biting my thumbnail, I stare at her name on my phone until it rings out. A beat and then it starts again. Surely, she won't give Daisy any trouble…will she? No, of course not. I'm being silly. Paranoid. She's a changed woman. *Come on, Bella, where's your sense of charity? The woman's bereaved, at a loose end.*

Fiona told me that Liam didn't have any life insurance, when I rang to offer my condolences, and if that weren't enough, her landlady was kicking them out at the end of the month. Finding a landlord who accepted housing benefit tenants was near impossible. 'I'm sorry for sending you those awful emails, Bella,' she admitted. 'Once the police identified the body, they gave me all his belongings. I went through his phone and when I saw your name I lost it. I thought you two were…you know.' I told her it was fine. That it was our fault. We shouldn't have liaised behind her back. 'I was looking for someone to blame for his death. I'm so sorry.'

Her dilemma played on my mind. She was grieving. Had just lost her husband. I couldn't stand by and do nothing. Daisy's flat is affordable and convenient for schools. I had to offer it up.

'Hi Ona,' I say now, 'everything okay?'

'Um…actually,' she begins, sounding breathless. I cross my fingers tightly, praying she's going to tell me she's found another flat.

'I'm running ten-minutes late. Is that okay?'

My shoulders sag. 'No problem at all,' I reply, uncrossing my fingers. 'Listen, Ona, just to let you know we've had a lot of interest in the flat, and I did say it's only a two-bedroom, didn't I?'

'Don't you dare let it out to anyone else before I see it, Bella,' she warns. 'It sounds ideal and the kids don't mind sharing.'

Clamping the phone between my jaw and shoulder, I assure her that I won't, as I hurriedly do up the zip of my skirt and dash to the bathroom.

'I'll see you soon, then,' I say. 'We'll be waiting outside.'

Linda looks at her watch and gives it a shake. 'What time is it? Is she late?'

'Ten past ten,' I say, glancing at my Apple watch. 'And here she is.'

We watch as Fiona rocks up along the shared driveway, tanned and groomed and cool as a cucumber. 'Sorry I'm late.' Fiona pulls me in for an air kiss. 'Noah couldn't find his PE kit. You look amazing, Bella.'

'Thank you. So do you. You haven't changed a bit.' Bar her chestnut hair, which is now platinum blonde.

'Gah.' Fiona gushes. 'Three kids and a dead husband puts a lot of lines on your face, but thank you.'

'This is Linda, my partner in crime,' I grin, and Linda gives me a look as she thrusts a hand out.

'And this must be...'

'Daisy Murphy.' Daisy takes Fiona's hand and they exchange limp handshakes.

'Are you related?' Fiona asks. 'I can see a resemblance.'

'We are,' I begin, as Linda urges us to all make our way inside, she'll be late for her eleven o'clock.

We walk along the driveway and as Fiona fires questions at Linda about the flat, Daisy hangs back, drawing me to her. 'You don't have to tell her about me if it's awkward,' she whispers. 'It's okay.'

I stop stock-still and look at Daisy. I get the feeling she thinks I might be ashamed to relay her history. But she's wrong. Daisy put her neck on the line for me and Zelda from the get-go

– kept our secret about Frank. Didn't tell a soul that Liam replied to her email on the ancestry website and gave her every single detail about me that she wanted. She even picked up the letter knife when I dropped it at the cashpoint, knowing full well what it was. Implicated herself. Protected me. Protected us. I'll never forget that. I cover her hand with mine and we start walking, picking up pace as Linda calls out to us.

At the front door, we pause while Linda pushes the key into the lock, all the while keeping up a commentary about how wonderful the flat is – it's immaculate – ultra modern – spacious, bright, has a balcony with side glass panels. A well-kept garden that backs onto Green Bay Gardens and Lake.

'Daisy's my sister,' I blurt to Fiona, realising this is the first time I've introduced her as my sibling and feeling surprised at how normal and natural it feels.

'Seriously?' Fiona says, disinterested, as we step inside the flat, 'I thought it was just the two of you.' Fiona takes in the bright hallway hungrily. I can see she likes what she sees already, and then Zelda thunders down the stairs in her cream loungers and animal slippers.

I watch as Zelda and Fiona exchanges pleasantries and my heart breaks a little for her. Although Zelda has moved on and seems more upbeat, I sometimes catch her in deep thought and wonder if she's missing Frank. Although I loathe to admit it, he was good to her. She was the happiest I'd seen her in years. Was I wrong to intervene in their relationship? Maybe. But the truth is, I couldn't bear seeing them together. The truth is…

'Bella, did you bring the particulars sheet?' Linda asks briskly.

Snapping out of my musing, I pull the A4 sheet out of my handbag. 'Here you go.' My phone buzzes with a text. Daisy glances up at me from her phone. It's from Georgia, pleading with me to join her and Tom for dinner tonight. I hesitate, type out *I'll think about it*, then press send. Thumbing the cracked screen, Frank's face slams into my mind and guilt claws at my chest. *I did the right thing. I was protecting my sister.*

Hastily, I slip my phone back into my handbag, making a mental note to get the screen repaired. This is no time for regrets. Frank would've destroyed Zelda, broken her. It was only a matter of time. How could I be so sure? Well, it's what irresistible men like him do, isn't it? They bewitch you with their charm and good looks, make you want to sacrifice everything for them – your marriage, your family, your life…and then they push you away. Just like Frank had done to me.

Chapter 68

Daisy

The chill bites against my ten-denier-clad legs as I yank the lever of the garage door. I don't usually show potential tenants the garage. It's my space. But Fiona, or Ona, as she insists on being called, asked about storage for her kids' bikes. I could see you were about to tell her she'd had to leave them in the hallway, Bella, but I also sensed a hint of anxiety in your deportment. Call it telepathy. A bond between sisters. I can't allow you to suffer any discomfort. Linda ushers us all back inside.

'It's very clean and spacious.' Fiona gazes around the open-plan kitchen, with its navy matt cabinets, shiny cream granite worktops and skylights. 'You've got a lovely home, Daisy.'

I thank her, explain that it's not my doing, the previous owners did a great job, and you jump in, say I'm being modest – the house is spotless – the interior and furnishings are my own vision.

'Is that an Irish accent?' Fiona folds her bony arms against her chest. She's not what I expected, with her long leather-clad legs and blonde waist-length hair – salon styled, you don't get results like that out of a bottle.

'It is Irish.' I toss a glance at you, but you're busy talking to Linda now who is showing you something on her iPad. 'I'm from Dublin.' I study Fiona's face – smooth and tanned without a wrinkle in sight. Botox, obviously, at her age. Hardly the grieving widow. How can she afford all that if she's on the breadline? You do realise I could get a grand more for this place if I rented it to someone else, Bella, don't you? Still, no matter, you want me to rent it to her and I will. I'd do anything for you. *Anything.*

'Wait…I'm slightly confused,' Fiona says. 'How comes you were brought up in Ireland?' I inwardly roll my eyes. I fecking knew it.

Your head snaps up at Fiona. You are listening, after all. 'Daisy was adopted,' you say, your expression set in defence mode. 'We've only just connected.'

I love you for it, Bella but you really don't need to fight my battles. I'm a big girl. I can handle myself. Trust me.

'Oh, how lovely.' Fiona turns to me. 'So, you've got two families.'

I think you were right about her, Bella, she's already annoying me. 'Three, actually. Biological mum, dad, and two adoptive brothers. My adoptive parents have passed.' *Thank God.* A phone rings. I hope it's hers, because I really need her to feck off now.

'I'm sorry to hear about your adoptive parents,' Fiona says, sounding sincere. *Really? I'm bloody delighted.* What's with all this empathy anyway? I don't care what she thinks. This is strictly a business transaction. You walk over to us. Linda glances at you, phone pressed to her ear.

'Can you try ringing the vendor again?' Linda huffs into her handset. She must be talking to Maggie, your PA. It was good of you to give Maggie a job at your agency, Bella. The increased salary will help now she's got a nipper, especially with the cost of living these days.

'Her adoptive parents were Irish,' you say tightly, and I can tell you're trying to protect me from Fiona the empress of nosey-buggers.

'Your mum was quite young when she died, wasn't she?' Linda asks, joining us in a waft of Fiona's pungent perfume. Feck's sake, now they want my life story. Well, I suppose I'd better get it out of the way. I'm surprised you all waited this long before quizzing me.

'Mid-fifties,' I explain and you all gawp at me as if I'm orphan Annie. 'I was sixteen. Mammy drowned.' Your frowns grow deeper. Apart from Fiona's, which is paralysed. Fiona gasps, tells me she can't swim either, a piece of information which I file in my brain for future reference. 'Mammy was an excellent swimmer. It was an accident in the bathtub – slipped and drowned.' My mother stood up and lunged at me in a rage for daring to answer her back. Reflexively, I took a step back and she skidded. Water gushed everywhere. It was like a tsunami. I watched in a stupor as she started splashing manically between gulps, begging me to help. She tried to get up but kept sliding back under the water, as if she'd lost total control of her limbs, and then she was still.

'Mammy had been drinking,' I explain. She was three sheets to the wind, as per. 'They had to break the door down to get in. It was locked.' After I watched her die, I climbed out of the window, the bathroom was located on the ground floor, and quietly slipped out the back gate that led into the woods. It was late, dark, no one saw me.

Fiona gasps, 'I'm never locking my bathroom door again.'

'What a traumatic experience for you,' Linda says, and you agree, come over to me, rub my back tenderly. 'Rotten luck that she was in the house alone. I've never heard of anyone dying in a bathtub before.'

'Nor me,' Fiona says, 'wouldn't the water wake you up?'

'It *is* extremely rare. The coroner said she might've fallen asleep or had some sort of seizure – neither of which could've been proven. A verdict of death by accident was returned after the post-mortem.'

'Wow,' you say, 'you must've been so terrified.'

I shrug, mouth drying. 'It was horrific. We were all shattered,' I lie, putting on my best devastated face. 'Dad was much older when he passed.' Clearing my throat, I slide the bifold doors open a fraction and breathe in some fresh air. 'He had a good, long life.'

I shepherd you all towards the lounge area. 'I was his carer until he died last year,' I continue, and you all ooh and ahh. Linda calls me a saint. I suppose I was a bit of a saint, cleaning and cooking and caring for him all those years, while his good-for-nothing sons strutted around Dublin, with their flashy cars and big houses. I'd gag when I loaded his piss-stained bedding into the washing machine. The shit stains on his pants wouldn't shift, not even on a 60-degree cycle.

'Father had a fall,' I say quietly. 'A heart attack.' I'd packed my bags to leave that day. We'd had the biggest brawl ever. I was sick of my life. Sick of him. I lied to you about only finding out I was adopted after my parents died, Bella. I'd known for months. The idiot blurted it out during a row. I couldn't stop thinking about them after that. Where were they? What were they doing? Did I have any siblings? Would I have had a better life with them, or were they a couple of useless bastards who could barely look after themselves? Something made them dump me. What was it? I was desperate to find out.

I plucked up the courage and questioned Da, asked if he knew anything about them and do you know what he said? Do you, Bella? He told me that Stanley *had* got in touch. Once. The hospital gave him our number, although there's no record of this. Da told Stanley I was dead. Dead, Bella. *Dead.* I didn't believe him, not until Sandra confirmed it. So, your dad wasn't lying when he said he'd made that call. But I haven't told you that. Not yet. I might one day, but then I might not. I mean, he did dump me outside the fecking hospital in the middle of winter. I might've died. Sandra was weak, letting Stanley give me away like that. I think I'll let her squirm for a bit longer. Guilt is quite pleasurable to watch. A bit like squeezing lemon juice on a laceration. Besides, I relish you all hating on your father - putting me before him – refusing his calls – his pleas. It makes me feel special. Wanted. *Loved.*

Anyway, I divert, Bella. Da telling Stanley I'd died was the last straw. A rage I'd never felt before tore through me. I'd had enough of being his servant. Needless to say, he didn't take it well. Who else would be his skivvy? Certainly not his stuck-up daughters-in-law, or precious granddaughters. He threatened to cut me off dry if I abandoned him – he'd left me the house in his will. All six-bedrooms of it. Old and dark and creepy. Worth a fortune.

But my freedom was worth more than that. I shoved past him, told him to do whatever he wanted, he always did. In his haste to stop me, he stumbled. I tried to help him, Bella, honestly. But he shook me off, said he could manage, thank you very much, in that brisk, self-righteous tone of his. Only he didn't manage because my foot came out – he tripped over it and collapsed onto the marble tiles, hitting his head. He was spark out. I don't know why I did it. Maybe watching Mammy die, all those years ago, and not lifting a finger to help her made me bloodthirsty.

'The paramedics did all they could,' I say now, 'but he didn't regain consciousness.' I don't add that I gave it ten minutes before ringing them, just to make sure the old goat had snuffed it. When they arrived, I told them I was in the shower upstairs, came down and found him lying there unconscious. I want to cry now. Why has Fiona dragged up my wretched past?

'Poor, love.' Fiona's mouth turns downwards, reminding me of a sad emojis. I'm not sure if you notice when I twist my lips to stop myself from laughing out loud. I can feel your eyes on me.

'It's fine,' I say to my feet. 'They weren't the best parents in the world.' Why should I protect them, or honour their memory? They were a pair of selfish arses.

You take a deep breath. 'Anyway, she's got us now, haven't you, Daisy?'

'I sure have,' I say, 'and this place.' I saunter back into the kitchen, run a hand along my bespoke granite worktop. 'I couldn't be happier.' Reflectively, I gaze out into the garden, and as I'm about to turn away I notice the garage door ajar in my peripheral. Perfect timing. I needed something to put an end to this morbid conversation. 'Can I leave you to it, ladies, I didn't shut the garage door properly.'

'I didn't expect the rooms to be so big,' Fiona trills, and Linda agrees. Their voices drown as I step outside, with you in my wake.

'Wait up,' you yell. I hear the clatter of your heels hitting the concrete on the driveway. I inwardly roll my eyes. Is two minutes of alone time too much to ask?

Chapter 69

Daisy

The two of us yank the garage door down. It was a two-man job. You were right to follow me outside, Bella. I'm not ungrateful. I'm just not used to anyone helping me. I take a step back and look up at the garage. The painters did a good job. I like green. Reminds me of Ireland. It's always been my favourite colour.

'Best get someone in to look at that door, Daisy. We don't want any accidents. I'll be inside. It's fucking freezing out here.'

You rub your arms and make a *brrr* sound. I smile, tell you I'll be in in a moment. Locking the door, I give it one final tug. I'm about to turn away when a shivery feeling courses through me. The last time I looked up at this garage was to make sure there were no security cameras installed. Frank didn't have a hope in hell after what Zelda and I did to him.

My mind drifts back to that Saturday barbeque at yours. Frank and Zelda are at the kitchen table. I'm sorting drinks out for everyone. Behind me, I hear them having a bit of a domestic, shuffling and murmurs. I spin round and catch him holding her by the wrist. I fight the urge to lunge forward and stab him in the eye with the teaspoon in my hand. Then they're back to normal and he's complaining of a headache. Zelda is concerned, offers him ibuprofen.

Of course, you know all this, Bella, because I told you, but what I failed to mention is the reason Zelda didn't come out to ask you for ibuprofen was because Frank reminded her of his allergy, asked if she was trying to kill him. Oh, the irony. My heart hardened then. I'd had enough of Frank Hardy upsetting my family. I pulled out a blister of ibuprofen from the kitchen drawer – what an odd place to keep painkillers, Bella. Using the pestle and mortar, I crushed them as best as I could and poured the grind into his coffee, giving it a good stir before placing it in front of him. He gulped it down gratefully, with two paracetamol tablets, which I also found in the drawer.

I wasn't sure how long it'd be before they took effect. I thought they'd give him diarrhoea or stomach cramps the next day. The symptoms kicked in faster than I expected, and Zelda bore the brunt of it.

I didn't want him dead, Bella. I'm not a *murderer*. I wanted to teach him a lesson, that's all. How was I to know he'd pump himself full of cocaine and attack Zelda?

He came flying out from next door's back gate like a rocket. The one I'm standing in front of now. It was so dark and quiet, he didn't spot me squatting by the window, eavesdropping on your conversation.

I stood up when I saw him staggering around, blood all over his neck and shirt, mumbling to himself like an eejit. He almost leapt for joy when he saw me, thought I was his saviour. Stupid sod could barely string a sentence together. I think his tongue had swelled up.

Frank told me Zelda tried to kill him to stop him from leaving her, and that you were in love with him, too, said he'd slept with Linda, and now the three of you were planning on finishing him off. He urged me to call the police, pleaded with me to be his witness, said he'd see me alright.

When I hesitated, he pulled out his wallet and gave it to me. Well, I was never going to call the Garda, was I? I couldn't let him put you all inside, not when I'd just found you. I feigned shock, told him I'd left my phone in the car, and, with a tremulous hand, he looked at his phone – face recognition. It didn't work, probably because of the swelling of his face. I watched him tap in the number, 666007, sweat trickling down his face, congealing with the blood.

I must admit, he looked terrified. I almost felt sorry for him. I jabbed at the screen, told him to hold on, I'd get help, and then, slipping his wallet into my pocket, I pretended to talk to an operator while he leant against the wall, eyes tightly shut. I started talking, breath ragged – *Ambulance please. A man has been stabbed, please come quickly, he's in a bad way. Yes, the address is* – and then his eyes snapped open. He was like, 'Hang on, what were you doing loitering in the driveway in your dressing gown?' And then he saw the screensaver on his phone. I underestimated him, Bella.

The words *evil, lying, bitch* spat from his lips as he lunged at me. For a moment, I froze, spiralling into the past. But the numbness thawed as quickly as it came. I slid his phone into my pocket, grabbed a wooden broom that was propped against the wall and blocked him with the handle before he could reach me. Fuelled with vicious energy, I pushed him as hard as I could, he lost his footing around some builder's gullies and fell backwards into the excavation.

I shone the torch from his phone on his still body, hair in my face, breath ragged. He'd landed into a curved cavity, almost as if it was a prepared grave. I stared down at his twisted body, eyes wide open, with a feeling of empowerment. He was dead. I'd killed him. *And I liked it.* But now I had a fecking body to hide.

Shrugging out of your dressing gown, I kicked off your faux fur slippers and placed them neatly by the garage door. I couldn't risk getting any grime or blood on your belongings. The sting beneath my feet was immediate. Stones, grit, slithers of wood. I knew I couldn't go down there barefoot.

I opened Zelda's recycle bin, hoping to find some plastic packaging to tie around my feet and that's when I spotted them. I pulled the wellington boots over my fleecy pyjama bottoms and made my way into the dark ditch. I checked for a pulse and any signs of breathing. Nothing. I was about to stand up when I felt moisture on my fingers. I stared at my blood-stained fingers. What was I going to do now, Bella? Looking around me wildly, I spotted a half-filled bottle of cola and an abandoned screwdriver, chucked in the ditch by the messy builders. I poured the cola over my hand and shook it dry. Noting his stab wound, I set the yellow handle of the screwdriver into the soil and rolled him onto it until his flesh met with the blade and penetrated the shank. He was bloody heavy, Bella, but I'm a strong lass –got trophies for weightlifting.

Satisfied, I was about to cover his corpse with builder's crates and rubble when something shone in the moonlight. A watch. I figured I could get a few quid for that. It felt heavy, expensive. I slipped it around my arm, and then I heard a rustle of movement and your voices in the garden. I covered his corpse as quickly as I could and got the hell out of there.

You were none the wiser when I turned up at the front door a while later, composure regained. I suspected the builders would find him the next day, of course, but figured they'd have thought it was an accident. I doubt very much there would've been an inquest, especially after discovering all that alcohol and cocaine in his system; or maybe the coroner would've ruled that the cause of his death was due to an allergic reaction. I'm not sure if you can die from an Ibuprofen allergy. Probably.

There was the little incident about the stab wound in his neck, of course, but I imagined the medical examiner would rule that it happened when he collapsed and fell onto the yellow screwdriver. Either way, we'd cross that bridge when we came to it. But, as fate would have it, a huge concrete mixer arrived the next day, who, according to Zelda, pumped the cement through a tube connected to the lorry like concrete ninjas and he was buried within half an hour. Job done.

Frank had his debit card in his wallet, Bella, with his passcode scribbled on the back of his business card. Why do people do that? Nevertheless, it came in handy when I went to St. Ives on a shopping spree on my day off. I bought you that perfume from *Icecube*, remember? It cost me sixty-five quid. You're wearing it today, bless you. Anyway, I digress. A homeless guy, sitting outside the station in a black hoodie, agreed to take two-hundred-and-fifty pounds out of the cash machine for me in exchange for fifty quid. And get this, he was the same height and build as Frank. Isn't karma lovely? Fortunately, he was a regular at the station and was happy to offer his services again on my next trip. Wearing Frank's watch, he held up a coffee cup, emblazoned with Frank's name, and took a selfie with Frank's phone. I gave him two hundred pounds for that. He deserved it.

The watch is expensive, Bella. A Patek Phillipe. I got it valued. It's worth between £170 and 200k. I'll flog it when I go back to Ireland to visit my loathsome brothers. I never let it out of my sight. Gosh, would you? It is very beautiful. I'm quite tempted to keep it. But I can't. It's too risky. Every now and then I pull it out to make sure it's still there. The emerald green strap is gorgeous. I've got a leather key fob in the exact same colour. Anyone would think it was a set. I pull out the wristwatch now and rub my thumb over the face with glee, and then…

'Daisy, what are you doing?' My heart stops. You've startled me, Bella. Creeping up on me like that. 'We're waiting for you. Fiona loves the flat.'

I spin round, almost dropping the watch in my haste to get it back into my handbag.

You frown, face hard. Shit. *Shit*. You saw it.

Chapter 70

Daisy

'What was that?'

'What was what?' I say coolly.

'What you had in your hand just now. It looked like a watch.'

'A watch?' I laugh incredulously.

'Yes,' you say, your frown lines intensify. 'I saw a strap. It was green.' You take a few steps towards me. 'Can I see it, please?' There's an undercurrent of anger in your voice. I don't like it, Bella. I thought you were nice. I thought you trusted me.

I swallow bile that is creeping up my throat and it pools into my stomach like vinegar. Feeling the dampness of sweat forming at my hairline, I move away from you. I need to think fast. If I tell you the truth, will you dob me in, or protect me like you did Zelda? Will you, Bella? Do you really love me as much as her? I mean, I know we share some DNA, about twenty-five percent with half siblings, I looked it up, but you've got history with her.

Our eyes lock and I feel my resolve dwindling. My nerves flutter under my skin as the all too familiar sensation of fight or flight slithers in. Swallowing hard, my eyes dart to the back gate, left agape for today's viewing, and the flight of steps directly behind you. Twenty-six. I counted them. I can't go down for this, Bella. I can't go to prison. You must sense my tension because you intuitively take a step back, but you style it out, as if you're leaning your weight onto one leg and fold your arms. I don't want to hurt you, Bella. You must protect me. You must understand why I had to kill Frank. *You must. You must. You must.* I open my mouth to speak when someone yells. 'What in the world is that?'

You jolt your head round. Fiona is pointing at the hot tub beneath my pergola as she makes her way down the flight of steps, leading to the lower level. My hand slides into my handbag and I slip the wristwatch into the hidden zip compartment, away from your prying eyes.

'A Jacuzzi,' Linda says, following Fiona into the garden, her Manolos click-clacking against the steps. 'Come on down, girls,' Linda calls out cheerily, waving us over.

'We'll be there in minute.' You spin round and nod at my handbag, jaw tight. 'Show me now, please?' God, you're like a dog with a bone.

'Seriously?' I say, but your face is deadpan. 'Okay, okay.' Unzipping my bag, I open it wide and your eyes dart around it suspiciously. 'Was it this?' I pull out my green key fob. 'I just used the key to lock the garage door.' This is true, Bella. 'It was still in my hand when you called out to me.' This *isn't* true. I slipped it back into my bag the moment I locked up.

The muscles in your face ease. I can almost see your body deflating with relief. 'I'm sorry. I'm sorry.' You pull me to you and squeeze me in your arms, kissing my hair, and I inhale the fug of your delicious perfume. 'I don't know what came over me.' You let me go. 'Actually, I do. For a moment, I thought I saw Frank's... Oh, never mind, my eyes are playing tricks on me.'

'Put Frank out of your mind,' I whisper, linking my arm through yours. 'There's no way he'll show his face around here again, and if he does, we'll deal with him. The four of us.'

We walk through the back entrance of the house and then you stop on Frank's grave and look at me. 'Do you really think he's gone for good, Daisy, because sometimes I just think...' You wrap your arms around yourself and look around you, a haunting look on your face, 'almost as if, you know, I can feel his energy.' A beat and then, 'Oh, ignore me. I'm being silly. I'm so glad you decided to buy this place and stay.' So am I, there's a corpse buried beneath it for a start. One that I put there. The last thing we want is some snazzy developer coming along and digging it all up again, and you know what they say, Bella – keep your friends close and your enemies closer.

'It's so good of you to give Zelda a home. It'll give the two of you time to bond.' Zelda isn't like you, Bella, she's more like me, I think. All that pent up anger and hostility. You must admit, putting me through all that DNA testing was a cunty thing to do. It was kind of you to offer the DNA proof I had. But I couldn't do it. I couldn't draw a wedge between you and Georgia. Anyway, the flat is an olive branch. Perhaps, in time, Zelda will accept me too. I think she's already starting to thaw.

'I still can't believe you're not charging Zelda rent,' you say. I tell you it's fine. I can afford it. Well, I will once I've sold Frank's watch and Fiona starts paying rent. 'Zee's so bloody jammy.' You roll your eyes but in an affectionate way. 'Could get away with murder, that one.' You realise what you've said and go a bit red. I scuff my shoe against Frank's grave.

'Anyway, thank you for giving Fiona a chance,' you add, swiftly moving on. 'I do hope you won't live to regret it.'

We descend the stairs, me behind you, holding onto the railing. 'We'll be fine,' I say in a musical tone, 'stop worrying. You're such a worrier.'

In the garden ahead, Linda is showing a very excited Fiona the hot tub, and Zelda has joined them, sitting on the cushioned-covered bench above the fairy lights looking at her phone. God, does she ever let go of that thing?

'I thought you were getting rid of the Jacuzzi,' you quiz, 'said it was tacky.' That's one word I'd use to describe it. I can think of several others, including sex pond. Bloody things are disgusting.

I squint up at the sunlight. 'It is. I was. But Zelda's fallen in love with it.'

You smile, in a grateful way. 'You do realise Fiona will be in it all day, don't you?' you groan, as Fiona takes selfies of the hot tub. 'We didn't call her the spa queen for nothing.' We're standing side by side at the bottom of the stairwell. 'Look, are you sure you want her to be your tenant? It's not too late to back out. She can be a bit of a handful.'

'Believe me, I can handle the Fionas of this world,' I say and you raise your eyebrows. 'I can always lock her in the hot tub if she gets out of control.'

You laugh when I say this. 'Oh, you,' you say, elbowing me playfully on the arm. 'You'd never do such a wicked thing.'

I would, actually. 'God, no,' I exclaim, laughing with you. 'Well, not on purpose.'

But accidents do tend to occur when I'm around, Bella, don't they?

I link my arms through yours. 'Come on,' I urge, 'let's go and welcome my new tenant.'

The Temp

Note from the author

Thank you so much for reading The Temp. I really hope you enjoyed it. If you did, I'd be grateful for a brief review or star rating on Amazon. Reviews and ratings help readers discover new books and make the author smile. They sometimes even make them do a little jig around the coffee table!

Thanks again for reading. You'll find more of my books on the next page.

Also by Kelly Florentia

The Magic Touch
No Way Back
Her Secret
Mine
To Tell a Tale or Two…

About the author

Kelly Florentia was born and bred in north London, where she continues to live with her husband Joe, and where her novels The Magic Touch, No Way Back, Her Secret and her psychological thriller, Mine, are set.

Kelly has always loved writing and was a bit of a poet when she was younger. Before penning her debut, she wrote short stories for women's magazines - To Tell a Tale or Two is a collection of her short tales. In January 2017, her keen interest in health and fitness led to the release of Smooth Operator - a collection of twenty of her favourite smoothie recipes.

As well as writing, Kelly enjoys reading, running, drinking coffee, gyming, watching TV dramas, and spending way too much time on social media. She is currently working on her next novel.

Website: www.kellyflorentia.com

X: @kellyflorentia
Facebook: @kellyflorentiaauthor
Instagram: @kellyflorentia
TikTok: @kellyflorentia
Threads: @kellyflorentia

A Stylo Publication

Printed in Great Britain
by Amazon